The Boy and the Brothel Madam

The Lost Diaries of Cyrus Kirkpatrick, Being the True Tale of his Travels from New York to San Francisco to China and back, his Abduction by a Notorious Brothel Madam, his Harrowing Escape from a Raging Fire, and Other Perils.

A Novel

Noel C. Cilker

ISBN: 979-8-9935121-0-5 (Kindle Ebook)
ISBN: 979-8-9935121-1-2 (Hardcover)
ISBN: 979-8-9935121-2-9 (Paperback)

Library of Congress Control Number: 2025927387

This book is a work of fiction. Any references to historical events, real people, or real places are used fictitiously. Other names, characters, places and events are products of the author's imagination, and any resemblance to actual events, places or persons, living or dead, is entirely coincidental.

Visit the author's website at www.NoelCCilker.com.

Printed in the USA.

The Boy and the Brothel Madam

Prologue

Befuddlement racked my imagination when I espied the package on the step, bearing my name.

What was it? Who'd sent it?

"Msr. Cyrus H. Kirkpatrick" was inked as the recipient in handwriting unknown to me, yet I hadn't placed any order. I picked up and fingered the soft, battered parcel which had by all signs been in transit for months, with numerous forwarding addresses scratched in various inks and scripts. It was bulky, weighty, and torn, containing volumes of some sort. They were flexible, and I could easily manipulate them into U-shapes without creasing the inside pages.

Something long dormant pushed itself up into my consciousness but I tamped it down. There was no way.

I brought it inside and stood at my desk, where I unfastened the string and broke the wax. A newspaper clipping fluttered out. The headline announced:

'CHINA MARY OF ALVISO' DIES AS CENTURY NEARED

It was from the *Oakland Tribune*, dated February 2, 1928. Just this year. I combed through the obituary, holding my hand over my heart. She had been alive all this time. I sank into my chair, stared into the distance, and took five deep, slow breaths to stave off the ringing that had started in my ears.

All this time.

I reached into the packaging and slid the volumes onto my desk, my long-dormant dreams spilling into a pile. I couldn't breathe at the sight of that which I had resigned myself to believe forever lost. My journals, lying in front of me, plain as the day on which I last saw them—the day I had fled San Francisco. By some miracle, no fire, flood, nor mud had claimed them, and though they were in a sorrier state than when I'd left them, yet here they were, as seemingly whole and complete as I could quickly gather. I closed my eyes and turned them over in my hands, feeling and smelling the worn, soft-bound leather.

Who had sent them? I shook the envelope and found no note enclosed. Their sender was a mystery, and yet that didn't stop a well of gratitude buried inside me from percolating over. My early life had been restored, risen from the depths where it had lain comatose and corroded, vanishing word by word with each passing day. I fanned through the crinkly pages and recognized the demented knitting of my teenage scrawl, and the clippings of frail, yellowed newspaper articles. There it was! That hole in my life was real, and that which had filled it had existed. It had mattered. Although my lost writings contained events I would rather have ascribed to some delinquent child, I needed to confirm they did, in fact, occur. I rubbed the inky markings above my wrist, which had long since faded, yet still were clear enough to undam the flood of memories.

C. H. Kirkpatrick

1928

Part One

THE GOLD IN CALIFORNIA
Brooklyn Evening Star
Sept. 9, 1848

The fact that gold has been found in such abundance in California will no doubt tend greatly to its speedy settlement. Multitudes will be tempted to quit their ordinary avocations with the idea of growing speedily rich, and the settlers being provided with a medium of exchange, there will be no lack of vessels with every article of sale which can aid in a wide dispersion of the precious metal. There will probably be many melancholy scenes resulting from the frauds and violence to which gold gives rise. A gold country is likely to be a barren country.

June 25, 1849
Panama City
Hot and sticky.

Lex shook me awake and shouted, "Let's go see the steamer!"

"Mmmphh," I replied, my face buried in a blanket.

The other passengers from our ship were about. I could hear them through the walls, too excited to sleep while their passage out of Panama City lay moored within sight. Some have been here for weeks, awaiting a steamer that was promised but always delayed. Boats coming around Tierra del Fuego, apparently, are always delayed. Naturally they neglected to tell us that before we left New York.

The newcomers—those who'd traveled with us from Manhattan, around Florida, skirting the edge of the Gulf to the Chagres River, then overland to Panama City—joined in the elation as if they, too, had been put out in Central America for weeks on end. It's only been a week and a half or so in our case, but I've learned that when the stars and the schedule refuse to align to a man's liking, no other foreigner can grumble like an American can. Everyone here is in a rush to reach California and I can't understand why. Scratch that—I *do* understand why. What I can't understand is what makes a full-grown adult slaver for it, uproot himself, sell off his life, muck through the jungle, and burn to a crisp (or freeze into ice) on a ship's deck to get there. I remember Mr. Payran's eyes affecting a distant look when Leland asked him where California was, the first time I'd ever seen our teacher's eyes gaze at something without their usual cold glint. Yet to leave home to travel half the world away to dig rocks out of the ground? *Voluntarily?* All the comforts of home are already at home!

I didn't want to wake, but Lex can be forceful. "Up, Cy. Let's go," he said and pushed me out of the Hotel Americano and toward the beach. "Take a few minutes and try an adventure!"

Stepping out of the room's stale air *was* a slight relief. The climate here is otherwise unbearable. The heat and sticky heaviness of the air is oppressive, like a wet, woolen blanket weighted with lead pressing me to the ground. Moisture is everywhere, and it leaves every surface, bit of food, and inch of clothing damp, and all of it rots if forgotten. I even wipe my journals every day so they don't molder.

The beach teemed with people in lifted spirits. They clapped each other on the shoulders and smiled, having already forgotten the resentment they held for this place in these last weeks. Lex espied some of his gambling boys and disappeared, leaving me alone in the crowd.

Feeling anything but festive, I returned to the room and sat amongst our things. We were leaving this damp town, but the joy that enveloped everyone outside stopped at my door. What was there to be joyful about? From one bad place to a California mystery; all we'd heard of it were reports from the gold fields, most brimming with optimism. But there was nothing in the papers about the climate, or the wildlife, or the food, or where we'd sleep. Lex says the hotels there must be decent enough since everything there is freshly built. As long as they're in better shape than the Americano, maybe I'll survive just long enough to turn myself around and head home.

Home. I tried my hardest not to think of Mother and Father. It's not their welfare I pushed from my mind, but the fact of their still living there. Lucky them, 'though they don't know it. By now, Father's business must be rebounding; it must, with all the hours he spends out of the house. He's more a boarder than a resident there. Mother would be complaining—to herself, of course, now that her "boys" are gone. Well, Lex at least. She and Father have sometimes called me their "little lass" since before I can remember, which, growing up, I used to think was a quirky nickname. But they persisted long after quirky childhood nicknames should be shed, and it's increasingly embarrassing and infuriating the more they refuse to let it go. And what has Mother to fuss about? A warm house, a cushioned bed, and vegetables, fruit, and meat? Give her a few weeks on a ship in the blistering sun, then let her tramp through the jungle and swat mosquitoes like the rest of us!

I lay back down, and the heaviness of my eyelids overtook me. Lex had awakened me far too early.

*　　　　*　　　　*

Something hit me in the shoulder and my sticky eyes flew open. The room was as stifling as ever in the morning heat. Lex had come back and was currently slurring a song.

"Hey," he said when he saw me awake. "Go find us breakfast."

"Me? What are *you* doing?" I asked.

"Packing," he said, stumbling slightly. "Steamer leaves in a few hours."

I closed my eyes and sighed. "We don't *have* to go."

"Really. You want to stay here?"

I looked out the window. The vegetation was enormous—large, flat fronds fanned out before us, behind us, to either side, slick with moisture, trapping the humid air, casting a green glow from the sun behind. A mosquito whined, and I slapped my neck.

"I hate this place," I said.

Lex rolled his glassy eyes. "You hate everyplace."

"Not home. Let's go back."

"Yes, we all know you want to go back. Pack it up." He pointed to my trunk.

"Why not? It's not as though we know what we're doing."

"We know exactly what we're doing."

"Sailing around the continent to stand in a river and dig in the mud all day? We could go back, live at home, I can go to school, you can get a job…"

"That's foolish, Cy," Lex said, shaking his head. "That wouldn't solve any of our problems."

"Mother and Father's problems."

A sharp rap on the door startled us. A man poked his face in: Mr. Jackson, one of Father's acquaintances, a sad-faced, watery-eyed man from our church. He'd formed a gold company back home, and for the following two weeks Father worked on him hard to accept Lex into the group. He, Father, and Lex had conversed deep into the night over piles of paper and cups of wine, and then they'd struck a deal. He never did warm to me, however. I think he saw me as a hanger-on in their gold venture.

Mr. Jackson entered with his hat in his hands. "Gentlemen," he said, "are we ready?" He glanced at our trunks and frowned. Taking out his pocket watch, he made a big show of studying it and looking out our window to the steamer. "Time is money, and never more than in California. We leave with or without you, but that doesn't absolve you of your financial obligations." He tapped his watch at us before bustling away.

Lex raised his middle finger at the vacated doorway. "I hate that man," he said, then turned to me. "But he's right. Pack it up."

I did, cursing under my breath the entire time, even as I pulled my trunk behind me onto the dock and into the ship. Ringing filled my ears and dizziness sat in the crown of my skull. I pressed my fists to my head and moved little the rest of the evening.

June 30, 1849
On board the Oregon
Hot and sticky. Some clouds.

Now I find myself aboard the *Oregon,* steaming toward California.

Not one person cares about the welfare of his fellow passengers; he thinks only of himself, even Mr. Jackson and the other gold company partners, so blinded are they by their lust to "see the elephant."

My head is aching terribly from clenching it all day. I need to find space on the deck to sleep; the heat in steerage is oppressive. The steamer is filled with passengers from stern to bow, and sleeping spots on deck must be bartered or contested for. The miserable losers are forced below. This is where I've slept these last few nights. A malaise has settled over me and I can't shake it; it's like a wet blanket wrapping itself over me and pinning me to the deck. Maybe it's the still, humid air, and the unceasing rocking of the ship. I have no energy except to read and to write here, though often it takes all my strength to do even that. I don't know what we'll do when we arrive in San Francisco—accommodations, provisions, &c.—so instead I sleep as often as I can.

I've seen little of Lex since our departure. I hear his laugh at times, yet it's difficult to pinpoint the source, even with the steamer as small as it is. They've really packed us in here, and he's fraternizing and making merry with all on board who will have him.

Just yesterday we came upon the Acapulco harbor. It's beautiful, and I wish I could have gone ashore to give my legs a stretch, yet that wasn't in the cards. We were greeted by a row of soldiers lining the beach and a message from the governor not to land due to our originating in Panama, which is known to be a haven for the cholera. We had to move on. I returned to my hammock to stare into the gloom, hoping to fall asleep and wake up in my bed at home.

Only forty or so days ago I was in New York, enjoying a fine Spring and looking out over the Hudson River. I've got to return home. As soon as we arrive in San Francisco, I'll purchase a ticket and take the first steamer back. Sure, I'll have wasted months of life sailing back and forth from one end of the country to the other and back again, but no matter, I'll be back where I belong. I'll make up for lost time.

July 1, 1849
On board the Oregon
Hot and sticky. Partly cloudy.

Today is my 16th birthday. It's the first birthday I can recall feeling worse than on a normal day.

In N.Y., I would've woken up before dawn to the sound of pebbles clattering on my window, and upon opening it, I would've seen Leland crouching behind a shrub, scratching at the ground in search of another missile. I would've sneaked out the front of the house and stepped carefully to the other side of that shrub, then launched myself at him. I would've seen him turn his shocked face before I collided with him and sent both of us sprawling upon the ground. He would've started laughing until I smothered his face with my hands so as not to awaken Mother and Father or Lex, and then we would've stood and run away from the house to the street, where we would've slowed down and walked side by side. He would've handed me a biscuit pilfered from his mother's kitchen and said, "Happy birthday."

We wouldn't have returned until the dark of the night, and I'd walk into the house alone, just before Father returned from work and after Mother had gone to bed, so as to avoid being questioned about "that boy."

July 15, 1849
San Francisco
Foggy and frigid.

I didn't sleep last night. Having yesterday passed the Farallon Islands—the "Devil's Teeth" according to the crew—we were only a day away from San Francisco. It made me want to shove my feet in the water and drag the steamer to a stop, impeding it from one more inch of forward progress. I should have sabotaged the engine room. I should have thrown something into the steamer wheel to jam it or heaved someone overboard to force the ship to turn and rescue. But I may as well have screamed against the tide. The steamer was pushing, pushing, pushing toward the coast like a relentless wave, with no sabotage or near-drowning to arrest it. Instead, all I did was thrash uselessly throughout the night in my hammock, like a desperate mouse held underwater, wasting precious energy, as if the town we churned for was my final destination, not just of this voyage but of my life.

The worst of this feeling passed in time, yet the vestiges of it lingered in my heart and my stomach. A heavy sickness settled in my bones.

Meanwhile, the excitement above deck was palpable. Energy built in the ship as the Golden Gate grew larger, not just among the passengers but the crew as well. Every person was above deck. They leaned against the side and strained their eyes. Men clapped each other on the back as if they'd really accomplished something.

The captain narrated to us as we entered the Golden Gate. I only half-listened. Angel Island here, Alcatraz Island there, Yerba Buena Island farther on, and some history no one listened to.

There were no signs of civilization yet—no streets, buildings, other ships, &c. No hint at all of a city, town, village, house, or even a single tent. Some passengers spotted an old building close to the water and gestured wildly at it; but it was only the Presidio, an old, neglected, and dilapidated Spanish fort. There was no gold nor anything shiny in sight, and the hills weren't glinting with gold as some expected. I laughed to myself. Some grumbled that this must surely have been the wrong entrance and began to curse. They believed the journey had become a mistake, a view I'd already formed long ago.

The steamer banked right to follow the beach and came upon the San Francisco harbor, choked with hundreds of vessels lying at anchor in no pattern or organized manner, with the flags of all nations flapping in the wind. The cluster of masts resembled a dead forest, and we discovered that the ships were deserted. The greed of gold is so powerful that many of the crew—and sometimes the captains—abandoned their ships for the gold fields. They left so quickly that the ships were still loaded with cargo.

Then we saw the town of S. Francisco. On the flat ground before us and up the sides of the hills are tents scattered about, of assorted sizes and colors, with no order or design in their layout. There are hundreds of them that fill the valleys. There are solid buildings too, though that's a generous description. Some are no more than frames covered with cotton cloth—creating the effect of an overgrown camping ground, a canvas city. I couldn't see how any of these could be considered home to anyone. Was I supposed to live in one of those?

We debarked, dragging our trunks behind us. I was pushed onto the Long Wharf and was hit hard by an awful stench of brackish ocean water, raw sewage, and sour garbage. Before I could recover, I became disoriented by the sea of people, though thankfully living in New York prepared me for the press of the crowd.

Yet even the mixed people of New York didn't prepare me for what I saw here. It's as though all the populations of the world have teemed into this tiny town. While some of these races can be seen back home, many more here are new to me. There are Mexicans who wear bright-colored serapes over their left shoulders. There are Englishmen and Yankees in black dress-coats, and Southerners and Frenchmen dressed as if they're off to the theater. Others are garbed in whatever scraps of clothing were nearby. California fashion is anything at all, with a hat of any shape and color, and pants stuffed into a pair of boots. Pistols and knives are worn in every belt.

Then there are the miners—bearded and muddy, wearing heavy woolen shirts and belted trousers. Their appearance is rough and savage. The strangest are the Chinese Celestials, who wear oversize blue cotton pants and shirts with sandals, and while they are bald on the front half of their heads, from the back they wear a long braid down to their waist. They walk in a funny way, like a duck, and carry a long pole on their shoulders, weighted down on both ends with their loads.

All around me swirled the noise of people talking, though I understand almost none of it. Some English; but the rest of it is like the buzz of angry bees. Spanish, French, and Hawaiian sound like words spoken underwater, while German sounds as if the speakers are choking on food. I don't know how people understand each other. Above all this fray a clear, deep voice boomed, "Mornin' papers! Mornin' papers!" Passersby dropped two-bit coins into the vendor's hand, then grabbed a newspaper and walked away with their heads buried in the news. Does everyone read the same language? What events here are considered newsworthy?

"Heya!" an accented female voice called out. "Heya!" Lex was already lost in the throng, and I had to step out of the column of unloading passengers to look around for him. There he was, off to the right, with a pair of women who appeared to be Chinese: dark hair, narrow eyes, small noses, faces made up with white powder and rouge, and dressed in silk pantaloons and silk jackets.

"Cy, come over here!" Lex called when he saw me. He swayed standing there, either "getting his land legs" or feeling his drinks.

Wary, I trudged to the group with my trunk.

"Heya!" one of the girls said, smiling, coming over to put her hands on my arm. I pulled it away.

"Isn't this great?" Lex smiled, big and sloppy.

"Uh huh," I said. "Let's go."

"Gentlemen," said a voice from behind us. Mr. Jackson joined us with the three other men in the gold company. I never bothered to talk with them because their conversation was insufferable: the price of gold this, the price of tools that, and weather predictions from the almanac to top it off. Never anything about anything else, so I learned early on to quickly say hello, down my meal, and get out of conversation range. It didn't take long for them to learn to ignore me. Lex, on the other hand, gave each a big smile and an unsteady handshake.

"Beat it!" Mr. Jackson barked at the Chinese girls, waving them away. They threw him murderous looks and disappeared, chattering to themselves. He cast an annoyed look at Lex and continued, "The status of our accommodations has changed. The hotels are booked up faster than we thought. We will have to scatter and find our own lodging, but we will reconvene when we sail for Sacramento. I hear there is a popular saloon called the Eldorado. We will meet there in two nights' time to plan our next steps. Meanwhile, start gathering your tools. There is a man here called Sam Brannan. He has everything you need. He is overpriced but it will be worth it, remember that." He held up his pocket watch and gave it a good studying. "Right then. Time is money here, so get yourself settled and find Brannan. In two nights, the Eldorado." He gave a final nod, and thus dismissed, the others dispersed.

"Hey, look." Lex pointed me to a man standing next to a wooden dray. "Let's use that."

"Do we have the money?"

Lex walked up to the guy. "Can you take our stuff up the hill?"

"Two dollar minimum. Where you goin'?"

Lex gaped. "Two dollars? You're not serious."

The man shrugged, and in the moment it took for Lex to pick his jaw up off the ground, Mr. Jackson shoved two dollars into the man's hand and threw his luggage into the dray, and off he went. Lex and I stood there, staring at the empty spot as if the dray had never existed.

"I *really* hate that man," Lex grumbled.

We lugged our possessions ourselves, like fools. Yet where to? Lex asked around for lodging and was pointed in the direction most of the passengers were already walking. We followed, managing to pull our trunks up the hill, and landed in a large space in the middle of the town called Portsmouth Square. "Let me see what I can find," Lex said, leaving me with the trunks. This gave me a chance to rest my legs and observe my surroundings.

The Square is ringed by buildings on all sides, a couple of them wooden, more of them canvassed, and the remaining mere tents. Within its boundaries the energy is like a railway terminal with all people moving in different directions, with no care, consideration, or even awareness of their fellow men. They carry luggage, food, shovels, rope, lumber, bales of hay, and one held a flapping chicken by its legs. Vendors with their stalls are stationed all about, selling everything under the sun worth selling: coffee, bread, beef, medicines, pickaxes, pie tins, boots, nails, cookery, sweets, insurance policies, land deeds, old newspapers, and some things not worth selling at all.

A completely empty booth advertised "all natural fish manure," with no potential buyers within thirty feet of it. Over the hum and clatter of human activity, an impeccably dressed auctioneer with a piercing voice was selling wares at a volume loud enough to give anyone a headache. "Gentlemen! Tobacco, two cents a pound!" he screeched. "Do I hear more? Going. Going. Gentlemen, what a sacrifice! Gentlemen! Coffee, Brazilian origin, twenty barrels! What is the opening? Gentlemen! Superior Fall River nails, eighty-five kegs, sure to go quickly! What is the offer? Gentlemen!"

Not far from him, French bootblacks erected stands in a long row, thirty to forty of them, and tended to the dustiest of boots. Many men waited their turn. Nearby was a man with a badge pinned to his shirt, a revolver hanging off his belt, and a pony by his side. A crowd surrounded this pony, and curious, I stood up a little straighter to see what the attraction was. The constable nodded, and a man stepped forward and placed a two-bit piece in the pony's mouth. The pony then turned and marched to the nearest bootblack stand, dropped the money into the polisher's hand, put one hoof upon the boot-rest, quietly observed the polishing, then raised the other and repeated, then walked directly back to his master to wild applause.

Something bumped into me roughly: Lex. "Twenty-six dollars a week!" he groused, "and another twenty for meals! Can you believe that?"

"For a hotel?"

Lex shook his head. "Forget digging gold, we should build a trash heap and charge an arm and a leg to sleep in it."

"What are we going to do?"

Lex looked around as if he was seeing it for the first time. "Isn't this place something? Expensive as hell, but look at all this!" His bad mood evaporated instantly. "Gambling tents and saloons everywhere. Did you see that horse getting his feet shined?"

"Yeah. A spectacle."

Lex beamed. "Incredible!"

"But where are we going to stay? How much money do we have left?"

"We'll figure it out. A guy told me there's some cheap places just up that hill a ways."

The wind started to pick up and kicked choking clouds of dust into the air. Lex and I had to breathe through our shirts while heaving our trunks up the street. It stung our eyes and caked our clothing, somehow swept underneath our hats and into our hair, and nestled in our ears. When I undressed for bed later, I shook my garments outside and kicked up a giant plume.

We stopped at every tent that gave any hint of possible lodging and inquired about vacancies, yet the answers never varied. Too many people have come for gold and the lodgings are rare and expensive, leaving Lex and me to journey farther and farther away from the Square and higher and higher up the hill. At last we came upon a neighborhood of tents called "Little Chile," all of whose colorfully ponchoed inhabitants spoke Spanish. They eyed our luggage and understood our pleas for lodging, and pointed to a cluster of tents close by. We were in luck. One worn canvas tent lay abandoned—perhaps the owner had left for the diggings—so we brought our trunks inside and collapsed. Lex desperately wanted to explore the Square and try his hand at the gambling tents, yet even he was exhausted and couldn't rouse himself for that noble cause. He fell asleep in an instant atop a pile of his clothes, while I sit here writing. It's not even dark yet. I remember the one camping trip Lex and I took with Mother and Father. I'd wanted to bring Leland, but they'd said no with disgusted looks on their faces.

I feel as if my spirit has left my body. I look around me and can't believe we're here. Am I walking in a dream? Every face is a stranger, and I can't be farther away from home on this continent than I am now. It's July, which means school has dismissed and Leland is probably wading in the Hudson River. I took the button out of my pocket and rubbed it. There's either too much ocean or too much land between me and N.Y. Everything here is too much.

I closed my eyes and listened to the staccato sounds of Spanish all around me, not understanding any of it, my ears begging for a comforting word in English. I was soon enveloped in the jagged rumbling of my big brother's snoring, which filled the tent, spilled out of the canvas walls, and was blown away by the frigid, dusty San Francisco winds.

July 16, 1849
San Francisco
Cold and sunny.

Yesterday was a grievous day.

After I drifted off to sleep last night, our first night in the Little Chile tent, panicked shouting startled me awake. I must have been dreaming, because I awoke believing I was back on the *Oregon* during the July 4th holiday. Some light leaked in from outside, but was it sunset or sunrise?

Lex shook me, yelling, "Get up!" and pushed a revolver into my hand. Where had he gotten that? He had wide eyes and a determined smile, as if he'd been created for this moment, yet I had no idea what kind of moment we were in. The blast of a gunshot nearby nearly jumped me out of my skin and sent me diving behind my brother, who immediately leaped up and out of the tent, leaving me alone with the revolver.

The screaming turned to roaring as I poked my head through the tent flap to see what I could see, though the combination of dusk, running bodies, and shouting kept me disoriented. When a second shot exploded followed by hysterical shrieks I ducked, withdrew to the back of the tent and hid behind my trunk. A man crashed into the tent and I raised my revolver with shaking hands, yet it was only Lex. He smiled and said, "Good boy!" and knelt beside me. "It's some sort of gang," he reported. "They're after a Chileno."

At that moment another man crashed through the tent with a raised club and looked wildly about. He was large, bearded, in tattered dress, and reeked of whiskey, sweat, and other powerful odors from a profound lack of a bath. His eyes adjusted, and he spotted Lex and me. "Two more over here!" he bawled and charged toward us. Lex jumped up to meet him, plowing his shoulder into the man's stomach and knocking him onto his back. But while Lex abounds in courage, he lacks in skill, so despite the man's drunkenness, after a short tussle, Lex found himself pinned to the underside of the intruder and taking a mighty pummeling from the man's fists. He called out, but I froze, so much larger was this man than I, and I remained rooted in my crouch.

Having subdued my brother, the man's gaze caught me behind my trunk. "Filthy Chileno-lovers!" he growled and charged again. He raised his club to strike and I raised my hands by instinct in defense. Then I jumped as the revolver fired, and the intruder fell. Blood spread into his shirt near his abdomen. The revolver fell out of my hand and I wondered how it had gone off without me pulling the trigger. I could only stare at the crumpled man, his life leaking out of his body. The metallic smell of blood filled the tent.

Lex, in his half-conscious state, slurred, "Did I get 'im?" His muffled words barely penetrated my squealing ears. I quivered as I peered at the man, thinking he would rise at any moment, yet no part of him stirred.

"You must go!" a singsong voice trilled behind me. A Celestial stood in the opening of the tent, an older man with loose-fitting clothes and a top hat with a braid peeking out from under the brim, his eyes moving from half-conscious Lex to the dead intruder to the smoking revolver at my feet. He spoke in a calm yet urgent manner. "Others are coming. If they see him dead, you will be next. Quick! Leave the trunks and go!" He reached down and lifted my brother up, then dumped him onto me. I nearly fell to the ground under his weight, though I managed to stay afoot, and shuffled him out of the tent while the Celestial moved aside. "Where should I take him?" I pleaded.

"The Square," he answered me. "No one will notice. Everyone fights there." He glanced at Lex's mangled face. "Fits right in." He picked up the gun, tucked it into my belt, and nudged us toward the Square. "Come back later for the trunks. Go!" He pushed us again.

We went. Lex and I stumbled down the hill, dodging men with clubs and knives, and when we reached the foot of it, I glanced over my shoulder. The Celestial had disappeared. At the Square, a host of S. Franciscans were gathered with horrified expressions, watching the fracas and muttering disgusted comments. I dumped Lex and myself down and watched in the same direction. There I could make out orange, flickering light and a plume of smoke beginning to rise. The screaming increased.

"You there, boy."

I tore my gaze away from the carnage and found a man standing before me, staring at me with unblinking eyes. He was young and nattily dressed in brown with a vest and necktie, his beard trimmed and complexion fair. He crouched in front of me clutching a pad of paper, which he shoved into his back pocket.

"Are you all right?" he askede, but before I could answer he spoke again. "Did you and your friend just now come from Little Chile?" My mind was too clouded to understand at first, though when he pointed from whence we'd come and said, "Over there?" I nodded.

"Are you from the States?" he asked.

I nodded again.

"Just arrived?"

I nodded a third time.

"How queer," he mused. "You're clearly not Hounds, yet two beaten Anglos in Little Chile!" He smiled at the thought.

"Hounds?" I asked.

"The very same." When he noticed my blank expression, he continued. "You must be new. They're our homegrown gang of depraved, ex-soldiers with no prospects in life. They take from anyone who has what they don't. A disgusting bunch." He spat on the ground. "Were you there when the mess started?"

"I suppose—"

"Was it Roberts?"

I furrowed my brow. "Who?"

"It has to be. He's been agitated all day like a ram in heat."

He took out his paper and a pencil and began to scribble furiously, with such pressure that he tore a hole through his notepad. He didn't seem to notice.

"Looks brutal up there," he said, head down.

"It is."

"Fire's already broken out."

The glowing smoke was now billowing from the tents.

"Any deaths?"

"Not that I—" but then I hesitated. He paused from his writing and glanced at me. I shook my head. He held his stare, then grunted, and went back to writing. Lex groaned, hugging his side.

"What's your name?" he said, eyes still on his notes.

"Cyrus."

"Last name?"

"Kirkpatrick."

"Age?"

"I just turned sixteen."

He pointed to Lex. "His name?"

"Are you a constable? Did I do something wrong?"

He didn't answer. After another minute and another tear in the paper resulting from an emphatically dotted "i," he folded his notepad, replaced it in his pocket, and held out his hand all in one motion as if he'd had considerable practice at this.

"I'm James King of William. I'm a banker but I report for the *Alta* on the side. I'm starting my own paper soon, and this—" he gestured toward the hill and the swelling smoke and flames, "—this is just a travesty." He grimaced with concern—authentic or fake, I couldn't tell—and took it all in like a king—aptly so—watching a tournament.

When he finally returned to me it was with an odd expression, as if he couldn't believe I was still there, or for that matter, that I was still on the ground with my bleeding brother.

"I suppose you'll need some help," he said, more to himself than to me. He looked around him and said, "Ah!" then pulled a man toward him. "Reverend, these two are up a creek. Is there nowhere for them to rest and recover?"

A shaggily bearded man lowered himself into my view. "Oh dear! Looks like you've had a rough day. Where are you lodging?"

"Up there." I pointed at the hill.

"Not anymore," said James King of William with a snort.

"Stay here," he added. "I might have some more questions." Then he melted back into the crowd.

The bearded man watched him go before returning his attention to me. "I'm Reverend Taylor. Let's see what we have here." He gave Lex a gentle and thorough looking-over. A groggy groan issued from Lex's lips.

"He'll be fine, no worse than you see every day at the Eldorado," said the Reverend. Then he asked me, "And you? Any hurts?"

I looked myself over. "I don't think so."

"Thank the Lord. You got lucky. You both did. The Hounds are a nasty gang." He rolled up his sleeves. "Come with me. I'll take you to the Garrett. We'll clean him up, then find someone to venture up the hill to retrieve your things."

"Thank you. Thank you so much."

Rev. Taylor smiled and led us through the Square.

Later in the evening, after we settled into a small, flimsy room in a "hotel" called the Garrett House and Lex was bandaged up and sleeping, the Rev. took a man and ventured up the hill to the tent I described for him. An hour later they returned, hoofing our trunks and panting.

"Lord, it's not a pretty sight," he said. "The carnage there is just awful. And something devilish occurred in your lodgings. Blood was all upon the ground, though the poor soul must have stumbled away or been retrieved. At any rate, G—d will not abide this violence. I'm only heartened that you two are unharmed. Relatively." He checked Lex one more time.

"I'm grateful. *We're* grateful. Can I repay you somehow?"

"No, no, there's no need. I'm only glad you're safe and well."

"But you've treated me nicer than anyone else here."

The Rev. put his hand on my shoulder. "My son, 'When thou doest thine alms, do not sound a trumpet before thee, as the hypocrites do in the synagogues and in the streets.'" He breathed deeply with a smile, then patted my shoulder. "But it wouldn't hurt to see you and your brother at next Sunday's service. Find me at the corner of Dupont and Washington."

*　　　*　　　*

I spent the night in an awful state. I slept poorly, if at all, clutching the revolver in my hand so tightly that my fingers lost feeling and the whites of my knuckles showed through my skin. Lex slumbered at my side, his breathing ragged.

Every click and sudden noise throughout the night—and there were many—caused me to flinch. The lodgings were so dark that if someone were to intrude, I wouldn't be able to see him. Screams echoed in my ears. Were they real? Were the Hounds coming after me? Was it something I'd done?

What *had* I done? My hands trembled. The warmth of the revolver made a permanent mark—not one I could see, but one pulsing in my nerves. The man collapsed again and again and again in my mind, and I couldn't figure out why. The revolver had fired. How had it fired? The last time I'd held a gun was when Father took Lex and me hunting upstate. I didn't want to go, but Father, like Lex, was forcible. We happened upon a bear cub that had broken its leg and was yowling from the pain. Father was on edge, as the presence of a cub means the mother is nearby, and he swung from left to right to intercept the angry beast we knew would be coming. But there was no sound at all except from the pitiful creature. After a while it became clear there was no mother, and just as clear that the cub wouldn't make it without one.

"There it is, son, handed to you," Father said to me and pushed the rifle into my hands. "Even a lass like you can-na miss." I don't remember firing then, either.

By sunrise I was a mess. I wondered how it would feel to have a club come down on my skull and crack it in two, to feel my own blood gush down my face. Would I black out? Would I gradually slip away? Would I be killed quickly enough to not know the pain from that first strike?

A foul smell drove those thoughts away, but provided no relief. I checked on Lex, who was still sleeping, then arose and discovered sewage floating through a ditch running in front of the Garrett House. I'm not sure how I missed it the night before in all our stumbling around, but there it was, collecting clouds of flies as the offensive objects made their slow path downhill. A dead, bloated rat soon followed. I didn't know whether to vomit or smile. Maybe this town is more like N.Y. than I first thought! I still skipped breakfast.

I met with the owner of the G. House. Because I couldn't find where Lex stored the money—assuming he still has it—in exchange for room and board, I'm put to work in the kitchen. And because Lex can't work due to his injuries, I'm also to do his part by sweeping out the rooms and changing the straw for the beds. I did all this over the course of the morning. Then the owner sent me to the Square to gather whatever vegetables I could from the peddlers there. I quickly learned that vegetables are nonexistent in San Francisco. Back home, a lack of vegetables would've been my dream come true. Here, it feels like a lack of civilization.

Other goods are available, however, and it's strange to see hundreds of abandoned ships sitting anchored in peace in the harbor, while on the beaches and in the streets, merchandise of all sizes, colors, and types lay out in the open, unguarded, for want of storage space. There's surprisingly little concern for theft, which makes no sense given the lawlessness of the previous night. But people leave everything unlocked and their goods unattended. I reckon thuggish violence is a larger threat than burglary. In as many ways as N.Y. is preferable to this overcrowded camp, this is one that my great home city would do well to emulate.

But let me be clear: S. Francisco holds no candle to home.

July 17, 1849
San Francisco
Cold and fog.

I awoke early this morning in the dusk, before my work was to start, and dressed quickly. Lex's snores sounded like the rattling of a carriage on cobblestones, so I felt safe enough to drop to my hands and knees and search through his trunk. I pushed aside his odorous, dusty clothes and felt around. Thankfully—and this is the only time I'll say this—most of his belongings were scattered around the floor, making my exploration much easier. My hands set to work feeling pockets, inspecting boots, burrowing into socks, probing past belts, suspenders, and shaving blades, but came up with nothing. Where else was there to hide money? My eyes fell on Lex's straw bed. I'd have to check that when he wasn't around.

I exited the tent and walked through the Square. Even now, just before sunrise, the place was humming. The shops and stalls were on the verge of opening, including the Old Adobe House and the alcalde's office, though the most popular establishments were already open, and appeared to have been the entire night. From these great tents, music, noise, and light issued forth and people passed in and out. The Eldorado is the biggest, rivaled by its neighbors, the Parker House and the Bella Union, and the men were considerably drunker in this quadrant than in the rest of the Square. I wonder what Mother would have thought of the wide-open sale of alcohol in these streets. I also shudder to imagine how Lex will take over the place once he's finally unencumbered by his injuries.

I made my way back to the Wharf onto which we debarked at

our arrival. Lingering at the end of the dock were the Chinese girls again, smartly dressed and made up. One of them saw me and called "Heya!" but I turned quickly away to the shipping office and found the agent there, going through the motions of readying his office.

"Good morning," I interjected into his routine.

"Not open yet," he grunted as he took a sign off the wall and began erasing its lettering.

"I'm only inquiring as to the cost of a steamer to New York." I peered at the board and discovered it was a menu of destinations and their prices. "Ah, there it is," I said, pointing at the line that read:

N.Y. VIA CAPE . . . 275$
N.Y. VIA PAN . . . . 420$

My heart sank. "Four hundred twenty?"

"Not anymore." Smirking, the agent erased the 2 and wrote a 5 in its place. "Those were yesterday's prices."

"But how—"

"Ships keep coming but not many leaving. Tomorrow will be $480. You gotta strike it rich to leave this place."

He may as well have written $1,000 or $10,000; those numbers are just as out of reach. But then a thought hit me. "What about overland? Do any wagon trains return East from here?"

"Any trains moving East are going only to Sacramento, and most are already there or in the hills. Everyone's coming West, clamoring to get where you already are."

I trudged back through the Square.

Breakfast was commencing when I returned to the G. House. The aroma wafting out of the tent betrayed heavy food inside, like most fare in S.F. Meals are dense and heavy: boiled and roasted meats, salted meats, potted meats, curries, stews, fish, rice, cheese, frijoles, molasses. It's filling but not satisfying, and as I've written before, there are no green vegetables anywhere.

I peered in but I was already too late to find a seat, the place swarming and food already flying. Meals here are contentious affairs. When ravenous men descend on a restaurant, it's as if they're at war. They obliterate all decorum as they attack the dishes and demolish their contents. The victor has the quickest eye, the longest arm, and the sharpest elbow, for everyone helps only himself and no attention is given to any request. "Pass the salt" and "A fork down here, please?" Forget it! I'm cursed to witness this bloodshed three times daily in the G. House's dining tent.

When the owner spotted me, he promptly stuck me in the kitchen to wash the dishes, which came in quicker waves than expected. I don't think any of those well-mannered diners gave their repast a single chew, choosing instead to inhale it. But even with licked-clean plates, the number that came through the door and stacked in front of me was so large it took hours for me to finish the job. By the time the owner came in and said "Take a break," my feet ached, my eyes bleared, and my fingers had turned completely to prunes.

"But don't go too far," he added. "Dinner starts in ten minutes."

I stumbled back to the room and collapsed on my mattress. Lex was awake and slipping his boots on.

"What's with you?" he asked.

I glared at him. "I just washed every dish in San Francisco. What have *you* done?"

"Convalescing."

"Where's the money? We should be paying instead of working. Instead of *me* working."

"I'd help you if I could. Honestly. But I've got to meet the company at the Eldorado. We could be leaving soon!"

"You're suddenly moving around well."

"Don't worry, Cy. You'll only have to worry about this place for a little longer. We'll be rich soon enough. We can leave this working business behind."

I closed my eyes, just for a few minutes, and my bedroom in N.Y. swam into my vision. I could almost reach out and touch it. Aching tore at my heart.

The clanging dinner bell brought me out of it and I almost cried. I rose and made for the door.

"Where are you off to?"

"To cover your share of the work. Unless you'd like to fork some cash over to pay off our boarding?"

"You're a good lad. Bring some food back when you're done. I'm starving."

July 31, 1849
San Francisco
Chilly with a medium breeze.

The number of people in this town has surely increased in the two weeks Lex and I have been here. I noticed it today while I was cleaning the breakfast dishes, that the pile was noticeably taller and listing slightly rightward. I've also been sent to the markets more often, since now my errands require multiple trips to transport all the supplies to the Garrett. Lex is grudgingly helping; at least he puts on a good show. The gold company has left him glum. The price of passage to Sacramento is enormous, and a few in the company have had to take on some work to pay for the ticket. We're stalled in S.F. for now.

At the same time, the Garrett owner has begun to grumble about our results, which have slackened in relation to our growing responsibilities. Today after dinner he made a comment about raising everyone's room rates and "taking only money" as payment. It's not lost on him that the majority of the time Lex is spotted, he is either on his way to or from the Eldorado. My brother claims it's for gold company meetings, but if so, they sure do meet rather a lot. Tonight after I finished the supper dishes, I snapped at Lex before the owner could.

"Am I the only one here who cares about our lodging?"

"What do you mean by that?" His eyes narrowed, which is a bad sign, yet I was too frustrated to take heed.

"I mean that I've been doing all the work here to pay for our lodging."

"*All* the work?"

"*All* the work! All the dishes from every meal. All the food shopping. All the errands!"

"I've done work where I can."

"You've been lying on your back for two weeks, then only get up to go gambling."

"I've been recovering from the worst beating of my life. I was almost done in! And you're lecturing me about working?"

"You were able to work a week ago, but I've been carrying the load for both of us!"

Lex sat up. "Maybe you *should* take the load. I was the one who got us here, remember? I took care of all the arrangements and got us here. Where were you?"

"Seasick on a boat, that's where. I could barely move."

"Ah. Well, it's a joy to see you up and moving again."

My face burned like a stove-top. "And what about you? How are we always out of money, but you're always out at night? Where do you spend it?"

"That's something that you'd best not know."

"Why not? You think I'm too young?"

"You're not experienced in these matters."

"I'm sixteen! What right do you have to withhold information from me?"

Lex only shook his head.

My head exploded with the high-pitched ringing. "You're just like Father! Nobody shares anything in this family. Am I your brother or not? I saved your life in that tent!"

"By accident, but yes, you did. That's why I'll make us rich."

"More likely you'll lose everything we have. I bet Mother and Father's money already belongs to that gambling den."

Lex jumped toward me and pinned me with his hand on my throat. I choked and couldn't breathe. "You don't question my loyalty to our family," he spat in my face. "I've only done right by you. You're only now just seeing how difficult it is to take a little responsibility."

"Go to hell," I gurgled. "I never wanted to come here. If you truly want to help, then leave me alone and let me find my own way home. I don't need you or the money you lost."

Lex growled and threw me onto the floor. "If you don't want

me here then I won't burden you." He snatched up his jacket and hat and stepped over me.

I kicked at him as he left through the door and I called after him, "It's a joy to see you up and moving again!"

Once the tent flap stopped swinging, I grabbed my own coat and stormed out in the opposite direction. Through the Square I raged, not watching where I was going, bumping through people and drawing curses from the offended. One called after me in a challenge but I stomped on, not turning back, nor did I until I somehow reached the edge of the water. I found an area to sit that contained the least amount of refuse and gazed out over the Bay. The view away from the town was beautiful. The water rippled; a fresh breeze blew; the weak sun tried to warm my face. Yerba Buena Island rose from the water in a serene manner with the Eastern Bay hills in the background—no tents, no ships, *no people*. I wondered how far away the island was from the town.

I thought of the day when Leland and I were killing time on the bank of the Hudson two years ago. We were skipping rocks and exploring the shore when we happened across some of Leland's friends, some fellows who also had just started high school. I didn't know them well, nor cared for them because they were loud and irrepressible, common boys, yet Leland knows and likes everyone for reasons I can't understand. It's his only obvious flaw. These boys, four of them I think, espied us and came over, hallooing and shouting all the way. I turned to disappear, but Leland made for them. I reluctantly followed.

"Hallo there, Possum! How's your poor feet?" one of them called when they were near. The other three swaggered behind him.

Leland smiled. "Davies! What's the news?"

"Naught. We filched a bottle o' tar water from Pike's. Wanna pull?" The kid named Davies shoved a brown bottle into Leland's hand. He was a medium-sized kid and thin like a rail; his stringy hair stuck to his temples and his face had more dirt streaked across it than a pig's. He and his gang belonged to a class of kid I didn't care to associate with. Leland swigged from the bottle and offered it to me, which I declined.

Davies squinted at me. "Aw, come on now! What's yer name again? I seen you at school."

"Cyrus," I said.

Davies snapped his fingers. "Right! Lee here talked about you. How's things, Cy?"

"Cyrus."

"Yeah, go 'head, have a swallow."

I shook my head.

He grabbed the bottle from Leland and took a long pull and winced. "Tastes like piss but gets 'er done, huh?" His three sidekicks giggled. He pushed the bottle into my gut.

I refused to take it so he handed it to Leland again.

"What are you two cavortin' 'round here for?"

Leland drank. "Just passing the time. You?"

"Naught. Tryin' to find a peaceful place to enjoy a drink." He looked around. "Found one!" He took the bottle back and sat down on a rock. The other three followed. "Kick up your feet!"

Leland sat down and I did the same, though I would've rather run in the other direction. For the next little while Davies and Leland talked nonsense, mostly about the teachers at school, the drunks in the neighborhood, and girls they thought were pretty—though that topic was mostly a Davies monologue. The other three laughed or nodded dutifully. Leland stole a glance at me and winked. After some time Davies said, "Hey Cy, wanna see somethin'?"

"Cyrus."

"Yeah, come look at this." He got up, steadied himself from the effects of the booze, and stumbled in the direction he'd come from. On cue, the other three rose and trailed after him. Leland watched me and shrugged. I sighed in exasperation and followed Leland as he followed Davies and the other three, like a column of ducklings after their mama. Davies stomped into a clump of bushes and rustled around a bit, then dragged out a splintery, sun-bleached raft. A paddle lay across the top.

"Lookie! Saw it the other day. Don't know whose, but let's take 'er out!" The three others whooped and dragged the raft into the water. Davies ran and jumped onto it, toppled onto his backside and laughed. The other three clambered on. "Come on!" he yelled at us. "Ship's leavin'!"

"Why not?" Leland asked me, then climbed aboard.

"Let's go, Cy! Ahoy!"

I groaned. There was no way that rickety raft would stay afloat with six of us atop it, yet Leland boarding it was an invisible tug, and so I, too, kicked off my shoes and boarded with great caution. The raft heaved and jerked, and I immediately crouched to steady myself. Being there felt like a mistake. As we floated away from shore, however, I calmed somewhat. I hated being on such a precarious perch with those four boys, yet Leland's presence anchored my nerves, and as time passed I thought that maybe, *maybe* I understood why the others found the thing enjoyable.

By and by we found ourselves in the middle of the river, pushed gently along by the current. The water was fairly calm and the sun shown down with its usual summer ferocity, so that by turns the boys jumped into the river to cool. Not feeling confident in the water, I remained on the raft. Finally I was the last still aboard, and Davies yelled to me, "In you go, Cy! Join the mob!"

"I'm happy here," I answered.

"Aw, come on!"

"No, thank you."

"It's cool in here. See?" Davies splashed me. "Don't be an ol' coot! In!"

I shook my head. Davies stared at me, his eyes slightly misfocused on account of that empty brown bottle.

"Boys?" he called to the others. "On the count of three, ol' Cy joins us!" He gripped the edge of the raft, and the other three did the same. Leland, treading water beside them, grew a concerned expression. "One! Two! Three!" The boys pushed up, and the raft tipped me to the back edge. I flailed and grasped for purchase, yet the boys continued to push, tilting the raft perpendicular and sending me headlong into the water.

"No!" Leland yelled as I sank like a sack of flour. Cold water rushed into my nose and ears—underwater is so *loud*—and I thrashed my limbs, yet they were of no use; I couldn't find the surface. Just as my lungs began to protest, something tugged at my gut. An arm heaved me upward and air rushed out of my mouth in gigantic bubbles. The arm heaved again, my face broke the surface, and I gulped in the hot, humid air and coughed.

"Kick!" Leland yelled as he strained to keep me afloat. I kicked my legs as hard as I possibly could because I wanted nothing else in the world than to abide by Leland and ease his burden. "Move your arms!" I flailed my arms. "Hug the water, over and over!" I tried, but I gave a poor showing. The water kept pulling me down. Seeing I was a more helpless case than he imagined, Leland slipped an arm each through my armpits, slipped underneath me, and pulled, both of us on our backs, faces to the sky. He strained under my added weight, yet his kicks were powerful and purposeful. I did what I could to help, though it wasn't much; nonetheless, Leland slowly guided me in the direction of the shore.

"Where's the raft?" I gasped when I caught my breath.

"Don't worry about them," Leland puffed, and sure enough, the raft was a ways away and getting smaller. I could make out Davies and the three others, looking in our direction and laughing. "Keep kicking!"

I kicked, but my legs dragged through the water, the water pulling at my pants and rendering me a dead weight. Leland, as always, was steady. "My legs are too slow!" I gasped.

He paused, heaving. "Take off your clothes!"

"What?"

"Take them off! We'll swim easier!"

My limbs were stones. "How?" There was no possibility of doing it myself without sinking. I'd never felt so useless.

He unwrapped himself from my arms and turned me toward him. "When I say to, take a breath, put your arms up, and kick as hard as you can!" Using only his legs to keep himself above water, he used his hands to unbutton my shirt. His legs pumped furiously. When he undid the last button at my waist, he yelled, "Now!" I kicked with gusto and raised my arms and sank, while at the same time Leland pulled my shirt up and over my head. As my nose sank below the surface Leland tugged me up again, and I threw my arms down to continue treading. The improvement was immediate; my arms moved with freedom and smoothness.

"Now your trousers!" Leland angled himself in front of me

and his hands went down. He pulled at my buttons while my limbs floundered. His panting hit my face. The riverbank and the wharves slid by. After some fumbling, he got the last one undone, then ordered, "Hold your breath and float on your back!" I did the best I could and held my breath as long as possible to stay above water. He tugged at one leg, then the other, back and forth until my trousers came free. My legs, liberated, moved like fish. I floated there for a while and attempted to use as little energy as I could.

"Onward!" Leland said. He, too, was stripped, and had tied our garments around his waist. He came up underneath me, hooked himself under my arms as before, and we continued on. His body was warm in the brisk water, and we made faster and more efficient progress toward the bank.

When we made it to land, we were hardly moving, so exhausted were we from all the paddling. We crawled up the rocks on our hands and knees and collapsed on the gravel, our chests heaving and panting for air. Leland rested his head on my stomach and we lay, soaking in the heat from the air and the sun, for what may have been hours. I could have lain in the sun like that until I died.

When we regained our strength, we walked home. Leland's house came first so I deposited him there. "One thing is certain," he said in that way I knew would conclude with a joke, "you swim like a brick." I gave him the biggest smile my worn-out face could muster. On my way back out to the street I noticed a button lying on the ground, and I picked it up. It was wet. Was it his? I made to knock on his door to return it but I hesitated. I rubbed the button with my thumb and carefully put it in my pocket. I'd return it to him later. When I arrived home stooped, damp clothes hanging off me, dragging my feet, and long after dark, Lex saw me and said, "This ought to be good." Mother stuck her head out of her bedroom and said coldly, "Your father will deal with you in the morning."

That night I slept like a brick, too, the sorest and happiest I'd been in a long time. I fingered the button in my pocket and fell asleep in peace.

Not knowing what San Francisco has in store for me, I could use some of that peace right now.

August 6, 1849
San Francisco
Weather same as yesterday.

Lex returned today from Lord knows where, the first I've seen of him since our row. He wouldn't say where he'd been, and though I didn't press him hard on it, the aroma of stale whiskey radiated off him so guessing wasn't difficult. He acted as though we'd been getting along famously the entire time. "Good news!" he greeted me. "The company is making for the diggings. We're leaving in two days!"

I stared at him.

"I'm off to buy supplies. We'll need shovels, pans, rockers, food, blankets, and a tent. I already have clothes. Brannan sells all these at inflated prices—everyone here knows it—but there's a fellow on Jackson Street who sells at a hair under. Ah yes, the steamer ticket too. One's departing this Wednesday, so I'll make my way to the office today and pick one up. That'll be my first stop. Those tickets will be snatched up, for sure. Cyrus! No time to dawdle! Money's being made while we sit here!"

"Wait!" I said, trying to shut him up. "Where? When? With what money?"

"Long Wharf. Wednesday. And…" He patted his bulging jacket pocket, grinned at me, and was out the door.

Only a minute later the owner poked his head through the flap. "Was that your brother just now departing?" he asked.

"I'm not sure," I answered.

Lex returned in the early evening laden with supplies. "The rest we'll get in Sacramento," he announced, dumping spades, pans, and sacks in the doorway and throwing himself onto the bed, but he soon rerose and paced the room.

"Where'd you get those?"

"Hush a minute and listen. Here's the plan. We'll take the steamer up the delta to Sacramento, unload, pick up some mules, and continue to the hills. Then stick shovels in the ground, set up the rockers, maybe build a sluice if the site shows promise, and start collecting! Do you know how much is up there? We'll live like kings!"

I was quiet. After a couple of weeks at the Garrett I'd picked up a fair share of stories around the dining room from miners returning from the diggings, pestered for advice by the wide-eyed novices who were trembling to head out. Occasionally an exhausted miner dug into his pocket to display a glittering specimen to impress his interrogators, and it was this image the hopefuls desperately clung to, ignoring most of the veterans urging that the heartache was not worth the meager returns and to forget the whole business.

"How do you know?"

"Look around you! Do you know who these people are? Teachers! Lawyers! Doctors! Politicians! All of them are here to pull some rock out of the ground, and look, they've struck it rich!"

"They have?"

"They've seen the elephant! And here we are, on the doorstep to the richest land on the globe. All we gotta do is throw a shovel into the ground, reach in, and grab it!"

"Wouldn't it be easier to just go home?" I said, starting to panic.

Lex waved me away. "It's there for the taking. You can pluck the nuggets straight from the river; all you have to do is bend down."

"Then why do you need all this?" I swept my hands toward the tools. "And how did you pay for them anyway? Did you raid a tent?"

"A bit of good fortune. Mr. Jackson fronted me the money at a very reasonable rate."

"The man you hate?"

"Turns out he's quite an admirable man. I can see why Father fell in with him."

My stomach dropped. "What rate did you agree to?"

"It was reasonable. Nothing we can't handle now that we have the tools. I'm telling you, the river is glinting with it!"

"Lex. What is the rate?"

Lex's expression clouded over. "What's wrong with you? Can't you see what we're trying to do? Why are you pestering me with all these questions?"

"We already owe them so much money. We can't get trapped under more debt."

"You don't think I can do it? You don't think I can stand in one spot, lean over, and pluck a nugget from the ground?"

I took a breath and rubbed the button in my pocket for strength. "Look, you know I'm not meant for this place. San Francisco already disagrees with me." I'm no sluggard when it comes to chores, yet digging rocks out of the ground would be the end of me. I held up my hands. "Can you imagine me in the diggings? I wouldn't last a week out there."

"Of course not. That's why you aren't coming."

I paused a beat. "Sorry?"

"You'd be laid up by day two, any fool knows that."

I didn't appreciate his emphatic agreement. "Then…who is 'we'?"

"'We'? Oh! No, not you. Me and the company. We'll be going at breakneck pace, rough work, really, and you…well, your hands are a bit more—*delicate*—than what we need."

I bit my tongue. He was extracting a bit of revenge from our row. But I couldn't help but feel a cold wave of something douse my insides. "So…you're leaving me here?"

"Just for a bit. I'll be back before the next Hounds riot." He must have seen something in my expression and added, "Promise."

I stared at the canvas wall. After a minute I asked, "Am I staying here while you play in the dirt?"

"While I earn us a living. Why don't you try to find some work and make yourself useful for once?" I clenched my fists yet his laugh stopped me. "You want to return to the States," he said, "but this is an adventure! Let me go make our fortune while you earn something here. We'll meet up again and have enough to buy our tickets to New York. Enjoy this loud, stinking, glorious town in the meantime. Collect some stories to tell your little friend back home. We'll be back there before you know it."

I shook my head and stared toward the Square. I hated the thought of remaining here a day longer, but maybe he had a point. With what money could I purchase a ticket home? My Garrett work was only for meals and lodging; I hadn't earned a single penny since we arrived. Even more dismaying was that the steamer price, like all other goods in the town, rose with every boat that disgorged its gold-seekers at the Long Wharf. What was once a $420 ticket home was now above $500. I had no other choice except to hope that Lex hit the motherlode before the price was unreachable. Still…I'd be alone. How would I make it?

"How long?"

"Shouldn't be too long. I'm telling you, the stories are endless. It's loaded out there. Probably take us a couple weeks to ship out and find a spot, another couple to load up, and then back. Two months tops. Of course, the longer we stay out there, the richer we get. I wouldn't guess later than October."

"October."

"Tops."

"Because the steamer prices rise every day. By October they may be $700."

"Look." He leaned toward me and placed a meaty paw on my shoulder. "By October, when I come back, the price of a ticket will mean nothing to you."

I wanted to believe him. I really, *truly* wanted to. What else was there? It was the quickest, surest way to get out of here. "Where will you dig?"

Lex got back to pacing. "Mormon Island."

"Where's that?"

"Outside Sacramento about twenty-five miles."

"Are there actual Mormons there?" Father reserved nothing but vehemence for the Mormons, and I made it my mission to hold the opposite opinion from Father whenever possible.

"Some, sure, but by now most will have pulled out and moved on. We aim to rake through what they left behind."

That didn't sound like a promising plan to strike it rich, but I held my tongue again.

The owner poked his head in with a triumphant "Hah! It *is* you! We have extra dishes to wash on account of additional diners. Let's move!"

"Yes sir, Boss Man!" Lex saluted him, then walked out of the tent toward the Square.

August 7, 1849
San Francisco
Weather same as yesterday.

The day passed as most of the days have, in that I covered the chores for both me and my brother. Apparently Lex believes that, because he's the key to our becoming rich and living like kings, he's earned an extension of his exemption from the hotel's daily duties. Instead he's occupied himself with writing in his notebook. I didn't know he even possessed such a thing, yet every time I checked in on him to inquire if *now* he could help with the washing, or the shopping, or the sweeping, or the clearing, &c., he dug his nose into the book still further, muttering such phrases as "Three ounces a day ought to offset the rocker" and "Find the quartz, find the gold" audible enough for me to hear.

When I returned to the room in the early evening and collapsed on the bed exhausted, he slammed his notebook shut and announced, "We're going out!" I turned away from him and closed my eyes. He gave me a shove. "Up! It's our last night!"

"It's *your* last night," I mumbled. "I work tomorrow."

"You work every day. There's plenty more waiting in the morning. Come!"

I refused to budge, so Lex dragged me off the bed. As I thudded to the floor, I called him a "raving cumberground," but he was in too good a mood to slug me for it.

"You're up!" he said. "Off we go, to celebrate the last night as a family!" My protests that I needed sleep went unheeded. Sleep was "merely an obstacle" and absolutely no obstacles stood in the way of Lex and a fun night out. He dragged me out of the tent.

"At least tell me where we're going," I said.

He only smiled. Just two minutes later he led me to a line of men that snaked about the block and ended at a small, canvas shanty. I'd seen this shanty before, but it was nondescript and forgettable. Lantern light flickered through its fabric walls and occasional loud crashes issued from its entrance, yet it was the whooping of men's voices that made the largest impression. We got in line. The length of the queue, though, was deceiving, for every few minutes a dozen or so men exited the shanty—wide-eyed, guffawing, slapping each other on the back, some returning to the end of the line to cycle through again—and the blocks-long queue would advance. In about thirty minutes' time we were within the doorway. After another round we stepped inside and were promptly blasted by a wall of heat and the crash of a gong that split my ears.

Lex pushed me forward. At a small table sat a Celestial. He was stocky, adorned with a long, black braid and a sullen disposition, with no hint of a smile to spare. Despite the din and the heat and the stuffiness enveloping him, he sat in a cocoon of serenity. And though he moved with deliberate intention, disconnected from all other beings, his hands moved at a whir, picking up the sacks laid down by the hopeful men, pouring the gold dust out opposite the counterweights on his brass scales. With no halting he then swept the shavings off to somewhere unseen and grabbed the next sack. The men, having thus paid, continued into the room. When Lex and I reached the table, the Celestial doubled the counterweights and grabbed the bag Lex held out for him. I glanced sideways at Lex.

"Where did you get—"

He shushed me with a finger on my mouth.

I pushed it aside. "Seriously, did you have this—"

"Later," he muttered and pinched me hard. As my eyes teared up, Lex plastered on a smile for the Celestial's benefit.

The Celestial didn't smile back. He emptied the bag onto the scale and the pans evened out, yet in that moment he slightly hesitated, giving a second look at Lex's offering. He studied Lex, the first time I'd seen him acknowledge the presence of another man in the room. Lex stared in return with his dumb grin. Something was off. A moment of annoyance stabbed me in the chest. Was my brother playing at something? How very much like him! Couldn't he just do something normal for once and *not* draw attention to himself? The Celestial scrutinized at him a beat longer, ignoring me completely, as though he already sensed who he'd have to deal with. Then two loud crashes from a gong broke the moment, and he swept the shavings out of sight. Lex nudged me into the room.

Inside the room the heat radiated still more, and I shed my jacket. In front of us, in the flickering lantern light, was a canvas wall with a dozen or so holes—about eye-height—bored into it. Half of them were occupied by other men, who stood peering through to whatever was on the other side. Lex spotted a pair of holes side by side and guided me to one whilst he shucked off his hat and took the other. The deafening gong crashed once more, and I jumped as the men around me raised a throaty cheer. Lex pointed to the hole. The other men were already peeking through, boyish and eager.

I peered in and saw a raised platform in the middle of the room. Lanterns stood in front and along the sides, yet there was nothing happening. "What are we looking at?" I asked Lex.

"That."

And at that moment, a leg knifed out of the shadows. Sharp and entirely naked, it explored the stage, probing for purchase, tapping here and bending there, sliding in and out of the light, until it issued forth and grew until whatever was attached to it slowly and silkily emerged from the shadow. The knee led, then the thigh, then the shin, then the ankle, all bare. Just this sent the men to full-mooned howling.

In the next moment a dress appeared, the borderline between flesh and cloth resting at the top of the thigh. One man whistled. The rest of the body poured out of the darkness like liquid and revealed a Celestial, tall and flawless, with not a blemish nor line on her golden skin, and lips painted the color of cherry. She wore a sort of silk robe with a flower print on it, yet the men weren't noticing her clothing; rather, it was that the robe couldn't contain the woman's appendages, which drew slavering from those in the audience. The men whooped with uncontained joy. Now in full view in the middle of the stage, the woman stood still, hands posed on her hips, never once peeping in our direction, waiting for something. One man exhorted her to "Take it off!" yet the woman batted nary an eyelash at the plea; only a slight smile played at her lips. I couldn't stop staring.

Someone began stomping on the ground in a rhythmic manner. The others joined in, creating a thunderous effect: STOMP STOMP STOMP STOMP STOMP STOMP STOMP. The woman responded. Starting slowly, with as smooth a movement as a ripple, she began to spin. Then again, then again, gradually picking up speed. Five times around she twirled, each revolution revealing more and more leg as the robe fanned out. Then, putting her foot down in dramatic STOMP of her own while the robe wrapped itself around her, she strutted across her stage, pushing each leg out as far as the slit in her robe would allow. The skin reflected the light as though it were another lantern, and the men hooted and hollered, and called out scandalous things. Yet nothing flapped her.

To cap it off she revolved once more, paused, waited for her robe to settle, and walked delicately off the stage, and out of our lives. The men stamped their feet and blasted shrill whistles. The gong crashed again and the next set of men entered the room, and we were pushed to the exit. When we made it outdoors, the frigid wind stung our faces with sand and the spell was broken. The whole thing took only a couple of minutes.

Lex flushed with excitement as we stood in the middle of Clay Street. "Whatcha think?" he asked.

"Well..." I replied.

"Isn't she something?"

"She is beautiful."

"Ha ha! Yes! That's my boy!" He clapped me on the shoulder and beamed, a wild glint in his eye.

I forced a brief smile and became serious again. "Lex. Where was that money from? How much do you have?"

Lex groaned dramatically. "Won't you hush up about that? Tonight's about having fun!"

"I'm working my fingers to the bone, and you're sitting on this money? We need that to live!"

"*This* is living! You're so cooped up in that 'hotel' you've forgotten that life can be fun."

"Because I'm supporting us!"

Lex rolled his eyes. "And *I'm* supporting your growth from being a priggish, henpecking nun into something that resembles a human male. But it looks like I need to open my wallet some more for that to happen."

I opened my mouth to return the volley, but Lex held up his hand and cut me off.

"Since you insist on ruining a fine evening, I'll tell you this: I'll make up for anything I spend—and more—with what I find in the hills. You have nothing to worry about. Now will you let me enjoy my last free night before I go off and make us a fortune?"

I glared at him.

Lex crossed his heart and put his hand up.

I shook my head and walked away from him.

"Goodnight, Sister Cyrus!" he called after me.

I raised my middle finger toward him, yet he'd already turned away to make for the Eldorado, awkwardly adjusting his pants.

August 8, 1849
San Francisco
Weather same as yesterday and day before.

I awakened early this morning. Lex was not in the room, which didn't surprise me; on the contrary, I would have been astonished to have found him present in the wee hours following a night out. With the sheer number of gambling saloons and bars available for his exploitation, Lex's proclamation that we should "spend the last night together as a family," I knew, would never be a serious one. Nonetheless, there I was and there he wasn't.

I ate, cleaned up the breakfast dishes, and swept the dining room. Lex hadn't returned. Then, after realizing that Lex had never told me *when* on Wednesday his steamer would depart, I journeyed to the ticket office to inquire. The agent told me 11:00 in the A.M., only two hours hence. There already sat the ship at anchor, awaiting her passengers. I returned to the G. House and saw that Lex's trunk remained untouched. I wasn't worried, exactly, yet my mood was darkening.

The owner, positively gleeful at the prospect of unloading a freeloader from his premises—despite my working double to cover Lex and me both—sent me out to purchase supplies, and the list was a long one, to my dismay: beef, pork, molasses, flour, ale, fresh water. All of it would take over an hour to gather in addition to carting it back to the hotel. So I set out in a rush, collecting all I could—and not attempting to bargain, which I knew would vex the owner immensely—in under forty-five minutes. I returned close to 10:30, and yet there were Lex's things, still sitting in a neat pile with no indication of being disturbed. Where in God's name was he? How did he expect to fulfill his grand plan of riches and tickets home if he wasn't even able to get himself on a boat? Just as I was about to spend the remainder of my free time pacing the room, however, the owner came by and requested that I join him in his office. I pressed my fists to my head—the ringing had already begun—as I followed him out.

The owner started blathering about how, as a newly single boarder, I wasn't let off the hook for Lex's contributions to the hotel. It was out of the goodness of his own heart that he had taken us in at our time of crisis, &c., and soon his lips were mouthing words that turned soundless and meaningless. I'm unsure why it meant so much to me that Lex made his boat on time. He could have boarded the next one out, or tomorrow's, or the next day's. All I knew is, Lex or no, I needed money. And so, with my thoughts buzzing about how to get it, I barely registered the owner telling me he was moving me to a smaller room. I stared out the door, tapped my foot, and rubbed the button in my pocket.

When I at last made my escape, I sprinted to our room. Lex's trunk was gone. The tent flap was swaying in the rising breeze.

August 16, 1849
San Francisco
*Warm midday, foggy and dusty on
either end of it.*

Today dawned with the town enveloped in a chilling fog with just a breath of breeze pushing up against the canvas tents. It was worse in the afternoon, when the wind picked up and the dust swirled down every street and into every niche, nook, and eyeball. The residents here pulled their jackets tight and shielded their faces with crooked arms and dried, cracked hands. In other words, what I've been told is a typical San Francisco summer day.

This past week has been a daze in my head, almost as though I'm dragging myself through a world with no color, painted with only a palette of grays. How could I have guessed that Lex's departure would affect me so strongly? I'd wanted him on that boat, after all, and he left when he said he would. But he didn't say goodbye. I've been sleepwalking ever since. My hands mechanically laid out the food, monotonously scrubbed the plates, and numbly cleared the gutter. I imagined him standing proudly in the middle of a sparkling river, the sun rising on his face and shimmering upon the nugget of gold he's holding up in triumphant delight.

This morning was no different. I, half awake, lugged food to the tables for the breakfast rush. It wasn't until I'd made my fourth trip when something snapped me into the present. "…in court, can you believe it?" a sunburned miner was saying to the table. "Who has ever heard of a Celestial doing *that?*"

The others in his audience shook their heads. "Against a white man? Nah."

"It is true, I swear it. He cheated her out of some money or something similar."

"Yeah? Where you heard it from?"

"Really? Half the Square is buzzing about it. Where have you been?"

"Makin' a livin', that's where. Anyway, who *hasn't* been cheated?"

"The trial is happening this morning. But mark my words, there is no way a judge will listen to a Celestial. Not against an American. I am surprised they will let her in the courtroom at all. Believe me, this is unprecedented."

"Unpressawhat?"

"See for yourself. I am on my way there myself. See some history. Why not?"

"Because I'm makin' a livin'. Ain't got time for that."

"Suit yourself. Hey, you there," the man called to me. "You ought to go down there. Get yourself an education on the law, see what happens in an American court. Land of freedom and justice, right, gents?"

"Whadda you know about the law?"

"Here we go," a third man muttered.

"I will have you know I read law at Litchfield."

"And yer now a half-baked lawyer lookin' for gold rocks!" The table laughed.

"Didn't that school close down?" someone else called, and the table exploded again.

The man's face reddened and he turned back to me. "You will not want to miss it. Celestials don't land in court every day." He smiled and spread his arms wide. "Where else but San Francisco?"

I ran through my chores list in my head. After getting the dishes cleared and washed, I'd be free for a couple of hours until dinner preparations. I might as well go. It left less chance that the owner would saddle something else on my shoulders. Court didn't sound like much of a thrill, but it *was* free. And anyway, I've always been fascinated by the idea of—

"Hey, boy. You gonna put that plate down or what? We're

starvin' here!"

*   *   *

An hour later, having reluctantly been given leave by the owner, I sat in the alcalde's office at the western end of Portsmouth Square. A sizable crowd filled the room, chatting and shedding their excess energy before the trial began. At the rear of the room stood some Chinese men, stone-faced and silent. When the door opened, the crowd hushed and turned to look. I did the same and froze at the sight.

There was the dancer, the same Celestial lady Lex and I had watched through the wall on Lex's last night in town. She stood framed in the doorway, pausing, looking straight ahead but at no man in particular. She was dressed exquisitely, in an apricot satin jacket over green pantaloons, punctuated by a colorful pair of socks that split at her big toes for her thong sandals to slip on. She looked young, so much younger than that night. Her cheeks were whitened with powder, which contrasted sharply with her thin, black eyebrows and her jet-black hair that she wore in a tight bun. It was as if she'd taken one step out of some faraway land and found herself in the middle of San Francisco.

After an exaggerated pause, she walked past the gaping men and into the center of the room. Someone let loose a sharp whistle, at which crowd chuckled, but she ignored it. Keeping her eyes above the heads of the onlookers, she sat down slowly and effortlessly into the vacant chair near the front of the room. All eyes, mine included, were glued to her. The half-baked lawyer sat a few rows away, his jaw nearly on the floor. The dancer allowed a small smile, clearly enjoying every second of the attention. In a chair opposite, a man sat quietly, looking bored and unamused.

The door banged open again. Someone shouted, "All rise and remove your hats! The Honorable George Baker presiding!" and the sound of dozens of scraping chairs filled the room as the crowd took to its feet. A middle-aged man in a black robe with a white collar made his way to the desk at the front.

"Be seated," he commanded, and the crowd sat. He did the same, his expression solemn, as if this gathering were like any other. "Welcome, everyone. It's a rare occasion to see a woman in court, rarer still that that woman is Celestial. Historic, really." The audience murmured.

"Now then," he started, wasting no more time and addressing the dancer. "What's your name, miss?"

She stood slowly and smoothly. "I am Ah Toy."

Her voice was soft but carried energy behind it. It was powerful yet muted. Effortless. Judge Baker stared at her and pursed his lips.

"Mr. Honor, sir," she hastened to add. The room snickered.

"That's enough," Judge Baker's voice cut through the hum, and the room immediately quieted. He turned to his deputy and gave a nod. The deputy rose from his chair and strode to Ah Toy. Holding a book in front of her, he said, "Place your right hand on the Bible and repeat after me."

Ah Toy shook her head.

The deputy faltered, glanced at the judge, and repeated, "Place your right hand on this Bible and repeat after me."

She shook her head again and looked at Judge Baker. "Why do this?"

Judge Baker's lips tightened. "Miss Ah Toy, we will not start the proceedings until you swear an oath."

"Oath?"

"Yes. You need to tell us that you'll be truthful. Truthful means you will not lie."

"I know this."

The audience chuckled again.

"I need..." Ah Toy looked around her for something, but seemed at a loss. A rustling then came from the audience, as well as protests of "Watch it!" and "Who's pushing?" Out of the sea of white men emerged one of the Chinese men from the back of the room. He hurried over to Ah Toy, dug into his pants, and pulled out a piece of yellow paper and a pen. She gave him a curt nod. The man dissolved back into the gallery. Ah Toy began silently writing on the paper. Over the next few minutes she wrote, filling the paper with inky marks. No one interrupted, not even Judge Baker with his put-out expression. They may have been afraid to.

Something mysterious and strange was taking place. When the paper was filled, Ah Toy placed the pen down and addressed the judge.

"Please, Mr. Honor, you have fire?" She mimicked striking a match.

Judge Baker glanced at his deputy, but the man only shrugged. "What for?"

"For oath, send to spirits."

"Will it speed things along?"

"Yes, very fast."

He didn't look convinced, but barked out anyway, "Which man here has a loco foco?"

Amidst the sounds of rustling clothes and murmuring, another Chinese man materialized at Ah Toy's side and handed her one; then he, too, disappeared. Many in the crowd stood to get a better look at what was about to happen. Ah Toy walked up to Judge Baker's desk. He watched her warily.

"This is for truth. Chinese way," Ah Toy announced. She then struck one of the matches.

"Easy, now," the judge said. "This is a wooden building."

"Yes, very careful," Ah Toy replied. The audience craned their necks to watch her pick up the yellow paper and ignite it. It immediately caught fire, and she placed it on the desk. The flames ate through the yellow sheet and twisted Ah Toy's writing into a small pile of black ashes. Only when the last of the sparks died out did Ah Toy look back to Judge Baker. "Oath to tell truth."

He leaned back and steepled his fingers, regarding her. The onlookers held their breath. "Very well," he said. "Let's begin then. Return to your seat." He waved his deputy and the Bible away. Ah Toy gracefully sat.

If the crowd was looking for entertainment, it wasn't disappointed. I admit that the proceedings were far more interesting than a stack of dishes after breakfast.

"Miss Ah Toy," Judge Baker said, "what is your grievance?"

She looked blank for an instant. "Please repeat?" she asked.

"Your grievance. What is your grievance?"

Ah Toy glanced around her and murmured, "I don't know this

word." More snickers from the gallery.

Judge Baker was not amused. "Quiet!" he barked, and the room fell silent again. "What is your...problem? Why are you here?" He sounded like an impatient schoolteacher, like Mr. Payran talking to a child.

"Yes, Mr. Honor." She smoothed out her jacket and once again affected an elevated air. Taking a deep breath, she began.

"Mr. Honor, I come because men cheat me."

"Very well. How are you cheated?"

"Some men pay brass but should pay gold."

"They should pay gold? Why is that?"

"Gold is best quality money." The audience nodded.

"Indeed," Judge Baker said. "No need to tell us twice."

"Tell twice...?" Ah Toy asked with a plastered smile.

Judge Baker waved it off. The audience chuckled, then quieted when the judge shot the crowd an impatient look.

"Miss Ah Toy," Judge Baker continued, "how do you know these men are paying you in brass?"

"I do tests."

"Do you? What tests are those?"

"I test weight. Gold very heavy than the brass."

"That is true, gold is heavier." Judge Baker folded his hands. "Miss Ah Toy, do you have the brass with you?"

"Yes, at my home."

"Not here?"

"At my home. I will take it here." She started to leave her seat and make for the door.

Judge Baker looked incredulous. "Hold on. How far away is your house?"

"Mr. Honor, three minutes I return with brass."

The judge sighed. "Fine. Be quick, I have a full docket today."

"Docket...?"

"*Go.*"

The audience laughed. Ah Toy walked out the door as serenely as she could with a half-smile set on her whitened face. When the door shut, the gallery erupted with chatter. What an unusual event! Was this a *real* trial? Was Judge Baker taking her seriously?

There was no possible way she could win, was there? No, impossible. But this was the Wild West, so who knew what scrambled-up law they practiced out here? The lawyer from breakfast caught my eye and shrugged.

I sank into my own thoughts. *Brass. Brass is lighter than gold. It takes more brass to equal gold.* I thought back to Lex's and my visit to the dancer's tent. *My brother miraculously had a bag of money. The Celestial had put Lex's gold on the scale. He'd hesitated. He'd looked at Lex a long while, as if something was off.* As I caught sight of the quiet, bored man sitting across from Ah Toy's vacant chair, a single thought fell over me like a curtain. *Should Lex be sitting in that seat?*

It suddenly didn't feel safe to be here, but before I could contemplate edging myself out of the room, the door opened, the chatter ceased, and Ah Toy reappeared, this time with the Celestial. He carried a pan full of sparkling something. I slumped in my seat.

"Bring that here," Judge Baker ordered. The Celestial laid the pan on his desk. The judge picked up a pinch of shavings and looked at them closely. He nodded and replaced them, then sat for a minute, staring at the pile and lost in thought. The room was quiet.

"Miss Ah Toy," he said suddenly, "why are these men paying you?"

The room exhaled and a few people snickered.

"Pay me?"

"Yes. Why are the good men of this town paying you?"

"Pay me for my business."

"And what exactly is your business?"

Many in the audience were grinning. This was the entertainment they'd come for.

Ah Toy gazed defiantly around the room with a nonchalant smile.

"I give look-see show."

"A 'look-see show'? What, exactly, is that?"

Ah Toy raised her head high. "Men pay. One ounce. I take off clothes. I give look-see show!" she said with a dignified flourish.

People in the audience laughed with more than a few hoots and hollers. "Give us a look!" one voice yelled out. "I've got real gold right here!" called another. Judge Baker had to pound the desk before the crowd agreed to calm.

"This is a court of law!" he bellowed. "Any other disruptions will result in ejection from this room!" The deputy was on his feet, trying his hardest to appear menacing. The laughter finally died down.

"Miss Ah Toy," Judge Baker continued in a flustered and annoyed tone, "you realize such activities are illegal."

She didn't answer. The audience hooted again and the judge yelled, *"Enough!"* and pounded the desk. The onlookers were having a marvelous time.

"Miss Ah Toy," Judge Baker said, his face flushed, "you said you've been cheated."

"Yes," she replied, calm as ever.

"Yes, *Your Honor.*"

"Yes, Mr. Honor."

"Who is it you are accusing?"

"Accuse...?" She cocked her head slightly.

"Yes, accuse!" Judge Baker snapped. "Who cheated you?"

"Yes. I know who cheat." She pointed at the quiet man opposite her.

"You, sir," Judge Baker said to the man. "Your name?"

The man paused and rolled his eyes. "Sam Carroway, Your Honor."

"Not only him!" Ah Toy butted in. "More!"

"Miss Ah Toy, are you accusing more people in this room? This is not the way this works."

Ah Toy turned and scanned the room. This time she made eye contact with several men, winding the room's atmosphere tight. A few of the men refused to return her gaze and became instantly intrigued with the floor.

"Miss Ah Toy."

The audience leaned forward, now still as she continued her survey.

The judge narrowed his eyes. "This court has a full day's work to complete."

Ah Toy spun and pointed. "Him!" she said, indicating a mustachioed man with a sun-worn, deeply creased visage. "He pay brass! He cheat!"

"What?" the man blurted, shocked by the accusation. But quickly his mouth curled into a grin. The audience cheered.

"And him!" Ah Toy wheeled on another man, younger with a baby face, who immediately turned red and sank in his chair. The audience cheered louder.

She found a third man. "Him! He pay brass! Criminal!" The third man didn't smile, laugh, or slump. He only gave her a wink. The audience howled.

Judge Baker was beside himself, trying to restore order in his courtroom, and his useless deputy only stood there puffing up his chest. Ah Toy's expression, for the first time, broke after the relentless onslaught of derision and laughter. She turned to the judge and pleaded.

"Bad men! They steal my business!"

Judge Baker appeared to be on the verge of defeat. When he focused back on Ah Toy, his expression was not one of understanding or pity. It was loathing.

"Miss Ah Toy," he said in a deadly tone. "You have come into this court and made a mockery of it."

"Mock—?"

"You have instigated these men into hysterics and accused men of a crime without any proof."

"I have proof!" Ah Toy shouted indignantly.

"You are speaking to the court in an offensive and disrespectful manner! Because of this and the other reasons just stated, this case is dismissed."

The audience clapped and whistled. When the Judge started to rise, Ah Toy seemed to sense she'd lost.

"What do you know?" she spat at him. "Crazy *gwai-lo!* This is justice? *Gam Saan* justice? Gold Mountain justice?"

The audience cheered her on. "You tell him, Mary! Give him a piece of your mind! Give him the what-for!"

"Deputy!" Judge Baker bellowed. "Get her out of here. And

clear this courtroom!"

Ah Toy disappeared into the crowd and didn't materialize after that. I felt a clap on my shoulder, and the half-baked lawyer was there, looking exhilarated.

"Well!" he said. "What gumption! To accuse those men like that? In front of everyone? A lot of embarrassed expressions on a lot of faces. A historic day for the law. What a show!"

"Not a good show for her," I said.

The lawyer laughed. "Not at all! Still, this is the type of event that can move mountains."

He saw the confusion on my face. "Yes, she lost today. But starting today, everyone here will start to believe that a Chinese in court is not so singular a thing. She nudged us in that direction. And anyway," he continued with a wink, "what an advertisement for her business!"

My gaze swept over the men in the courtroom, all laughing raucously while the deputy struggled to herd them through the door. The Chinese men had already filed out. Before I knew it, I was swallowed in the crush and spat from that room of enlightenment and into the Square. I walked quickly as I could back to the Garrett House. There was work awaiting me; it wouldn't do to dally and have the Celestial recognize me from that night. I returned to my room and shut the door, suddenly relieved that justice had slipped from the dancer's grip.

August 20, 1849
San Francisco
Commonly breezy.

Yesterday was the most grievous day ever.

It's difficult to know where to begin, and in truth I'm still shaken. A month has passed since my arrival in S.F., a week and a half since Lex abandoned me for the diggings, and yet a thousand days must have transpired in that time, none of them worse than the one before today. I'm fortunate that I'm able to write this at all, though I should wrap this up and have it away by the time they return.

I had a rare day off, it being Sunday, and thus I designed to walk through Happy Valley and sit on the shore to face Yerba Buena Island. I carried my journal and writing implements with me to practice illustrating, and after a simple breakfast I departed the G. House and looked forward to a morning of clearing my foggy-of-late head. The Square had few people, though was not empty—it never is—and those who were present were meek enough, taking care of their personal business. The Rev. Taylor was preparing his "church" at one corner of the Square, where he always holds his outdoor sermons. The Celestial, the money-taker from Lex's and my last night out, emerged from the dancer's tent. I turned sharply away from both and hoofed it in the opposite direction.

One small errand I needed to tend to was the replenishment of my writing supplies. I'd picked up from the dining room chatter that Woodworth & Morris on the Long Wharf was a prime seller of such things, so I hiked circuitously down the hill, past Montgomery and onto the Wharf. Few merchants were open this early, but I knew they would soon be, despite it being Sunday, as San Franciscans care less for the Almighty Father than they do for the Almighty Dollar.

Woodworth & Morris was indeed not yet open, so I meandered about, keeping distance from the Chinese dock girls at the far end of the pier and taking in the morning scenery of abandoned ships bobbing upon the water. Something about the pattern and repetition of the naked main masts against the backdrop of the Contra Costa hills captured my eye. I had set myself down on the edge of the pier and withdrawn my pen and journal to capture them when the creak of a footstep on the wooden boards caused me to glance back. There was the Celestial, pattering about. He appeared not to notice me as he continued down the Wharf, peering into the shuttered stores, obviously of the same mind as I. I turned back to my scene and opened this journal to a blank page, then inked my pen and commenced sketching. The quiet enveloped me, and only the lapping waves, the cry of a gull, and an occasional, vague wondering of Lex's current state reached my awareness.

I was putting the finishing touches on my third ship when, rapider than my brain could comprehend, this journal was ripped out of my hands. In the next moment I was weightless, my stomach crawling into my throat; then the shock of freezing water knifed me in the face and limbs. I flashed back to the Hudson River as I beat my arms and strained to stay above the surface, yet when I gulped for air something else kicked in, a sort of muscle memory, and I found myself, quite without meaning to, moving my arms in looping patterns under the water. Thank you, Leland.

But I was failing fast. In the frigid S.F. harbor, I spent all my strength to keep my head above the water. My arms and legs were like numb lead. The ringing in my ears needled into my brain.

Something slapped near me. I turned, dazed, to see the paddle side of an oar hovering near my face. I instinctively grabbed for it. As soon as I did, it pulled me to a skiff that had materialized beside me. As my arms cradled the gunwale, two hands clamped down on me, heaved me into the boat, and I splayed on the floor, sputtering and sopping wet. I coughed and wiped my eyes. When I focused, I took my first look at my rescuer. It was the Celestial.

"What?" I gasped as my chest heaved and my hair dripped. "How…?"

He didn't say a word, nor did he for the entirety of his mission; he only regained the oars and rowed toward shore. His betrayed no emotion, and his braid swayed with each stroke. When we made land, he threw my arm over his shoulder, helped me out of the craft, and walked me up Clay Street. I probably could have walked under my own power, but since I was shaking so hard and he had such a strong presence, I let him guide me up the hill and to the Square. "Thank you," I said through chattering teeth once we came to it. "I can walk the rest of the way." Yet he held on and continued in what he must have thought a helpful manner. As he was the first person since Rev. Taylor to assist me so generously, and not wishing to appear an ingrate, and furthermore surmising that the language barrier played a role in my inability to relieve him of his zealous chivalry, I let him lead.

He led me directly into the dancer's tent. It was warm, thankfully, though I hardly recognized it; the peeping wall and the stage were both gone and the tent was cavernous. Then he led me to a chair, pushed me down on it, and with a rope and surprising dexterity, tied me to it. He left the room and I sat there—stunned, alone, shivering, and dripping bay water onto the packed dirt floor.

*   *   *

I didn't know where the Celestial had disappeared to. He'd bound me so quickly that it wasn't until he exited the tent that I realized my hands and legs were immobile, and it was by promptly falling sideways onto the ground that my situation was nastily confirmed. My wet clothes squelched into the ground.

"Hello?" I called out and waited.

No one responded.

I turned my head away from the dirt. "Hey!"

I waited a full minute. Nothing.

"What is this?!"

There was no response. My face warmed and a soft ringing

began to pound in my head. Little fires of rage ignited in my gut, and I clenched my fists. I gathered air in my lungs like giant bellows, then pushed it out with all my might.

"WHERE ARE YOU, YOU DIRTY CELESTIAL?!"

The tent was quiet save for the sounds of the Square outside: conversation, exclamations, business, laughter, horses clopping, wagons squeaking. They all went on, indifferent. No one came.

"Goddamn this cursed town!" I bleated, panting from exhaustion.

From where I lay, I blinked away freezing drips of salt water rolling down my forehead as I attempted a more thorough survey of the room. It was entirely unrecognizable from my last visit. For one, it was morning, so the room was illuminated by daylight rather than strategically placed lanterns. For another, I was on the floor and sideways; what I *did* see was at a distorted tilt. And third, the layout—that which I *could* discern—had changed entirely. The Celestial's gold-counting table had disappeared, in addition to the partition and stage. In their places stood a bed, a small table for dining—maybe *that* was the Celestial's table?—a chair, and a washbasin. If I hadn't recognized the tent's location in the Square when I was led in, I would've believed myself to be in another abode altogether. It was as if an auctioneer had sold the place off and a new party had taken up residence.

When I next opened my eyes, the light shone at a different angle and the sounds of the Square outside had increased, which meant I must have fallen asleep. I studied the room again. No one appeared to have been in; I'd been deposited into a bank vault and summarily forgotten. Life continued around me, but for me there was nothingness. I would have pressed my fists into my head but for the fact they were bound to my sides. The ringing, instead, pressed on.

The sunlight burning through the tent aggravated me and so, with great coordination and all the strength I could manage, I closed my eyes, pushed my head into the ground, and rolled on my stomach to rest on my other side. My eyes cooled with relief. When I opened them again, the young dancer was sitting there, watching me. I yelped and jumped out of my goose-fleshed skin.

"Dirty Celestial? Cursed town?" she said in a soft, dangerous voice before I could gather my wits. She stared at me with dark, unblinking, unsettling eyes. She wasn't made up as she had been on the night Lex and I watched her dance, nor when I saw her in court. Her face was plain, her dress common, her hair in no special arrangement, and yet the totality of her was as striking as any of the fashionable ladies-about-town at home. How long had she been in the room? Had she watched my every desperate move, and heard my every pleading cry? She had materialized like a ghost.

The dancer stood and walked toward me. Even from my warped perspective I could tell she was a tall woman, much taller than the Celestial, and the other China folk around the town as well. Standing directly over me, she stared at me down the length of her body, making the effect especially pronounced.

"You thought you get away?" she said with a sneer that uglied her face in an instant.

"Get away?" I rasped. A salty drop seeped into my mouth.

She gave a quick jerk of her head, and a cold, metal point pressed against my throat. I jumped out of my skin a second time, which caused it to prick my skin, and presently warmth trickled down my neck. The Celestial money-taker had returned.

The dancer crouched down to my level. "You," she said, "you cheat me. You and other man." Every word was deadly quiet yet filled the entire room.

I squirmed to move away from the man's knife but without success. "What do you mean?" But I knew it must have been true.

The Celestial's dagger pressed harder into my flesh. "My man he know gold," the dancer said. "You pay with other kind. Too light."

"I…" I tried to swallow, "I didn't cheat you. Maybe my brother did, but I had no knowledge of it. I didn't want to be there at all!"

"Brother."

Lex. In that moment I could have torn him limb from limb. "I'm not the one who paid! It was him!" I felt no qualms ratting on that derelict.

She cocked her head. "He is where?"

The dagger dug in all the more. I winced and swallowed shallowly. "He…he's digging for gold."

"Not here?"

"He went to the hills."

"Too bad."

The knife pierced my skin and fire burned my throat as I cried out.

"No, please! I didn't know he'd cheat you!"

"He cheat. You with him."

I knew I must be done in or at the least mutilated, if Celestial law were anything like N.Y. Tears welled in my eyes.

"No cry," she said calmly. "You very lucky."

There was no way that was true.

"With you I make the deal. You work, pay full price back, for all the *gwai-lo* cheat me."

My eyes bulged.

"Agree?"

"I…" The knife pressed in. It stung like a hornet.

"Agree?"

The Celestial began to twist it. My vision turned gray and glittery. My ears screamed. I tried to choke out the words, "…'gree…'gree…"

The dancer nodded, and the Celestial pulled the knife away. I gasped for air.

"Good." She patted my face. "You sleep with 'Dirty Celestial.' Awake, you work." She took my head in her hands and made me look directly in her face. "My man always find you. Good with the knife." I winced from the pressure in my head and she smiled.

The man unbound me, and when I turned back she'd gone as silently as she appeared. The Celestial threw something at my feet. It was my journal and writing implements, no worse for wear. I looked back up and the man, too, was gone. I was alone again, with only a bleeding wound, sore wrists and ankles, a pounding headache, and my thoughts, such as they were.

I held my aching throat with one hand and my shrieking temple with the other, and I stayed in this position, with barely a movement, for over an hour. If only there were some water. I needed air. A soft mattress, a seared steak, dead silence, an eternal night…

I should escape, I thought. But though I couldn't see nor hear them, I knew both the dancer and the Celestial must not have gone far, based on their quick appearances from nowhere, and on the fact that they'd left me unbound and wouldn't permit me in this state without supervision. So how to make my exit? My headache was on the wane, at last, which allowed my thoughts to entertain nascent external ideas. A few floated into my head:

1. This setup must be a test of sorts, or a trap. How could a hostage be left like this, unbound and unsupervised? But was I *really* unsupervised? Maybe they lurked just outside, listening, alert to any chance that I'd moved from my spot.

2. The Celestial was armed and quick with a knife. If he truly was hidden just steps away, I had no chance of exiting the tent unscathed.

3. Yelling for help would be fruitless. The S.F. public was remarkably deaf, except, of course, my two captors.

4. I was wet, cold, and hungry. Through my shivering, clammy skin, my guts twisted in their emptiness and my head felt faint and dizzy. The last time I had eaten was at the G. House that morning, yet the ensuing events stretched the day into a year, and it felt that way to my poor stomach. My mind could now think of little else. The white canvas walls became giant biscuits. The brown ropes at my feet became fat sausages. And then, God knew that that very moment was the one in which to torture me, for all the aromas of food from the Square wafted into the tent with a slight change in the breeze. Boiled meats from the American stands ravaged my nose, followed by savory curries from the Celestial eateries and the overwhelming pungency of freshly baked bread.

Not knowing what my next step should be, I searched the room, first with my eyes, then with my hands, for a bit of food. There was none. Nor did I find any water, which made me think of it all the more and added to a growing parchedness in my throat.

If they were so serious about my servitude, what were they playing at by leaving me here? I'd read accounts of kidnappings— like the Cynthia Parker girl in Texas—yet even her Comanche abductors fed, clothed, and watched over her. So where had these Celestials gone off to?

Time passed, who knows how much. I can't recall how I spent it, but I remember my heart pounded at every rustle and footstep. I didn't dare set foot outside the tent, though at one point I peeked through the opening—just enough to get a view of the outdoors. People hustled and bustled as always, with no time to care that a boy was held prisoner just feet away. Would they have cared if they'd known? I swept my gaze across the Square, past the merchants, past the miners, past the bootblacks, past the church congregants…and glimpsed two Celestials walking across the Plaza.

I froze.

Their backs were to me and they were across the Square near Washington Street, so I couldn't make out their features well enough to confirm if they were *my* two Celestials. I stared hard until my eyes watered. Maybe? I scanned the rest of the Square, but espied no other Chinese, and when I turned back the two were gone. My heart fluttered and my pulse pounded in my ears.

Should I?

I surveyed the scene. The dancer and her man weren't in sight. My clothes weren't dripping anymore, so no trail of wet dirt would tell where I'd gone. *Now.* I took one ginger footstep out of the tent. *Now!* I pricked up my ears. I took another step. *Go now!!* I paused to take in the Square. But where should I go? *For God's sake, RUN!* Something flickered to my right. I turned to the left, toward the direction of the Garrett House out of habit, and collided into the dancer.

"Oh, lucky woman!" she cooed loudly, wrapping me up in a firm embrace. "Handsome man!" A couple of Mexican men walking by chuckled and nudged each other.

"No! Please! She's kidnapping me!" I yelled at them, but they smiled.

"No English!" one of them said.

"Gringo loco," the other replied and they walked on, laughing.

The Celestial clapped his hand over my mouth, stuck his knife at my back, and ushered me back into the tent while the dancer followed, all smiles and simpers.

Bound all the tighter to the chair with double the rope, I watched the dancer—who no longer smiled—and the Celestial move about the shanty, gathering items in their hands until they both stood over me.

The dancer said something to her man, and he threw something in my lap. She picked it up and dangled it in front of my face: a newspaper, thin and crinkled with tiny type. "Read," the dancer commanded, holding the paper at my eye level and pointing to a short paragraph.

I didn't dare take my eyes off her.

"Read!"

I reluctantly glanced at the newspaper. *Miss Atoy was brought up on a charge of keeping a disorderly home*, the story read. Disorderly... *that* was true enough. And they're calling this tent a home?

"Loud."

I glanced up at her then back to the story. It was written by James King of William, the reporter from the Hounds attack. I read out loud, trying to keep my voice from shaking.

Recorder's Court
by James King of William
Daily Alta California

Miss Atoy was brought up on a charge of keeping a disorderly home. The house is on Clay Street, opposite the Post Office, and is supposed to contain a number of valuable Chinese curiosities which cause a crowd there continually, which necessarily causes a row, so that the neighborhood is disturbed.

"See?" Ah Toy said.

I didn't, and I didn't care.

"See? They cheat me. I go to court. Mr. Honor say no case. All laugh. Now," she hit the newspaper. "American justice, huh?"

I didn't answer. They should have thrown her in the bay.

She left for a moment, then returned with two small pots. "Now, Chinese justice."

The Celestial kicked my chair over, and I landed on the floor with a painful thump. Then they bent down over me, and with surprising strength she gripped my right arm and placed her weight upon it.

"Old China criminal get tattoo. All people know the crime."

Her man took the knife and, with the focus of a surgeon, scored four troughs into the back of my forearm, just above my wrist, in the shape of a square. I arched my back as a white-hot, fiery pain seared my skin, and I cried out in agony. My two captors, though, took no pains to gag me, likely because, as I had already realized to my horror, they knew no one would run to my rescue. Yet they weren't finished. Poising his knife once more, my torturer carved out two more strokes in the shape of a mountain, and although my cold and hunger had been swept away by the clarity of the pain, my eyes blurred with tears and I couldn't fully see what his design was.

"You very lucky. Old China criminal get tattoo on the face."

Her man then lay the knife down and took up the two pots. He uncapped both, and while warm blood trickled down my hand and wrist, poured a bit of one into the other, swirled it, and dripped the solution onto my raw wound, using his thumb to rub it in. I clenched and yelled again at this fresh abuse. The dancer gripped me all the stronger.

It must have been an hours-long ordeal, yet couldn't have been any more than just a few minutes. When I dared to reopen my eyes, the two fiends had released me. I peered at my arm, which now throbbed in an unbearable ache. They had defiled it. The cuts were welted, raised and red, but where blood should have seeped was instead greenish-blue. Blinking away the tears, I focused on the image the Celestial had carved:

I didn't know what to make of it; the symbol held no meaning for me except for the agony it inflicted on my wretched limb. I turned away, not able to bear the ugliness. Yet there was the dancer instead, wearing a smile that said, "Well?"

"What have you done to me?" I growled, my eyes sending her daggers of hatred and loathing.

"Chinese justice. I tell you, he very good with the knife." She reached over to her table, grabbed a handful of rice, and dropped it on the floor near my head. I spat at it—or at least attempted to, yet instead my saliva dribbled down my chin.

She stepped over to me. "You now eat, then sleep. Tomorrow, many works."

No one cares that I'm missing. Maybe the owner of the Garrett House? It wouldn't have taken him long to clear out my belongings and fill the room with another hopeful prospector. He could find anyone to complete his chores. I looked away from her to my sore arm, and her gaze followed mine.

"You know it?"

She took my wrist and held it delicately, and because they'd rebound it to the chair, I couldn't snatch it away.

"You run, you hide, no matter. You always know. 'Prisoner.' My prisoner."

She gave it a squeeze and the wound screamed anew, then she blew out the lantern.

I felt into my pocket to rub the button, anything for comfort, but my fingers grasped only cloth and lint. *It must have fallen out in the bay at Long Wharf.* I shut my eyes and tears leaked down my face.

September 3, 1849
San Francisco
Cold evening wind.

The dancer doesn't allow me much idle time to dwell on my condition. The day following my marking, after her man escorted me behind the tent to relieve myself, she put me to work. The Celestials showed no consideration or accommodation for my injured hand. Under their stern direction and watchful gaze, I washed every surface: dishes, cups, cutlery, table, desk, bed frame, tent walls, tent ceiling, dirt floor, and yes, the very chair to which I had been bound. At the end of that first day, I collapsed and fell asleep without eating, clutching my hand.

The next day, incredibly, she had a new set of chores: emptying and scrubbing the bedpans, scraping dried rice from the bottom of the pots, darning the holes in her man's garments, beating the rugs, refilling the lanterns, washing the sheets, and changing out the straw in the mattresses. The third day contained still more.

At the end of each day during these past two weeks, the dancer inspects my work. What she doesn't deem satisfactory she orders me to redo, and what she does, she ignores and moves me on to the next job. I'm allowed no questions, save for clarification on a task. When I lag, they withhold my meals. When I *am* fed, the rice is dry and stale.

Since that first day, they no longer leave me unattended. Mostly. On rare occasions when the dancer was out in the Square, her man stepped out for some air, but only briefly. I'm accounted for every other minute of the day. One might conclude that the tattooing knife hangs threateningly enough over my head to dissuade any further attempts at escape, yet they seem convinced that I'm an ever-present risk for flight. But their methods are working; I'm too exhausted to attempt anything.

When I awoke this morning, therefore, to find myself alone in the tent, my heart skipped. *No, it's only another trick.* I sat, waiting for them to return. Preferably with a bowl of rice for me.

But they never did.

Don't get your hopes up. They're outside like last time, I know it.

Shadows of strangers moved past the shanty, but I dared not call out to them, knowing that somehow the Celestials would know. Yet an hour later I was still alone, and the anxiety was working on me. My ears started to ring. I pressed my fists into my head and the shadows unceasingly passed in front of me, some moving left, some moving right, all with someplace to go.

My captors had never left me alone for that long before. *Maybe I should call out.* The knife pierced my throat again, and my hand ached with red puffiness. Shouldn't my wounds have healed by now? What did Mr. Payran teach us about infections in school? *"Breathe a vein to ease the pain."* I could stand to lose a pint or two.

A commotion to my left grabbed my attention. Voices, a lot of them, murmured, with a few shouts punctuating the shift in energy I could feel through the walls of the tent. I glanced around and tiptoed to the opening. Taking a breath to calm my head, I peeked through the flap, then stepped gingerly into the doorway. I wouldn't have done it were I thinking clearly.

A small crowd gathered around the alcalde's office and was making noise, standing on the balls of their feet to better view something out of sight to me, and others walked, then jogged to the rapidly swelling crowd. I stood on my own toes, but too many people choked my view, so I instead turned to my right. Fools with necks like rubber ran by me; the Square was alive with skittering little ants. "Is it the alcalde?" someone yelled. "The Hounds are after him," someone else answered. "He's barricaded himself!" I took a breath. My head momentarily cleared while I focused. *Now,* or else no one would be left to cover my escape to the right, and with any luck, the dancer and the Celestial would be too drawn to the distracting cacophony to notice me.

I hesitated a second, then another second, then retrieved my journal—now my only possession other than the clothes on my back—stepped out, turned toward Long Wharf, and ran. I dodged and weaved through the current of people pushing against me. "Wrong way!" someone yelled. I pushed and stabbed my elbows through the throng, each of my footsteps pounding 'tween my ears, till I saw daylight through the mob, which spit me out onto Kearny Street. I didn't dare look back. My legs flew me down the hill until I landed, panting, at the shipping office on Long Wharf.

"What's happening?" the ticket agent asked, coming out from behind the window into the street.

I gulped at the air in reply.

He walked by me a few paces and craned his neck. "Come, boy, what's the ruckus up there?"

"I need your help," I coughed. "I've been kidnapped by two Chinese. I need to get out of here fast!" How could a downhill run wind me so?

The agent furrowed his brow. "Kidnapped?" He looked past me, up the hill, to the left and to the right. "By Chinese?"

"I've only just escaped. They'll find me." I scanned the shore frantically. "I must get out of here. Can you hide me until the next boat leaves?"

He watched me a moment, taking his time, glancing behind me as if to verify that I truly was on the lam from two foreigners.

"Please, they did this to me"—I thrust my hand in his face and showed him the angry welt from the tattoo—"and this." I revealed the scar on my throat.

The agent frowned. "Apologies, but I've seen worse wounds on a monte dealer at the Eldorado."

"They threatened to kill me!"

He puffed up his cheeks and blew them out, then gazed up the hill toward the excitement. No one had followed me onto the dock. "Look," he said, "like most people here, I'm no defender of the Celestials. You can hide in the office for a bit, but you'll have to leave when I close up. And if your two Asiatics—if they ever get here—get violent, don't think I'll be your number two."

I scrambled into the office. He followed me in while I shoved myself under the counter. "Thank you," I whispered.

"You just stay under there. As long as they don't come in, they won't see you." He went back to craning his neck to the sound of the hubbub. "If only I could see..." he muttered.

Ten or fifteen minutes went by, and he never asked me about the dancer or her man. In fact, he was rather nonplussed by the whole situation, as if I were just another willful youth up to no good. Soon my legs started cramping and I had to contort myself to allow them to stretch. "Sir," I said up to him. "Do you know anyone who needs a sailor?"

"A sailor?" he asked distractedly. Half of S.F. was moving toward the Square with an excited hum. "What is going *on* up there?"

"I just need a way out of here. I'll do anything. Are there any boats leaving today?"

He brought his hands down but never took his eyes off the hill. "First of all," he affected a put-upon air, "it's a 'ship.' A boat is a log in a sewage gutter. Second, only women say 'sailor.' For you"—his eyes gave me a once-over—"it's 'deckhand,' or more likely, 'cabin boy.' Third," he swept his arm over the Bay, "what ships do you see preparing to embark? Which are loading up? Go ahead, point them out."

"What about that steamer parked there?" I pointed to the vessel through the wall. "Where's that going?"

"Nothing but questions, eh?"

"Do they need an extra man?"

"'Man'? Boy, that *ship* currently *moored* is *bound* for Sacramento. If you need out of here, you can pay for a ticket like everyone else. Then you can disappear into the hills for as long as you want. If you can survive the heat, dust, bandits, wild animals, Indians, and whatnot. But you won't get there quick. Captain won't be here for at least another four hours, so you either wait for him *quietly* or scoot and come back to talk to him later."

A loud roar rose from up the hill in the direction of the Square. The ticket agent paced, checked his pocket watch, and made up his mind.

"All right, out you go," he said, waving his arms toward the door.

"What? I just got here!"

"Tough. Out you go."

"But..." My breathing came shallow and fast and my ears rang. "Where should I hide?"

"Wherever, but not here. I'm closing up."

"I won't touch a thing while you're gone. I promise."

"No doing. Time to go."

"But they'll find me! Do you see them? Are they coming?"

"Out."

He grabbed my arm, shoved me out of the office, slammed closed the door, locked it, and trotted up the Wharf, forgetting me completely and leaving to me the entire pier. I scrambled behind the building and scanned the shore for my captors. There was no sign of them, though my heart thumped and sweat soaked my forehead. Seeing nothing for it, and no one else around, I launched myself up from my spot and darted across the pier to the immobile steamer. "Heya!" one of the Chinese dock girls called to me as I crossed the gangway, peeked over the edge for any sign of life, and finding none, stepped onto the main deck. Still exposed, I quickened to the nearest door and found it unlocked, thank God, so I slipped in and shut it behind me, ensuring its click.

I'll wait here until the captain returns, I thought, looking around what appeared to be the ship's dining room, *and I'll beg for passage if I have to. In the meantime I'll be out of sight of the shore.* Yet just to be sure, I ducked behind a side table out of view of the window. Finally, as my heartbeat quieted, I allowed myself to breathe and take in the room. *This could be the steamer Lex boarded for the diggings. He could be out there now, plucking one golden nugget from the ground after another.* I lingered on that for a moment. *Or he could be soaking in a ditch somewhere, tools gone, pockets empty.* If only I had a coin to flip, I could have decided which was the likeliest. *In fact, I may be the closest anyone in my family has achieved to reaching the gold fields.* That said more about my family than it did me.

Something rustled to my right. I turned my head sharply and panic stabbed my stomach so hard I almost cried. It couldn't be. *How had he...?*

Standing up from a dining room chair was the Celestial. With deliberate speed, calm, and the knife in his hand, he walked toward me.

*　　　*　　　*

The dancer said nothing for a long time. Instead she stared at me, unblinking, her gaze burning into my skin, her eyes squinting periodically as if trying to piece together a particularly challenging puzzle. I sat in the chair, but with no binds or gags, my arms and legs free to move, my mouth free to speak. But I too was still and said nothing. The dancer's man sat behind me in the corner of the tent, cleaning his fingernails.

The minutes ticked by in silence. A goat bleated in the Square. On a normal day I would have cursed the absurdity of living with livestock in a town, yet at that moment I was too exhausted—in my head more than my body—to feel anything. A horse whinnied an answer. Nothing inside the shanty made a sound, and the canvas was like a membranous barrier to the outside world. I was neither separate from it nor part of it; I languished in some in-between world. Purgatory, perhaps. In fact—

"You break the deal," the dancer said, splitting the silence. I flinched. She moved nary a muscle for the next minute.

I stared at my knees. Her gaze was too intense to meet straight on.

"How say?" she said. "How say, you no win, I no win?"

Was she asking me or asking herself out loud? I waited.

"How say?" Her tone was hard to place. Assertive, yet this time not so threatening. I glanced left to right.

"'Stalemate'?" I asked warily.

"Stalemate. You and me stalemate."

She paused for me to agree. I waited for her to continue.

"Two time you escape. Two time I catch. You very sneaky, I very sneaky. You win, I lose. I win, you lose. Forever, always, like cat chase the rat." She pointed at me. "You run, I find. You again run, I find. How long to run? Always? Who know?"

It could have been another trap. Another in a series of constant, endless traps, so I didn't dare say more. With Lex, I learned early on that you let a talking person talk, and often their true intentions come tumbling out. Yet she went silent and waited for me to respond. Despite her broken English, she was a much sharper conversationalist than my blusterous brother. I didn't want to yield and ask what she was playing at, yet neither did I wish to further stoke her anger.

"So," I ventured, not feeling that this was a stalemate at all, "now what?"

Her face was unreadable, though at one point, for only an instant, a slight grimace curled her lip. Was it intentional? What did it mean? It may have been real, a betrayal of her disbelief that she was parlaying with a young mischief-maker just out of her control. Or perhaps it was triumph?

"You break the deal," she said, nothing else but her mouth moving. "Now we make new deal." She took a slow breath. Her hatred rippled through the canvas walls.

I swallowed.

"You work, pay the cheating. Then you are free. Or stay, work more, and earn money to keep. Your money for whatever to need. Who know? Clothes? Gamble? Send to your parent? Or maybe somewhere to go?"

I met her gaze. "I can leave after I pay off my brother's debt?"

"Yes."

"Or I can earn money for myself."

"Yes. After pay the cheating."

I nodded slowly. New York. Leland. *Home.* I stretched my arms and legs. "Why don't I just leave now?"

"Stalemate." She nodded toward her man. "He always know. Always see."

I glanced behind me at the Celestial but he was gone. When I turned back he was at my elbow, calm as ever. I started and had to keep myself from falling. How had he done that?

The dancer's expression was inscrutable.

I refocused. "Why do you care so much about me?"

"I care about money. You cheat, you pay."

"People are cheated all the time. They get over it."

"You believe?"

"I do. It's a better use of your time to move on. The world is not always fair."

Her eyes narrowed. "What do you know?"

"Well, before my brother took me away from my home in New York, I had a friend…" I shut my mouth. She was letting a talking person talk.

When she saw I wouldn't answer further, the dancer said, "New deal, you agree?"

"Or what?"

Her eyes gestured to the binds, limp on the floor.

I raised my aching, tattooed hand. "Am I still your 'prisoner'?"

"Until you pay."

Home. Eventually. I sighed and nodded.

She stood abruptly and pointed to herself. "I call Ah Toy."

"Ah Toy," I tried the words.

"You. What call?"

"Cyrus."

She nodded once. I looked over at the Celestial, who was back in his original spot, napping.

She shook her head.

What was I getting myself into? I didn't know how this journey to San Francisco was supposed to go, but absolutely not like this. Somewhere someone caused something in my life to veer sideways while my back was turned, without my agreement. *This isn't what my life was meant to be. But what choice do I have?*

"Do you have my button?"

"Button?" Ah Toy shoved a broom in my hand. "Work now."

Part Two

TERRIFIC GALE!
by James King of William
Daily Alta California
Dec. 17, 1849

Our town and bay were visited by an extraordinarily severe gale from the southwest Friday, about 1 o'clock P.M. Very little damage was done in the city, or to the shipping in port, though the gale was the severest experienced this season and accompanied by lightning, thunder, hail, and rain. The little steamer Mint, which started at 11 o'clock in the morning for San Jose with freight and a great number of passengers, was obliged to return to her dock, which she reached about 2 P.M. Shortly after this had been done, the squall struck her in all its fury, attended with much lightning and thunder, and a mingled shower of hail and rain.

December 24, 1849
San Francisco
A slight break from rain

Today started with two revelations. First, that it's the eve before Christmas. The holiday has sneaked upon me. There's been some preparation around the town, though mostly in the number of the Rev. Taylor's sermons and in the increase of alcohol-infused incidents. As S.F. is a mostly masculine town, there's little feminine influence to check the inhabitants' boorish behavior: gambling, drinking, fighting, womanizing, and just plain making *noise*. Those few ladies that do exist, such as my "employer," profit from the men's baser instincts and thus encourage it. With so many wives, girlfriends, mothers, and sisters thousands of miles away, the impending Christmas holiday has become an event of melancholy and mischief for many. There's more than the usual imbibing, and though I don't take drink myself, I understand the sentiment. So many are orphans out here, separated from their families by thousands of miles, and the nostalgia and the sentimentality are running syrupy thick.

The holidays have also brought a shift in the weather in a truly Californian way, unlike anything resembling N.Y. In October the cold summer metamorphosed into an oh-so-brief Indian Summer (oh sweet, blessed warmth!) and banished the chilling fog. Then the short spell of autumn deteriorated in a rapid fashion into winter, though here it's more accurate to say "the rainy season." S.F. doesn't entertain the traditional four seasons, rather, just two dominate the climate: Wet and Dry.

Wet has currently taken over, and hard—harder, the old-timers say, than anything they'd seen here before. In mid-November the rains commenced and haven't concluded since. Some days mist, some days sprinkle, some days unleash torrents that soak into the canvas tents and flood the ground. There's no blue sky to be found. Ceaseless gray clouds hang over the town and repress the sun, and the constant condensation pounds into the ears and the heads and the souls of the weary residents.

The effects of such a damp drubbing have taken a filthy toll. The streets are a disaster. Dirt has turned to mud, and rainwater streams downhill, washing out tents and flimsy buildings, loosening and carrying refuse and sewage past dwellings and into the bay. Now, a month and a half on, San Francisco floats on an ocean of mud, which has grown thick, sticky, and hazardous. The ground is so soft and so churned by the stream of men, horses, and carts, that it's impossible to move along without sinking up to the knees. Some enterprising citizens have placed small beams or boards so that traffic is not completely backlogged; but it's your misfortune if your foot misjudges the proper place to step. Woe unto the inattentive townie who disregards the warning staked at the corner of the Square on Kearny and Clay: "This street is impassable, not even jackassable."

Second revelation: I now know how good the dancer Ah Toy is at holding secrets. "Come," she told me this morning with a beckon of her hand. Exiting the tent, she offered no explanation. This in itself was remarkable. In the four months I've been living and working in the shanty, I've been an extremely busy man, always at her beck and call, morning, noon, and evening, to fulfill whatever fickle feelings filled her fancy. Mostly this work has been mundane, the same type of work I described earlier. Other times, the requests have been odd, such as rubbing her feet after an evening of stomping and twirling, and yet others are baffling. Among the strangest: blocking passersby's view of her while she does nature's business behind the tent; assisting her in the fastening of her robe before she slides on stage for her peep show; and venturing alone into Little China, the Celestial neighborhood very close by, for ginseng root, having not the slightest grasp of Chinese.

Could I have escaped on some of these occasions? Possibly. But for how long, and to what end? Ah Toy's man utilizes the properties of a spirit or the gifts of an illusionist; one never knows where and when he'll materialize, yet it's always at the point one feels they've gotten away with it. The man, I swear, can read minds. Perhaps that's why he never talks, so he can listen to one's thoughts all the better. I feel at all times that he's just over my shoulder. Sometimes he isn't. Yet unnervingly often he is. That, more than anything, causes me pause, and any hesitation in an escape attempt will doom it. But almost as big a factor for my staying put in Ah Toy's service is that I have here a means to an end. Maybe I could earn a higher salary as a merchant's assistant, or a deckhand on a steamer, or even a dishwasher in a hotel. But these are big *ifs*. *If* I am hired. *If* I can stand the work and I'm paid on time, *if* at all. *If* I can evade Ah Toy's and her man's supernatural detection.

And if I were to skip town, how would Lex find me when he returns? It's two months beyond his October promise and he could arrive anytime, laden with gold, to whisk me home again. Of course he's delayed—that's his way—and I'd love nothing more than to let him taste my knuckles. But even more aggravating is that I'm anchored here awaiting him. I'm as much a prisoner to him as anything else.

"Come."

Grateful for any change of scenery, and really, having no other option, I followed Ah Toy out of the shanty and up Clay Street. The mud, rendering the street unfordable, forced us to leap, like scotch-hoppers, from dry item to dry item that the populace has hurled into it: wood, cement, iron, leftover refuse, a half-buried wagon wheel, the top of a metal stove, and crates of unsold tobacco, beans, salted beef, shirts, and nails. We made Pike Street and turned left into the alley. Down the block we toddled, and after nearly missing the pile of broken chairs that saved her from an earthly, sloppy disaster, Ah Toy stopped. She stood, quite still, and gazed upon a wooden building. What was inside I couldn't tell —there was no merchant's signboard nor hint of habitation, so I could make no sense of her preoccupation. Turning finally toward me, she pointed at it—marked number 36—and announced, "Home."

It was a modest building—small, two stories, unassuming and

rather unremarkable, blending in with the rest of the new construction around S.F. It elicited little emotion from me, yet clearly pulled at the dancer's heart. She gazed upon it with admiration. She had, after all, been living in canvas these many months. This was wooden, one of the first signs of permanence in this tarpaulin town, and it dawned upon me that she must have been here, supervising construction or generally admiring the building, for all this time with no word of it to me. *Home,* she had said. *I might finally bed down in a structure with proper walls and a functional roof. Oh, to sleep on dry ground!* As we looked upon it now in the early morning darkness, the building stood highlighted by a warm glow emanating from the sky beyond, a sign, surely, from some divine place that the future would be an improvement over the present.

"Move everything here," she said.

In the distance men's voices called to each other. Usually their bombastic greetings and ugly braying set my teeth to grinding. But the anticipation of a warm, dry place deafened me to the usual morning clamor. Ah Toy glanced one last time at her future home, then crisscrossed back up Pike toward Clay Street, with me close behind. The men's voices grew louder and more numerous. Some mornings in Portsmouth Square sounded as if the night had never ended. It was a miracle anyone could sleep.

The voices increased in volume, and I thought it must have been yet another brawl. Soon there was panic, however, similar to the day of the Hounds attack. *That* was a grievous day, an awful way to be introduced to a new place. And then the crazed man, and the revolver...

Now, as we climbed up Pike Street, the din transformed into sustained, full-throated screaming, which, even at the town's most cacophonous, was unusual. I lunged and landed on an empty wine barrel. What were those fools yelling about so early in the morning?

It sounded like...liar?...pyre?...sire?

I turned my head.

"FIRE!!!"

Ah Toy was already running. I leaped off the barrel and squelched up the hill after her. When we made Clay Street, we turned the corner and saw down the hill to the water. The sky's warm glow was not a divine sign at all; rather, it was a sign from Below rather than Above. On the earthly realm, it came from the eastern edge of the Plaza. Smoke was already belching into the air.

Portsmouth Square was aflame!

Ah Toy bolted down the hill as rapidly as her boots could negotiate the mud, and I trailing in hot pursuit. Enormous waves of heat slammed against us as we descended into a scene of chaos, pandemonium, and noise. Horses and men scattered in all directions, maneuvering piles of goods into the muddy streets and down the hill. The hot wind assaulted my face. When we gained the tent, Ah Toy surveyed the room and retrieved her silken robes folded on a dresser in the corner, and I hunted down my journals and writing instruments. She then rescued the scales and followed her man outside and down the street toward the water.

The soft streets combined with the half-buried refuse made the going treacherous, exacerbated further by the panicked horses struggling to flee. Men tripped and dropped their cargo, then rose once more, covered in the stinking mud, straining to make the bay. We lost the trail of the Celestial again and again as swarms of people crossed our path and obstructed our vision. At last we espied him standing near the Long Wharf. We pushed our way through the crowd, inch after inch, and when we reached him, he set her chest of gold on the ground and ran off, to where I don't know, possibly to tend to his own possessions. Ah Toy's most prized belongings and her earnings were secured for the time being, as were mine, and so, catching my breath, I had the chance to fully observe what surrounded us.

Madness, all madness. The fire spread with fearful rapidity, and within a quarter-hour it had risen into wide, sparkling columns. The shore, bay, and air glowed orange, as though in an early sunset. Every gambling saloon along Kearny Street was engulfed, and the buildings adjacent, leading down to Montgomery Street and the water, were consumed as well. House and tent gave way to the unchecked flames like matchsticks. Men shouted in great confusion and helplessness as the canvas walls shriveled away and the wooden frames collapsed. Bells and gongs clanged and trumpets blasted to sound the alarm, and underneath the pandemonium was the deep roar of the furnace punctuated by the pops and cracks of splintering lumber. The inferno spread in all directions with sickening speed. I remembered the Great Fire of 1845 in New York, including the saltpeter explosion, yet I didn't recall the fire there spreading with such ferocity as this.

An hour into the blaze, explosions pounded my ears, and buildings across the Square collapsed. In a desperate effort to stay the flames, some men threw mud, of which there was ample supply, at the houses across the street, but there was nothing more than that to do. It was a curious sight: thousands of men compelled only to look on and watch the fire's course, with not a single fireman's tool at their disposal.

A wall of heat pushed against me. I raised my arms to block it, while the smell of the char and the smoke attacked my nose and lungs, and I coughed violently as the thick haze swirled in my face and stung my eyes. Sitting near the Long Wharf with hundreds of other townsfolk—many of whom sat on their pile of belongings and watched the blaze as if at a theater—I was intrigued by the awesome power of the fire and the resignation of those waiting for the blocks to collapse. The murmurs and cries of my fellow refugees washed over me as the carnage played out. Ah Toy, meanwhile, sat upon her chest of gold, clutching her knife, watching not the blaze but the crowd around her for looters and derelicts. So far, her tent had been spared the wrath of the flames, but I couldn't see for sure, and she wasn't about to abandon her life savings to investigate.

In the midst of the tragic show, Ah Toy turned to someone behind us and spoke in rapid Chinese. I shifted my gaze and beheld two young female Celestials. They weren't the same girls from the dock. The taller of the two appeared close to my age, while the smaller was perhaps a handful of years younger. Their manner was cowed before Ah Toy, who did most of the talking, and they gave only clipped responses to my boss's verbal assault. Of what they spoke, I couldn't tell, but the tone resembled a parent questioning a guilty child—though the two girls were torn between answering Ah Toy's entreaties and gawking at the inferno before them.

When the fire at last died out, and the Celestial arrived to help me retrieve the chest, the two girls followed in our wake. They ate supper with us, silent as stones, though the younger one's eyes—full of energy, fire, maybe anger—darted around the room without rest. Ah Toy then ordered them to wash and prepare for sleep, and as I close this entry with the smoke from a thousand campfires burning my nose and itching my throat, the three women have bedded down in Ah Toy's side of the shanty. The dancer made it clear to the Celestial, in Chinese, and to me, in English, that we weren't to go near them, and for the first time I felt an odd sense of brotherhood for the mute, knife-wielding henchman.

But who are these girls, and what have they done to find themselves so unfortunate as to be in Ah Toy's care? *Whatever dreams they had before today,* I thought as I drifted to sleep, *have gone up in flames like this shanty town.* I wondered if they knew it yet.

Christmas Day, 1849
San Francisco
Cloudy but dry (much to my relief).

Today is Christmas Day, normally a day of rest and celebration, but one wouldn't know it in S.F. First, the Chinese don't celebrate the Lord's birth, so the morning in the tent was like any other as far as they were concerned. One change, though: this evening, Ah Toy bid me to her room and handed me a newspaper. "Read," she ordered me, and sat back with a cup of tea to await my narration.

I skimmed through the headlines. "It's all about the fire," I said. "We saw it all."

"Read. 'No limit to learning.' Big Chinese saying."

I found the big story and read aloud.

APPALLING AND DESTRUCTIVE CONFLAGRATION!
by James King of William
Daily Alta California
Dec. 26, 1849

Our city has been visited by fire, and we are called upon to record the disastrous career of conflagration. The fire originated in Dennison's Exchange, and, it is said, in the second and upper story. The morning was still, scarcely a breath of air swerving the fiery columns; soon came thronging to the scene our affrighted citizens, and then commenced the din of a thousand voices, the crash of property, jingling of battered windows, the quick, sharp sound of axes, plied vigorously in cutting away encumbering timbers; and yet, above this the roar of the devouring element, which now surged wildly around the Parker House.

Portsmouth Square, in front of the burning buildings, was crowded with anxious spectators, when an alarm was created of stored powder in the Parker House. A stampede of six thousand human beings then added to the terrors of the spectacle. From the El Dorado's windows and doors was seen to issue the thick, black smoke, premonitory of a burst of flame. Ladders were reared, the glass crushed in, and the El Dorado shot forth darts of fire, followed by an ignition of all parts of the house at once. It was when the flames of this towering pile rose highest that the general pulse quickened and the hearts of the thousands assembled throbbed wildly with fear and anxiety.

"Lex would have throbbed wildly with fear and anxiety to see the burning Eldorado," I muttered.

"Your brother?" Ah Toy asked.

I nodded and continued.

An unfinished brick store, owned by Burgoyne & Co., stayed the fire at the corner of Washington and Montgomery Sts., and by vigilant and energetic exertions, the flames were prevented from spreading further. At about 12 PM, the last burning building came down, and the conflagration was considered at an end.

An additional police body has been added to the town, and watchmen stationed on the ground burned over to prevent sly operations in petty larceny, at which many persons have manifested themselves adept. It would scarcely appear credible that men, if so we must call them, when required to assist at the late fire, could demand pay for their services, yet such is the fact. We hope they were not Americans. The indifference displayed by too many of our countrymen in rendering assistance, is bad enough.

I closed the paper and put it down.

"See? We learn more," she said, finishing her tea.

"What new was there? I already know a bunch of buildings burned down."

"You now know what the men do. Never trust. Take care yourself."

*   *   *

There's no rest in this town, not even for the Baby Jesus. The banging of hammers and tools awakened me. Exhausted and reeking of ashes, I walked outside to a surprising and eerie scene. Atop embers still smoking, and in some spots still glowing, men erected the frames of new walls. The heat from yesterday's blaze still shimmers from the ground, yet the town of S.F. is already in a state of rebuilding. It was a small miracle that Ah Toy's tent survived, especially since we hadn't had time to retrieve all our belongings. The entire block from Kearny to Montgomery and Washington to Clay Street was reduced to smoldering rubble. The shanty stands less than one block away, and while buildings across the street from the burnt district had ignited, the flames had been stayed before they reached it.

The speed of recovery is perplexing. Less than twenty-four hours removes me from the disaster, and yet I'm looking at new skeletons of small houses, shops, and stalls rising out of the ruins. The single-minded determination to press on in the name of profit has possessed the residents here. It's a grand atmosphere in many ways, feverish though it seems to me.

In that same spirit, I started my responsibilities of hauling all manner of possessions from the tent to number 36 Pike St. Having procured a dray, the Celestial loaded it with the dancer's belongings. As he did *not* procure a dray horse, I, then, was tasked with pulling it uphill through the mud-softened, litter-strewn streets, with the Celestial pushing from behind. The result was a mess. I sank to the top of my boots with every step, and worked just as hard to clear my feet from the morass as I did to pull the cargo. The street litter offered little in the way of traction, as it just as often impeded my progress as aided it. The only blessing was that it wasn't raining, nor conflagrating! At any rate, the span of one full workday netted only two transported loads. Ah Toy scowled when the sun began to set. Not only was she expecting to bed down in her new abode this evening, I suspect she is also none too pleased to have to rent the dray for another day.

The two Celestial girls ate and stayed through the previous night. I'm trying to puzzle together who they are and what their designs might be. They don't talk, and Ah Toy volunteers no information, so it's up to me to solve it. Are they family? Friends? No, they don't interact in any warm or familiar way (though when has lack of warmth disqualified families?). Are they fellow dancers? Perhaps. They're certainly young and lithe enough, though no dancing took place last night to confirm it. Stranded souls in need of shelter? Possibly. The town now has plenty of those. In any case, Ah Toy has only ordered, "No talk. No touch." Her man, too, gives them a respectable berth. So this must mean they're somehow delicate or valuable. Hostages? Prisoners? Unlikely; they're not treated roughly or with scorn. Are they harlots? Conceivably, but no men pay them any visits.

I wonder if Mother and Father are thinking of their sons this day, toiling on the opposite end of the continent. I should be at home, eating chestnuts by the yule tree, inhaling the aroma of roasting turkey and baking mince pies, and listening to Father read from the book of Luke (soporific though it is). Instead I'm spending my holiday pushing trunks through the mud, wondering about two foreign squatters and whether or not they're here to butter their buns.

And so, with that, Merry Christmas to one and all.

January 18, 1850
San Francisco
Rainy.

It's still raining. How is it still raining? In N.Y., periodic storms dump their snow and move on, unlike here, where the gray clouds form a blanket over the town with no seams or breaks. Onward and ceaselessly it stretches, and rain—the never-ending rain.

The only comfort is the roof over my head, though little good that does me while I'm retrieving supplies from the Square. Most of the buildings eaten up by the fire have now been rebuilt, to the point where, not only does the place look as though no fire had ever happened, but the structures are larger, taller, and more decorative, as if the fire had given permission for their inhabitants to grow and stretch. The most important structure in the place, the Eldorado, stands completely roofed and weatherboarded, and will soon be ready for reoccupation.

And here we are in our own building, number 36 on Pike St., spared from the flames and feeling grand as the raindrops stop at the roof and penetrate no further, except as mud forms on the floors. These will soon become wooden floors with carpeting, I'm told.

While I clean, Ah Toy arranges and adorns the house in ways that are foreign to me. Day after day she receives crates, boxes, and barrels bursting with goods: furniture, linens, plateware, rugs, curtains, silver, trunks, oil lamps, vases, mirrors, and bedpans, to name a few. And pillows—more pillows than I've seen in my lifetime, all stacked and ready for distribution around the place. The dancing business, it seems, which she's now quit, had been lucrative.

I'm tasked with placing these items around the house at her whim. Other crates reveal far stranger contents: lanterns made of paper, sticks that give off a pungent aroma when burned, and a wooden altar with a carved, intricate design. These she has only her Celestial transport, as though I, a Westerner, couldn't possibly comprehend their significance and worth. Even the two girls, who have yet to lend any hand to the house, showed reverence by bowing to the alter. It's a mystery where Ah Toy sources these goods.

She also follows something called *fung soy,* which is a sort of Chinese guide to laying out a room. She directed the arrangement of furniture in the most precise spots, and mirrors at off-angles, and placed a small fountain in the corner of the parlor. This is supposed to allow the energy to flow—*chi,* she calls it—while deflecting the evil spirits away. It all seems excessive to me.

In this same room, the walls have been painted red with gold trim, so that the bold colors punch at my eyes each time I enter it. It feels gaudy, like a carnival. Ah Toy also managed to procure Eastern décor, and decorative plants to adorn the entrance, which looks more like a portal to the Celestial country itself than an abode to settle down in.

My room is not decorated in such a manner, to no complaint from me, and neither is the Celestial's, although Ah Toy's is, as are the rooms the two girls inhabit. They now have a surprising quantity of goods arrayed in a similar, showy way, like the front room. They are opulent, more so than a normal bedroom. Is this typical of Chinese women's quarters? Perhaps it's a necessity for a woman and nothing more.

And yes, the two Chinese girls are now living with us. We make an odd family, the five of us. The girls are both beautiful, in their own way: one is tall, graceful, and demure, barely a strand of her straight, black, shining hair out of place. She whispers through the house on feet that must be padded and she takes up no space, clinging instead to the walls and traveling through each room via its perimeter. Her name is something like "Ah Loi," though I'm not certain because she rarely speaks. Her communication consists of nods and slaps at the younger one to pay attention and mind herself.

The younger one, Ah Si, is a tiger. Or a bear. Or a bull. She's loud, short, clumsy, and devoid of womanly manners. She's quick to anger and cannot conceal her disgust, which often earns her that aforementioned slap. Her laugh, however, fills the house, and is so infectious that my face takes on a life of its own, stretching itself into an ear-to-ear grin. Her beauty is somewhat plainer than Ah Loi's. Yet there is something within her—spirit, I suppose—that shows upon her face, so that when she's angry, her face contorts into that of an ogre, and when she's pleased, her visage sparkles and she becomes the most beautiful creature in the town. She is a wonder.

No confirmation yet of why they're here, but I can make an educated guess. They have no freshly inscribed tattoos as I do. They don't contribute any chores. They don't dance. And they never seem to leave the confines of number 36. This lack of activity keeps them soft and pure, and what man can resist that? This is probably the one good result of Lex not returning yet; he would turn into a clown around these two, like a fox in the chicken coop. The purpose of this chicken coop is coming into focus for me, after suspecting it these past few weeks: the girls, the overly-decorated house, the many rooms… Ah Toy must have designs on a "boardinghouse." But what do I know about such things, and how am I supposed to fit in to it?

January 29, 1850
San Francisco
Cloudy but not rainy.

The clouds never cease yet the rain has, briefly, to everyone's wild relief. Ah Toy has been looking chipper lately though her commands are coming quicker, sharper, and more specific. I tend to most of them while her man completes most of the tasks requiring strength. Leland sometimes bantered with me about my frame; he is slim yet strong, while I am slim and not. Were he here, he'd have been outside with the Celestial, carrying, pushing, beating, building, while I washed and folded the linens and scrubbed the floors. I attempted to blacken his eye once when he wouldn't let up. "No," he laughed, "like this," and taught me a proper hook.

This afternoon I did assist in one masculine task: the Celestial and I affixed to the front entrance a signboard he'd painted in a remarkably calligraphic hand, reading *Garden of Fragrant Flowers*. A curious name for a house. Later in the evening, while I broomed the floors—the mud is ever-present, regardless of the weather—the door opened and a sharply dressed Western man walked in, took off his hat, and stood in muddy boots on a just-swept spot. I glared at him. He coughed and cleared his throat.

"Yes?" I asked, clenching my teeth.

He looked down at me and scoffed. "Unless you are the mistress, run and fetch her for me."

I narrowed my eyes just as Ah Toy breezed into the room. "Mr. Alderman, welcome! Please come, find comfort!" She slipped a glass of whiskey into his hand, then nudged me with her foot and, with eyes on fire, hissed, "Work in the kitchen!"

I scowled and made my exit as unhastily as possible. Once I achieved the kitchen, I peeked back through the doorway to see what business this stranger had here. The man downed his drink and, out of nowhere, Ah Toy produced a bottle and refilled his glass.

"Heya!" I looked up to the stairs to see Ah Si, the tiger, leaning suggestively over the railing. She called out to the Alderman. "Chinese girl kitty go east west, you know? Not north south like white kitty. You know?"

"Aiya!" Ah Toy muttered fiercely. She snapped something to her in Chinese, and the girl wilted and disappeared. "Many sorry. Not dirty girl house, not here," Ah Toy gushed to the Alderman. "Only best, most polite!"

Ah Loi, whom I only see but once a day, then appeared at the top of the stairs as if on cue. She was dressed much like Ah Toy was when she traipsed across her dancing stage: a silken garment, her hair up in a tight bun, her face white, and her lips bright red. She paused there, lingering at the steps, moving her head languidly like a feline's. She was truly, stunningly beautiful, and the stranger could not take his eyes off her. Ah Toy was pleased at his reaction.

"Ah Loi, come see the dear guest," she called up to her.

The girl poured like molasses down the stairs. Time became sluggish. As she alighted from the last step, Ah Toy took her hand and placed it into the man's, then delicately let go.

"Ah Loi take good care," she said, all warmth and assurance. "Only ask, she will do." She handed Ah Loi the bottle. The man, somewhat awkwardly, attempted to hand something to Ah Toy, but she demurred. "Mr. Alderman, you come is our pleasure. Please feel comfortable." She withdrew quietly as Ah Loi led him up the stairs.

Hours later I was in bed, going over my journal, when footsteps echoed through the house and the front door opened and closed. A minute later a sharp rap on the door startled me. Ah Toy opened the door, and in a voice cool with efficiency, in complete contrast to her earlier demeanor, barked, "See Ah Loi. Bring hot water, sponge, and towel. Change sheet, change bedpan, clean up lemon, bring whiskey, open window." *Now?* I set my journal aside and stumbled out of bed. "Make sure she wash all inside," Ah Toy said on her way out. I climbed the stairs, left the bathing supplies at Ah Loi's door and knocked. She opened and grabbed the bucket.

"Um, she says to make sure you wash all—" but she'd already closed the door again. In that brief moment she looked ruffled, her hair strewn around her shoulders and her red lips pale. She'd clearly been through an ordeal.

"Are you all right?" I whispered to her, the first time I've attempted to communicate with either of the girls.

"She need rest only," Ah Toy said as she came up the stairs. She pushed past me, opened the door, handed Ah Loi a brown medicine bottle with a cork stopper, said something in Cantonese, then closed the door.

It all makes sense now. The girls, the furniture, the plush surroundings, the feminine house name, the experience Ah Toy has with slavering men. I saw houses of ill repute back home on one occasion, when Lex dragged me through Chatham Square. Never the inside, of course, yet it was remarkable to me how ordinary they appeared (though the leg draped out the window gave a mighty clue to their true purpose). And now I understand what kind of "family" we are in the *Garden of Fragrant Flowers*: the young, blemish-free girls, the "heavy" for security, the hired help (me), and all of it overseen by the acute, no-nonsense madam. Whether or not I'll play a greater role than housekeeper in all this is hard to say, as are my feelings about being a part of it. I don't think I like it. To be associated with prostitution...

But what's my choice? Ah Toy and I circle each other in a state of stalemate, and I'm afraid I'll become a new pincushion for her man's sharp toy if I disrupt it. So for now, toeing the line is the safest bet. And it *does* pay. After hounding her for the number, she told me I'm about one third of the way toward paying off my debt —"my" debt, which is really belongs to four or five other, scot-free men. Of course, I would have been done with it by now if it were Lex's alone.

Lex, meanwhile, is three months past his October promise.

Keep your eye on the prize, Cyrus. You have to troll through the muck to get there, but you'll get there. One dirty deed at a time.

March 5, 1850
San Francisco
Cold sun in the middle of day.

In the last month, as the Garden's routine has fallen into place, I've gained an education that would make even a teenage schoolboy blush. Due to its late-night nature, the house sleeps until the middle of the day. Ah Loi and Ah Si bed down in separate rooms, which are also their working quarters, and likely are, ironically enough, the most hygienic in the Garden. I cleanse them constantly, every afternoon and between every visitor.

I awaken before the girls and, while the Celestial cooks, I wash the laundry early so it has time throughout the day to dry. Linens are the bulk of it, but I can be rough and quick with those. I have to be, because of the various stains they hold: some pale yellow, sticky when wet, and crusted when it dries; some red, either from a wound or "moon leak" as Ah Toy calls it; and some brown and odorous, and best not thought of. The hairs I must pick out with my fingers.

I use a finer touch with the clothing, and I do mean *all* the clothing. Not only do I wash the girls' and Ah Toy's dresses, but also their stockings and undergarments, which the boys at home would scarcely believe. I was squeamish about it at first, handling a woman's private garments, but now I scrub them and pound them like they're nothing. The novelty wore off quickly.

The chamber pots still make me gag, however, and I suspect they always will. It's not so bad when the entirety of the nightsoil is contained in the pot, but occasionally Ah Loi and Ah Si host a guest who, due to drunkenness or a faulty eye, exhibit bad aim. Cleanup at that point becomes a miserable affair, which is why I try to get it done and out of my way first, before emptying each girl's cold bathwater and seeing to the rest of their room. The one thing I don't touch, however, is the wooden altar tucked in the corner of the parlor. A bowl of rice sits at its base with sticks of incense rising out of it. I'm not sure of its purpose, but occasionally Ah Toy and the two girls bow to it when they walk near it. Only the Celestial tends to it by dusting it, which he does gently and fastidiously, and replenishing the rice and sticks. I steer clear so as not to ask for trouble.

I then set up for midday dinner—after washing my hands. By that time everyone is awake and at the table, ready to ingest the Celestial's creation: rice, boiled meats, curry sauces, &c. No one really talks—the women are still rubbing sleep from their eyes, and the Celestial never says a word. Only Ah Toy will sometimes make a terse comment in Cantonese to the Chinese or in English to me. Otherwise, it's a muted affair.

After the meal I clean the dishes and the kitchen while the Celestial tidies outside; then he and I are sent to the Square with our list of errands. Each day's is a little different. Yesterday, for instance, we departed the house, he with a tin and a small package and I with a list of groceries for the afternoon dinner to keep the girls nourished, along with jujube, ginger, and peony to keep them from "overheating their system." Diseased girls and pregnant girls, Ah Toy says, will sink a house faster than stones, and as such, she insists that Ah Loi and Ah Si wash between each visitor. The little brown bottles we pick up at the apothecary help with that. The little slices of lemon, though astronomical in price, do too.

"What's that for?" I asked the Celestial when I noticed the tin in his hand. He pointed to the alcalde's office at the western end of the Square, and that's the direction we made for. I followed him into the building.

"Ah!" a voice to my left boomed. "I won'red when yuh'd come in!"

I turned to behold a thick man striding our way. He was middling in height but his straight-backed posture, his thick, chinstrap beard, and his steely eyes told everyone in the room that he was in charge. My eyes traveled from his collared shirt and black vest to his puffed-out chest, and the glinting metallic star that settled there.

"Howya doin', John?" He clapped the Celestial on the shoulder.

The Celestial's face didn't move.

"Talkative as ever! Love it." He turned to me. "You know, John, like John Chinaman? Anyway, who've we here? Got yerself an apprentice? Hey there, kid." He grabbed my hand and pulverized it in a bone-crushing grip. "Jack Hays. Got yerself a good teacher here'n John. Don't talk, of course, but don' you mess around with him. You blink'n he'll have you trussed on the floor with knife t'yer throat. Don' test it!" He laughed and clapped me on the shoulder, making my knees buckle.

"Say now," he returned to the Celestial, "y'came at the right time. I's just startin' t' think about how much I miss those dumplings o'yours." He eyed the tin in the Celestial's hands and lit up. "Looks like you'n'me on the same level."

I wasn't sure the Celestial was following this at all, yet with both hands he passed the tin and the small paper package to the sheriff.

"Susan'll be anxious fer these," he said, placing the tin on a desk. The package he slipped into his vest. Then, in his signature move, he clapped both of us on the shoulder, stumbling us forward. "It's a fine thing fer you t'come'n' visit." He guided us toward the door. "Don' be strangers now." He nudged us out into the Square, and just before closing the door on us, he concluded with, "An'you, boyo, always watch yer backside. Crazy town out here!"

After the evening dinner we relax a bit. The girls play cards or chatter—despite Ah Loi becoming more talkative, it's Ah Si doing most of the chatting—while I write in my journal, and Ah Toy seals herself away in her quarters to balance the books. The Celestial simply disappears. When Ah Toy finishes her counting, she calls for me to bring her tea and the day's *Alta California*. "Read," she commands, and for the next half hour we sit in the parlor and I read her the news of the town. She doesn't say a word, only listens while she sips. When I come to the end of the shipping traffic report, she nods, rises, and leaves, and I'm left to clean up after her. Then comes a light supper, then a final freshening up, and then the business begins at the opening of the Garden door.

Every night the house welcomes in the men of San Francisco. Most of them are Western, though several are Celestial, Mexican, or Chileno. It's not strange to see such diversity in S.F., though at home the races never mix as they do here, and while in theory I can tolerate the intermingling, in practice, having them in the house—the house where I live and work—puts me on edge. I avoid the more populated rooms when I can and skirt around the edges of them when I can't. Ah Toy can't be more at home. She breezes through the house with the grace and confidence of a socialite—all smiles, a ready laugh, a constant pourer...and a keen memory of what to put on the bill.

Some of the men divulge their names, yet most remain mum about their identities—save for those who are already known throughout the town— and prefer to talk instead of gambling, gossip, and girls in other houses. Some make repeat calls, though a fair few are still new, and many of them appear to be of at least middling class. Occupationally, too, the visitors are of some import: successful merchants, gambling saloon owners, aldermen from the town council, a judge, a constable, &c. They all have some money, which they surrender to Ah Toy, who by now has stopped declining their offers.

One of the many visitors is a Celestial named Henry Conrad, who, like many of the other men, has begun making regular appearances here. He's a dapper man—collared shirt, tie, bowler hat, fashionable boots, not dressed at all like the Chinese laborers around the town. He's clearly a man of business, a merchant of some sort, yet I know nothing else about him, only that he stands out against the grungy, the self-important, and the oleaginous who frequent the place. He always regards me and never visits the girls. He arrives, nods in my direction, makes small talk with whomever's in the room, then enters Ah Toy's chambers. I never hear the grunting or anguished sounds that typically issue from Ah Loi's and Ah Si's chambers, only serious conversation in Chinese. I'd wonder more about his business, but there frankly isn't time with all the chores to be done.

It all adds up to a buzzing house and, for me, barking feet when I'm finally through with my work in the deep hours of the early morning. Nightly I collapse, exhausted, onto my bed. Ah Loi and now Ah Si are each busy with up to three visitors per night, each completed rendezvous requiring fresh hot water, a bedpan flushing, a change of linens, and opening the windows for *"toe-goo-nahp-san,"* as Ah Toy says, which means something about ridding the place of stale air and bringing in the fresh.

But I still have a lot to learn. Tonight, as usual, the Garden received its visitors. Ah Toy gave her boozy welcome and sent them off with Ah Loi and Ah Si, while I got along with my work and the Celestial tended to the door. At some point I had cause to walk upstairs and down the hall to fetch one thing or another, and as I passed by Ah Si's room, someone shouted from within. I stopped, curious, and listened further. The sound came from a man. Then a female shrieked in response, whom I had to assume was Ah Si, yet I'd never before heard her at such a pitch. That was followed by the sound of a violent slapping, and then a scream even higher than before. I grew rather alarmed, and when came an even louder slapping, I lost my mind and rushed into the room.

I discovered the man naked as a jay, kneeling on Ah Si and slapping her left and right with great gusto. Flecks of red spotted the sheets. Before my common sense could kick in, I launched myself at the man, wrapped my arms around his torso, and gave a mighty heave, which toppled me over, with him rolling over me. He was sour with whiskey. His surprise turned quickly to rage, and he hurled blasphemous invectives. He made a move toward me with ill intent, yet came up short. I grabbed the empty whiskey bottle off the nearby stand and wielded it as threateningly as my body would allow—my body, which my mind had temporarily left.

"Go on, take a swing at me, boy!" he growled. "Finish what you start!" He lurched toward me and I swung the bottle, connecting with his head with a hollow sound. He fell sideways and crashed into the bed. The bottle didn't break, but caused great damage to the man's face, which now sported a gash above his nose that immediately soaked him in blood. In that moment a strong fist latched onto my collar and pulled me back with force. I turned and raised my bottle again until I saw it was the Celestial.

He grabbed my arm and pinned it to my side, then chopped at my hand until I released my weapon. He pushed me to Ah Toy, who'd just arrived, and she, quick as a cat, grabbed my ear and twisted. I yowled in pain as she dragged me out of the room, down the stairs, and into the kitchen, where she sat me in a chair and unleashed upon me a ferocious slap.

"You do what?" she yelled in my stinging face.

I looked at her with tearing eyes, attempting to regain my senses. "He was hurting her."

She slapped me again. "Hurt? You know what you do?"

"I got him off her! He was pinning her down and hitting her! She was bleeding!"

Ah Toy went to the stove, grabbed a wooden spoon, and struck me with it. "Are you stupid?"

I clutched my hot cheek so she rapped me on the hand instead.

"He high-pay guest!"

I clutched my hand, which gave her another shot at my face. "She was in danger!"

"*Not* danger!"

"She was! I pulled him off her."

"You make him bleed!"

"He made *her* bleed!"

"Are you stupid?" she snarled again, striking me again with the spoon. "Look around!"

I didn't. I wouldn't give her the satisfaction. I returned her glare.

"What is the house?"

"A harlot-house," I fumed. I was wronged. I'd saved a frightened girl from a brutal thug and I was somehow paying for it. My world, all I knew and had grown up with, my framework of right and wrong, was now being tipped off its foundation. The savior was being punished. Should I have beaten Leland for saving me in the Hudson River?

"'Mist and flower' house. Use your monkey brain! Men come here. They pay me for desire. I give. Some gentle, some rough. They pay, get what they want."

I pressed my fists to my head and wiped my tears away. "He was hurting her," I said weakly.

Ah Toy shook her head. "You dumb child," she said. "The man pay extra for the big treat. The girl play along. You go now, give money back. Invite to come again, our pay. You pay the bill."

Ringing filled my brain as I walked up the stairs and knocked on Ah Si's door. She answered, the welt under her eye already clotting, and behind her the foul man lay on his back on the bed, stickiness dried on his belly. I couldn't bear to look at her. She reached for my hand and took the money, and just before closing the door she gave me a kiss on my raw cheek and a smile.

March 6, 1850
San Francisco
Cold yet dry.

I avoided everyone for as long as I could today, steering clear of any occupied room. Every facial expression disguised a smirk or a grin, all of them I know making fun of me. The rest of the time, when I was in danger of encountering any of them, I cast my eyes downward and imagined them in fits of giggles. At dinner, however, Ah Si scooped extra food onto my plate, and later Ah Toy tracked me down for our nightly news reading.

Still, I'm grateful Leland isn't here with me at this moment. One day after school last year, he walked home with me, as he normally did, but continued past his house because he hadn't wished to go home yet. He came home with me instead and, as he was neither in the mood to go swimming in the river, we spent the afternoon in the yard of my house, discussing people at school, his family, &c., and generally avoiding my own parents, although, truth be told, they were likely avoiding me.

After some time like this, we heard the pitiful sounds of a moaning woman. "Who is she? She must be in pain," I said, concerned, and I jumped up to locate the source of the sound. Leland also jumped up, yet rather than one of concern he grew a sneaky grin across his face. I couldn't make sense of his reaction. The woman, however, continued with her sorrowful moans, and concluding her to be in peril, I hunted her down. Leland was on my heels, still wearing a diabolical smile. I'd always known him to be compassionate, understanding, patient, and careful, and so his obvious pleasure at the sound of this poor, distressed woman unnerved me. It must have been a joke and I the butt of it. My first instinct, however, was to come to her aid and soon, and after some minutes the crying increased in volume as I neared a garden shed in my backyard. The sound was coming from within.

What was a crying woman doing in there? I pulled open the door, and there was the familiar shape of Lex, face down on top of a girl, her pale knees in the air. She whimpered but made no effort to fight him off. Once it dawned on me what was happening, Leland, stifling a laugh, pulled me from the door and off across the yard, finally bursting into laughter when we landed side by side beneath a tree. It stung that he was laughing at me, yet he assured me it was Lex he found amusing. "Your brother is such a saucy oaf, I'm surprised he found a *human* woman to mount!" He wrapped an arm around my shoulder, saying, "Don't you worry. That's not me."

Perhaps Leland *is* the person I most want here with me at this moment, and I felt a pit in my stomach knowing how far away he is. And so, looking for anything to keep myself away from the others, I decided to try my hand at letter-writing. Strange to say, however, that, despite all my writing in this journal, I found writing to a person an unusual challenge. I hadn't had to do so before, since Mother did all the letter-writing to distant relatives, so the process was a mystery. It was curious, too, how I was able to tell Leland almost anything in person, yet in writing there seemed to be barriers that blocked our free and easy conversation. Maybe because he wasn't here to respond, and I depended so much upon his reactions. But I wanted to write *something,* no matter how wincing, because he knew me and would listen to my tales. I wanted also to tell him how much I miss him, but I know that men don't say such things to each other, so I attempted to write in the formal, hinted way I saw Mother do. I dipped my pen in ink and wrote him the following:

March 6th, '50

This letter is for Leland Sampson in Manhattan, New York.

Dearest Leland, this letter is for you. It is probable that you already know of my having reached California, maybe through word of the gold company; however, in case you don't, let this letter be proof of my safety. I hope you weren't overly distressed waiting to hear word of my fate, although maybe you were too occupied with school and holidays to give me a second thought.

Lex, my brother, whom you already know, has departed for the hills in which he will attempt to find gold, that same substance that Mr. Payran, our school teacher, whom you also know, also departed for here for. I didn't go with him, for various reasons, and now I live in a boardinghouse with some interesting characters. My jobs are many, but nothing I'm not able to complete, though not often with happiness or contentment in my heart. If only you were here, you would understand, since I cannot explain all of it to you and do any of it justice—

At this point I reread the letter and was so disgusted with it—the vagueness, the ponderous phrasing, the dull boringness. I sighed.

I went to bed in a state of mind lower than ever. I could try writing again soon, but I wondered if there was any point to it. Maybe there's no use. I haven't received anything from him, after all. My foul mood pushed aside the inconvenient thought that it was nearly impossible for him to contact me. How would he know where to write? *But at least he could have tried! He's probably moved on and stopped thinking about me entirely. And why not? There are plenty of other friends on the Hudson River.*

I rose from my bed in the dark, found the letter, and ripped it up.

April 15, 1850
San Francisco
Mild.

Outside the house today, in the Square, was held an election for county offices, of which a big deal was made: banners, flags, free liquors, meals, torches, musicians, a parade, &c. Ah Toy closed the Garden while this hubbub took place, then disappeared on some business. I used the opportunity of a rare free day to steal away to the steamboat ticket office to inquire about N.Y.-bound prices. The ticket agent was just closing up due to the voting festivities. When he saw me approach, he snickered.

"Still here, boy? Couldn't shake them two Asiatics?"

I waited until he finished laughing. "I came to see what a ticket to New York is."

"More than you can afford." He closed the door and locked up. "No matter how much those kidnappers are paying you." He turned the sign in the window to *CLOSED,* then walked up the Wharf toward the Square.

"But how much?" I called after him.

"Come back tomorrow!" he called back without turning around and gave me a wave.

I wondered if I should stow away, yet that thought didn't go far. The penalty upon a stowaway's discovery is said to be arrest and surrender to local authorities; but I've heard stories of ship captains dispensing with the formalities and heaving the offender overboard. With my lack of swimming skill, it's one more obstacle I'm unable to conquer.

I sighed and trailed in the ticket agent's wake up the Long Wharf. Just as I reached Montgomery Street, I caught a movement in the corner of my left eye and turned my head in that direction. Disappearing around a corner was the swish of a black braid and the glint of something metallic. Was it the Celestial? I looked behind me to the far end of the Wharf and saw the Chinese dock girls there. None of them seemed to be missing, so it wasn't one of them.

Despite the mildness of the day, my body gave an involuntary shiver. I pushed my feet forward and struggled back to number 36 Pike Street.

May 22, 1850
San Francisco
Warm midday, cool evening, wind
returning.

God help me, the wind is returning, just as the town has dried out from the winter soaking. The streets are solid enough to walk upon, yet the afternoon winds blow the dust with as much ferocity as when I arrived here with Lex ten months ago. The S.F. weather cycle is exhausting. So is waiting for Lex. He's seven months past his due date.

While cleaning up the parlor this morning, I found a copy of the *Alta California* left behind by a guest. My eyes caught this quick item:

MARRIED

In this town, on the 16th inst., HENRY CONRAD, to the well known China woman, named ACHOI, from Hong Kong.

Achoi—Do they mean *Ah Toy?* There are very few women, let alone Chinese women, in S.F. *Maybe. But if so, married? She and the well-dressed Celestial are married?* Henry Conrad is a regular at the Garden, visiting only Ah Toy in her chambers. And while they always close the door behind them, there are never sounds remotely amorous, and nothing at all approaching affection. No warm embraces, no pecks on cheeks, no excited glint in either's eyes. I'll be the first to say those aren't prerequisites for marriage

—just consider my own cold parents. Nonetheless, I wanted to acknowledge it, so I brought the paper to her. She asked me to read it to her, and when she heard her name in the report, she ordered me harshly to reread it. This time her eyes narrowed, and she calmly took the paper from my hands and crumpled it into a ball.

"Who know? Who tell?"

I scratched my head. "Is it bad?"

"Very bad!"

"Why?

"I cannot be marry!"

"You can't?"

"No!" She rapped her fingers on the table and glared a hole through the wall.

"Why...?"

"Think. Many man want girl, other man want madam. Higher price. Better to be unmarry. Marry is lower price."

Many men do leer at Ah Toy, that's true. Despite her experience and wisdom as businesswoman, she's still very young, and she plays that to her advantage. I took a breath and said, as neutrally as I could, "So why *did* you marry him?"

Ah Toy narrowed her eyes again. "I want my business grow very big. Henry have big business."

"You married him for his money?"

"I marry, he keep the promise."

I nodded. "When was the wedding?"

"Too many question!" she snapped, getting up and clearing the table. I know she's upset when she starts doing other people's work.

Growing up, I gave little thought to marriage. Men and women bore children, that's why they married. Lately, however, the idea of pairing up has crossed my mind; I can't say why. But I know that I notice people more, and their faces, and their shoulders, and their legs, and the shapes of their bodies. Feet, even. How that connects to marriage, I'm not sure, yet these thoughts increase and jumble at the same time. Leland says it's the same for him. It's a thought that first came upon me as he dragged me from the river.

He's the only person I've asked about it.

There was a loud knock at the front door. Then another knock. Then another. It was as if the person outside was running from a pack of thieves and was desperate for safety. Ah Toy was unperturbed by the insistent rapping, caught up instead with wiping the table. "Tell them closed."

The rapping only ceased when I opened the door.

"Good morning!" greeted a man in front of me, as pleasant and unhurried as could be. He was a Celestial, older than the others I've seen, the wrinkles etched in relief on his face shadowed by the midday sun. His eyes, however, were alive, observant, and cunning, and his movements quick and light. He was dressed in a strange manner: a baggy suit of cotton clothes, boots, a shaven head with a queue in the back, braided with strips of silk, and a stove-pipe hat perched on top. The hat was familiar. *Where have I seen that?* I would have remembered a man dressed as oddly as he. However, it was he who took one glance at me and pronounced, "I know who you are."

I stared at him.

"You are the dancer's servant."

"I'm not a servant."

A placid smile played across his lips, and he slightly nodded his head. His eyes never blinked. "I am Norman Ah-Sing. I am looking for your...for Ah Toy, the dancer." His English had a slightly British intonation, mixed with his Celestial accent, and his words were very considered. He'd clearly been schooled in our language.

I opened my mouth to answer but her voice came instead. "No more dance." We both turned. Ah Toy had framed herself in the opposite doorway. I've long ceased being surprised at her sudden materializations, and her somehow knowing everything that was said and done preceding her dramatic arrivals. I often imagine her just on the other side of the wall, spending the day cupping her ear to the walls or peering through some concealed slit, waiting patiently for the cue for her grand entrance.

"Ah Toy *taai-taai.*" Norman Ah-Sing clasped his hands together and shook them in front of his body—a Celestial greeting? "Mrs. Ah Toy. So nice to meet you. My apologies for not calling on you earlier."

Ah Toy sniffed the air. She looked at me, as if I had put her up to this, but I was still trying to place his face from my memory. *"Siu-je.* Miss. No husband."

"My misunderstanding. You do not mind, I hope, that we converse in English? I've lived around the world—Europe, Charles Town, and—" he winked at me—"New York. My Chinese is degrading, but I prefer English anyway, as it is becoming the global language of commerce. I need the practice. 'With familiarity you will learn the trick,' as Chinese say, eh?"

"You are who?" she asked.

Norman Ah-Sing hesitated. "But do you not know?"

"I should?"

The old man gave an unctuous smile. "Not to worry. It is becoming a large town. I am Norman Ah-Sing. I own Macao & Woosung Restaurant and I head the Chew Yick Gung Shaw Association. I am pleased to meet you." Having not been invited in, Norman Ah-Sing continued to stand outside.

"Very good. So sorry, closed." Ah Toy began to push the door shut but Norman Ah-Sing put his hand out to stop it.

"'A door closes, yet a window opens,' they also say!" Norman Ah-Sing gushed with a smile.

"My window don't open."

"Perfect! Then we shall not be overheard."

She raised an eyebrow. I noticed that her man was not in the room. I glanced around for anything I could use as a weapon, if it came to that.

Norman Ah-Sing took off his hat. "Ah Toy *siu-je*, I have very important information for you."

She raised the other eyebrow.

"It is about your business, your wellbeing, and perhaps your very survival."

"No need. Very alive."

"For now." Norman Ah-Sing's smile was bright.

Sighing deeply without bothering to hide her annoyance, she opened the door and walked to the table. I mumbled that I would leave yet she said, "You still work. Not take long."

Norman Ah-Sing removed his boots and came inside. "Thank you. It is a pleasure to meet you both!"

I didn't reply and grabbed a broom instead. He took a seat.

"Many sorry, no tea," Ah Toy informed him as she drained the last of her cup. His eyes flicked to the steaming tea pot on the table, keeping his smile plastered to his face.

"You have a nice home," he began, gazing around the room. "How much did you pay for it?"

"Some."

Norman Ah-Sing smoothed his shirt and rested his silk hat on the table. He then reached into his clothing and produced a small red box, which he placed on the table and slid to Ah Toy. "First, may I offer my congratulations to the bride!"

She said nothing and left the box untouched.

"It is my wedding gift to you. If I had known of the happy occasion, I would have been there."

"No one come."

"Is that so? No family? No friends?"

She didn't respond.

"A shame. I would have brought the most delicious cake!" He turned to me and explained, "At Macao & Woosung we make excellent confections," then winked. "Not even your servant was there?"

Ah Toy's eye twitched. "You also very busy," she said and waved me toward the door.

He paused, and something shifted in his expression. After drawing out the moment, he spoke. "Ah Toy *siu-je*, you are a very hardworking woman. You started from nothing and look what you have done!" He was all smiles again, warm and engaging.

"'Good thing through many suffering,' Chinese say."

"Yes!" He was pleased. "And 'Everything is difficult at the beginning.' And now, the most successful Chinese woman in San Francisco!"

"'Not best but not worst.'"

"Ah, but 'comparing yourself to others will only make you angry.'"

"Who compare? You?"

Norman Ah-Sing smiled. "Indeed. But it is true, your success is well known, which is why I have valuable information."

"Say quick. 'Gold don't buy time.'"

My head spun from the rapid back-and-forth. Something was happening that I didn't understand, as if they were speaking in quasi-riddles.

Norman Ah-Sing opened his mouth to respond, then appeared to think better of it. Instead he nodded and said, "You run a very successful house and your business will grow even greater, more lucky and more prosperous! You are already becoming very well known around town by the white men and very many Chinese."

Ah Toy shrugged.

"Does this not worry you?"

"Worry for prosper?" She laughed. "I get prosper first, worry later."

"Yes. 'A poor man can stand by the roadside, but no one will ask how he is. A rich man can hide deep in the mountains, but distant relatives will come to visit.'"

"No family here."

"Again, a shame." Norman Ah-Sing sighed. "So many of us are here without our families."

It was clear Ah Toy would have liked nothing more than to send him packing to whatever distant place he still had relatives.

"The point is, you are better off than most Chinese here, and you are well known because of it. People will come to you— white, Chinese, Chileno, Mexican, everyone. That makes it extremely dangerous for you. You could be robbed, hurt, even killed." He twisted an imaginary teacup in his fingers. "Tell me, do you keep your money in a bank?"

Ah Toy answered with only a thin smile.

Norman nodded his head. "Good, you shouldn't. I don't trust the banks either. That means," he looked again around the room, "somewhere here?"

"Time for leave," she said, moving to get up. This time she meant it.

"Not to worry," Norman said, putting his hands up in surrender. "I am rich myself. I am not a threat. But other people are. Peasants who are lazy and would rather steal than work. They are in China and they bring their poor habits across the sea. They will take the money you earned and hurt you in the process. They don't care. What would you do if you lost everything? How would you take care of yourself? How would you take care of your man?"

"He protect me. I don't worry."

"I'm sure he does a wonderful job." Norman smiled his slick smile. "But he is only one man. What if the Hounds return? What of your girls?"

"No more Hound." She glanced at me. I gripped my broom.

It was Norman Ah-Sing's turn to raise his eyebrows. "Do you really believe that?"

"Why you say this?" she asked.

"We Chinese all live hard lives already, and I want to make it easier. I want to make sure all of us are safe. That's why I'm leading the Chew Yick Gung Shaw. It is an association that does many things. It helps those of us who arrive from China. It delivers us back home to our families. It sends our deceased back home to rest in peace. And it protects us from people who want to rob and injure us."

"You *very* good man." It was clear she didn't believe this.

"I am just trying to help my people."

"Your people?" She took a minute to inspect her nails. "What more?"

Norman folded his hands. "Ah Toy *siu-je*, there are great opportunities here in Gold Mountain, but Gam Saan also contains great risks and dangers. I would love to help you, your girls, and your business by protecting you from these dangers. I can ensure that you will never be harmed or robbed."

Ah Toy laughed. "Ensure? Very foolish to say."

"I have many people who will see to it."

"Who?"

"I am friends with many *gwai-lo*," Norman said, sitting up straight. "They keep the others in line, away from us."

"Bah!" she waved at him. "You say white man bad, then you say friend. 'He near red turn red. He near ink turn black.'"

Norman's smile began to look forced. "I can assure you that these are good men."

"They cheat, give fake gold!" she cried. My face flushed.

"Do they? I will make sure that never happens again."

She shook her head. "I say yes and you help?"

"That's it! You just pay me a small fee, a bit—"

"*Aiya!*" Ah Toy scoffed. "Old way come to the new world."

"It's the way it's done. As you know, 'Cheap things aren't good, and good things aren't cheap.'"

"Friend is free! But you don't give me the friend." She poured fresh tea into her cup.

"Ah, but I do!" He slid the red box to her again, triumph on his face.

Ah Toy ignored it.

A cloud just briefly passed over Norman Ah-Sing's eyes. "But you must see it. It's lovely!" he said, then shoved the box into my hands, and I instinctively dropped the broom and took it. "Open it," he said.

I looked at Ah Toy, who softly shook her head. They both watched me.

"Go ahead."

I stood frozen.

"You must not refuse a gift!"

Ah Toy then stepped forward, took the box out of my hand, calmly placed it on the table, and pushed it back.

Norman Ah-Sing struggled to maintain his oily, unctuous demeanor. "You refuse the traditional bridal gift?" he asked, eyes flashing.

Yet Ah Toy was more than his equal. In a quiet, steely tone, she said, "Best gift is give peace to me!"

By now the Celestial had slipped into the room. He quickly judged the situation and fingered his knife.

Norman Ah-Sing recovered his composure. He rose, picked up the box, and turned to face us. "Perhaps I should mention, I am good friends with a well-respected newspaper reporter. He is widely read. A thorough, tenacious man. The kind who can get to the bottom of any truth. Someone who can poke around and discover, say, the origin of those who live in this house, and how they came to be here. I wonder, how would the news be taken, here, in California, a free territory after all?" He gathered his things, but left the red box behind. "Thank you for seeing me. I will give you some time to think about it. I do not want anything to happen to you, your business, or your...many friends."

He tipped his stove pipe hat to each of us. "Sir," to the Celestial. "Madam." He turned to me. "Servant." Then he turned and walked out the door.

Ah Toy took three deep, long breaths, looking calmer and more serene with each one. "I breathe for calm. For when men yell," she said when she caught me looking. Meanwhile the Celestial went into the kitchen and retrieved a bucket full of water. Ah Toy took it and splashed it over the threshold in Norman Ah-Sing's wake, washing the old man's bad energy away.

"Always think," she scolded me as she stalked toward her quarters, her serenity vanished. "Last saying: 'Gift reflect giver.' Now clean the mess!"

May 23, 1850
San Francisco
Weather similar to yesterday.

"I know who he's talking about," I said to Ah Toy the next noon at dinner. "The reporter. I met him the night I landed in San Francisco. He had a long name."

"I don't worry," Ah Toy answered, taking a bite of pork, thoroughly unharried. "Old dog always bark."

I wasn't so sure. "Reporters can cause trouble. They find things that outrage people. If it's scandalous enough, the government can close a business."

"We have sheriff."

Have the sheriff? I thought back to our errand to see Sheriff Jack Hays. So *that's* what the package was for. I sighed at myself for being so slow on the uptake and went back to my meal. Ah Toy, however, looked thoughtful, and after a while she placed her chopsticks down.

"Good to have heart. Have care." When I glanced up, she'd made up her mind. "You go to news man. Tell him our house very clean."

"Clean?"

"No dirty. All girl very clean, never mind. Tell him before the old dog bark. 'Quick foot arrive first.'"

"Won't that make him suspicious?"

"Better to tell first. For story." She took her last bite and cleared her dish. "If he give trouble, give the little package."

Half an hour later, with a lumpy envelope pressing against my leg, I was at the door of the *Alta California.* I was alone—"One is less trouble," Ah Toy said—but I knew her man was close by, watching. I took a breath and knocked.

Nobody answered. When were newspaper offices open, anyway? Didn't they work 'round the clock? I stood there, unsure what to do.

A man walked briskly past me, opened the door, and went in. I sheepishly followed him inside. A hum buzzed in my ears—loud, fast talking, and clacking footsteps across the floor, all swirled in a fog of cigar smoke. A printing press stood in the center of the room, at rest for the time being. No one paid me any mind, so intent they were on their work, the stories that would be coming out in tomorrow's edition.

"Excuse me," I said to a young man who flitted by me, but he was already gone. The environment was becoming overwhelming, so I stepped backward toward the door, and in doing so collided into another man passing behind me.

"Watch it!" he cried, dusting off his vest.

"Sorry," I said.

He finished putting himself in order. "Do you have the steamer schedule?"

"Steamer? No...I...I'm looking for James...William...?"

"James King of William?" He rolled his eyes and lowered his voice. "Awful name. It's as pretentious as *he* is."

"Yes, him."

"Unfortunately, he's too good a reporter to get rid of."

"Um..."

"In there." He pointed to the next room. "And watch where you step." Then he was gone.

Minding my path more carefully this time, I edged my way to the next room, where a sole man sat at a desk, looking at strange, looping symbols in a notebook and writing longhand on a sheet of paper. I recognized him from our brief encounter on my first night. He glanced up at me, then back to his work.

"You didn't stay," he said to the paper in front of him.

I furrowed my brow. No one else was in the room. "I didn't...?"

"Stay." He continued deciphering his indecipherable script. "I told you to stay in case I had additional questions. I did, and you didn't."

"I…well…"

He put his pen down and glowered at me. "You were running from the Hounds, were you not? You and your brother?"

"Um, yes, that was us."

"And now you live with that Chinese harlot."

Had Norman Ah-Sing told him that? No, the Garden is full of comings and goings, so a good reporter would have already known.

"Why didn't you stay? I had questions."

As it came back to me, I became bolder. "I'd answered your questions."

"But I had more." He sounded like a child on the edge of a tantrum.

"I remember you'd left."

"Yes, but I asked you to stay. That was a big story."

"I'm sorry. My brother was injured and needed attention." *And I'd just killed a man.*

James King of William shook his head. "Well. I had to instead interrogate some Chilenos who managed to squeak out of that mess. I couldn't get more than two words out of them."

I shrugged. "Sorry."

"So now you're finally recovered enough to give me a few answers?"

I felt pressure in my head, so I tried Ah Toy's technique. I took three long, deep breaths, filling my lungs to the limit of their capacity, then exhaling until my chest was like a vacuum. Then, twitching my nervous fingers, I took the envelope out of my pocket and passed it to him over the desk. "This is from Ah Toy, the madam of the Garden of Fragrant Flowers." He scoffed. I continued, "She wishes to let you know that, whatever you've heard from other people, her house is clean. Nothing to get excited about."

"Really." The reporter smirked. "And she sends you with a gift to keep me away? You know what the Chinese say about gifts."

I'd handed it over too soon. *What was I doing?* "She only wishes for you to—"

"You see, gifts always come with baggage. They're all wrapped up with pretty bows to hide some ugly thing inside. That you're here now, with a pretty bow, tells me there's something disturbingly ugly underneath. But what is it?" He stood up and walked around the desk, eyes on me the whole time, and smiling. "What is it? Are half the judges and aldermen in the town being paid to turn their eyes away? That's common enough in the wild west. Sheriff Hays too? Typical, for a drifter like him—no morals. No, perhaps there's some uglier thing. Why come to me of your own accord, unless heading something off? A murderous madam, perhaps? The mysterious past of her henchman? Or—" He moved to the front of the desk and sat on it, crossing his legs and looking me full in the face. "—unsavory circumstances surrounding the girls of the house? Scandalous? Unmentionable? Harrowing? Something to rile up the bleeding hearts and the pious?"

I couldn't get a word out. Just when I wrapped my head around one accusation, another came right on its heels. I searched for some rejoinder, anything at all, when I detected a brief movement just outside the window. Noticing my focus shift, the reporter turned to the window as well and we both beheld a long, black braid just visible at the edge of the glass. It wasn't moving now. At that moment, however, I snapped back into place.

"No," I said loudly, "that's all false. Whatever evil you're implying, you're wrong. I refuse to tell you anything more, as there is nothing more to tell."

The reporter turned back to me, then placed the envelope in my hands. "Then I refuse to take this."

He returned to his desk chair, sat, and picked up his pen. Dismissed, I replaced the envelope in my pocket and made for the exit.

"Again I say, don't stray too far," James King of William called to me as I glanced back at the window. The braid had vanished. The reporter resumed work with his symbols. "I most definitely will have more questions."

I braced for James King of William to arrive at the Garden's doorstep, notepad in one hand, pen in the other, eyebrow raised and mouth full of questions. The other shoe must drop, either in the form of the reporter or the old Chinese restaurateur, yet though my heart has this past month dreaded every knock at the entrance, that doorstep has been at ease.

Not that there hasn't been activity like a full-scale breach of the Garden's defenses; no, business here has only hummed along all the more. Men with lascivious appetites nightly cross the threshold and occupy Ah Loi and Ah Si. Ah Toy is all abustle in positive energy, feeding off the house's, and even spares me a friendly gesture from time to time—a knowing wink, a friendly smile, an extra bit of rice at dinner. I can only guess that her man reported that I didn't divulge anything troublesome to the reporter. They don't know that my taciturnity was due largely to my ineptitude with bribery and lack of any concrete knowledge. Just because I've wondered at the origins of the Garden's two hardest workers doesn't mean I've uncovered any secrets dark enough to keep hidden. Not that I've strenuously tried. But again, I do wonder. The girls themselves are untroubled by the bump in business. They know that a busy night means more pay, better meals, nicer clothes, all that an employee longs for.

At dinner they attempted the hardest work they've encountered so far at the Garden: teaching me to use chopsticks. Ah Si pulled my hand out in front of me and threaded my fingers with one stick between my thumb and forefinger. "Like paint stick," she explained. Then she slid the second stick behind the base of my thumb. It promptly fell to the table. Ah Si smiled, picked it up, and shoved it back into place. When I tried to clamp the two sticks together, the second one fell out again. Ah Si repeated the step. This time I held on to it, but the sticks were uneven. She then showed me how to push the points against the plate to even them out, which I precariously succeeded in doing. "Now eat!" she ordered, pointing to a dumpling. I looked warily at it, distrusting it, then gave it a try, but its slippery skin resisted my attempt and it sat there, stubborn and mocking. Ah Si laughed and Ah Loi, the withdrawn one, couldn't resist the fun and put in her two cents.

"This here." She moved one stick to the left of the dumpling. "This here." She moved the second stick to the opposite side, then made a squeezing gesture. I squeezed the sticks and punctured the dumpling's skin. Juice gushed out, and Ah Si and Ah Loi exploded into a fit of giggles. Fed up, I wielded my sticks like a spear and impaled the blasted thing, then triumphantly brought it to my mouth, satisfied with my ingenuity.

"*Aiya!*" the two girls yelled, giggling out of control. The Celestial gave me a look of disgust, finished his bite, and left the room. Chewing victoriously, I decided to ask them how they felt about the work they're in, only to be met with expressions of puzzlement.

"Job," Ah Si answered. "*Louh Ma,* Old Mother, give for hard work."

"Then why do you sometimes cry out in pain?"

"Big show. He like weak. Want to help. Want to save. Want to 'buy freedom.' We play. 'Oh, save me!' Many moneys."

"Do you *want* anything?" I asked after Ah Toy left the table.

"Want?" Ah Loi smiled at me, almost pityingly. "Food. Husband. Home. But China, very danger."

Ah Si said, "*You* save!" and they both laughed.

I glanced at the door and lowered my voice. "How did you come here?"

Ah Si followed my lead and leaned forward conspiratorially. "Boat."

"Yes, but I mean, was it voluntary?"

They looked at each other, puzzled.

"As in, on purpose?"

"Purpose?"

"Yes," I whispered. "Did you *want* to come here? You *chose* to come here? Did anyone force you?"

Ah Si opened her mouth right when Ah Toy stuck her head through the door and barked at them in Chinese. The girl closed her mouth around her chopsticks instead, slurping down her breakfast with no further word. "You," Ah Toy said to me, "come."

The whole business confuses me. In Sunday School I learned about the evils of whoring, that harlots debase themselves before God and soil the sacred temple of their bodies. Yet Ah Loi and Ah Si don't seem soiled to me, and their reasons for working in this way are practical; they're not evil; they haven't cast Him aside and welcomed in the Devil. Then again, excepting the missions, God and the Devil aren't known in China like they are here. The girls could be offending whatever Celestial spirits and idols reside there instead. I cannot imagine such sweet girls as these being doomed, though I guess that's not for me to decide. But what part do I play in it? My participation is likewise practical, but does my work here contribute rungs to the ladder for their souls to descend upon? Ah Toy may have gotten them here, yet do I lead them by the hand to the mouth of Hell, or whatever version of it their souls are bound to?

When I reached the parlor, I found Ah Toy sitting with a stranger, and her man standing off to the side as he does. The stranger was a bearded fellow, fairly well-dressed in nice trousers, a starched shirt, and a vest with a watch chain looping from the front pocket, classier than many of the mining sort who frequent the Garden. Yet plenty of his ilk—politicians, constables, judges, the like—make the Garden a regular stop. He stood to shake my hand, and in so doing towered over me. He appeared to be someone important.

"I am Selim Woodworth. I own a goods store on the Wharf, but presently I call in the capacity of a liaison between the Chinese people and the Western. My pleasure to meet you, lad," he said, and retook his seat. "I would have read this to the

Chinalady myself, but she insisted you do the honors. You must fill a significant role here." He scrutinized my appearance, perhaps uncomprehending what a teenaged Westerner was doing at an Eastern boardinghouse, before moving on. "Unfortunately, the content in this page does not offer the honor one desires in a letter."

Woodworth unfolded the paper. It was delivered to him, he explained, from her husband.

"Henry Conrad?" I asked. "But he's here in town. He doesn't live with us but he's not far."

"Here? No, not so," he answered. "Perhaps he was once, but he must have returned home. This letter is from Hong Kong."

I looked at Ah Toy, puzzled. Her expression mirrored mine. "You say what?" she asked. "Henry is here. Not at Hong Kong. I call him."

Now it was Woodworth's turn to look confused. He handed me the letter. "I think it's best you read this so we may get to the bottom of whatever this is."

I took the paper and read aloud:

To the Honorable Liaison Selim Woodworth, Mandarin in San Francisco:

I write to you both with earnestness and trepidation. I am an aggrieved man residing in Hong Kong who is in desperate need of your assistance. My wife, whom I dearly love, has injured me by taking leave of me. I am not sure why or where she has gone to, but I am in need of assistance to locate her and bring her back to me. She is a Chinese lady called Atoy, young, rather tall for someone of her type and stunningly handsome. I understand that this is a daring request to ask, but as your town is well-known as a port of debarkation for those voyaging from Canton, I humbly implore you to help me find her. I am willing to take any steps necessary to ensure that she is returned safely, and I have conferred with Hong Kong church authorities to apply for the same to their counterparts in your land. I cannot bear the thought of a life without her. Until we are reunited and Atoy return to her home and her duties as wife, I remain,

Gratefully yours,

Atchoung.

I glanced around the room. Woodworth was solemn. The Celestial was inscrutable. Ah Toy was furious. "What is this? Not true! I have no husband in Hong Kong!"

"Please forgive me," Woodward said, "but are you married."

"Yes. But my husband not in Hong Kong. This letter is someone else."

Woodworth retook the letter and read it. "This is your name, is it not?" He showed her the text.

"It is," I said.

"Who is this liar? I don't know Atchoung!" said Ah Toy. "My husband is Henry Conrad."

"It was in the newspaper," I added.

Woodworth furrowed his brow. "It very clearly states your name."

"Someone else! Ah Toy very common name."

"I am certain it refers to you. Mr. Ah-Sing confirmed with me that you are the only Ah Toy is existence in San Francisco."

I winced.

She narrowed her eyes. "Ah-Sing? He give to you?"

"Not quite. I received it first, then informed Mr. Ah-Sing of its contents. As a liaison to the Celestial community, it is my duty to report such correspondence to its leadership."

Ah Toy shook her head and aggressively waved him off. *"Aiya! A trick!"*

"A trick? How so?"

"No Atchoung. No Hong Kong husband. Ah-Sing make it up!" She grabbed for the letter but Woodworth leaned away.

It was his turn to narrow his eyes. "And why would Mr. Ah-Sing do something like that?"

Ah Toy burned. "Old dog want my money. I say no. He punish! Take me to China!"

"I admit that Mr. Ah-Sing is an unusual fellow." Woodworth frowned. "But to fabricate a letter for the purpose of deportation? That does not cohere with what I know of him. It is his mission to *help* the Celestials in this new land."

Ah Toy scoffed. "Chinese justice. I don't know Atchoung. All make up!" She wagged a finger in his face. "You tell Ah-Sing I stay!"

Woodworth set the letter down and wiped his brow. "This is a problem. This Atchoung fellow, whomever he is, has consulted with the church to order you there. I brought the matter to the attention of Mr. Ah-Sing, and he has generously organized a collection to financially assist you on your voyage back. My understanding is that your people have raised an impressive sum of money, and in very short order at that."

Ah Toy was silent, finally, and for a full minute. She stared through Woodworth, through the wall, and into some infinite distance. Then her eyes refocused. "Not my people."

Woodworth sighed, looking regretful at what he was about to say. "You should know that an application was made by Mr. Ah-Sing to the town council, to order your return."

"Aiya! See? You understand? I say no one time! He think he is the mandarin, but what does he know? Only the old dog!"

"Unfortunately, there seems to be a dearth of your—of Celestials—who approve of your line of work, and Mr. Ah-Sing, we both know, can be very persuasive. He has achieved much for the Chinese people here. Even you must admit the Chinese are currently in good graces with the West."

"They hunt me like pack of dog; he is the wolf!"

Woodworth leaned back and sighed again. "I cannot presume to know whether Mr. Ah-Sing arranged this entire matter. The man is an upstanding member in the eyes of the town. Regardless, I urge you to fight it in a Western, civilized court. The sooner you do this, the better. Your life and career could depend on it. This town has expelled its citizens before." He looked at her with something resembling sympathy. Then he gathered himself up.

"One last suggestion. Find a witness to testify on your behalf. As you know, as a Celestial, and a woman at that, your word alone will not be enough."

He bid her good day, gave me a nod, clicked the door shut, and was gone.

July 1, 1850
San Francisco
Cool and cloudy.

Today is my 17th birthday. One year ago I was on board the *Oregon*, angry at Lex for having disappeared. Today I live in a harlot-house. There's really no other way to state it, whether one calls it a "boardinghouse," a "disorderly house," a "bawdy house," a "sporting house," a "Garden of Fragrant Flowers"…it is a house and harlots live in it. Well, maybe the house as a *whole* is a harlot-house, though I hesitate now at labeling Ah Loi and Ah Si harlots. I can't say why. Earlier on I would have had no trouble in that regard, but now…now there's something different. They are victims of other people's decisions and actions, aren't they? Or are they here of their free will? Didn't they arrive at that beach on Christmas Eve, unbidden? Maybe they really are harlots, ugly a term as that be.

I don't know what to think nor how to feel. Though my eye is ever trained on home, I've become accustomed to the Western way of life. Everything is a bit seat-of-your-pants and do-whatever-it-takes, truly an *American* style, though it's hard to know what rules there are to govern this chaos. People here frown upon murder, so that's one, and you are to practically prostrate yourself before a woman. Outside of that, who really knows? The harlots hole up in luxurious houses and the ministers preach in the streets. The lawmen are just as gold-struck as the miners. The gangs maraud the town, yet valuable goods pile in the streets and no one locks their doors. I stumble about in these chasms between the ambitions and the morals of this place.

On my birthdays, Leland used to spring me from my house

before dawn and spirit me to safety. We would spend all day together, it being summer and school being closed, and that entailed wandering around the city, visiting bakeries to acquire edibles, and ending up at the bank of the river, where we'd spend hours talking, playing cards, shooting dice, skipping rocks, soaking in sun, all the activities I would dream of while sitting in a hot classroom in June. On my birthday, Leland made it all happen.

This year I'm here, while Mother and Father remain at home, free to visit *their* friends and do the things *they* want to do, and loving the empty, child-free house. Lex too; I'm sure he's living up my birthday in my absence, boozing it with his gold company friends in some small-town gambling saloon, the gold slipping through their fingers just as fast as they'd found it.

My only birthday gift offered up at the Garden was the privilege of reading Ah Toy her nightly news. She took her cup of tea and said, "Read," and with zero gusto, I did.

ENLARGEMENT OF SOCIETY
by James King of William
Daily Alta California
Jul. 1, 1850

We are pleased to notice by the arrivals from sea Saturday, the appearance of some fifty or sixty of the fairer sex in full bloom. They are from all quarters— some from Yankee-land, others from John Bull country, and quite a constellation from merry France. One Frenchman brings twenty— all, they say, beautiful! The bay was dotted by flotillas of young men, on the announcement of this extraordinary importation.

This is the most gladdening intelligence of the day, and what is still better, there is no mistake about it! The girls are coming, and the dawning of brighter days for our golden land is even now perceptible! The day of regeneration is nigh at hand, and we shall look trustingly forward to the advent of that glorious epoch. We shall begin to count confidently upon the stability of California affairs, and prepare ourselves to witness the great change which is shortly to follow, with feelings akin to hilarious joy.

In a word, the girls are coming…

I looked up and noticed that Ah Toy hadn't sipped from her cup. "'Fairer sex in bloom'?" she asked.

I shrugged.

She put her tea down. "So many girl." She scowled and sat in silence for a while, staring into the distance. I didn't move on to the next story. Bad moods filled the room—mine from my birthday ruminations and Ah Toy's from the newspaper—icing the atmosphere and seeping into the adjacent rooms. After a while, she stood. Without giving me another glance, she muttered, "So many," and left the room, a cold wake swirling behind her. Not to be outdone, I rose and left in the opposite direction, letting her tea freeze into a cube the shape of its abandoned cup.

July 4, 1850. Independence Day.
San Francisco
Mild and breezy, foggy in evening.

"What the *gwai-lo* do not realize, lad, is that no Chinese woman would leave her husband to sail across the ocean to try her hand in a different land. Either she would come with her husband or be left behind while he made the voyage alone."

Henry Conrad wiped his mouth with a napkin and took another swig of tea. We all—he, Ah Toy, the Celestial, Ah Loi, Ah Si, and me—were sitting at the table, eating our dinner. Henry Conrad did the talking. He was in the midst of explaining to me why the man named Atchoung didn't exist, or even if he did, why the letter was a fraud.

"*Gwai-lo?*" I asked.

"Foreigner. All Westerners are *gwai-lo.*"

"But aren't *you* the foreigners here?"

"Mmm. And you, are you native?" Henry Conrad refilled his cup, took a sip, and replaced it on the table. "This is one of the nicer ways we refer to Westerners."

He'd arrived last night and had spent the evening in Ah Toy's quarters, as usual, but rather than go home at first light, or wherever the Chinese businessman goes, here he was, diving into a lecture presented for the benefit of his captive audience. Ah Toy's expression was particularly pained. From the way she ground her teacup into the table, it was clear she didn't like having her situation bandied about in conversation by the rest of us. Yet she didn't deny any of Henry Conrad's assertions.

"Thousands of men have left their parents, wives, and children behind to sail to Gam Saan—Gold Mountain—to make their fortune and return home. The financial burden prevents most men from bringing their wives along with them for the rugged adventure. A wife's job is to work for the family—especially serving her mother-in-law—while her husband farms or sells goods. It is not her job to earn money. One of the very few ways a woman can, if she absolutely must, is as a *baak-haak-chai.*"

There was a shifting around the table. "A what?" I asked.

"Us!" Ah Si piped up.

Henry Conrad nodded. "A 'hundred men's wife.' Yet only an unmarried woman would do this, not a wife. There is too much shame for the husband."

"But she *is* married," I said.

"Married, yes. But her *baak-haak-chai* days are past. Now she is the madam."

"What do you know?" Ah Toy grumbled from the other end of the table. "You tell my life story?"

"I know that you have caused Ah-Sing to lose face. He is a strong man, and he is no doubt lashing out at you."

Ah Toy gave him a look that said, *I already know this.*

"But you are the defendant, which means Ah-Sing must provide the proof. You only must create doubt in the judge's mind that Ah-Sing is correct. You can do that by telling your side of the story—"

"The truth!"

"Yes. Though that Mr. Woodworth is correct. You need someone to testify on your behalf."

"Who?" Ah Toy challenged him.

"Why don't you send the judge a small package?" I asked.

Ah Toy's raised her eyebrows to Henry Conrad.

"It will work one time, maybe," he said. "But what's to stop Ah-Sing from accusing you again and again? He will bleed you dry. And you can bet Ah-Sing will be sending small packages as well."

"Find a *gwai-lo!*" Ah Si snorted dismissively. Ah Loi giggled.

Ah Toy glared, and they quieted immediately. For a long, torturous minute, Ah Toy's stare bore into them. The two girls cast their eyes down.

"You." Ah Toy shifted to me.

I glanced around. "Me?"

Ah Toy nodded. "You do it."

"Do...what?" *Testify?*

"Can he handle it?" Henry Conrad asked the madam.

"What can be me? Handle what?"

Henry Conrad gave Ah Toy a look that said, *See what you are working with?*

Her expression became pained. "I don't have the *gwai-lo* friend. Customer only."

"And none of my contacts would risk their reputation to defend a madam," Henry Conrad mused. "It is not ideal," he added, inclining his head toward me.

"Nothing ideal here for the *Tang-yahn.*"

"The Chinese person," Ah Si explained before I could ask.

Ah Toy pointed at me. "Only choice."

Henry Conrad was quiet for a long while, appraising me, while I stared blankly at him. He sighed, coming to some reluctant conclusion, and addressed me. "A Chinese voice in an American court carries little weight—"

Yes, I'd seen that in Ah Toy's brass case.

"—but a Westerner's voice is weighted at full value. And you are a man. Well," he gave a wry smile, "a male."

"*Gwai-lo* always believe each and other," Ah Toy said.

"But I can't testify," I protested, wanting nothing more in that moment than to wipe the smile off Henry Conrad's face. "I don't know what to say!"

"It is simple. You say you know Ah Toy to be married, which you do."

"But I don't know anything about her life in China."

"You also say that Ah Toy has told you on numerous occasions that she was unmarried when she had to flee for her life from China and landed here. It is becoming dangerous in China, and you can play that up for the judge."

"But won't I be under oath?"

"You only tell the judge what she has told you, and she has told you she was unmarried and had to flee for her life, and that she wishes to make this land her new home. You will have told no lie. Isn't that all true?" he asked Ah Toy.

She nodded curtly.

I thought in sullen silence. My nerves shook, thinking about answering a judge's questions at the front of a courtroom. That judge in the brass case was an intimidating guy. What if he thought I was lying? Would I be jailed? Would I be incarcerated on the gaol ship *Euphemia* in the middle of the bay and left to rot? Could they hang me? *No, no, I can't, there's too much at stake. I'd never leave this place; I'd never see home again, due to imprisonment or the noose. I might be roughed up for refusing to play along, or find myself at the wrong end of the Celestial's knife, but I have to take that risk. I must live to find my way home, somehow, some way, either whole or broken, it matters not. There's no reason for me to get tangled up in all this.*

"I want something."

Every pair of eyes in the room bored into me. What was I doing? What was I saying?

"Want something?" Ah Toy said, dangerously soft.

I gulped and pushed my panic down. My shirtsleeves stuck to my armpits. "My um…my pay. I want…double."

Nobody said a word.

"From now to the end of my service, when I've earned enough for passage home."

The room was oppressively still. Ah Toy stared at me, unblinking, cold, and unmoving. Henry Conrad, Ah Loi, Ah Si, and the Celestial watched her, loath to distract her away from me, morbidly curious as to what her reaction would be. Time crawled, and no one breathed.

A minute passed. Or an hour? Or a second? What happens when time slows? I could smell my sweat. I wanted to wipe it off, to close my eyes, to run outside and breathe in deeply, but a vise on my chest, nay, the whole of my body, forbade it.

"No."

I refocused my eyes. Ah Toy hadn't moved. Had she said it? Was I in the clear? Would everything return exactly to what it was before, me cleaning the girls' rooms between guests, Henry Conrad and Ah Toy counting their money, the Celestial running errands and flexing his knuckles on his knife? I hesitated, then pushed myself up from my seat, ready to exit from the conversation I wasn't sure actually happened.

"Sit," Ah Toy commanded, and I was back in my chair. "You will do it, but no extra pay."

I sat there, stunned. So that was it? All she had to do was say no and that was that? The room slowly came back to life, and everyone started to rise from their seats. Ah Toy had spoken. Time to get back to business.

"No."

This time it was my voice. The room froze again. Ah Toy's eyes flashed. "What?" she said without moving her lips. Henry Conrad's eyes were as large as saucers. Ah Loi looked like she was going to be sick. A smile played at the corner of Ah Si's mouth.

"I want something in return," I said. Sweat dripped down my sides. "Give me something. Part of the business."

"You realize you are asking for something large," Henry Conrad said. "Be more specific."

"I want a percentage of the Garden. Any client that pays, I want a piece of it."

"Why you deserve this?" Ah Toy asked in a serious voice.

"Because," I said, diving into the pool of no return, "you need me. I clean the rooms, wash the linens, go to the market for food, empty the chamberpots."

"Anyone can do this."

"Yes, but I also talk to reporters, deliver packages to the sheriff, read the news to you every night, and now you want me to testify for you in court. And," I paused, ready to throw my best argument onto the table, "I am a *gwai-lo*, the only one you have."

Ah Loi and Ah Si still hadn't moved. Henry Conrad leaned toward her and said something in Chinese. Ah Toy answered him with a nod, and he sat back up.

Ah Toy stared at me a long while and tapped the table with a finger. No one around her moved.

"How much?" she asked.

I blinked and gathered my thoughts. "Oh. I'd say…" *How much is enough? Will I insult her by asking too much, or will I earn her disdain by asking too little?* "Let's say…one percent?"

"One percent?" Henry Conrad cried. *"Aiya!* Do you understand how generous that is? This is the most profitable Chinese brothel in the town, and you want one percent of its earnings!"

I didn't reply. I noticed that it was Henry Conrad who answered me, whereas Ah Toy hadn't, and she continued to watch me with curiosity, as if she no longer knew the boy in front of her, the one she had bound to a chair and intimidated into involuntary employment. Henry Conrad picked up on it as well and stopped talking. All attention was back on her.

Ah Toy stretched the silence long and hard. Henry Conrad's indignance dissolved into the air, and Ah Loi and Ah Si stood rooted to their spots. Their legs had to be tiring. The atmosphere of the room was hushed yet charged, waiting for something to fall.

Finally Ah Toy spoke. "You say you very important," she said to me. "Big man, big work, many responsibility. Big help. No one else can do."

No one else spoke.

"But you only start. Very much to learn. Not so valuable yet, but one day, maybe. You talk in court for me."

It remained quiet. Ah Toy said no more, and after a few moments, Henry Conrad pushed his chair back to rise. "Well, lad, it was a valiant effort. I give you credit for the attempt. But in the future, you may want to—"

Ah Toy flicked her hand, and Henry Conrad, silenced, returned to his seat. She regarded me for another moment, and at that instant, a hint of a smile played at the corners of her cheeks. It was almost imperceptible, and when I blinked it was gone. Her face was all somber business.

"You talk in court for me, I give two percent."

Henry Conrad's jaw hit the floor. *"T-two?"* he stammered. The two girls shared a look with each other but didn't otherwise move. I wondered how much they were understanding. Even the inscrutable Celestial looked more serious than usual.

Still focused on me, Ah Toy said, "You talk in court for me; you keep me in Gam Saan; I give two percent. This is high price, you understand?"

All attention shifted to me. I stood up. I don't know why, but it had an effect on the room, as if I was taking charge of something. Ah Toy, not to be outdone, stood up with me. I looked at her, and she at me, and when I nodded, she nodded in return, with a gleam in her eye, which told me I'd done something right. What it was I didn't fully know, but something momentous passed between us, something I'm not able to put to paper, but somehow feels tangible and solid. At some future date, when I have occasion to read through this journal, the thing will likely be obvious to me, yet for now I can only say that it is some sort of translucent understanding. I may not know the full power of that which I wield in my hands, but it is there, and I can wrap my fingers around it.

Henry Conrad spoke next. "Why two when he only asked for one?" he asked with an incredulous expression.

She looked not at him but the over the whole room. "'Peony in bloom very pretty, but need green leaves to support.'"

A sudden understanding dawned on Henry Conrad's face as if he'd just stumbled on an obvious point. It gave him a superior expression, as if he'd finally been let in on a joke. He didn't say anything for the rest of the evening.

"One more thing to know," Ah Toy said to me. Henry Conrad nodded. He seemed to know what was coming. "Sit. I tell you about first husband."

This morning we awakened early to attend the court. For a normal person, rising with the sun is nothing unusual; in fact, the Square is always buzzing with activity in the pre-dawn hours. For those who tend a boardinghouse, however, it's agony. We bed down while the rest of the world rises. Ah Toy, the Celestial, and I ate and prepared in dour silence. Only Henry Conrad was amused by it all. "The Chinese have a saying," he said to me as we walked through the Square toward the alcalde's office. "'A crisis is an opportunity riding the dangerous wind.'"

"What does it mean?"

"It means what it sounds like. When you are in the middle of a crisis, there is always some way to take advantage of it."

We arrived at a court filled with Celestials, all with disapproving faces, judging her and her business as we entered the room and started walking the gauntlet. These were the same people who'd so quickly raised the funds to send her across the ocean. Only James King of William, sitting in the front row with his notebook and pen poised, kept a neutral expression.

Ah Toy walked through the assemblage with subtle, fluid movement, her back straight and her nose slightly lifted, as though to keep it clear of the rabble beneath her. The room around her didn't exist. At the front, in a raised chair, sat Judge Baker, stifling a yawn.

And across from us stood none other than Norman Ah-Sing. Begowned in robes and sporting his silk top hat, the old man allowed a serene smile to play at his lips, leaving little doubt that he had orchestrated the whole affair. Ah Toy proceeded as if he were a mere phantom.

"Back so soon?" Judge Baker asked when he saw her. "Has the courtroom life given you a yen for a return visit? This time I expect more decorum in this courtroom. Do you have all your evidence with you this time?"

"Yes, Mr. Honor."

"Then let us start. I know you want to write and burn your own oath." He motioned to the deputy, who handed her the necessary materials.

"Come now, just make the oath!" Norman Ah-Sing interjected. "We are on American soil, so make the American oath. They are disrespecting the court and its customs, are they not, Your Honor?"

"Thank you for your efforts, Mr. Ah-Sing, but this is not your time for speaking."

As the judge finished, a Chinese man whispered to Henry Conrad and handed him something. Henry Conrad nodded and spoke up. "Your Honor, we are not technically on United States' soil—"

"We will be soon enough. It's already before the Congress," Norman Ah-Sing interrupted.

"Mr. Ah-Sing, not another word," Judge Baker scolded. Norman Ah-Sing inclined his head. "Miss Ah Toy, please make your Chinese oath and be done with it. We have already eaten through valuable time."

As before, Ah Toy wrote her oath and burned it, sending it to the spirits.

"The backward ways should be left behind," Norman Ah-Sing murmured from his seat. The judge ignored him and got down to business.

"Mr. Ah-Sing, what is your case against this woman?"

"Where to begin, Your Honor?" he cracked. "The house of prostitution? The disrespect of the court and its time? The excessive makeup?" Some in the room chuckled. "As to this case, I have a duty to ensure that the lady is returned at once to her pining husband. The poor sir is out of his mind with grief at the loss of his wife and is begging that all effort be put forth to return her to him. As leader of Little China, I have an interest to see the two reunited."

Ah Toy sat stone-faced, moving no muscle.

"Mr. Ah-Sing, why should this court become involved in this matter? There is no statute violated by Miss Ah Toy's remaining here. Would it not be more prudent to allow the Hong Kong authorities to pursue this according to their rules and regulations?"

"I do not think so, Your Honor. Since Ah Toy is not on Hong Kong property, the British government must appeal to the United States for help in her deportation."

"Has it done so?"

Norman Ah-Sing paused. "Not yet, Your Honor."

"There are numerous Christian missions with autonomy in the region. Has Mr. Atchoung appealed to any church to assist in his wife's deportation?"

"He had written that he would, Your Honor."

"Has he yet?"

"Not that I'm aware of, Your Honor."

"Has Mr. Atchoung made any appeal to any governmental entity in California regarding Miss Ah Toy? The governor, the alcalde of this town, or the sheriff, or a judge?"

"He has not. You must understand, Your Honor, that a man living in Hong Kong will not have knowledge of these people."

"And yet he knows who *you* are?"

Norman Ah-Sing smiled. "Well, yes. There are many lines of communication that run across the ocean. We Chinese are but small parts of a vast network. We call it *gwaan-hai*. I have ties to gentlemen in Hong Kong, and many men in Hong Kong have ties to me. It is only natural for a man to turn first to his network when a problem arises. It is much the same way here, Your Honor, with the political machines."

Judge Baker rubbed his chin and turned to Ah Toy. "Miss Ah Toy, your husband in Hong Kong wishes you home, yet you will deny him the right to have his wife with him?"

Ah Toy looked at him with a hard calm. "No husband in Hong Kong, Mr. Honor. Here only."

"Please elaborate. Explain," he added, in case she didn't understand.

"I marry in Guangdong."

"Where is that?"

"In English it is Canton," Henry Conrad explained.

"Ah, yes. Where is your husband now?"

She hesitated, closed her eyes, and inclined her head. "Die. He come with me on ship to Gam Saan, very sick and die." She opened her eyes and stared straight ahead as before.

"My condolences. Was his name Atchoung?"

"No."

"Did he ever live in Hong Kong?"

"No."

"Have you remained unmarried after his death?"

"No. I marry this man." She gestured to Henry Conrad.

The judge turned his attention to him. "Have you ever lived in Hong Kong?"

"No. Only visited, Your Honor."

"Have you ever gone by the name Atchoung?"

"No, Your Honor."

"Did you write this letter?"

"No, Your Honor."

"Thank you. Be seated." The judge turned to Norman Ah-Sing. "Mr. Ah-Sing, does this Atchoung truly exist?"

"Yes, Your Honor. It is easy for them to say a man on the other side of the world does not exist."

"Just as easy as it is to say he *does*. What evidence do you present to verify Mr. Atchoung's existence?"

Norman Ah-Sing held up the letter. "Your Honor, here is evidence."

"Anyone could have composed that. What else?"

Norman Ah-Sing swallowed. "Your Honor, if you can allow me to present evidence in the next forty-eight hours, I will be glad to collect it and present it."

"This case will be decided by that time." He turned to Ah Toy. "Miss Ah Toy, I believe you have a witness to present?"

"Yes."

"You may present him."

Henry Conrad turned to me and gestured for me to rise. I did, without any feeling in my legs. Bees buzzed angrily in my stomach as I braced myself against the table. Every single eye was on me, and added weight and heat to my skin. The door that led to the Square, to freedom, was miles away. My knees began to shake.

The judge smiled. "You may relax, son, this will not be difficult. First, what is your name?"

"Cy—" My voice croaked and I coughed and cleared my throat. "Cyrus Kirkpatrick. Sir."

"Mr. Kirkpatrick. Do you know Miss Ah Toy?"

"Yes. Yes, sir."

"In what capacity?"

I licked my dry lips. "She is my boss, sir."

"Your boss?" He raised an eyebrow. "And what is it you do for her?"

I glanced at Henry C. and he nodded encouragingly.

"I clean the house for her."

"Is that a full-time job?"

"Yes. Yes it is, sir."

"Has Miss Ah Toy ever mentioned the name Atchoung?"

"No, sir."

"Were you aware she was married?"

"Married now, sir?"

"Married in Canton."

Ah Toy continued to stare ahead.

"Just recently, Your Honor."

"Before that, did you believe she was unmarried?"

"I didn't think about it, sir, until she married him." I pointed to Henry Conrad.

"I see." Judge Baker made a note. Out of the corner of my eye, Henry Conrad gave me an urgent look. *Tell him more!*

My mind went blank. *What should I tell him?*

"If there's nothing more, we can conclude this proceeding."

"Your Honor," Henry Conrad stood up. "Apologies, but Mr. Kirkpatrick would like to say a few more words."

"Would he? Then let's hear them."

What should I tell him? My vision flickered. *How long have I been standing here?*

"Take your time, but not too much. Other cases are waiting."

A ringing started in my ears. I pressed my fists to my head, then quickly pulled them down again. I breathed in and breathed out. In, and out. In, and out. Percentage signs danced in front of me. I answered before I knew I was answering. "I've known Ah Toy for almost a year. She was born in Guangdong and lived there, then came here with her husband, but he died. His name was not Atchoung. She came here to improve her life because China is dangerous right now. What *gwai-lo*—what Westerners don't realize is that no Chinese woman would leave her husband to sail across the ocean. The man would go instead. Either she would come with him or be left behind."

I glanced at the judge. He was listening. I took another breath and, a little more calmly, continued. "Thousands of men leave their wives behind to come here. They can't afford to bring their wives with them. A wife's job is to work for the family. But she wouldn't leave her husband's family to go alone. Ah Toy was married, but they both came."

"In essence, you're saying there is no man named Atchoung waiting back home?" Judge Baker asked.

I nodded. "Correct, Your Honor."

"Fine. Thank you for your testimony. On its face we have a 'he-said, she-said' situation here, with a letter as the only proof. These are the types of cases a judge doesn't envy another judge. But here we are." He paused for a moment. "And with that, I am ready now to announce my ruling."

The room became still. "So soon, Your Honor?" Norman Ah-Sing asked, with a touch of nervousness.

The judge cast him a withering glance before continuing. "As to the fate of Miss Ah Toy, I proclaim—"

"He threatened us!" I blurted out, my pointer finger squarely on Norman Ah-Sing. "He came to our house and demanded money for protection!"

The courtroom went cold. Judge Baker stopped mid-sentence. "Excuse me?"

"That's a lie!" Norman Ah-Sing said. "I went to your *whorehouse* with a wedding gift, nothing more. Don't slander my name, boy!"

"Mr. Ah-Sing!" the judge thundered. "Control yourself or be expelled from this courtroom!"

Norman Ah-Sing gathered himself and bowed, then sent daggers in my direction. "My deepest apologies, Your Honor."

"You." Judge Baker glared at me. "You have disrupted my courtroom in the middle of my ruling. Your opportunity to testify has passed, and your wild accusation does not please this court. You will keep your mouth shut for the remainder of this proceeding, or be held in contempt. That means jail. Understood?"

Horrified, I nodded.

The judge rubbed his eyes. "Always with this Chinawoman," he muttered, then waited until it was silent, then waited some more, daring anyone else to speak up. It was deathly quiet.

"Miss Ah Toy," he finally said, "I can see no reason you should leave this country, your chosen occupation and the quality of your witness notwithstanding, nor can I see why this court should become drawn into this provincial dispute. As far as the state of California is concerned, there is too little evidence to deport you. You may go."

"Thank you, Mr. Honor."

Norman Ah-Sing clenched his jaw. There were angry murmurings in the audience. Perhaps to them this was their best shot to rid them of their countrywoman. As they stood to go, Judge Baker spoke again.

"Mr. Ah-Sing, remain here. Miss Ah Toy, you are dismissed. I look forward to seeing you in a more friendly environment."

Without giving him a second chance to call her back, Ah Toy bolted up and whisked through the room to the exit. I lingered a bit to see what would happen next. The Chinese in the audience whispered to each other, not sure if they should make their own exits or stay to support the Little China leader. Before he approached the judge, however, Norman Ah-Sing found me in the crowd and set upon me a stare so cold it could freeze the bay.

"Come along, do not linger," Henry Conrad said, pushing me along. "Justice may be about to take place, and we should not interrupt it with our presence. Besides," he winked, "the Garden is where news comes first, even before any newspaper, is it not? We will find out soon enough."

I thought it perplexing, however, and entirely appropriate for the town of San Francisco, that we should sit in a courtroom, under the stern gaze of a judge, not for our base role in the hiring out of a woman's body, yet for something as trivial as a counterfeit letter.

Part Three

CALIFORNIA ADMITTED INTO THE UNION!
by James King of William
Daily Alta California
Oct. 19, 1850

We are at last enabled to send the news so long awaited by our fellow citizens on the Pacific coast. California is admitted into the American Confederacy, and today takes rank as the THIRTY-FIRST STATE OF THE UNION! The bill for her admission was brought up in the House on Saturday, and after a short discussion, passed as it came from the Senate.

The news had been received everywhere with most unbounded satisfaction. At Washington, 100 minute guns were fired on Saturday evening, followed by a display of fireworks. In this city, many of the hotels and public edifices hoisted the national flag in token of rejoicing. Let us all unite in a demonstration of gladness, congratulation and pride for the new glory now enwreathing the brows of our loved State, that shall carry happiness and joy to our relatives and friends and brethren beyond the mountains and the deserts, and make the hearts of our Senators and Representatives glad, and strengthen their hands and their arguments by our unequivocal response to the entry ticket which Congress has given us.

The Utah and New Mexico bills have also passed, and the organized members of our confederacy now span the Continent in one unbroken arch, whose base is washed by the world's two great oceans. May it so stand through the coming centuries.

October 29, 1850
San Francisco
Finally cooling.

Last October I was caught by surprise by the strange climate this town was built in. This month is the summer month, more so in the first couple of weeks, and it's when the residents shed their moleskin jackets and boots and let their skin bake in the sun. It's a strange and wonderful sight in this town: bare arms swinging to and fro in the midst of work or the simple act of walking.

A few weeks ago the heat affected the atmosphere of the Garden of Fragrant Flowers as well. Firstly, it wasn't the flowers that were fragrant but the ripeness of bodies—men's bodies, to be exact, since Ah Toy requires the women in her house to be bathed and scented for the guests. I'd also taken up the regimen when I could, though water is a scarce resource, and the Celestial and I were often out of luck at the end of the day. We gave each other a wide berth whenever possible. The climate has dramatically cooled since, and after their short respite the jackets are again called into service.

It's been so remarkably busy that by the time I was finally able to crack this journal again, I was astounded that over three months had been shaved off the calendar since I last picked up the pen. I would not make a good reporter, whose job it is to tenaciously write and fill space, regardless of the import of the story or the gossip. James King of William can keep his job. However, where I *do* best a reporter's skills is in my knowledge of the goings-on of the town. The Garden, as I'm sure is the case with other boardinghouses, is a clearinghouse for news. Ah Loi and Ah Si can only see to one man at a time—unless there is an agreement by all parties for more—so the men spend a good amount of time in the parlor, conversing and drinking. Ah Toy is a master of never letting a glass sit empty, and it's in this sloppy state that the talk most readily flows. Clients share the news, negotiate business deals, slander officials, defend their honor— since many of them *are* officials, though I will abide the boardinghouse code and not divulge names—and spout off the most salacious of scandals and gossips. I am in and out of the parlor in the service of my work, it's true, but I hear a fair amount.

I learned, for example, what fate Judge Baker imposed upon Norman Ah-Sing after the trial three months ago. He was made to sign a bond for $2,000—two thousand!—to keep the peace. He's been quiet since, not a peep, and so, while we don't want to let an enemy out of our sight, the more immediate day-to-day demands of running the Garden have pushed him out of our minds for now.

I also discovered, sooner than most, that the California territory joined the Union in September. The debates had been ongoing for months, and at the highest levels of Congress. The guests here talked of Henry Clay, Henry Foote, and Thomas Benton, the latter two apparently having some firearm-fueled altercation on the House floor, and some sort of compromise between the slavers and the abolitionists. The news came officially on the *Oregon*, believe it or not, the very same steamer that brought me here from Panama City, and, as Ah Toy's is commonly the first stop for freshly-landed crews, we were some of the first San Franciscans to hear the report.

The mood in S.F. has been jubilant over the past week and a half due to the news, and so the powers in the town planned a grand parade to celebrate the event. Ah Toy predicted a high demand at the Garden once the parade finished and the drinking really got going, so she and the Celestial stayed behind to prepare. Ah Loi, Ah Si, and I went to the parade. The men ogled my two companions as we strode through the Square, which was exactly the point.

The crowd buzzed with talk, cheer, and drink, much like a county fair at home. Important men gave speeches, and then the fun began. A parade full of banners, politicians, military, and bands started up and snaked its way across the town. Cheers arose at every moment and a cannon boomed very, *very* frequently. American flags draped over balconies and flew from any vertical space that could accommodate them. The German, Spanish, and Italian contingencies all had their moments of glory, yet no group attracted as much attention as when the Celestials made their appearance. There were about fifty of them in number, and they carried a banner of crimson satin, inscribed with Chinese characters and the inscription "China Boys." Their costumes were rich, much more colorful than their everyday cotton, and they appeared genuinely pleased to be part of the proceedings. And there at the front of it all, waving his fan and doffing his silk stovepipe hat, was Norman Ah-Sing.

"Him!" exclaimed Ah Si.

"Yes," I said.

"*Louh Ma* chase away."

"That's him."

Norman Ah-Sing, without losing a step, turned his head and stared right at us. Ah Si gasped as he winked at her.

"Time to go," I said, and turned the two girls around.

*   *   *

Tonight was the busiest night the house has yet seen. Ah Toy was right; the celebratory mood from the day translated into a bonanza for us. The Garden was packed. I had to squeeze through the door and edge the perimeter of the parlor to get to my quarters. The room smelled like sweat, feet, incense, and booze, and a jaunty, slightly hysterical tune was being pounded out on a piano. The piano and the player are new, rented for the festivities. "Can you believe?" Ah Toy marveled, materializing out of nowhere at my side. "Long line, like when I dance. Big payday!" she said with a wink. It took me a moment to remember that I, too, would profit from the surge. Suddenly some oddly positive feeling arose in my belly, a swelling of pride, perhaps, and I attempted to remember how to calculate percentages.

"Oh," she said. "Maybe you know. Reporter, long name. He earlier come here."

I frowned and scanned the room.

"Maybe leave now. Be careful. Don't talk."

James King of William. What was he sniffing around for? Odd that he should show up just after we'd seen Norman Ah-Sing in the parade. I hadn't told Ah Toy about that. I turned and she was gone again, dissolving into the crowd to refill whiskey glasses, and before long the demands of the house drove the reporter from my mind.

The night was a series of errands and emergencies. Other than servicing the two girls, I cleaned glasses, wiped up spilled whiskey, washed vomit from the floors, smoothed the reused linens—I didn't have enough clean sets to keep up with demand, and I cringed at what would accumulate in them—and changed out the water. The Celestial did what he could, yet he had to set up guard at the stairs to keep the men at bay, who otherwise would have wandered up on their own. Two rival aldermen had to be separated at one point due to differences of political opinion, and Ah Toy flitted between the men all night, serving, laughing, flirting, really playing up her hostess role. As for Ah Loi and Ah Si, I couldn't see how they could possibly work through the backlog of guests. I was exhausted on their behalf.

At one point late in the night, probably 2 or 3 o'clock, I stole away to my quarters for a moment of respite. I sat on the edge of my bed and fell back, and for the first time was aware of the ache in my feet. I was on the verge of falling asleep, lulled by the muffled din outside my door, when I heard someone come into the room. I sat up and beheld a man standing there. He was young, maybe in his early twenties, and his eyes were glassy. He swayed slightly. "Hope you don't mind," he said and shuffled over to my bed and collapsed down next to me. "Too loud out there. Ears need a break."

I tensed up. These were my quarters and a stranger was in them. He smelled like booze.

He lay there a while I sat, unable to relax. He looked at me. "Need a break too, eh? Yeah. I've seen you working all night. Your feet must be killing you." He then leaned over and picked up my left foot in his hand. I instinctively pulled away but his grip was firm, and he started to knead it like a pile of dough. I didn't know what to do next. Exhaustion had been pushing relentlessly into my brain, yet now my thumping heart drove it away. He then took my other foot and did the same. *Is this something men do together?* I'd never heard of it, and Leland and I had never done this, yet this man was older, and thus, maybe, more experienced? It didn't feel bad, though my nerves prevented what I presumed was supposed to be enjoyment.

Then he did something else. Not letting go of my foot, he worked his hand up my ankle, then my calf, then my knee, all the while kneading my flesh.

"Umm," I said, and I noticed I was shaking.

"Relax," he said in a soft voice, not pausing even a second. His hands then moved even farther up. I jerked myself away and rolled off the bed, crashing to the floor. A pain shot from my elbow, and I jumped up. I had to get out of there; I had to get out of my own room.

"Hey now!" he said, startled. "Hey! What are you doing?"

I moved frantically around the room, my hands fumbling under my pillow to grab my journal.

"Come on! The wait is too long out there. Hey, slow down, you little twit!"

My journal and pen in hand, I rushed for the door and stubbed my toe on the bed post. So much for my massaged feet.

"Hey!" he called as I escaped the room. It wasn't until halfway down the hall that I realized I should use my journals to cover up my trousers.

When I returned to my room hours later, after the house had quieted, the man was gone. Under my pillow was a package filled with coins. Inside was a note with "Big payday!" written in childlike scrawl.

November 3, 1850
San Francisco
Still cooling.

With autumn in full swing and the wind mild, the townsfolk are out and about again in a much-improved mood, if from nothing else than the cooling air neutralizing some of the nightsoil stench from the open gutters. The Celestials of the town move about at the same speed and routine as always, with nary a lull or break in their constant rhythm. Perhaps they are immune to weather, from harder stock, too concerned with making a living to be bothered by such trifling matters as climate.

Perhaps, too, I am unsettled by Ah Toy's news. She announced it at midday dinner. Ah Si and I are always bleary-eyed from the nights before, yet Ah Loi and the Celestial are awake and alert, ready to receive their marching orders. And today, Ah Toy's were something to behold.

"We have the problem. Good problem, but still the problem," she announced between bites of curried rice. "Ah Loi and Ah Si. Very strong, many talent, but only two! The business always go up. Need more girl."

It made sense, but there wasn't much to do about it. "Where do we find them? There are hardly any Chinese women here."

She nodded. "Two day later, we leave."

I put my cup down. "Leave? Where? Who?"

"Guangdong." She took a sip of tea. "You and me."

"Me?" I looked around the room. No one else seemed to think this news was out of the ordinary. Indeed, all had returned to their meals, ready to move on to more interesting conversation.

"Henry the boss," Ah Toy said to the group. "We return with

many girl. For now, make the men always happy."

"What about me?" I asked.

"You go with me," Ah Toy said between bites. She said this as though she were discussing the weather with one of her clients.

"Why me?"

"You very useful. Safety."

I nearly choked on my food, but before I could raise an objection, she said, "Pack for tomorrow night," and that was it.

*   *   *

China? *China?* It's a place so distant that I can't be sure it even exists. I can point it out on a globe, but its only mention in my education was a school lesson on the merits of European imperialism. The rest I've heard in bits and pieces here in San Francisco. I know there are Christian missionaries there, though that is the limit of my knowledge. The enormity of such a proposition, that I'm to travel abroad to that exotic land, hasn't yet fully sunk its teeth into me. The weight of it has not yet pressed down upon my shoulders.

And "safety"? *Me?* I must be an unknowing participant in a ruse. It can't possibly be that I, a seventeen-year-old East Coaster, could fulfill such a need. What weapons do I own? What muscles do I possess? What alien language skills can I boast? And yet, I'm to have my trunk packed by tomorrow night, and in two days' time sail to the other end of the world. But I couldn't go. There was no way I could go. I could barely make it to S.F., and now I'm circumnavigating the globe?

"You go," Ah Toy repeated when I told her she'd have to find someone else.

"It's just that…I'd be of more use here. I don't even know Chinese."

"No need. I talk *Guangdongwa*."

I tried a different tack. "Look at me. I'm not someone you want protecting you. I can barely protect myself."

Ah Toy raised an eyebrow. "Barely?"

"Fine, I *definitely* can't protect myself. Why not take him?" I gestured to the Celestial.

"I decide okay."

"But…isn't it better to take someone who can actually protect you, and speak Chinese as well?"

She squinted at me. "I there live many year. I know Guangdong."

"Yes, but—"

"You afraid of what? You own the business. This good for the business. What?"

"Nothing. I'm just that, wouldn't *you* be protecting *me?*"

"Afraid so many Chinese?"

"What? No!"

Ah Toy smiled. "All Chinese work hard; too busy, don't bother skinny *gwai-lo*."

True, *most* of the Chinese here hardly glance my direction. Yet —

"Too busy to feed family. Fight the war, too."

I choked. "Fight the *what?*" Henry Conrad's words came back to me: *It is becoming dangerous in China.*

At a knock on the door, Ah Toy waved me out of the room with conversation-ending finality. "You pack."

A *war?* I stumbled down the hallway, trying to wrap my head around that word and nearly collided into Ah Si descending the stairs. "Be care!" She grasped my shoulders to steady herself and then held me there, looking me over. The top of her only comes up to my chest, so it was an odd feeling to be handled in this way.

"You, have care," she said. She squeezed my arms. "Danger. Big fight."

"Yes, well…" I tried to squirm out of her clutches, "I will just refuse to go. I am a part-owner too, you know."

Ah Si laughed. She turned me around to face the kitchen, then swatted me on the rump as if I were a horse. My cheeks reddened. I made my escape, with Ah Si laughing behind me, and decided instead to seek out Ah Loi to inquire about this war. Ah Loi was more serious and would give the matter the solemnity it deserved.

I knocked on Ah Loi's door and a muffled reply came from within. I opened the door slowly and peeked in. She sat on her bed looking out the window, so I went in and sat in the chair next to her, staring out the window as well. I haven't spent much time with Ah Loi, and something told me not to disrupt the atmosphere. After a while, Ah Loi gave a shuddering cough and pulled something from under her bedspread. It was a lumpy package, filled with jingling coins, which she placed into my hand and closed my fingers around it.

"Father Mother," she said, gesturing to herself. "Find. Give." Of the four Chinese speakers in the house, Ah Loi is the most limited in her English—if not counting the mute Celestial—yet she is the sweetest, and I immediately knew her wish.

"Where do I find them?"

"Hong Kong."

"How will I find them?"

She opened the package and pulled out a slip of paper with Chinese characters written on them. "Name," she said.

My heart fell. The writing was indecipherable to me. "Does Ah Toy know them?"

Ah Loi shook her head.

"I don't think I can help," I said, feeling a deep sorrow in my gut. I handed the package back but she refused it.

"You," she said. "You."

"But how will I find them? What do they look like?"

Ah Loi shook her head again. *"Louh Ma* no." She gestured to the door. "You."

She looked so heartbroken that I did the only thing possible to do. I accepted the package and nodded. She rested her hands on mine, then turned back to the window. I took that as my cue to leave and left her there with her faraway thoughts.

Ah Loi's gold reminded me of Lex. October has passed, which means he's been absent now a full year. I suppose there's no risk now to leaving the town; Lex can't still be alive at this point, or perhaps he's already returned home and dumped his earnings at Mother's and Father's feet. They'd welcome him back into the fold and hoist him upon their shoulders, the savior who'd also managed to ditch that useless leech of a lass in California. A double triumph for the Kirkpatrick family!

"Good?" Ah Loi asked, and I snapped out of my head. She'd come out of the room and found me at the head of the stairs. I nodded and quickly turned my head, then hurried away.

November 19, 1850
On board the Golden West
Cool and breezy.

Two weeks have passed since we departed San Francisco, and this is the first I have summoned enough of my energy to write. The morning of our embarkation I awakened early, partly due to the steamer's departure schedule, mostly due to a queasy stomach. The night before I'd put off packing as long as I could, imagining that at any minute Ah Toy would inform me that the voyage was called off. Maybe the fighting had gotten worse, or Norman Ah-Sing's *gwaan-hai* network had presented too much of a threat for Ah Toy to risk landing. Would Atchoung be there? *Maybe he's real after all?*

But the voyage was still on. There I was that midday, pulling the dray downhill to Long Wharf, my trunk upon it and filled. At dinner everyone had acted as if it were another ordinary day. Ah Toy was all business. Ah Si was all yawns. Ah Loi was all prim, proper, and ready hours in advance for her clients to arrive. The Celestial was stoic, unreadable, his usual mask in place. The atmosphere nearly had me fooled, but there was Ah Toy's trunk by the door, telling me the whole venture wasn't a figment of my thoughts. My unsettled stomach lasted all that day. Whereas in previous months I would have leaped at the chance to board a steamer bound somewhere—*anywhere*—my feet were like lead as I clattered our trunks down the Wharf.

Upon reaching it, the Celestial presented our tickets at the office—the ticket agent, seeing whom I was with, gave me a wry smile—then deposited Ah Toy and me on the ship. Without any word or second glance, he walked back up the pier to Clay Street, then became lost in the crowd. Ah Toy, wasting no time, had me hoist our trunks onto the ship for the crew to take below deck. With nothing to do afterward while the other passengers loaded, I wandered aimlessly, noticing all the water surrounding me—*so much water*—until one of the crew cuffed me on the shoulder and informed me that if I did not clear the deck, the next blow would land me in the bay. I hastened below and found my hammock. *I am on my way to China. Lord deliver me back safely.*

There's been plenty more of note to write about: the Farallones, a pod of whales migrating southward, a squall that pitched the ship for twelve hours, and a drunken man falling down the deck ladder. I didn't see most of it because I'm bound to my hammock. My queasy stomach has gone into full revolt and protests every roll and pitch of the ship, and only between bouts of sickness do I arise for meals and relief breaks. The steamers from New York to San Francisco also gave my constitution a fair test, so I can't tell why this particular leg is doing me in. The swells must be larger, or I've grown weaker. Everyone else, however, seems to be getting along fine. All I know is that there's no desire, no will within me to join the world topside.

Two days ago Ah Toy brought me a meal and exhorted me to eat. I know I'm in a sorry state if *she* is serving *me*. She set it in front of me without a word and walked off. She's staying in the Captain's quarters, having made an arrangement—one I wonder if Henry Conrad would approve of. When she returned at the end of the day, with another plate in hand, she landed it with a piercing clatter. I hadn't touched the previous meal.

"How come?" she barked.

I didn't want to move. Against all my will and my innards' protestations, I rolled over and stared at her vacantly.

"You eat. I don't like come here." She crinkled her nose at the staleness of the steerage.

I didn't want to eat in front of her, so I turned away. She left without further word.

This morning a bitterly cold wave of icy water dragged me under, and frigidity sliced into my skin. Gasping, I bolted up out of sleep, my heart pounding and blood pulsing. I lurched like a startled beast, flinging droplets all about, my head on the verge of freezing.

A man in the hammock behind me, now soaking as well, shouted in Chinese.

"Finally," Ah Toy said, giving him no thought, and when I wiped my face dry and calmed enough to focus, there she stood with a dripping bucket.

I glared at her, shivering.

"So angry!" She smiled. "Up! Eat! You have work."

"What did you do that for?" I snapped.

"Up. Walk around to feel better."

"I'm sick."

"Every day sick. Up and walk. You get better. Stomach grow strong."

My guts lurched and my teeth chattered uncontrollably. "I can't."

"You can. You think no need to work?"

"To do what?" I made a big show of looking around. "We're on a boat."

"Always work. You need healthy. No good sick."

Nostrils flaring and gooseflesh flaring on my skin, I climbed down from my top hammock, opened my trunk, found a linen, dried my face and hair, climbed back up, and lay back down. She said nothing, and a minute later she picked up the bucket and climbed back up to the deck.

I knew I shouldn't celebrate, for I knew this wouldn't end in my victory, but I couldn't help a flutter of defiant joy rippling through my gut. I savored it while I could.

Sure enough, only minutes later footsteps came back down the ladder. Refusing to grant her the pleasure of my concern, I stayed put.

A second icy wave of water cut me to the bone. I yelled out in agony.

"*Aiya!*" the sopping Chinese man behind me screamed.

I turned, drenched, to see Ah Toy dipping my face linen into the remnants of the bucket water. "Up," she said calmly. "You have work."

Christmas Day, 1850
On board the Golden West
Warm and tropical.

Two weeks ago we landed at the Sandwich Islands to take on fresh water and supplies. The warm air, heavy and sticky, drew me out of my cabin, and I stepped onto my first steady land in almost two months, though for the two days we were laid over there I felt as though the whole island would tip me over. "No land legs!" Ah Toy smirked at me while I stumbled for a place on the dock to sit. From there I took in the tropical surroundings: green hills, turquoise water, blindingly white clouds, and frond-adorned trees with long, skinny trunks that bent in the wind. Out past the harbor, clouds of mist from migrating humpback whales puffed from the water's surface. On the dock, brown-skinned kanakas with minimal, loose clothing and sacks of possessions clambered past me onto waiting ships—all on course due East to California, while ours pointed the opposite direction.

After weeks of cloistering in the bowels of the ship, I couldn't get enough sun. I was a cold-blooded reptile upon a rock, soaking in every ray of heat, feeling it on every hair on my skin. The soft breeze lulled me into drowsiness, and the next thing I knew something stung me on the arm. I yelped and sat up too quickly, nearly falling over as my stomach flipped.

"Too long sun!" Ah Toy laughed. "So much burn!"

I looked down at my skin, bright red now and still stinging where she'd tapped me. My body radiated heat.

"Time for shade," she said, grabbing my arm to pull me up. I howled in pain.

*   *   *

Since then, nothing except a vengeful stomach, flaky skin, and "haole rot" spots on my neck. And the sea. Sea upon sea upon sea, the only changes registering as more sun and humider air. I'll never admit it to her, but getting up and walking *does* help. When I'd finally dragged myself up the ladder above deck, the breeze hit me in the face and, for the most part, calmed my nausea. The rocking of the ship still does a number on me, and with no permanent point to affix my gaze to, I've resorted to staring at the clouds to anchor myself. The worst days are the ones with clear blue skies and nary a puff of white in sight. That's when I spend much of my time hanging over the railing and doing my damnedest to avoid looking at the water, a tricky proposition given my positioning. In late November we ran into a stretch of four straight cloudless days, and I spent so much time folded over the edge that my nickname among some of the bemused crew and many of the nose-holding passengers became "Sick Cy." Ah Toy finds this particularly amusing and can't help laughing at my expense when this sobriquet is invoked. "'Sick Cy' sound like Chinese 'finish eat,'" she explained, leaving me to find the irony in it.

*   *   *

Yes, it's Christmas Day. I should be sitting in St. Patrick's church listening to the Christmas message, then walking home to the smell of Mother's spiced butter-roasted chestnuts. Rather than sinking into happy thoughts and merry feasts, however, I'm here, tossing my guts while the ship endlessly rocks. It's been a year since last Christmas—naturally—a year since my first Christmas away from my family, and a year since the great fire. The entire year, it feels, has been a trial by fire, or a sinking in mud, or a choking in dust.

I've been thinking about Jesus this day. Some time ago, it must have been Easter, Rev. William Taylor preached in the Square about the passion of Christ. The disciple Judas, he said, was a traitor through and through, betraying Jesus to the Abrahamites for thirty pieces of silver. Rev. Taylor continued on to lambast the gold seekers, saying that their drive for riches turned them unforgivably evil. The fire from a year ago was proof of God's wrath, he claimed. I don't know. If that's true, it seems to me that the enterprising folks of San Francisco quickly built over God's punishment and are only thriving all the more.

I mistakenly glanced at the infinite expanse of water, pressed my fists against my head, and slowly breathed in and out five times. What will a Godless China hold for me? Damnation or relief?

January 1, 1851
Hong Kong Harbor
Mild.

We've now docked in the humid port of Hong Kong. Here I am, then, on the other side of the globe from where I ever expected I'd be. Still, I couldn't help but become awed by the beauty and strangeness of the Far East. Here is a whole other world where life plays itself out. Some of the passengers, mostly Chinese, wept at the sight of it, and it was a sight to see, too. Fervently green hills arose out of the sea, while the aroma of marine salinity wafted through the port. Piers jutted out up and down the shoreline, some filled with the shipping traffic of a major European city. Mid-size junks dotted the bay, their sails shaped like bat or dragon wings, and many were colored in bright red hues, while British ships crawled through. Small skiffs laden with strange goods sidled up to our ship, and their owners called out in babbling tongues. The passengers were too preoccupied to pay them much mind, though, the gathering of their trunks and possessions and getting to shore as fast as possible taking precedence. When it was our turn to debark, Ah Toy led the way while I dragged the trunks behind us. Long-queued Celestials with drays swarmed us on the dock to offer their services, and Ah Toy obliged, to my relief.

The place was aswarm with people. Men and women with long cotton shirts and baggy cotton trousers pressed in everywhere we went, many of them carrying ridiculously large loads, some of the women holding the arms of tottering children or letting them trail in their wake like ducklings. The men with long poles on their shoulders, their cargo balanced on either end, were particularly impressive and dangerous. One swing to the left or right was bound to take out any pedestrian in his radius. Yet nothing of the sort occurred; the people were far too experienced and nimble to incur that embarrassing fate.

In fact, business was carrying on. The crowd at the port numbered more than San Fran. and more than New York. I said as much aloud, mostly in awe to myself, and Ah Toy responded, "Hong Kong very crowded, but this more than normal. War chase people here." And on cue, I bumped into Ah Toy in front of me without looking. She'd been forced to stop suddenly by the crowd, and a murmur buzzed front to back.

"Down," she hissed, and I did without questioning. Through the limbs of the people I saw a gang of a dozen or so men with bamboo hats and gently curved swords. They were walking on the street, which had been cleared by their presence. Nobody else moved.

"Who are they?" I whispered.

"Taiping fighter. Bad for *gwai-lo*."

I watched as their eyes darted this way and that. They were scanning the crowd—for what, I couldn't tell. One of the fighters looked behind him, and in his visual pass his eyes met mine for the briefest second before moving on. Then they darted back, a double take, and his eyes found me again. He whispered to the man in front of him, and that man found me too. They muttered to each other, and the meaning was clear. I was caught. My face burned, my heart thumped in my ears, and a sudden acid churned in my stomach. I didn't know why I should be considered their enemy, and a thousand thoughts and regrets rushed through my head. Why had I come here? I'd let myself be tricked! My ears rang in my head.

The gang of fighters turned and strode toward me. Ah Toy said something harsh under her breath. The crowd parted before the Taipings, and Ah Toy smoothly, and almost imperceptibly, shifted her body in front of me as she tried to melt into the nervous pedestrians. The crowd, however, wouldn't let her, and a hand clamped down on my wrist and yanked me forward. Ah Toy suddenly, with great force, brought her elbow down upon the arm whose fingers gripped me. The man to whom the arm belonged yowled in pain, but didn't let me go. Ah Toy, transformed by the fury that overtook her, wound up for another blow, but was restrained by a Taiping who rushed forward to aid his comrade.

Shouting erupted from the contest, and hands flew in—I don't know from where—to assist on both sides of her. I was still attached to the first man, and I cowered on the ground, trying to drag him down with me so I at least stood a chance at flinging him off. He was shorter than me, and wiry, yet his grip was iron and he refused to be shucked aside. Another of his compatriots secured me by the opposite arm and hoisted me up. I wriggled and flailed the best I could, yet it was Ah Toy who put out an effort twice mine, a display so impressive that my two captors and I paused our struggle to watch her attempt to throw off the now four warriors straining to subdue her. This the four eventually did, though not without injury to themselves, an inventory of which included many deep scratches, welts, a stomped foot, a bloodied nose, and one very visual bite mark on one poor soldier's forearm. She stood there heaving, a murderous look burning in her eyes, and spat something out to them in Chinese. One of the fighters, whom I took to be their head, answered her equally harshly, grabbing my arm, pulling up the sleeve, and revealing my tattoo. A couple of the others noticed the inky character and glanced at me with expressions of bewildered accusation, as if I hadn't been forthcoming with them and had some explaining to do.

Ah Toy launched Chinese words at him thick and fast, and it was a wonder to see her command a conversation in her native tongue. My two captors kept their hold on me but their attention was focused on the drama. My tattoo was quickly forgotten, and after Ah Toy's second verbose volley, the head fighter began to look overwhelmed. He stared at her for a moment, then looked around him at the crowd and seemed to lose his resolve. He muttered something to my captors, and much to my amazement they released their hold on me. I took in the full scene. The warriors surrounded us. Dread still filled my chest, yet it abated somewhat when I had a realization: They had yet to draw their swords.

The man who'd first grabbed me stepped in front of me. He glanced sideways to Ah Toy, and gave her a small smile before turning his attention to me.

"God man!" he said in an accent almost too thick for me to understand. He bent his head, then clasped his hands together and shook them, much like the gamblers in S.F. do to prepare to throw dice. Then he grabbed both of my hands, shook them, and released them. He then made, in the Catholic manner, the sign of the cross with his right hand and stepped aside. Then the second man came to me and did the same; he took my hands in his and shook them, signed the cross, then stepped aside. Then the third man, then the fourth man, then the fifth, until all the fighters in this small squad had paid me their respects, even those restraining Ah Toy—although they had to jump out of her reach after releasing her. By then she had cooled to the point of wavering passivity, though her face remained hard. I didn't know what to make of any of it. The Taipings moved on, and the crowd resumed its movement. No one else was shaken by what had just occurred.

"What just happened?" I asked, short of breath, my body still humming.

Ah Toy didn't answer. Maybe she couldn't. We'd survived something we hadn't expected to, not more than twenty minutes after setting foot on solid ground.

Maybe I'm some sort of god to them. No, that's blasphemous. I couldn't be the only pale-faced Westerner here; the British had recently taken over.

Ah, maybe they think I'm British! I wasn't dressed like one, but it was hard to compare. No other Europeans walked in the crowd, but everyone knows the Brits are snooty, so maybe they steered clear of the commoners, the "riffraff" as Father used to say.

No, the soldier said 'God man' and they all crossed themselves. They must think I'm a missionary. This made the most sense, and I chewed on that for a while. If I signed the cross every now and then, maybe I could get through this war-torn country alive after all. Though, in truth, I wasn't so sure it wasn't my business partner and her combat techniques I should fear more.

We are now lodging in downtown Hong Kong in a secretive location I'm not allowed to know the way to. Despite the reverence the Taipings showed me, I was blindfolded for the journey from the street to our quarters by a man who materialized out of the shadows. Ah Toy appears to know him, but not well. They don't talk together much, at any rate. He deposited us in our quarters—Ah Toy in the nicer of the two, as usual—and left without fanfare. Fifteen minutes later a very young girl came in to serve us tea and a meal of rice and vegetables, then she, too, disappeared. It's now late, and though my body is weary, my mind is buzzing, and I can't recall all the unique sightings I would've normally marked.

On top of all this—and I had almost forgotten—it is the new year. Another anniversary to mark off.

January 13, 1851
Hong Kong
Warm yet comfortable.

For all the excitement of our first day here, the subsequent twelve days have been a bore. Well, not at first. For a week Ah Toy showed me around the city. Excepting the strange incident with the Taipings, she's been upbeat. She clearly feels at home. We've spent the days at food stalls with steaming pots of seafood and rice, on the docks watching the fishermen land their bounty, and wandering through alleys where women hang their wet laundry while children with shaved foreheads scamper around them, all of which infused her with a happiness and comfort. There's a bounce to her step, and she's even genuinely smiled from time to time. I imagine she's feeling similar to how I would, were I to set foot back in New York.

When I asked her if we'd do anything other than tour the city, she said we'd also go to the surrounding countryside, but there is Taiping activity in the area, so we are stuck here for now.

I asked her the thing that had really been on my mind. "While the Taipings are the subject," I said, "who are they? What happened when they grabbed me? What did you say to them?"

She put down her tea. "Qing is Manchu, China leader. Emperor. Bad leader—no food, many tax. Taiping is Christian. Hong Xiuquan, crazy leader, think he is God, want new China. No Qing. Very many fight, getting big, take over. No one can stop. They see tattoo." She pointed at my arm. "Think you bad criminal. Take you to jail or kill."

Gooseflesh spread across my skin and I sat down. *Was I really that close to death?*

"What did you say to them?"

"I say, 'He God man. Many pray, many talk to *gwai-lo* God. Here to say God teach.' They like very much. Taiping is Christian."

It wouldn't hurt to add a crucifix to my wardrobe, just to be safe. And then another thought came to mind. "If I'm in their good graces, then they'll let us travel without trouble?"

She shook her head. "Taiping yes, but where Taiping, also Qing. Don't like *gwai-lo.*"

I frowned.

"Danger for you," she said. "Still, you can help."

Whatever I can do to bring her an advantage, I know she'll make me do. But really, all I care about is surviving this journey and returning home in one piece. *Yes, a crucifix and a little divine protection wouldn't hurt.*

I wondered one more thing. "If one side is bad and the other is crazy, whom do you support?"

She regarded me, almost with pity, as if I didn't see the obvious. She glanced left and right before saying, "No matter."

"No matter? Surely one of them must be even slightly better than the other! One side taxes the people; the other side starts a war. And the Brits, you can't be happy they've taken Hong Kong, can you?"

She shrugged. "No matter."

I couldn't believe it.

"Is it that you live in San Francisco and not here anymore, and don't care?"

"Not true," she said sharply. "Very care. My mother live here, very suffer. No money, no food, very poor, lose all the thing. Get very sick. Don't say don't care."

"Then..." A wall seemed to be blocking my understanding "... then why do you say, 'no matter'?"

"Chinese believe 'Ten thousand thing, all because fate. Nothing because one person.'"

"But you didn't accept your fate when your husband died on that ship. You came to California and worked hard to get rich."

"That my fate."

"No, you *worked* to do that! *You* did that!"

"My fate very small, my work very small. Easy. In China, Qing and Taiping very big. No person control. Too big fate for one person control. Survive only."

"But *someone* must control it. Things don't just happen. Maybe you can control a *little* bit of fate, if it's small enough? In America, we don't believe in fate. If we want it, we work to get it."

She gave me a sly look. "You not before like this. Before, very sad, very lazy, do nothing."

"I worked then like I do now!"

"No. Before, you give up, follow fate. Now you change, you work hard, you control."

I couldn't tell the difference. I shook my head, but she shrugged at me as if I was an oblivious child. She seemed very sure of herself, seeing something in me that I couldn't.

"What about you? You don't live like you're resigned to fate."

She thought about that. "In China, very old country. Very old history. In Gam Saan, very new. *Gwai-lo* not listen to fate. Gam Saan not Chinese place, maybe fate don't follow. Who know? I work hard, maybe control a little bit. Maybe Chinese saying a little bit right."

She smiled and sipped her tea.

January 14, 1851
Kau Pa Keng
Same as yesterday.

As it happened, while we breakfasted on rice and pickled vegetables this morning, our host, whom I've barely seen these past two weeks, came to us and conversed with Ah Toy. At one point as they talked, he looked over at me with a dour expression, until Ah Toy reached over and placed a golden coin in front of him. Apparently that convinced him of something, for he left the room without saying anything more.

"This morning we leave," Ah Toy said, finishing her food.

"To the countryside?"

"He take us. He not want you with us, too danger. But I change his mind, so no trouble."

"But the Taipings love me!" Over the past two weeks, the warriors had stopped me several more times, shaken my hands, and signed the cross.

"Your head too big. Maybe Taiping like, but Qing don't like. We go to Qing area. Less fight. Good for safety, but danger to you."

"Then why should I go?"

"Useful. You see. Many thing to see."

*   *   *

Our trunks packed, we left late in the morning. It was a six-mile journey, first across the harbor, then by foot through Kowloon, along the western side of the peninsula, and through a small valley to a village Ah Toy called Kau Pa Keng. The trek was a strange one. Ah Toy dressed in ratty cotton, "peasant clothes," she called them, "so Qing don't see rich." Bribery and extortion run as rampant here as anywhere; however, that didn't dissuade Ah Toy from hiring some locals to transport our luggage. Some luxuries are difficult to surrender.

We formed a small traveling band: our host at the lead, followed by Ah Toy, followed by our porters, and I was in the middle of this group, shielded, the hope was, from any Qing lookouts. Along the way we saw the estuary to our left while we passed old temples and numerous food markets, and then the buildings grew smaller as we reached the outskirts of Kowloon. Fields spread out before us, filled with thin-stemmed plants topped by green, round pods. Farmers scraped the oozing, milky substance secreting from the bulb.

Ah Toy pointed. "Opium. Bad plant."

In the late afternoon our guide stopped. We'd apparently arrived. There wasn't much to take in, just a cluster of shabby dwellings surrounded by green, tree-smothered hills. No one else was around. We were soaked in sweat despite it being the milder season, yet we pressed on until our guide led us to a worn, nondescript house. A man walked out to greet us, a man just as taciturn as our Hong Kong host—how does Ah Toy find these men?—and he showed us in. Tea and food were served by yet another incredibly young girl. She couldn't have been even half my age, yet there she was, padding silently around the room, pouring tea with downcast eyes, then disappearing as if she hadn't existed. Only Ah Toy watched her as carefully as I did, not out of curiosity, but with a more critical eye, sizing her up like the New York bettors do a prize fighter.

Although the last two weeks have put me at some ease in China, my nerves keep me on edge. I draw a lot of attention based solely on my appearance, especially in the countryside, with far fewer British here than in Hong Kong. Both hosts—in Hong Kong and here—don't speak a word to me, but their expressions scream their discomfort. I wish I could tell them my feeling is mutual.

January 15, 1851
Kau Pa Keng
Humid.

The girl had just gone into the house. Ah Toy stood just far enough away, watching her, fidgeting with something in her pocket. I thought I detected the jingle of money through the soft, warm breeze, even as I stood a fair distance away, out of sight for the time being.

This morning over breakfast, Ah Toy had given me my orders. Today we were touring the village, going house to house, but only Ah Toy would approach. I was to allow myself to be seen by the villagers, "but I go in the house," she instructed me. "You are outside. I call you to come." I wasn't to say a word the entire time. She attired me in brown missionary's garb, procured from who knows where, and sandals upon my feet. A crucifix on garish display around my neck completed the costume. I assumed the purpose of this was to appeal to any Taipings roaming the area, yet I also recalled Ah Toy's comment about this being Qing country, and that they didn't kindly suffer foreigners. It didn't help my anxiety that our previous day's traveling partners didn't join us for this errand. It was just the two of us. I felt glaringly exposed. I was about to say as much, but Ah Toy only shook her head and put her finger on her lips. My role in this ruse had apparently already begun.

The girl was a tiny thing, brown-skinned and skinny as a junk's mast. Her bones were the most prominent of her features. So malnourished was she that the edges in her face were visible, as were the knobs in her elbows and knees. Her attire was clean, but threadbare and ill-fitting. It hung about her as a farmer's old coveralls do on a scarecrow. A knot of pity settled in my stomach. I didn't know how to proceed. If I'd scooped her up, the tiny force of that act would've snapped her in two pieces or more. A puff of breeze would've caught her and blown her away. Her fingertips were scabbed nubs from clawing in the dirt, for that was what she was doing when we arrived, and she fled into the house. A shack, really, a clue that this was a family of intense want.

Ah Toy walked up to the entrance and called out. I planted myself just to the side.

A man answered. He was rail thin and slightly stooped, with brown, cracked skin. The years of farm labor had been hard on him, and hunger gnawed at his haggard face. Ah Toy greeted him politely. I couldn't decipher the subject of the conversation, as it was spoken in Cantonese. He said nothing at first, reading her with glazed suspicion. Ah Toy asked him a question, and he responded in a raspy, impatient voice. He gestured to me and made some sort of demand. Ah Toy had a smooth-sounding answer, and I burned at that moment to know Chinese, since it was me they were discussing, and with vehemence on the man's part.

His face darkened as the conversation continued. Ah Toy didn't give an inch—that is her way—and the man became increasingly agitated. The chatter of rapid-fire Chinese continued, increasing in volume and speed, until finally he roused enough energy to a crescendo and hurled some invective at us, turned around, and walked back into his hovel.

"That didn't go well," I opined, yet Ah Toy only smoothed her sleeves.

After a minute she said to me, "Come when I call," and, to my surprise, walked into the house after him.

I expected an explosion, so sure I was that the man's indignance would ignite at the sight of Ah Toy following him into his own home. Yet through the doorway there was only murmuring. Was the previous argument just for show? Was this how interactions played out here? I listened for my name and hoped that I didn't miss it in the stream of considerably calmer Chinese issuing forth.

As I waited, I let my gaze take in the view of the house and the surrounding land. It was dusty, with dried-out husks of opium flowers waving in the breeze. These desiccated versions were obviously not cultivated properly, and I wondered why a farming village had failed at farming a crop, while those only a few miles away were flourishing. Was the soil or the water supply so drastically different? Where were the food crops? What were these people eating?

Bored from waiting, I wandered around the house to explore. A sound reached me as I drew around to the rear— a grating *scritch, scritch, scritch*—and upon turning the corner I came across a woman, as skinny and malnourished as the man, grinding two bricks together and producing a rough powder. Next to her, lying on her side with a bulging belly, was a small child, a toddler perhaps, with not even the energy to lift her head. Neither appeared to notice me or couldn't be bothered if they did. The woman stopped periodically to scoop the powder onto a dish and then resumed her work. The child barely moved. In fact she hardly seemed alive. The woman herself wasn't much better; her movements were mechanical and her eyes distant, staring at something only she could see. I followed her blank gaze and found nothing of any interest to rest upon.

As I was about to turn away, the woman's gaze caught and held me. I was frozen not by her expression, which was as still as mine, but her eyes...her eyes haunted me. They were empty, hollow, deflated, a dried-up riverbed or burnt-out tree, stripped of all essence, as though whatever soul or spirit had once resided there had fled, leaving the doors open and the lanterns extinguished. And yet as her eyes locked onto mine they searched me, padding around to see what they could find, like a detective with a torch—opening drawers, inspecting footprints, peering under the rocks and into the crevices of my insides...

I heard my cue and I gave a huge shudder, sloughing off the woman's vacuous gaze. Ah Toy beckoned me inside. The squatting woman looked away, which was a good thing, since I couldn't have torn myself away under my own strength.

I stepped into a room with a cook stove and a pile of bedding in the corner. The man was sitting on the floor, and the girl, the knobbly-kneed one, sat next to him. The man eyed me with suspicion. Ah Toy sat on the ground across from him, and I followed her lead.

The conversation continued. Ah Toy did most of the talking, presenting me and gesturing to me from time to time. The man was struggling with something, and as Ah Toy pattered on, a little boy lethargically tottered into the room. He was a skeleton.

Ah Toy's voice became sharp as she pointed to the boy and berated the man, from which he shrank back like a scolded child. Then she beckoned the girl over. Slowly, apprehensively, the girl approached the madam and stood in front of her with eyes cast downward. Ah Toy dug into her pocket and pulled out some gold coins. She took the girl's hand and placed the coins into her palm, then closed the girl's fist around them. She whispered into the girl's ear.

Released, the girl walked to her father and shoved them in his hand. He stared ahead at nothing. Ah Toy gave him all the time he needed. She already knew the outcome. He closed his own fist around the money. Then he took his daughter and led her to the sitting madam. Ah Toy took her by the hand, and the girl recoiled. Ah Toy smiled. The man walked over to the boy and led the toddler out of the room, looking back not once at the girl.

Ah Toy rose. "We go now," she said to me, switching to English. She moved toward the door, and I followed. The girl halfheartedly pulled away, having no energy to do more, but Ah Toy held fast and dragged her forward. "Come," she told her and continued walking. The girl went limp and attempted to grab onto the door, but Ah Toy ripped her away. The man never returned.

Neighbors' heads peered in our direction as Ah Toy led us away from the farm, yet none came forward to assist the famished child. This kind of thing seemed to be normal. The girl began to cry, quietly but enough for me to hear the gulps in her throat. A pit in my stomach formed, and I refused to look at her all the way back to our quarters in the village. But I couldn't close my ears. The girl wept and whimpered the entire walk, jarring my bones and nerves. I winced but there was no escaping the torture. *Did Ah Loi and Ah Si experience the same thing?*

Once back, Ah Toy brought her into a dark room, sat her upon the floor, glared in her face, and spoke harsh words of Cantonese.

I missed all of it except *"Louh Ma."* Then she got up, left the room, and closed the door. The girl's tears continued for hours. I stuck my fingers in my ears in vain.

February 1, 1851
Hong Kong
Lightly humid yet not uncomfortable.

I haven't been able to sleep much. Ah Toy has kept us persistently on the road these two weeks, traveling from house to house then village to village, the names of which I've forgotten, always on the search for impoverished families with little girls. She skips over some of them, using some internal measuring stick, but when she finds one worthy, she throws the brown robe over me, hangs the crucifix around my neck, and in we go. The missions, she tells me, run the best schools in this part of China, and families are desperate for their children to attend, if not for the education, then for the room and board they provide.

"They truly believe I'm a missionary recruiting their daughters?"

"Send the girl is more food for the boy. They don't ask question," she said.

My insides feel like they're tearing, and my thoughts are swirling like dust and catching in the ragged, torn edges. *What am I doing here? We are actually buying children. She must have fooled me as well.*

No. She told me the purpose of this journey before we departed, that we need more girls. I had my reservations yet here I am, along for the journey. There was nothing tricky, nothing hidden. Even the starving parents here probably see through my disguise.

Still, this is her doing. I look at these girls and I see Ah Loi and Ah Si. I see their origins. I see their families, houses, food, and villages. I see their best friends coming by, confused and questioning. "Where is she?" If they had a choice in their fate, would they still be at home today?

Their parents gave them away so willingly, so easily, like a farmer's livestock or a merchant's good. How can this happen, their own flesh and blood? Would they release their daughters to us unhesitatingly if they knew I wasn't a priest? All it had taken was a brown robe and a cross. They had no idea where their children were really going. Did they?

My thoughts won't land. Every day I press my fists to my head and breathe deeply, but the fury in my ears won't leave me this time.

My only relief is that we've seen no war, though the Taipings have materialized briefly from time to time, followed by the Qing, who are more sumptuously dressed than their rivals, being the emperor's forces. They disappeared just as quickly, however, drawn on by the pursuit. We were briefly stopped by two Qing soldiers about eight days into our wanderings, during which I broke into a cold sweat, certain it was me they were after, and though it was true that they weren't pleased to see me, they moved on rapidly enough after a talk and a gift from Ah Toy. They didn't even regard the two sobbing girls we had with us.

Now we've returned to Hong Kong and are once again quartered at the shadow host's house. We have six girls with us. They are quartered in other rooms nearby, and I hear their voices on occasion. Sometimes one of them cries, and Ah Toy disappears to deal with it. "Miss the parent," she always says when she returns. I'm not allowed near the girls, which is fine with me, for I can't communicate with them, nor would I have anything to say if I could.

In contrast to my mood, everyone around us is joyfully preparing for the Celestials' season of the New Year holiday. The entire city is abuzz about it. The merchants have closed their shops, and instead of dealing in goods have spent great time cleaning their houses and festooning them with bright red cloth. The color red is on full display, including in the banners adorning the entryways, which carry messages for a better year ahead. Ah Toy even affixed the scarlet strips above and to each side of her room's doorway. I asked her what the calligraphy said, and she responded, "'Welcoming New Year, everything goes well,' 'Career rises step by step,' 'Good things around the corner.'" But what would these girls' parents be posting at their doors this year?

Ah Toy stopped fussing about the girls long enough to take me to one of the many temples in the city. These temples are ancient, smelling of history and centuries, and hold within a spiritual power that's impossible not to feel. The Chinese don't quiet their voices in the temples as we do in our churches; nonetheless, I can't deny the majesty of these places. Strips of red paper have been added to the walls here as well, and paper lanterns dangle from the doorways in celebration of the season.

Whatever peace there was to be found in these ancestor temples, however, wasn't to be enjoyed for long during this celebratory season. Throughout the day, in all the neighborhoods, firecrackers snapped like an ogre's knuckles. Yet these were only preliminary, for this evening, around midnight, explosions rose in such force that it sounded as though we were caught in a war. Indeed, if I hadn't been aware of the holiday, I should've thought a Taiping horde had finally attacked the city and a great battle had begun. Bombs, gongs, drums, and unceasing fireworks blew up the night sky, followed by the incessant clanging of pots and pans. The goal was to drive away the evil spirits to prevent them haunting the new year, and if their nature is to be driven away by an ear-splitting racket, why then, there is *no* chance of a misfortunate Year of the Pig!

At midnight, after the feast held in our host's home and the incense and prayers—and amidst the awful street ruckus—the climax of the holiday arrived, in the form of a great Chinese dragon, ribbed in silk and over a block long, parading through the streets, waggling to and fro by the numerous Celestials within it, who shouted in piercing voices to aid in the banishment of the aforementioned spirits.

Following this sacred creature came merchants, women, and others, just as in the statehood parade in San Francisco. The men, robed in gorgeous, shining silks, mingled in the streets and exchanged well wishes such as *"Gung hay fat choy!"* and *"San tai geen hong!"* Here were people genuinely enjoying each other's company. It was much like New Year's Day in New York, though even there one must be observant for pickpockets; here, I'm pleased to say, it's rather safe.

During this happy time, at least, there's a broad feeling of brotherhood and friendship. I suppose everyone here, me included, has a vested interest in keeping the spirits at bay for another year. How could I help but find myself wrapped up in the generous spirit of it all? Though I'm not of the people—I'd describe it as a glass wall between them and me—I felt in my bones a piece of a larger whole, part of a bigger picture more important than just me. I only wish I could pack this feeling into my trunk, load it onto a steamer, and sail halfway around the world, nonstop, until I land in New York and unload it—open the trunk and let it fill me, first in my mouth, then my chest, then my arms, legs, and finally my gut. I would smile at everything around me. I would greet all as my brothers and sisters. I would laugh at the smallest joys to be found in life. What a changed man Leland would find me.

And as she flowed down the street in a silken robe, even Ah Toy had a glow about her. I found her radiant and stunning, and any sour feelings I felt toward her diminished as the evening wore on. Toward the end of the night, or rather the start of the dawn, as the few remaining fireworks stubbornly crackled and popped in a last stand against the creeping peace, Ah Toy bade me goodnight with unexpected parting words.

"Tomorrow dress nice," she said, sweeping toward her room. "We visit my mother."

February 2, 1851
Huangpu
About the same as Hong Kong.

Long before the sun emerged over Victoria Peak but long after I had awoken, one of the young girls who serves in the house entered my room with tea. Her eyes were puffy, so she had clearly risen just to serve me. That caused me a second pang of guilt. The first was already gnawing at me.

Ah Toy's mention of her mother had thrown me into a state of panic. Ah Loi's money, which she had entrusted me to pass on to her parents, still sat at the bottom of my trunk. Amid my sickness at sea, our arrival, the Taipings, the Kowloon countryside, and the New Year festivities, my promise to her had completely slipped my mind. What was I to do about it?

I couldn't ask for help from Ah Toy—Ah Loi was expressly against that—but in Hong Kong I knew no one else, which left me precisely no one else to turn to. When the bleary-eyed girl walked in with the tea, I dove for my trunk, fished out the piece of paper with the Chinese names written on it, and thrust it into her startled face. "Do you know?" I shouted. "Where?" Alarmed, she set the tea down and hurried out of the room. I sighed. What was the use? There was no way to find these people in a city this size, and we were departing Hong Kong this morning besides. I had failed.

I gulped down the tea to clear my head. I then did my best to look as if I knew how to dress for an important occasion—slacks with a collared shirt and a vest. When I stumbled out of my quarters with my trunk, there was Ah Toy, in a surprisingly demure dress, yet still commanding attention in the way only she knows how to do. She, the creature of the night, was as trim and alert as if it were the middle of the day.

The day itself was exhausting in the way all-day travel can be, despite sitting for most of it. First Ah Toy pressed me into service loading the trunks onto a Chinese junk at the Hong Kong Harbor. Then we sat, and sat, and stood up to stretch, and sat. I'd become spoiled on the steamer; these junks, I'm told, are the quickest of the un-self-propelled vessels. But next to a steamer, the thing barely moves. For twelve slow hours we crawled—up the South China Sea to the Pearl River Delta, and up that to the Port of Canton. As we prepared for landing, I could barely make out, in the far distance, the American flag, perched atop one of the famed Thirteen Factories, which Mr. Payran had taught us about, those administrative and custom houses run by various European countries and the United States. What a strange sensation, glimpsing the Stars and Stripes on the other side of the world in the Far East, and not only that, the thirty-first star, California's, already upon the banner!

It was early evening as we landed, and, thankfully, Ah Toy paid two porters to transport our trunks. That wasn't all she paid. At the pier and again at the Custom House, Ah Toy met with official-looking men in robes, and she handed them, in a rather conspicuous and un-sly manner, bags of what I imagine was gold dust. "Now, free to travel," she said as we started moving again. "Walk two hour more."

And walk we did, through streets not dissimilar from Hong Kong's. Soon we were out of the city and into the countryside, Ah Toy sprightly gaining energy, me grumbling and dragging my feet, and the two porters behind us suffering silently. As it was when we departed Hong Kong, the buildings lessened in height, number, and beauty, and the roads grew more narrow and ill-maintained. The weather was quite pleasant, but I had no patience for anything during those two hours on foot. This day of traveling was never-ending.

To top it off, we began climbing a hill, gradual at first, then steeper as we neared the middle of its elevation. To top it off yet further, Ah Toy, in the middle of the dirt road, with no discernible landmark or reason for doing so, halted our little band of travelers. She placed some coins in the hands of the porters and shooed them away. They bolted before she could change her mind. There we stood, two walkers with two trunks and a hill in front of us. She turned to me and said, "Almost finish. Bring the trunk."

I frowned. "The trunks?"

"Yes. Bring."

The two trunks were packed full. "But the porters were just here. Why did you let them go?"

"My mother will like to see *gwai-lo* carry the trunk."

I stared at her.

"Come. Bring the trunk." She started up the hill but stopped when she saw I hadn't moved. "Come," she repeated.

I shook my head. The exhaustion from the long day left me in no mood to cooperate.

"You come now. Bring it." She pointed at the trunk.

I refused.

Her eyes narrowed. "What wrong with you?"

The porters were far down the hill now. I took a wavering breath. "I am not your servant anymore."

"What? You always do the work: sweep the room, wash the sheet, clean the dish, wear the God man robe. Always."

"Yes. But…" But what, exactly?

"'But?' No 'but.' Come with the trunk."

I shook my head again.

She waited this time, with a hard look. Waiting for a talking person to talk.

"All the work I do for you, it helps us both. Clean rooms keeps the clients paying higher prices. Food from the markets keeps the house running smoothly. Testifying in court keeps you in business and me a part of it. But this…?" I gestured to the trunk. "…this only helps you. You're doing this to make me look bad. For your mother's entertainment. I own part of the Garden now."

She shook her head and waved me off. "Come."

I sat down on the trunk.

Eyes flaring, she came up close to me, so close that she could just as easily kissed me as slapped me. I held my breath, but she did neither. A long minute passed. "You." She pointed at me.

"You don't want to lose the face."

"Lose the face?"

"Yes. Bad look in front of the other."

"You mean, being embarrassed?"

"Yes. Embarrass."

"That's right. I do a lot of work for you. But not that."

Ah Toy closed her eyes and breathed deeply three times. When she opened them and saw me still sitting there, it seemed to confirm something to her. "Okay," she said, more to herself than me. "Okay."

She took another deep breath and exhaled. "Please."

Her face was still hardened, as if daring me to say something—anything—to close her back up again. I didn't.

"Please," she said again. "Do one time. One time only."

I regarded her. Here she was, about to return triumphantly to her parents. To her birth home. How many opportunities would she get to do this in her life? How many times do *any* of us have to make a grand re-entrance to those we've left behind?

"Never again," I stated firmly.

"One time only, no more later."

I scrutinized the hill in front of me. "I can't carry both of these at once."

"You later come for your."

I grabbed her trunk and she pointed to mine.

"Hide; here many thief."

Fifteen minutes later—an hour by my feel—we arrived at little more than a shack in the side of the hill. Ah Toy stopped, smoothed her dress, and continued to the entrance.

She took a deep breath and cried, "Ma-ma!" A tawny-visaged woman with wrinkled skin appeared in the frame. I wished to see what would happen next—I'd never imagined Ah Toy's mother's appearance—yet I was mindful of my unsupervised luggage, so I turned and ran down the hill to retrieve it. When I arrived back at the dwelling, heaving and sweating, Ah Toy wasn't in sight. Voices wafted out from inside, so I wandered to the entrance and stood tentatively by, curious about the interaction yet not wishing to interrupt it. Ah Toy espied me, however, and waved me in. Her face, usually inscrutable, morphed into an expression of slight relief. Ah Toy's mother glanced at me, and I inclined my head in greeting, but she didn't return it, reserving for me only a frown as she returned to address her daughter.

Their conversation continued, and, not understanding it, I took the opportunity to let my eyes wander around the house. It was nearly bare, on par with the villagers' quarters we visited in Kau Pa Keng, with very few possessions, only some cookware piled on a table.

Another woman—about the same age and of similar appearance as Ah Toy's mother—shuffled into the room. She gazed around absently, out of focus, not seeing us. A drip of saliva clung to her chin.

"Ma-ma!" Ah Toy said. She jumped up and moved toward the newcomer. The woman looked at her, startled, and backed away as though under attack. The startled expression turned into a snarl. So *this* was her mother. Then who was the first, equally charming lady?

"Ma-ma!" Ah Toy said again, knelt in front of her, and grasped for her hands. Her mother snatched her hands away and yelled, and the first woman rushed over to stand between the two. She slapped Ah Toy's hands away and turned to the mother, soothing her and leading her back out of the room. Ah Toy leaped up to help, but the first woman slapped her away again and produced her own snarl. They were clearly related.

A strange chorus of yelling mixed with soothing emanated from the other room, and after some minutes the sound stopped and the first woman reemerged. Ah Toy had remained frozen in her spot. I believe she'd forgotten I was there.

The first woman began to berate Ah Toy. I couldn't understand what she said, and it's probably for the best that I didn't, for the biting, harsh tone that issued forth from this woman's mouth made her mood very clear. Ah Toy, for her part, shrank to half her size. I'd never seen her react with such submission before, this same woman who dressed down Norman Ah-Sing, yet here she was, diminishing before my eyes.

After the lengthy diatribe the woman gestured violently to the doorway. There was no question what that meant. Ah Toy didn't move, staring instead at the bare dirt floor. Fuming, the woman walked over to the table, opened a clay jar, pulled out a coin, and threw it down at Ah Toy's feet. Ah Toy lifted her head, turned around, and walked toward the threshold. As she reached it, a yell came from the mother in the back room.

Ah Toy stopped in her tracks and closed her eyes. The angry woman left the room to tend to her, which left me and my employer alone. Without a word or a glance in my direction, Ah Toy walked out. I followed at a distance. Outside, I made to lift her trunk, but she waved me away. Bending down, she lifted it herself and started down the hill. I watched for a moment, then gathered my own trunk. At least the downhill would prove easier than the uphill.

Halfway back down Ah Toy dropped her trunk, and it rolled onto its side. I set mine down and, arms shaking from exhaustion, righted hers. I didn't dare look at her directly as I did so, but from the corner of my vision I saw her stare into the sky. I began acting as though I were only tidying up my own things, but as I did so, some courageous force invigorated me, a surprising feeling that gifted me with sudden clarity and strength for what I must do next. I hid both trunks nearby, then continued down the hill without looking behind me, knowing she wouldn't move any farther than the two pieces of luggage. Not a word or look passed between us.

I descended, scanning every building and person who swam into my field of vision. The houses were similarly ancient, held up by wooden pillars worn smooth by countless years. There was a remarkable beauty to some of the others: the temples with tiled roofs and curved eaves, the shops dangling lanterns and ducks by the neck—each displayed its own dignified grandeur beneath the years of wear. But I was hunting for something specific, something to help at this late hour. The sun had already dipped below the trees, and the darkness was quickly falling with it.

There! In between two merchant shops, a house larger than a house yet obviously not a shop for goods. A man swept the doorway. I called out to him as I came closer.

"Hello! Sir, excuse me! Sir!"

He looked up from his work, then ceased his task and rushed

inside, closing the door with the punctuating click of a latch. I stopped only when I reached the entry and pounded on the door with urgency. "Sir! Sir! Hello? I need some help! Hello?" All the Celestials in the vicinity kept their distance and watched me make a fool of myself. The door didn't reopen, and when I stepped away to continue my search, those who'd stopped to witness the *gwai-lo's* commotion rushed away to avoid becoming his next victim.

I continued down the street until I found an older man who'd not yet made his escape. "Excuse me, sir," I said when I was next to him. I put my hands under my cheek and said, "Sleep?" He stared at me and shook his head, not understanding. I pointed at myself, then put my hands back under my head. I even closed my eyes to add dramatic effect. "Sleep?" Again he looked confused. I stood for a moment, thinking hard about what other actions I could use to convey my question. I came up blank, however, and could settle only on repeating my actions and question. "Sleep?" The man shook his head as before and walked away. I cursed in frustration.

My fruitless search went on. The darkness continued its fall, and whatever Celestials were still out allowed me a wide berth as I came near. I performed the same routine of charades for an unsuspecting woman and a young boy; both skittered away from me as though I carried the plague. For over an hour I searched, and my task became all the more challenging due to the near completeness of the night, which chased everyone else indoors. By this time my feet were sore and my legs ached. Soon there was no one remaining outside for me to inquire to.

Down a narrow lane I wandered, bleary-eyed and hungry, when a voice called. I stood, looking around, then heard it again. "You hear?" It was a soft, female voice, in heavily accented English, and I followed its tones to a second-story balcony. There, leaning against the railing, with her bosom on full display, was a girl gazing at me. She was dressed beautifully, in a shimmering cloth that tightly wrapped her body. Around her hung lanterns, which gave off a red glow that shrouded the place in playful mystery. Below her, at the ground level, was a door with Chinese characters bordering the entry. The whole effect was remarkably similar to the Garden of Fragrant Flowers. "You hear?" she called again. "Chinese girl have kitty go east west. You hear?" It was confirmed: I was back in San Francisco, and for the first time I was relieved to come upon a place like this.

I stepped through the door into red warmth and the bustle of bodies. Out of habit I didn't let my gaze linger too long on any one person. I knew the madam would find me, and find me she did, mere minutes after I entered, but not before the girl from the balcony came downstairs and attached herself to my arm.

"You have good taste," a voice breathed into my ear. I turned to a rotund Celestial putting on a naughty smile. Her English was exceptionally good. She must have received foreigners often, and sure enough, there were faces like mine. "She is a delicate flower who wants so long for a man to take care of her. What luck a strong man comes to take her in his arms! Come in, rest yourself, and get to know my poor, lonely child."

I knew the talk and it rolled off me. Still, I had to act like it had an effect. "She is very beautiful, and any man would be lucky to have her." The girl smiled and clung harder to my arm. Her jasmine perfume wafted into my nose, almost concealing an underlying aroma of stale sweat. Almost.

The madam put her hands to her mouth in delight. "What a man. What a strong, charming, handsome man. Oh, Li Fen, the gods smile upon you tonight!" The girl giggled with delight.

"Thank you. What a lovely palace!" I said.

"Oh, you flatter us! Li Fen, where are your brains? Do not stand there like a dumb statue. Bring your guest in!"

The girl tittered and pulled my arm, but I resisted in order to say more to the madam. "I am grateful to be here, thank you. However, I ask only for two rooms, one for me and one for my traveling companion. She and I are both very tired."

"You already have a woman?" The madam frowned. On cue, Li Fen pouted.

"I—"

"You bad boy!" The madam's face brightened again. "You wish to add a third. You will find your wish here! You do not need two rooms for that, but we accommodate any desire." Li Fen smiled once more.

"Thank you, but we don't need any services tonight. Only two rooms, please, and dinner."

The madam's smile faltered, and Li Fen's followed. "No service? No company? I am sorry, but times are tight, as you can see. I cannot afford only to rent you rooms without extra services. You understand. How else do I stay in business? See these fine people, who are waiting for a good time?"

I didn't want to continue my search for lodging. My eyes were burning from exhaustion. I thought for a moment, then offered, "We will pay full price, and Li Fen can continue to comfort the others. It's much better for all of us, yes?"

The madam smiled at the thought of the extra income. "But I only have one room free. Li Fen needs a room for her other guests, doesn't she?"

I didn't like the idea of sharing a room with Ah Toy, but it was too late to search any further. I agreed. I left the house to gather my boss and found her exactly as I'd left her, staring into the distance. I'd been gone for over an hour, yet she'd moved hardly a muscle.

"I've found lodging," I announced. "This way." She rose without a word, picked up her trunk, and followed. She was so surprisingly compliant that I knew she must have some ailment, either physical or spiritual. But when we arrived back at the brothel and the madam saw her, she shook her head and pushed her toward the door.

"No! You find somewhere else to turn your tricks! Not my house!"

I shoved myself between them. "She doesn't turn tricks."

"Yes she does. Look at her. Smooth face, sharp eyes, following a *gwai-lo* around. I recognize a whore anywhere!"

Ah Toy, incredibly, didn't react. Normally an insult like this would have earned from her a walloping, but now she'd become deaf and dumb. I came to her defense.

"She is no whore!"

A man came up to us, attracted by the noise, and spoke to the madam. He must have been this madam's version of our Celestial. She replied in Chinese and he began pushing us toward the door.

"Wait, wait," I said, appealing to the madam. "We can pay extra. We can help any way we can. We will not be a nuisance."

The madam said something to the man, and he backed off his task. She scratched her chin.

"Only two nights," I said.

She made a big show of thinking, then came to a decision. "You get one room but pay for two."

I had no idea how much money Ah Toy had left, though I figured that, with Ah Toy in her current catatonic state, I was, by default, permitted to make her financial decisions.

"Up front."

I didn't like the idea of displaying our money in public. "Please, let us settle ourselves, and I'll pay at dinner."

"Dinner is extra."

"Of course it is."

The madam's simpering smile returned. "Welcome!" she preened. "You are family here. Call me Auntie!"

Li Fen had already departed, looking for new business.

February 3, 1851
Huangpu
Comfortably warm.

I'm amazed how quickly I realigned with the old brothel clock. Maybe we were exhausted from the twelve-hour boat ride, the hike up the hill with the trunks, the interaction with Ah Toy's mother and the other lady, the hike *down* the hill with the trunks, and the search for lodging in the course of one day; yet something about the late morning rise and the late breakfast meal felt natural. Not *right,* but *natural.*

Even so, despite the silence of the brothel house in the morning hours, my awakening preceded my mistress's. It was impossible to relax with her in the bed next to me, and I couldn't help rubbing the tattoo on my hand. Now that I was fully awake, I quickly exited the bed. I left the room on tiptoe to avoid waking her and slid down the narrow stairs into the main room. Nothing and no one stirred; the windows and doors were shut up tight, casting an oppressive, tomblike curtain over the house. The staleness of bodies filled the place, which I was used to yet still repulsed by, so, with the house still sleeping, I returned to my room and spent the time going through my journals. I cracked a window to allow in the morning air. Ah Toy didn't move.

By and by the house awakened. First an efficient *thump, thump, thump* which I took to be the man from last night. He must have the same job as Ah Toy's man: cleaning, cooking, keeping an eye over the girls, always up before the rest of the house. This man moved around with purpose. I wondered if there was some special school that turned out silent, observant, fearsome men like them.

Half an hour later came heavier steps that could only have

been those of the madam. She must have already finished the counting of the take and was roaming around for breakfast. The steps bumped up the stairs and beat a path to my door, and before I could rush to intercept her, there came upon the door the most thunderous pounding, enough to startle the dead back into life. I jumped out of my skin, though Ah Toy's bed twitched not at all, leaving me wondering if its occupant was still alive. I opened the door to find the madam, dressed in plain clothes and hair thrown together in a ragged bun on top. "You slept well?" she said.

"Yes, thank you."

She peered around me at Ah Toy in bed. "She sleeps well too. You tired *her* out." She winked.

I opened my mouth as my face blushed hot red. She laughed and said, "Come eat!"

Still no movement from Ah Toy, so I stepped out of the room and followed the madam to the dining room. The girls were already around the table, grabbing bits of fish and vegetables with wooden chopsticks. I looked around for Li Fen, just to recognize anyone, but the girls were without makeup and none appeared to be the girl who'd clung to my arm the previous night. At first I felt shy, sitting at the table with so many strangers. Then I realized they were in too groggy a state to care who sat among them, just like Ah Loi and Ah Si at home. I ate, then made a bowl to bring up to the room for Ah Toy.

I considered asking the madam to send up a bucket of ice water, and grinned.

*   *   *

In the evening, the madam announced, "You have been such charming guests, and how well you care of your companion! Tonight's supper is no cost to you." She flashed a winning smile as I thanked her. Afterward, she stopped me on my way back to the room. "Clean up yourself, then come down to the entry." I'd planned to turn in early and get a full night's rest, but I did what she asked, soothing myself with the fact that we had only one more night; then we'd be off to Hong Kong in the morning. We had to keep everyone happy until then, and with Ah Toy indisposed, that burden rested upon me. I'd also gotten a free meal, after all, so after I washed my face, I retrieved Ah Toy's untouched dish and descended the stairs once more. The madam was there to greet me.

"I need a favor. Please, sit on the couch when the men come, but give them the seat when they want it."

I knew what she was doing. She was using me to make the brothel appear busier and fuller, which was fine with me because it permitted me to sit and rest my sore legs. Soon enough, however, her man shook me awake and forbade me to sit any longer. I walked around to stay awake. The men trickled in, but only when the sun had fully set and the darkness took over did the place really get to bustling. Westerners and rich-looking Chinese filled the house, all but one ignoring me, having eyes only for the girls who'd made themselves up and donned their coquettish masks. The one exception was a middle-aged Spaniard with slightly tanned skin, who caught my eye and smiled briefly before disappearing.

I had to pinch myself to stay awake. When the room began to fully buzz and the girls were full into their jobs, I glanced around for the madam and, having not espied her, made my way upstairs and closed the door. I collapsed on the bed next to Ah Toy, without undressing, and fell asleep before I was fully horizontal.

*　　　　*　　　　*

We sat by the edge of the river, absorbing the sun and relaxing. The warmth just filled me, like drinking hot tea, or better yet, pulling from one of Lex's whiskey bottles. I couldn't imagine anything more delicious on my skin, folding me up as in a blanket heated upon the hearth.

Leland looked over at me and smiled, himself drinking it in, and then leaned back and closed his eyes. I stared at him with such sorrow that I knew I'd break from it. With each passing minute he absorbed the heat, he had no idea. But I had to tell him. He would never forgive me if I didn't.

"I'm…I'm…I…have to…leave," I tripped over my tongue.

He opened his eyes and, still reclined, gave me a questioning look.

"Not 'leave' like right now, but…soon."

He waited.

"Soon." I sighed. "To California. Mother and Father have this whole stupid plan to get rich from California gold, but Father's trying to revive his business and Mother of course won't leave without him, so they're sending Lex and me with a group of random people and some man named Mr. Jackson, and they want to sail to Panama or something, then walk through the jungle, then sail to California, buy a bunch of tools, and go dig in the ground for rocks. It's stupid, I don't know whose idea it was, probably Lex's because he always thinks of dumb things, thinks he can make a quick buck by barely working. And now I have to go with him and I hate it."

Leland sat up. I couldn't look at him. The corners of my eyes began to prickle.

"It's stupid, completely unfair. It's as though they don't know I have another year of school to attend. Not that they'd care anyway. You know how they are, completely oblivious to everything in front of them. They barely know I exist. And when they remember, they push me out of their way." I pulled at my hair and growled. "Why are they forcing me to go with him? It doesn't make any sense. Do they think I'm going to shovel dirt? Look at me! Do I look like I can work a spade?"

I pressed my fists to my head.

"They can't wait to be rid of me."

My eyes burned and blurred, and my throat caught. The wave eventually passed, and I started to regain my breath.

"What if I come live with you?" I perked up. "I can live with you in your house, leave those rotten people behind, and then nothing has to change. It'll be fun! We'll go to school together, go to the river—well, not *in* the river, but you know—and I'll help you with your chores and sleep on the floor in your room. Forget about Mother and Father and Lex. *This* is home and I'm not going to leave it, I'm going—"

A hand on my knee shut me up. I stared at it. There he was, sitting, attentive, a serene smile on his face.

It made me hopeful and miserable. Why was my life becoming

this?

I reached out to—

A sharp voice sliced through my head, and my eyes flew open. It was dark, no sound of the river, yet Leland was still there. I could feel him. Movement rustled all around me, sheets, clothes, and cloth filled my ears and scraped my skin.

"Off!" The voiced seared through the dark; then it rang again in Chinese. Flesh struck flesh, and the weight on my body was released, followed by stumbling and thumping on the floor to my left. A second strike, and this time an angry, female scream came from my right, then the scrape of nails. A male bellow filled the room, and I pulled my knees up to my chest, not knowing where in the dark the next blow would land. I couldn't discern to whom these disembodied yowls belonged. I peered into the gloom, and in the first moments of adjustment, I caught a glimpse of a figure stumbling away. A door opened, and the light outside presented the figure in silhouette before it disappeared.

A loco foco was struck, illuminating Ah Toy's face. She brought the flame to a lantern, and the world crashed back in.

"Pack the trunk," Ah Toy ordered. She moved in a flurry, at a speed I hadn't seen since before we'd left S.F. She'd been catatonic for so long that her purposeful movements suggested to me that some soul-sucking spirit had finally been sloughed off.

"What's happening?" My head spun like a top.

"She soon will kick us out. We must ready. Pack!"

She was back in her bossy form, and I fell into my old role and did as she bade. My questions had to wait.

I was close to finishing my trunk, mind still reeling, when the thumps of footsteps sounded on the stairs.

"She come," said Ah Toy.

The door burst open, and the madam exploded into the room. The Spaniard followed her, his hand covering his face and blood peeking through his fingers.

"You two! Get out of my house."

Ah Toy stood up straight, ready for battle. Her eyes narrowed and her nostrils flared, and her voice grew dangerous. "Very happy to leave cheap house."

"Now the whore speaks, to insult me!"

They groused at each other in English, which struck me as odd. It's strange, the trivial details that become memorable in a moment of crisis.

"They attacked me!" cried the Spaniard in a heavy accent. "You promised me!"

The madam snarled at Ah Toy and me. "You attacked my customer!"

"What? I didn't—" I started, but Ah Toy shushed me.

"The man come and play with my friend. You send him?"

"I do what I want in my house! You owe me for the meal, but you insult me and my customer, whose business I will lose!"

"I will never come here again!" the Spaniard chimed in.

"You gave us supper for free!" I said.

Ah Toy shushed me again. "You sell the boy, but not for sale. You sell the guest. Very bad. Bad business."

"Don't now get high and moral, whore! You know how a house like this works!"

"No. You dishonor the guest. Dishonor the house, but very difficult to do. Already no honor."

"You insult me, who took you in when you were desperate! It is *he* who dishonors himself," the madam jeered, pointing at me. "Look at his pants."

All sets of eyes looked down. A wet circle spread there, already beginning to dry. I was horrified. *How? There was no way!* The heat from my face threatened to melt me. I shifted my clothes to cover up, but it was no use. I glanced up, and the madam stood there, arms crossed, a wicked smile on her face. "I should charge *you* for *his* services!" She jerked her head toward the Spaniard.

"Now you insult and shame the guest?" Ah Toy continued in her dangerous tone. "Big mistake."

"My mistake is letting you low-class garbage in here. Get out!" She called into the hallway and her man appeared, ready. He was holding a cudgel.

"Yes indeed, get out!" the Spaniard added, his hand still clutching his bloody face.

"Or," the madam's voice suddenly became sweet and cajoling,

"you can finish the business. You can stay, everyone ends happy, we can forget it all. Why end on bad terms?" The Spaniard looked surprised through his bloody hand, even a little hopeful.

I gaped at her. Her man's fingers drummed on the cudgel.

"No one scared by small girl and thug," Ah Toy breathed to the madam, then turned to me. "We go."

"Yes, follow your whore like a dog!" the madam mocked, turning nasty again.

Deliberately, Ah Toy took up her trunk and dragged it toward the door. I followed her with mine, but as we neared the hallway, Ah Toy stopped at the malevolent little group. She turned to the madam and said, "Everything you say, everything you do, you soon regret."

"Leave my house, filth!" the madam sneered.

Ah Toy turned to the bleeding Spaniard. "You," she said. "Filthy man play with a boy. You also soon regret." Swift as a cat, she kneed the man between the legs so sharply that he crumpled to the ground. Over his yowls and shrieks, Ah Toy, at the same deliberate speed, walked past the Celestial with the cudgel and down the stairs.

"You will not get your money back!" the madam yelled after us.

Ah Toy spat upon the floor, then calmly walked out. I trailed, careful to avoid the insulting glob she left behind. The sound of water splashing over the threshold followed us out the door.

*   *   *

We ended up in an alley, a narrow one between two worn-out buildings. The sharp smell of fish was all around us, and a pair of rats a few feet away nibbled on something slimy. Our trunks barricaded us from the street. Ah Toy was surprisingly upbeat.

"Better than *baat-po's* nasty house," she said.

"What does that mean?"

She smiled evilly. "Very bad word." She laid out the blankets from her trunk and folded up some clothes for her pillow.

I followed suit. The madam had expelled us in the dead of

night, so we had no chance of finding any available lodging. Ah Toy, though used to the comforts of life, being among the richest Celestials in San Francisco, was not put out; rather, she was invigorated to have a task to take in hand, that being our safe passage through the night and onto our scheduled junk to Hong Kong in the morning. I didn't fully know what it was that jolted her back into the world, though I felt at ease with her having awakened from her coma.

"Why didn't you come back?" I asked her, feeling bold.

"I come back," she answered.

"No, why didn't you come back after your first husband died? You stayed in San Francisco. Why?"

She repositioned herself on her blanket. "You know already. Husband die. In China, no life without husband, only take care of his mother. I stay in Gam Saan."

"Don't you miss your home?"

"My mother, yes, but not healthy. Father, yes, but he die. Auntie, no good." She shook her head. "Sometimes, I very miss everything in Guangdong. But *li-douh m-joi hai ngoh uk-kei.*"

I tried out the words. *"Li-douh..."*

"Oh, now want to learn Cantonese?" she asked, a sparkle in her eye. "Why not before?"

I shrugged. "I didn't like anything Chinese at first, remember?"

"Yes. 'Dirty Celestial,' I remember."

How long ago that was. I felt embarrassed that I'd yelled out such a phrase, but I had been tied to a chair at the time. *"Li-douh..."* I repeated.

"'Here,'" she translated. "Can also say, *'hai li-douh,'* or short, *'hai-douh.'"*

"M-joi hai..."

"'No more here.'"

"Ngoh uk-kei..."

"'My home.' 'Here no more is my home.' *Li-douh m-joi hai ngoh uk-kei.* Life now very better in Gam Saan. I make my own life. More happy."

"Isn't it difficult starting over in a different country?"

"Very hard. So many difficulty. But also many success. I need to try. Who know? *M-ging yat si, m-jung yat ji.* 'Not experience one thing, not gain one wisdom.'"

I stared up at the stars, which were sharply clear. After a few moments, when the only sound was her breathing next to me, she suddenly stood and broke the silence with, "Return soon," and sauntered out of sight.

I thought about the turns my life had taken over the past near-on-two years. From a cloistered, insecure boy to an international lad and part-owner of a Chinese brothel in the Wild West. And of course now, at this moment, alone at night in a fishy-smelling alley in a village in China. How did I get here? And yet how strange, then, that this is the first genuine sense of contentment I've felt in my body since before departing New York. How—and in what world—does this make sense? I wonder if Mother and Father have ever felt something similar at any point in their lives, and for one instant—but only one—I pitied them for having stayed behind. A night in a Chinese alley may have done them some good.

Ah Toy returned with something in her hands, and when she sat down she revealed a sheet of paper filled with Chinese calligraphy and a pot with steam curling out of its spout. Next, from her trunk, she dug out two cups, filling them both with hot tea and handing one to me. She then smoothed the paper, held it out in front of her, made herself comfortable, and through the dimness said, "I read news to you."

The night among the stars in the village of Huangpu passed without further incident. Although the early clattering of street merchants woke us before dawn and the noisome fish re-assaulted our noses, we were alive and unmolested by the elements, the people, and the scurrying fauna in the outdoor darkness. We snapped the blankets clean and repacked our trunks, then waited until the village declared itself open before finding a bit of rice porridge to break our fast.

At the conclusion of our meal, we took the final short walk to the port and set up our vigil by the dock of our departure. All that remained was to sit upon our trunks and watch the sun rise in the east. There were a few clouds in the sky waiting to burn off; otherwise the sky was clear and brightening. It was a beautiful sight to take in, the sun peeking over the green hilltops, and I was reminded that even a town as filthy and flawed as San Francisco could appear beautiful and tranquil wrapped in morning light.

I turned to Ah Toy, only to find she'd disappeared. Her trunk was there but she had vanished. I wasn't concerned, knowing we had an hour or so until our ship was to board; but when that hour came and went, I went from fidgeting nervousness to full-blown panic. Other passengers who'd arrived after us were now boarding, their porters stowing their trunks on deck, and still Ah Toy hadn't reappeared. I paced on the pier as my pulse raced. I don't know why I was so fussy; if we missed the junk then we missed the junk, and we'd just have to wait a few days for the next one. But something about seeing our transport there and not being able to board it fluttered my heart.

To make matters worse, a Celestial came up to me and said something in Chinese. I could only stare at him blankly. He pointed to the junk and repeated his inquiry, then pointed to my trunk and back to the ship. I shrugged my shoulders helplessly. He said something else and waved me off dismissively, then walked away to the vessel and began untying the rope knots from the pier. Just then I heard a shout. Ah Toy ran down the pier, her dress bunched up and held in one hand. Someone was following her, followed by a porter with a trunk, trying to keep up with the first two. The people on the pier grudgingly moved aside, some muttering imprecations, and Ah Toy rushed past me and beckoned me to follow without slowing down.

The second person, a young woman perhaps, and the porter with the trunk, also broke through the crowd. Dragging both my trunk and Ah Toy's, I followed to where she finally stopped at the Celestial who was untying the ship. A loud conversation in staccato Chinese instantly followed, with much arguing and gesturing. The second woman and the porter stood back to let the exchange unfold so I did as well, but after some minutes of this, something changed hands from Ah Toy's to the Celestial's, and we were given the signal to board the ship.

I moved quickly as I could. The porter unloaded his cargo and received his fee from Ah Toy; then I settled all three trunks below deck. When I returned topside, I found Ah Toy and the second woman leaning against the railing, resting themselves. The second woman turned and I started, at which she laughed. It was Li Fen, the girl from the brothel. She was dressed in shabby clothes yet her face was bright, joy sparkling in her eyes. Ah Toy smiled too, a victorious shine upon her face. Then the three of us gazed toward the shore as the junk slipped its berth and slid into the Delta.

February 6, 1851
Hong Kong
Mildly warm.

We spent only two nights in Hong Kong, in the same lodgings as before, which required the same blindfolded abundance of caution. The girls we'd transported from the villages, about whom I had forgotten over the past two days, had disappeared in our absence. I puzzled about that and asked Ah Toy about it, but she only put her finger to her lips and shook her head.

My mind is occupied with returning home; I've seen enough of China for a long while. I yearn for a steak and potatoes. External events have also signaled that it's time for our departure. Word has spread that the Taipings overtook a town called Jintian, roughly 270 miles from here. No one here is currently fretting, yet all the same I'd rather put China behind me as I sail into the Pacific. Even Ah Toy is anxious to depart, and she didn't wander the city nostalgically as she did upon our arrival a month ago.

By the time the sun showed itself this morning, Ah Toy, Li Fen, and I were situated on the pier, trunks at our feet, tickets in hand, and Ah Toy with a sack of gold dust for the inevitable payouts for our boarding. I hadn't been aware that the Emperor of China has forbidden women to exit the country, and although Hong Kong is now under the rule of the British and plays by a stricter set of more civilized rules, there still exist lower-level Chinese officials who take matters into their own hands: hence the need to grease the gears.

Ah Toy and the customs officer came to their agreement, and we loaded aboard with our trunks. It was hard going, due to the crowd, and at one point I stumbled and nearly fell upon a woman sitting on the ground near the steamer's gangway. I caught and steadied myself, then picked up my trunk to continue boarding. By happenstance I glanced back at the woman and noticed a young girl with her. They were both dressed in rags, torn and filthy, and their skin was browned from heavy exposure to the sun. The bowl they'd placed in front of them held not even a grain of rice. The woman was busy vying for people's attention and having no luck with it, but the girl turned her head and locked on to me. I saw her dark brown eyes for only an instant before the crowd blocked her out and I was forced onto the ship. Refocused, I took the trunks one at a time and heaved them down the stairs below deck, to where we'd be living for the next two months.

"Ho there, watch yourself!" a gruff voice called out in English, and I had only a moment to jump out of the way of six hulking, rough-looking crew members pushing three large crates marked "Fine China." Ah Toy stood motionless at the railing, watching with rapt attention. It wasn't a lustful gleam in her eye but an expression of concern, maybe nerves.

"What are all these?" I asked, sidling up to her.

"China."

Something crossed my mind. Lowering my voice, I said, "Where are the…you know…? From the villages?"

Ah Toy only stared at the crates.

My eyes widened. "Are you saying—"

"Read the label."

I didn't expect a wink or an elbow nudge; that's not her way, and sure enough she continued her vigil in silence. I thought it best to leave her to think in peace, so I moved a safe distance away and rested my elbows on the railing, gazing back at the pier. China is, on the surface, a strange country, but is it really that different than my United States? One is ancient and one is brand new, yet they're both large countries, both with a population bent on earning a dollar, both willing and desperate enough to bend and break the rules, selling even human chattel to do it. Both with established governments, yet both, of course, on the verge of some momentous split. *Which would I rather be a part of?*

At that moment the crowd on the dock parted, and I saw the woman and the girl again, the woman calling out to would-be passengers and the girl playing with some sort of doll. I felt the weight of something in my pocket, and I suddenly stood upright.

"Wait!" I cried. I bolted across the ship to the gangway, then across back to the pier. I stopped at the two seated figures, dug into my pocket, and pulled out Ah Loi's package. Through the rough cloth, coins and small pebbles rubbed against each other. I didn't know how much was in there, but it wasn't some small amount, and I passed it all, unopened, to the woman. She let it fall into her palm, weighing it, and gawked at me with suspicion. I gave her a solemn, knowing nod, which, now I realize, was probably too melodramatic. As it was, I had to get back to the steamer, which I did just as the gangway was about to be withdrawn and the lines untied. Once aboard, I looked back. The woman hadn't opened the package. It wasn't the swooning reaction I'd hoped for, but I knew once I'd sailed out of sight that she and her child would be better off, and who knows what that would mean in the long run? Perhaps the girl would avoid her own china crate.

Perhaps. I was certain of one thing only: the sun rising in front of us as we slipped Victoria Harbor was large and beautiful. Freedom is a beautiful thing. And an adventure. When I'm old and my grandchildren are upon my knee, I'll have plenty of tales to regale them with.

February 7, 1851
On board the Golden Mountain Breezy.

This morning, having awakened in a gently swinging hammock below deck, upon a steamer heading east, I was feeling generally well. My sea nerves were so far, to my grateful relief, steelier than on the voyage here. I leaned over to peer at Li Fen's hammock below me and found it empty. No matter. In fact, perfect. I eyed the remaining hammocks; not a single one stirred other than the normal swaying. I settled back in, ensured that I was covered in blankets, closed my eyes, and allowed my mind to wander.

I was on my way back to San Francisco. I wouldn't have previously allowed this to cheer me, yet every mile passing under this hull was another mile closer to home. It won't be New York, though N.Y. can only be an easier journey to undertake with S.F. as my point of origin. Details will come later. For now, any mile closer is a good mile.

My mind shifted to my dream of Leland. I'd told him I was leaving while we were at the river, but he never asked me about it, just as he never said anything in the dream. He must have been upset, but...*was* he? We were together all the time, telling each other anything of importance, and much of no importance, yet he didn't say *anything* about me leaving. I couldn't bring it up either, because how weak would that sound, a guy asking that of his best friend, and did it even matter to him? Yes, it had to. It *had* to. But *did* it? God, why didn't he just *say* something?

I'm being stupid. Thick-headed. Why do I have to make everything so momentous? Why can't I let things be to develop on their own? Why can't I say what I mean? What's wrong with me?

I bit down hard on my arm, driving my pointed teeth into my flesh and drawing small dots of red. Teeth really are sharp and unyielding.

Am I losing my mind? I have a sick mind, a troubled mind, a mind tricked, and deceived, and strained, and longing for any shred of normality. I've been too long from home, that's it, without proper guidance or influence. I'm still young, after all; no wonder I'm straying with such ease! I need to be home, where I can be watched, and taught, and guided, and...

My eyes unexpectedly filled with tears. Mother and Father were home in New York. What fools they were to believe they could pack off their two sons across the country to dig in the dirt. I had a house, I had food, and friends, and enough to sustain a happy life. And yet there I was, slipping away from New York on a ship, further and further from my life and everything I'd known. Why had they done that to me?

I wiped my eyes. All I wanted to do was jump into the Pacific, ride the currents around Cape Horn, and float into the Hudson River.

I couldn't help but wonder, and wonder. It was still tomblike below deck. My wonder grew. I moved myself to a more relaxing position. I closed my eyes. Here I was, just me, my hammock swaying rhythmically, back and forth...back and forth...back and forth... Sadness was rocked aside. Shame was more stubborn, yet I pushed onward.

And onward,

And onward,

Back and forth,

Back and forth,

Back and—

"Good, awake!" Ah Toy's voice rang in my head and I froze. I rearranged my blankets and took a few breaths. When I peeked over the edge of the hammock there she was, watching me. My face was oven-hot. "Put on the clothes and come down," she said and strolled away.

*   *   *

"All finish?" Ah Toy asked when I found her above deck. She was holding a small box.

"I—"

"Good. Many thing to do. Follow."

Shutting my dumb mouth, I trailed behind her into a decently furnished cabin. She closed the door behind us and latched it, then placed the box on a small table and pulled up a chair. She gestured to me to do the same. When I was seated across from her, she opened the box. Inside were two small burlap sacks and a small set of scales.

"Travel almost done," she said, setting up the scales and laying out the weights on the table. "Tell me how much remain. You can use the scale?"

"I've used them at school."

"Good. I trust you for this. I have coin and dust. First, count the coin." She set the first burlap sack on the table with the jingling sounds of metal. "Then count the dust. Gold very heavy, one ounce look like this." She opened the second sack, took three pinches of gold dust, and dropped them on the tray, then balanced the second tray with a weight. "See how much? Less than brass, right?" She rose from the table. "Count total coin and dust. Tell me when finish." She unlatched the door and left.

I sat there alone with Ah Toy's scales, weights, coins, and gold dust. My pulse pounded in my ears, and the vision of these valuable items swam before me. At the Garden, all the money-counting was done behind closed doors, doors I wasn't to enter nor even knock upon. Now her gold sat in front of me. Was this a test? Although I'd lived in the brothel world for a while now, I was still not completely fluent in the secret communications of unsaid words and wink-wink messaging. For instance, was I to understand that Ah Toy was allowing me to take some gold for myself, to get that much closer to a ticket home? Was it a thank-you for taking charge and finding lodging when she was at her lowest? Or should I leave it all there, all ounces and coins accounted for, to demonstrate my loyalty and trustworthiness? Surely she'd counted beforehand and was handing me the opportunity to ruin it all, and then she'd nullify our agreement and hold me as her prisoner forever.

I opened the door and scanned the deck. Just the normal activity from passengers and crew; Ah Toy wasn't in sight. I returned, latched the door, and took a deep breath. I couldn't take the chance. I counted the coins and weighed the dust. A few minutes later there was a rap at the door. Ah Toy stepped briskly into the cabin when I answered it and said, "The total?"

I told her. She gave a curt nod as though she'd expected it.

"Here is a trick." She rounded the table and sat next to me. She took a gold coin out of the pouch and pulled out a small file from the box. Then she brought out a piece of parchment and laid it in front of her. "Call it 'sweating,'" she said. Holding the coin in her left hand, she took up the file in her right and proceeded to file the coin's circumference in an even manner, letting the filings drop on the parchment. She handed me the coin and, at a quick glance, it appeared unchanged. Ah Toy poured the filings from the parchment into the bag with the rest of the dust. "Little bit add up."

I spent the rest of the morning sweating coins.

*   *   *

After a small meal of bread and weak tea, I intended to go watch some of the Celestial passengers play Fan-Tan, a betting game in which the number of beans or other small objects are guessed at and then counted. The Celestials play at this all day, and why not? There's nothing else to fill the time, and it's so much more civilized than the Western way of filling time—all whiskey, dice, and firearms. Before I got to the nearest game, however, Ah Toy, with a metal bar in her hand that had materialized from somewhere, stepped into my path. "Come," she said. We descended the ladder below deck and turned away from all the hammocks toward the cargo.

In the dusky gloom I made out Li Fen, standing quietly with a basket. I looked around me. This was a dustier, grimier part of the hold, stacked with crates away from the passengers. The sound here was muffled and the light was dim, and this raised my hackles, being a New Yorker who knew to avoid spaces such as these. I instinctively backed away and scanned my surroundings for pathways out. Li Fen lit a lamp, and her face illuminated while the background blackened. I could feel Ah Toy moving around. "Come," she said to both of us, lighting her own lamp. "Find 'Fine China' crate."

Not having my own lantern, I joined Li Fen as she and Ah Toy split up to search. Down the rows of crates we strode, holding the lamp up to each of the boxes, searching each one for any identifying label on its surface. Most had the names of owners transporting them or the export companies that sold the goods inside. Others were completely blank, their contents a mystery. After three long rows and nothing to show for our efforts, Li Fen gave a muffled cry and pointed up. There they were, the same three "Fine China" crates that had been manhandled by the crew. In a blink the mistress was there. The three of us gathered around one of the crates, and Ah Toy gave me the bar. "Open," she ordered.

I worked the bar around the edges, prying the side of the box inch by inch, the nails squealing in protest as I forced them loose. At about the halfway point a rustling startled me. Li Fen and Ah Toy didn't appear worried, however, so figuring it was rats, I braved onward until I was able to pull the side of the crate away, and then I truly did have a fright. A foul stench of excrement and urine gagged me. Then, out of the box's opening, poked a head. I stumbled backward and tripped over Li Fen's basket, causing me to sprawl and land on my backside. Ah Toy only shook her head and retrieved the basket, which she opened and withdraw from it chunks of bread. Into the crate she went, with her lantern held high and her hand offering bread to the living thing inside. I recovered my faculties, rose, and crept up. Inside I espied the shadowy silhouettes of two humans. My stomach dropped.

I edged closer and stood by Ah Toy's light. The figures were the small, Celestial girls, recognizable from the villages, with hungry eyes clutching at the proffered bread and water jug. It was as though they were a menagerie from the savanna wild animals *en route* to the circus. Ah Toy turned and looked at me, unblinking as she stood with the lamp illuminating my face, not moving a muscle, waiting until I gathered myself. Li Fen waited too, with cool professionalism.

"Some girl come to the house," Ah Toy said in a businesslike manner. "Other work for *gwai-lo*. All need train."

I couldn't say anything. I knew this whole time what the purpose of our voyage to China had been, but seeing them here like *this*, on this ship back to San Francisco, I experienced a gut *feeling*, for the first time, that this was wrong, all wrong.

The girls devoured the bread.

I shook my head as my ears began to ring.

"What?" Ah Toy said.

"Crazy. It's crazy."

"Crazy?"

"All of it. The girls, the sneaking, the disguises, the bribery, the...the...*trickery*, all of it. Everything you did."

"*I* do?" I couldn't see Ah Toy's eyes narrow but they froze me, like iced water dripping into my shirt. But I didn't care.

"Yes! You took six girls away from their families."

"They give me all the girl."

"You tricked them. You made them think I was a missionary."

"To save their face. They know what they do."

"That doesn't make it right. These are humans. They're *children.*"

"I know they the child!" Ah Toy's voice was getting louder. "You know why we go to China."

"I never wanted to come. You made me."

"This the business. You work with me. You do the work, you are part. You have the guilt; don't blame me."

"Don't blame you? Don't blame *you?*" I couldn't believe it. "Have you forgotten? *Your* man abducted *me*, tied *me* to the chair, and permanently branded *me*. And you say don't blame *you?*" I snorted derisively. "I always knew you were crazy, but now I know you're completely off your chump."

Something smashed into my head and white lightning dazzled my vision just before I thumped to the floor of the ship. The world tipped to the left, the right, and forward. I reached my hand out to find only air and instead felt around for my face and found it. Warmth trickled down my cheek. There was already a massive ache.

A minute passed, maybe five or ten, and hands dabbed at my face and breath puffed in my ear. "No more talk," a whispered voice pleaded.

"Go away from him," Ah Toy said in front of me somewhere, and footsteps hurried away.

A lantern rose and moved closer, and suddenly Ah Toy's face was inches from my own.

"You know what of China?" she said, voice calm and deadly.

I didn't answer.

"Huh? You know what?"

"A fair amount," I slurred. "I've just been there."

"China very poor country in the whole world. England—your ancestor, huh?—bring opium. Men get drug. Poison. Under spell. Cannot work. You believe it? The man job to feed the family. Very much shame if not feed, but he poison and cannot do it! Think, the mother with children and parent, all living on the man, he come home, bring no food. Or not come home anytime!"

I couldn't follow her. The ache spread across my face.

"Emperor, he stop the opium. England start the war, but China too weak. England take Hong Kong, and now people not eat. You see hungry person? They do everything for food. Kill elder's pig. Eat bark from the tree. My mother take brick, make into dust and cook bread. She give to my brother first because he is the boy."

She paused and took a breath.

"I go live at flower boat. Finally enough to eat."

I couldn't help myself. "Flower boat?"

"Parent cannot feed the child. Cannot feed own self. Now a war. Everyone very hungry! Who feed the child?"

I couldn't answer.

"You want child to hungry?"

I didn't answer that either. "What about the missions?"

"Full. Too small number."

"An orphanage then."

"Too many child. No food. You understand? *No food.*" Ah Toy moved her face closer. "We work business. You don't like, but everyone win. The family eat. We get the money. All the girl live."

She reached into her dress and pulled out a small sack, the same that contained the coins I'd just sweated earlier, and tossed it at me. It landed next to me with a clinking crunch. "No more debt. You all pay. This first pay, two percent. Don't like the work? Take and go, no more work. Like the money? Want more? Do the work. Stop your complain."

A silence fell between us. It stretched the length and depth of the boat, up to the deck and to the sky above, and through the hull to the ocean's floor itself. I was suspended in it, unable to respond. What was right and what was wrong had taken on the fuzzy quality of fog, and I floated, unmoored, in space. I closed my eyes and sensed the weight of the darkness pressing on me. Here they were, eating and drinking, hidden away from the crew, another mile closer to servitude and debasement. And I'd played my part. On my left side was darkness, on my right, a void.

Something stung at the corner of my eye; I blinked quickly and it passed.

Ah Toy stood up. "Up now. Two more crate." But before she turned away, she said, "You call me crazy again, you not go home."

*   *   *

Li Fen is to train the girls in the art of harlotry and obedience. This involves how to dress, how to apply makeup, how to talk to a man, how to give looks and glances, how to arouse interest, how to accept a man's body in all forms and functions, how to keep clean, how to keep free of diseases, and, above all, how to follow orders. Ah Toy's word is final, and she won't waste time comforting them. "You cry one day," she said to them in Chinese, which Li Fen translated for me. "Then no. Your parent sold you to me. I am *Louh Ma*. You my daughter. Do what *Louh Ma* say. I save you. I feed. Now you pay back to *Louh Ma*. Make *Louh Ma* happy. If bad girl, I give to *gwai-lo*. *Gwai-lo* like eat very little Chinese girl!"

I sat there and listened as the girls trembled, not taking one step left nor right. She was right. Most of the *gwai-lo* I know are very hungry.

April 2, 1851.
On board the Golden Mountain
Cold and breezy.

Today we sighted the Farallones. The "Devil's Teeth." This is the third instance I've come upon these hellish rocks, more than enough for one lifetime. I hope to see them only one more time after today—as I'm waving goodbye to San Francisco for good. For now I'm once again greeting this town on the bay, and I admit this time I'm somewhat glad of it. I'll be back, at least, on the same continent as home.

Although the start of this return voyage provided much drama to fill these pages, there's been little to write of otherwise, and I mean it. Yes, it has been weeks. In that time, I've fed the girls so they're no longer skeletons, and Li Fen has done a bang-up job of training the wretched stowaways in all the techniques of harlotry. From time to time I checked in on the girls in the "Fine China" crates—out of a sense of guilt and to bring any extra food, I suppose—and occasionally one of them—sometimes two—were missing. The first time, I panicked. I scoured the ship for her until Li Fen informed me the girl was not lost, merely in the Captain's quarters for a little "education."

Ah Toy was right. They are alive. But better off?

The Devil's Teeth indeed.

April 3, 1851
San Francisco
Cold and breezy.

This was my second time entering the Golden Gate. The air was just as cold, just as foggy, and just as biting through my cotton jacket as my first time through. But the town has changed immensely in the five months since I last saw it. This time the hills are dotted with whitewashed wooden houses, churches, shops, and now a signal building that stands atop Goat Hill near Little Chile. The streets are more crowded and bustling. Tall buildings carpet the hillsides—some even made of brick. The men dress better. There are even some women walking around, and I had to stare at a child waiting on Long Wharf. A child, in San Francisco!

The briny stench of the shore attacked my nostrils as the ship approached land—that hasn't improved—and gulls screamed in my ears. Celestials swarmed the dock the minute the plank dropped, calling out *"Saam Yup!"* and *"Sei Yup!"* to the dazed passengers filing off the vessel.

"No good," Ah Toy grumbled.

"Heya!" a voice crooned behind me, and when I turned there was one of the Chinese dock girls sidling up to me. She gave me a small smile, tilted her head, and clasped my arm.

Ah Toy barked something sharp in Chinese, and the girl dropped my arm and backed away. With curiosity I watched her go, wondering for the first time where she'd come from. She and the others had been at Long Wharf since the day I'd arrived. How did they come to be here? What hardships had they endured to stand and work this very pier?

"Girl here no good," Ah Toy stated with finality.

None of the other Chinese on shore gave Ah Toy, Li Fen, or me a second look. Li Fen kept her emotions in check; she'd already cemented her status as a cool customer. Then I spotted the Celestial, Ah Loi, and Ah Si, waiting off to the side with a couple of Chinese men holding two horses connected to drays. Ah Si smiled at me and gave me a small kiss on the cheek. The Celestial and Ah Toy shared not even a nod as if almost a half-year hadn't passed since their last meeting. Not skipping a beat, she gestured to the crates resting on the Wharf. The Celestial and his two men, without question or curiosity, loaded the crates into the drays.

Ah Loi came up to me softly and pulled me aside. "Father Mother?" she asked, searching my face. I held her hands in mine and smiled. She smiled in return, pulled away, and left the group to walk back up Clay Street to the *Garden*.

"Queen Room," Ah Toy told her man, and the odd caravan moved up the Clay Street hill, up past Washington to a narrow alley and a small, barely visible door. Ah Toy stopped, causing the group to stop too. The Celestial took Ah Toy's bar and pried the crates open. The girls inside winced and cried at the brightness of the day, then stumbled out and huddled behind the mistress like baby ducklings. They smelled of sour body odor.

Ah Si, I noticed, didn't seem at all affected by the scene in front of her, and I again wondered at her own journey here. She caught me watching and leaned toward me. "Long name news man, go to house many time."

"James King of William? He went to the Garden? When?"

"You go China. He say many question."

My mouth went dry and my heart pumped in my ears. "What did he ask? Did you say anything?"

She shook her head.

Ah Toy dismissed the two men. I took three deep breaths to quell my rattled nerves as we followed the Celestial through the door, down a stairway, into a cold, dim, musty-smelling corridor, and into the first room to our left. Four half barrels sat upon the ground, and a full barrel with water sat off to the side. Four older, grim-faced women entered the room and each grabbed a girl by the wrist, ignoring the yelps and whimpers, and with astonishing dexterity stripped each girl of her clothes and pushed them into the barrels. They then scooped the water, dousing each girl, and scrubbed them so violently that the girls wailed in agony as their skin turned red and raw. Flakes of dirt sloughed into the brown water, collecting at their feet. At the end of this torture, the women took up shears and cut the girls' hair and nails, handling their limbs roughly but never making the slightest nick upon their skin.

Ah Toy watched in silence for the entirety of it. When all were bathed, she fished for something in her dress, pulled out a bottle, and uncapped it. She moved to each pitiful girl and poured perfume into her hands, then slapped each girl on the neck, under the arms, and between the legs. The smell of jasmine wafted toward me.

"Listen!" she barked, facing the girls. They clustered together and cast their eyes to the ground. Ah Toy then lectured them in Chinese.

"What is she saying?" I asked Li Fen.

"She tell them be quiet and stand straight, or they never again see parent."

"But they won't anyway, will they?"

Li Fen didn't answer.

Ah Toy circled the shivering girls, looking them over. She paused to consider, then grabbed the tallest girl by the wrist and pulled her to my side. The girl, lip quivering, flopped like a ragdoll. The rest of them were to follow Ah Toy. The Celestial led all of us further down the corridor and into a wide, low-ceilinged room lit with oil lamps and populated by a dozen or more men, some Chinese, some Western.

"What is this place?" I whispered.

"Queen Room," Ah Toy said.

We waited as the girls trembled. It was dim and dank where we stood, the air stale and stagnant. Voices came disembodied out of the gloom. I shivered. This place, whatever it was, felt heavy and oppressive.

A crusty, stooped, old Chinese woman with a hard face lurched into view. Saying nothing, she pulled one girl into a shadowy clearing in the center of the room. With shaded faces, several of the men sidled over and strolled around the girl, visually taking her in while we watched from the side. The girl kept her eyes cast down and shivered. One by one the men manipulated her, gripping her chin and angling her head left and right in a rude inspection. They lifted her arms and pushed her legs apart. One put his hand between them, scowled, and walked away. The girl was too petrified to resist. I wanted to rush in and bash his hands away from her. But this was clearly part of the process.

One man produced a bag of gold coins and took out a handful. He counted them deliberately, took the girl's hands, and filled them. The old woman pushed her toward Ah Toy. Without a word and without meeting Ah Toy's eyes, the girl placed the gold in her hands, turned, and allowed the old lady to lead her to her new owner. My stomach dropped as I realized it was the second time she'd had to perform this twisted money ritual. The woman then slid a piece of paper and ink in front of her. The girl couldn't read it but it didn't matter. The woman inked the girl's thumb and pressed it to the paper.

Then they disappeared into the darkness. Soon enough the woman was back to grab the next girl. In this manner the others were sold off one by one.

When only the tallest girl remained, Ah Toy retreated to the door. The girl and I followed silently. But then behind me I heard a movement and the shout of a woman's voice. I turned in time to see a girl—one who'd just been sold, whose mother had rubbed the bricks together to feed her siblings—run at me and clutch my shirt. She cowered behind me as the old woman tottered toward us with an expression of impassivity. She had a leather strap in her hand, wrapped around her wrist. The girl trembled and sobbed, my shirt growing wet as she buried her head there. I looked to Ah Toy, yet she only watched with a somber face.

The old woman reached me and stopped. "Give her," she rasped.

The girl shrank into my back. The old woman bored her cold eyes into me. Around me everyone stood, waiting. I radiated heat. At any moment someone must step in to do something, but all was quiet, everyone anticipating the next move. I lost feeling in my body. I wasn't present, as if it was all happening above or below me. Nothing I did mattered, except it did—it all came down to me. But I couldn't do it.

The girl gripped me tighter. *No, I can't let that woman have her.* She already had the others; what did one more matter?

What will you do with her?

I'd take her to the Garden to live with us.

That will improve her life? It's a brothel.

We'd treat her better than any of these lecherous men would.

She's lost her family. Her life is already over.

No. There'd be life for her after her family. We'd become her family.

You think the madam will allow that?

We're all orphans. That would mean something to her.

She cares only for business.

No, we know each other now.

You know it's only about money. She wants it and you want it.

I'd convince her another girl in the house is good for business.

She already has her new girl. This one isn't needed.

But it's wrong! She's a child! We owe her her life!

What will you do with her?

Ah Toy cleared her throat, explosive in the silence. I turned and saw her holding a bag, this time the dust I'd weighed. "Second pay," she said.

I stared. I couldn't doom this girl to a life of misery, alive though she was. Had we saved her? Were we saving her? My head started to ring as my mind shifted, like a boulder teetering on the edge of a precipice. It balanced precariously, ready to be swayed one direction or the other—toward safety or toward the unknowable chasm below. A soft draft ruffled my hair and the boulder tilted, yet rather than rebalance itself, it slid slowly and noiselessly off the ledge and disappeared.

Ah Toy took my hand and set the bag in it. Then, while I watched paralyzed, she methodically unfastened the girl's grip from my shirt, led her around me, and placed her hands into the old woman's. The girl never resisted. Neither did I. The woman pulled her away down the corridor, the girl never once looking back. Then the darkness swallowed her.

Part Four

THE INCREASE AND IMPUNITY OF CRIME
by James King of William
Daily Alta California
Apr. 8, 1851

The fact that scarce a day passes without the occurrence of one or more bold and extensive robberies, and as frequent attempts upon life, is creating a very general alarm and rendering the practice both necessary and common for the citizens to carry arms for their defense. We are inclined to believe that there is an organized band of robbers, who have come in upon us from the penal colonies of Great Britain, and who have, on system, established the means among themselves of shielding each other from arrest, or from conviction and punishment, if arrested.

But so long as the Police force remains as it is, and the courts so lenient, there remains but one other way of protection, and that is for every man to institute a watch over his own property and arm himself for personal defense. To that end, we understand that quite a large party banded themselves together at the California Engine House on Monday night, for the purpose of punishing incendiaries and other criminals. The members of this society or club were all pledged to secrecy, though as near as we can understand, it is a protective force, the members of which have determined to see the laws enforced if they consider them adequate, and if not, to mete out such punishment as they deem proper.

It is deplorable that a state of things should exist in a civilized community rendering it necessary for citizens to band themselves together for the purpose of protecting their lives and property and visiting retributive justice upon the guilty.

April 11, 1851
San Francisco
Cool and breezy.

The Celestial had been a busy bee in our five-month absence, expanding the back of the house to accompany the additional girls. Li Fen fits into the Garden like a seasoned professional. The tall girl is completely lost, but Ah Loi, Ah Si, and Li Fen have taken her in and immersed her in the routine of the house, and she tags along behind them like a gangly gosling. I haven't been able to pry her name out of her.

I'm also unable to look her in the face. I stare at the floor when she passes or just turn another direction all together. There's too much of the knobby-kneed girl there, the one who'd clasped at me in the Queen's Room. I can feel the hatred burning off her, and I know at least part of it is directed at me. Ah Toy bought her, but I was the missionary who stood by and did nothing. I try to avoid her when I can.

I've reaccustomed myself to daily brothel life, though now I tend to new responsibilities much higher up. I'm fully in charge of delivering envelopes to Sheriff Hays and Mayor Geary, and I scour the *Alta California* for items that may have some influence on the Garden, whether it's some new, reform-minded alderman or a whiff of anti-Chinese sentiment, either in California, the hills, or right here in San Francisco. For instance, the debate over the Foreign Miners Tax has held Ah Toy's interest. It's been repealed for now, but as she says, "Tax for Chinese miner, tax very soon for *all* Chinese." And yet Chinese folk continue to land on our shore.

Ah Toy slipped back into her routine as well, as though she'd been gone only a day. The Celestial, Ah Loi, and Ah Si had done a decent enough job running the house in her absence, but they didn't possess the magnetic draw of their madam. That was apparent on our first night back, when the Garden positively spilled into the street with so many men. Smiles and mirthful energy—and booze—flowed when word reached the good men of this town that the famous madam had returned.

While the lustful desires of its men has remained, the town itself transformed for the better in the months we were gone. It's as if S.F.'s residents have decided to give this place an honest try and make a home of it. Many wood and canvas buildings have been replaced with brick and iron, which gives the town a more permanent appearance. There are firefighting crews now. Workers are digging wells to help fight fires, and I'm charged with yet another chore: keeping our six mandated in-house buckets always filled with water.

Even better, there are wood planks across the roads. No more mud-splattered skirts and trousers! And lastly, bath-houses have popped up—many, in fact. It's made for a much nicer smelling Garden. One of the guests even suggested I try one, saying that it's a pleasure I ought to enjoy at least once a week. He was adamant about it, and Ah Toy emphatically agreed.

June 6, 1851
San Francisco
Warm yet chilly in the evenings.

It turns out that not all is well and good in this burgeoning city. A hideous bit of news was relayed to us from multiple guests yesterday evening, which I picked up while passing through the parlor on a sweep for liquor glasses and cigar butts. A merchant near the Wharf was brazenly attacked—Jansen his name—by a thief who battered him with a slungshot. I know nothing of the poor man but he must be fairly well known, as many of those in the parlor were deeply affected by it.

Today the town was on edge. Merchants talked of Jansen and little else. Men cast wary glances as though on patrol and hurried what few women there are to safer ground. Stores closed earlier, before the complete fall of night, save the gambling saloons—they do a roaring trade regardless of danger—and of course the Garden. We may as well have closed, though. The guests clustered into groups for conversation rather than seeking out their favorite girls, which led to comical scenes of Ah Si and Li Fen resorting to ridiculous methods to get their attention. Ah Si feigned a faint onto one man's lap, who obliviously patted her rump and continued to converse. Ah Toy pivoted, as a master does, and pushed the booze instead.

While the town buzzed about the attack, a different scoundrel made his way to the Garden. Tonight, while Ah Loi and Li Fen stood unoccupied and perplexed, and while Ah Toy hurried drinks to the guests talking animatedly in the parlor, a tall man with a wild, bushy beard and a stained coat banged open the door and strode into the house with a flourish. The guests, accustomed to dramatic entrances, paid him no notice. He stood there, presumably expecting the madam to rush to him to tend to his needs. When she didn't materialize, he looked around the room, confused. The two girls raced over to him instead. I carried on with my work. Ah Toy had ordered me to teach the tall girl how to prepare a room, but with the language barrier it was proving challenging; sometimes it was easier to just do it myself, against the madam's wishes.

I was upstairs in Ah Si's room, pulling new linens over the bed while Ah Si, bored, washed herself with a pan of water. I've grown used to the girls carrying on important bodily tasks in front of me with no modesty or concern for privacy. It's all part of the job, after all, from the flirtation to the preparation, to the deed itself, to the cleanup. I've often been in the presence of the girls during their many stages of undress, and I've ceased noticing them, as they have me. When the door opened, however, and the bushy-bearded man stomped in, Ah Si covered herself and put up a wail.

"Aiya!"

"Oh, hush yourself!" the man growled. "I'm here for him," he pointed at me, "though maybe if you want to have a go afterward…"

I tensed. *Me?* Ah Si held a dress over herself and hurried out, yelling down the corridor, presumably to find the Celestial. I hoped she'd hurry because I was now alone with this filthy character. I flashed back to the man who felt up my leg. I backed away and put a chair between us.

"What do you want of me?" I asked, my eyes darting from him to the door Ah Si had left ajar.

"I have important news you'll want to hear." The man smiled a mischievous smile.

"I don't know you."

"You do. I'll tell you, but first you've got to come out from behind that chair. It's rude to treat a guest this way, like he's going to bite you!"

"I'll stay here. I've been bitten before."

"Unfortunate, but you'll hug me once you hear what I have to say."

There was something about that voice yet I couldn't think clearly with this interloper blocking the only exit. My best bet was to keep him talking so he wouldn't come closer. "Who are you?" I asked.

He laughed. "Has it been that long?"

I glanced at the door, measuring the distance. What was taking the Celestial so long?

The man spread out his arms and twirled around, then closed and locked the door, and turned back to me.

The hairs on my neck bristled. I clenched the chair. *Is it possible to jump out the window?*

He shook his head. "Mother and Father would be so disappointed that you don't even recognize family."

I cocked my head and squinted. His horrible beard made for an admirable disguise.

"Lex?"

He wiped his hand across his crusty forehead. "Thank God! This game was becoming tedious! Now how about you release your death grip from that poor chair and come say a proper hello to your brother?"

I didn't move.

He raised a dusty eyebrow. "What's the matter? Is this how you greet me?"

I tightened my grip.

He sighed and let his arms fall to his side. "Look, I know it's been—"

"Two years."

"Two? No, it can't have been—"

"Two years."

"Are you sure? I can swear—"

"'Two months tops.' That's what you said."

A long minute passed.

He broke eye contact and took in the room. "You got nice digs here. And all this flesh at your fingertips! Look how well you did, little brother, you're finally a man!" He laughed heartily.

I didn't say a word. His loud laugh died in the room.

He cleared his throat. "So. How are you holding up?"

I let the moment draw itself out. Then, with a staccato punch, I bared my right hand to him.

He squinted at it from across the room. "Nice, a tattoo! What is it?"

"Prisoner," I growled.

He frowned.

"I had to pay for your sin two years ago," I said, keeping the chair in front of me. "I was kidnapped and enslaved here. Kept prisoner."

"A prisoner? Here?" He looked around. "Come on."

"Do you remember that you brought me to the peep show, the night before you left for the hills?"

He burst into a smile.

"Remember how you paid for entrance?"

"Nah," he shook his head.

"You've already forgotten? You passed off a pile of brass for gold."

Lex laughed. "Right! I forgot about that! What a lark that was!"

"After you left, I was set upon by that dancer and her Celestial, bound and gagged, and made prisoner. I worked off *your* debt. Meanwhile, you've been chasing your little gold dream, doing what you do and forgetting all about me. But that's okay, Lex. That's fine. I've made my own way here."

He gave a whistle. "I had no idea. This is the *dancer's* house?"

"It is. And I've helped make it what it is."

Lex's eyes flicked around the room. "Huh. And what do you do here? Powder the girls? Fluff the pillows? Tickle the men to get them ready?"

"What do you know of it?" I rolled my eyes. "You've been prancing about the hills, playing in the river with your little friends, and I've been here working out a way to get home."

"Look at you, growing a backbone!" He smiled. "Sweet Lord, the miraculous has occurred! That'll make your little boyfriend back home happy. What was his name again?"

I reared back and punched him in the face. He closed his eyes and flexed his jaw.

"You *have* grown." Quick as a cat, he uppercut his fist into my stomach, and the air whooshed out of me. I crumpled to the ground and wheezed for breath. "And so *you* know, I *have* been working," he said, standing over me and watching me struggle to fill my lungs. "I've been toiling in the sun every day these two years, fulfilling Mother and Father's obligation to the gold company. But the gold has dried up, thanks to your little slanty-eyed friends who've taken it all. My skin's been blistered, my fingers mangled, my toes rotting away in the river, only to have what little gold I found snatched away from me by the company or thieves. You want to switch places? I'll take a roof and a hot meal any day of the week. How about *you* go dig *your* own gold and buy that precious ticket back home? See how you do."

He propped up the chair next to me and sat down. I managed to pull myself into a sitting position and breathe in deep lungs full of air. "You know that'd never work," I said when I found my voice again. "You'd find a way to sink a brothel in a city full of men."

"And you'd cry the moment you'd have to pick up a shovel."

We sat there a while. I stole a glance at him and saw deeper wrinkles than before. His skin was spotted and discolored. His hair was long and matted and he smelled of the ripe outdoors. The time in the diggings had taken its toll on him. We sat that way for a long time.

"Be level with me," Lex said. "You're a young man who can get work anywhere in this town. I get it, you have your room and board here. But two years is more than enough time to pay off my debt, blow out of here, and earn a respectable wage to get your ticket. What's keeping you here?"

"Maybe I like the work."

"You? Mr. Uptight likes working in a whorehouse?"

"Parts of it are decent."

"Uh-huh." He looked at me sideways. "Is that Chinese dancer paying you?"

My face went warm. There was no way I was telling him about my two percent deal, not in his ratty state. I was done being screwed over by him. "Some," I said.

He looked me over. "Hmm. Unless you've found your calling

working here, I find that hard to believe. Still here after two years. You're not chained to a wall or anything. I don't get it."

I was quiet.

"So which is it? She's paying you too much for you to leave? She has you by the balls? You've fallen in love with someone? Or are you trapped here? 'Cause if you are, I can have some guys bust you out of here first light tomorrow morning. Which is it really?" His expression was like Mr. Payran's at school, trying to stump me in front of the class. "Well?"

"Well what? What about *you*? What are *you* doing here?"

"You're switching the topic, but fine. I came to see my brother."

"Yeah? And what about the diggings? Have you come back rich?"

He hesitated. "Rich enough."

"How much is 'rich enough'? And what about your gold company?"

"What about it?"

"You paid back Mr. Jackson with that amazing rate you said you had?"

"That all ended a while ago. Everyone split, went their separate ways."

"Do you still owe them money?"

"No."

"No? You're sure?"

"Cy, enough, all right? The diggings weren't as prosperous as I thought they'd be; that's why I took longer to get back. But we have nothing to worry about!"

I eyed him. "Why don't I believe you?"

"Because," he grinned and slugged me on the shoulder, "you're Cyrus Kirkpatrick and life must always be miserable."

I scoffed in spite of myself, and he relaxed. "So how much did you come back with?" I asked.

The locked doorknob jiggled, followed by pounding. "He gone?" came the high-pitched voice of Ah Si through the door.

"I will be soon, sweetheart," he answered her. He stood up. "I'll not keep you from your important work any longer. But I will be back. You're my little brother."

He walked to the door, then stopped and fished for something in his pocket. He withdrew his hand and produced a shiny medallion.

"Look at this. I joined the Vigilance Committee!" he said, holding up the medallion for me to see.

I frowned. "The what?"

"Everyone's upset about the Jansen thing, so a bunch of guys got together and formed a committee. We're rooting out vice and protecting the good citizens." He smiled as if it was all a big joke. "Don't want to miss out on the fun!"

"That's rich, you rooting out vice."

"You remember Mr. Payran from back home? He's the head of the whole thing."

"He made it out here, did he?"

"The role fits him. Always a self-righteous antagonizer."

As he put his hand on the doorknob I said, "How did you know to find me here?"

He stopped and turned. "Some reporter told me. Had a weird name." He opened the door.

"Hey Lex. I *have* used a shovel before. Except it was for nightsoil, not gold."

Lex broke into peals of laughter. "Makes sense, you playing with other people's shit!"

He caught his breath and wiped his tears on his filthy sleeve. "I'll come back for you, Cy. If that's what you want." He turned, brushed past a wide-eyed Ah Si, and was gone.

June 7, 1851
San Francisco
Wind and fog in the afternoon.

Today I sleepwalked my way through my work, completed it as though I were moving through the fog that spills over the town on summer afternoons. All the while my mind was on Lex. Where was he staying? How much gold had he found? What exactly did he mean, that he would "come back for me"? Would he take me home? And the bigger question: Would I actually go with him?

At one point in the midday, Ah Toy stopped me and asked, "Last night, who with you?"

I shifted my weight. "Someone from town."

"Who?"

"No one important. Only someone who wished to say hello."

She gave me a searching look. After a moment she said, "Guest see me first." She stuck an elegant finger out at me. "Next time."

I nodded. "Next time."

She turned away and left. I hurried in the opposite direction.

Of course Lex had crossed paths with James King of William. He'd met both of us on our first night in San Francisco, and Lex must have remembered him. My stomach churned. What was it the reporter asked me last year? *"Unsavory circumstances surrounding the girls of the house? Something to rile up the bleeding hearts and the pious?"* That was a year ago. *Relax, Cyrus. He would've sniffed around long before now.* But he had been sniffing around while I was in China. Now he'd seen Lex, connected him with me, and he already knew where I was living. And Lex was part of the Vigilance Committee, some over-enthusiastic posse taking law

240

enforcement into its own hands. Were they sniffing around now too? My brother *was* asking me a lot of questions. *I'm becoming paranoid.*

What could a reporter offer Lex Kirkpatrick in return for a scoop? Publicity, probably. Lex lived and played hard; what wouldn't he do for a hero's profile in the paper? He'd then look for a way to turn that into money. And then find a way to lose it again. In the meantime, the Garden would be exposed and Ah Toy run out of town. It would make the posse look good, and there were still other brothels for the town's lonely men to frequent. Would he rat on his own brother? Would Ah Toy implicate me? Would I lose it all, along with all my savings, and be stuck in California for good?

No, I'd find another job. Or I'd follow my mistress to Monterey or San Jose or…Hong Kong?…and earn the money back.

Sure, after another two years.

Sometimes I feel my life is controlled by a Master Narrator who moves the pieces around on his board, chuckling to himself as I find myself in precarious and compromising positions—abandoned, kidnapped, captured, recaptured, in China, seeing my boss's demented mother, stealing young girls, at the whim yet again of my brother…

That's God at work for you. In my Sunday School lessons we learned about Job, who'd endured all that the Lord had thrown at him. It was a morality tale of never losing faith, and he passed that test to find himself handsomely rewarded. Yet I could never move beyond one thought that stood as an obstacle between me and devotional understanding of the story, which was, how could a loving God rain such cruelty down upon a man just to test him? What a sick way to treat your own creation. I've not suffered as Job did, but I feel that significant portions of my life aren't in my control—that people, obstacles, and situations are pushed in front of me to deal with, and the Being doing the pushing and toying is doing it all for His own amusement.

That's called life, you dumb blunderbuss.

But would I pass the test as Job did?

June 17, 1851

San Francisco

Temperate midday, frigid afternoon

The town is a beehive of Vigilance Committee activity. Patrols sweep the town, check in on merchants, lurk down alleys, nod to each other knowingly in passing, and generally make themselves as ubiquitous as they can. When they come across someone they judge to be a ruffian, they stop the fellow and surround him, and there's no lack of backup from other Committee members, for so many of them exist, scores at least, that there's inevitably one in the vicinity to jump into action at the first whiff of trouble. For larger confrontations, the church bell summons the whole throng of them. There's a tense excitement in the air and an aura of self-importance that pervades the group. Each member wishes to be the one to catch the next villain!

The townsfolk too are caught up in the frenzy and are encouraged to make reports to the nearest Committee member, who then brings it to the headquarters for deliberation and execution. And neither are thievery and assault the only misdeeds worthy of attention. Any nefarious or indecent act is subject to review, which includes such malpractices as corruption, bribery, and adultery. Naturally, harlotry in S.F. is suspect, with rumblings growing that the town should be "swept clean of these frail women." Though I know that the authorities won't let their favorite brothels be run out of town, they also must take heed of the public's momentary anti-vice sentiment.

At first the Committee raided and shuttered the low-class bordellos. Some at the Garden didn't take that as a serious sign, but Ah Toy thought differently. "We not very special," she warned us. "Always someone replace us. Chinese go soon." She ordered the Celestial and me to increase the gifts to those in power, including several Committee members who are now happily on the take.

Today at dinner Ah Toy was in a sour mood. When Ah Loi, Ah Si, Li Fen, and the tall girl came into the dining room, she set down her chopsticks and glared at them. "Why last night no many men?" she barked at them, even as she knew the answer. "What is wrong? You lazy and I work?"

The girls said nothing, so I answered for them. "It's the Vigilance Committee. Guests are afraid to be seen here."

"I know!" she snapped at me and scowled. "All coward. Three time I drop the price."

The girls put their heads down and nibbled at their food.

"No worry," she said, wagging a chopstick at them. "No man ignore the naked woman forever."

Later that evening, as I was in the parlor with little to do, the door opened and a trio of men walked in. Lex was at the front. I winced as Ah Toy rushed over, lipsticked and begowned in her hostess-wear, and greeted them with a seductive smile. As she looked him over, I held my breath, waiting for the recognition and the resulting explosion. It had to come at any second. Would she bind him to a chair as well, in fine Kirkpatrick family tradition? The Celestial slowly made his way closer to the group. He reached his hand into his robe. Ah Toy put her hand on his arm. She gazed at Lex and cocked her head.

"You want good night? How many, three?" she asked.

The two men behind Lex snickered. I let out my breath, but my heart was pounding. Lex stepped forward. His beard was thick yet tamed, unlike the time of his first visit a week and a half ago, though his walrus mustache completely annihilated his upper lip.

What is he doing here?

He met her eyes and doffed his hat. "Ma'am," he said, all courtesy, "I am Head Brothel Inspector for the Vigilance Committee. I'd love to have a talk."

Head Brothel Inspector? I groaned. Of course.

Ah Toy waved off the Celestial. I marveled that neither she

nor her man recognized him, but then again, my brother had two years' worth of beard on his face. "No criminal here," she said. "Come, look!" She opened the door wider.

Lex nodded politely. "I only have a few questions, then we'll be on our way."

"Very good price," she said in a lowered voice, then moved around him, drawing a finger over his shoulder. I silently gagged.

One of the men behind him hooted from the doorway. "Charge it to the Committee!" The other fellow laughed.

Lex continued to smile. I watched him carefully. I knew he'd always gone out of his way to find girls; he was renowned for his smooth talk with women. But this was the first time I had an opportunity to watch him operate in the flesh. Would he seduce her? Would she seduce him? I wanted to turn away, but my eyes were glued to the scene. Was this what Lex meant when he said he'd "come for me"? What was he playing at?

"Just a few minutes is all I need," he said.

"So quick?" one of the men taunted. The other one guffawed.

Ah Toy stood silent for a moment. She was not getting his business tonight—to my surprised relief—yet his invoking the Vigilance Committee was serious. She eyed the men behind him, then looked Lex over. Did she recognize him as her cheater from two years ago? Lex, for his part, stood there with a courteous smile and all the time in the world. She finally relented, stepped aside for only him, and closed the door upon the others, to their audible groans. She ordered him to take off his boots and chased the girls out of the room. Her man left too but I knew he hovered close by. I lingered behind a lamp.

Lex slowly walked around the room, taking in the plush surroundings and the incense burning on the table, relishing his role as someone who held control. "A lot of people," he explained in a voice he affected to command respect, "are concerned about criminality in the town. Very concerned, and not just about killing and thieving. They want to clean out the whole town."

"No good," Ah Toy said, watching him carefully. "Gambler too? Drinker? No, too much money."

"Maybe so, yet a lot of them think whorehouses are a problem."

"Whorehouse very dirty. This boardinghouse."

"Boardinghouse, then. They call it a bad influence. It distracts the men."

"Men need distraction." She fingered her slender neck. "No wife here."

"No, but enough folks don't like it anyway. Church folks especially."

Ah Toy laughed a high, tinkling laugh. "Church men best customer!"

"Sure, but at the moment they are swept up in the mood. It makes them feel important." I had to hand it to him, Lex was putting on a half-decent show. It was a revelation to see him in action. "You are now in their sights," he continued, "and the Committee wants me to do something about it. So here I am to inspect."

"See anything you like?"

It was too wonderful that of all the posts available in the Committee of Vigilance, my brother should end up as Head Brothel Inspector. He must have made friends in high places. Regardless, I followed his charade with horrified fascination. He was playing with fire and loving it.

"Whatever I recommend, the Committee will carry it out," Lex said. "If I tell them to close your 'boardinghouse,' they'll close it. If I tell them to back off, they'll back off. It's down to me. Now, what I must decide is if you're operating a whorehouse in San Francisco or you aren't."

Ah Toy clenched her jaw, and her expression was one of pure iron. In that brief moment, I felt for her. To have fled her home, lost her husband, sailed across the ocean, established her business, rebounded from cheaters, and thrived in an outlaw town—to have experienced all of that, only to end up at the whim of some ne'er-do-well Westerner—my brother, of all people—who thought it amusing to play dress-up and throw his weight around, well, it was unjust. *But what am I thinking? The pilfered girls would have a thought or two about injustice...*

Ah Toy was silent, but it was a smoldering, resentful silence. The room filled with it. We all felt it, with the only exception being the man who put her in this position, the one talking to her right now.

Lex fished a paper out of his jacket. "There's been a report filed against you at the Committee yesterday by a concerned citizen. I'll read it to you:

I know one individual named Conrad. I know him to be a reprehensible man who keeps a house in this town. He has with him a woman of bad repute, known as Ah Toy, a known reprobate. I also know their house is filled with frail women who they may have brought to this country against their will. It is dangerous and immoral to the community for these individuals to remain, so I solemnly request, for the health and wellbeing of this great town and state, to return Conrad and the woman Ah Toy to their original home in Hong Kong. I will pay all expenses in keeping them and procuring a passage for them.

Signed,

Norman Ah-Sing, respectable citizen of San Francisco.

It sounded just like him—the pompous, for-the-good-of-the-community tone. *Are Lex and Norman Ah-Sing working together?* So many separate parts of my life were now colliding. The old Chinese man had an ax to grind, and Lex would do anything for a bit of fun.

"I guess what I'm trying to figure out," Lex said, refolding the paper and returning it to his pocket, "is what should I do with this complaint?"

Ah Toy sat stone-still. All eyes turned to her, and the room held its breath. Would she tell him off like she had—satisfyingly so—Norman Ah-Sing or the brothel madam in Huangpu? Would my brother be verbally smacked like a misbehaving child, realizing too late that he'd pay for his antics?

Instead, she unclenched her jaw, rose from her chair, left for the kitchen, and returned with two glasses and a tray loaded with bottles. "You walk all this way. Maybe very thirsty. No pay."

Lex smiled. She was speaking his language now.

She had a drink whipped up in little more than a heartbeat. She took it over and sat next to him on the couch, resting a hand on his shoulder. He gulped it down, briefly abandoning his gentlemanly aura.

It was her turn to ask the questions. Such a big title for a big man! How difficult was his work? How did he deal with angry people? What did he think about being bossed around by the muck-a-mucks at the Vigilance Committee? More importantly— and this with a hand on his arm—did he tire of women telling him how handsome he was? Did he have a woman here? And so on. She switched out the empty glasses with full and reached up and twirled some of his hair with her finger.

I scowled.

Lex clearly wasn't leaving anytime soon, and when Ah Toy put her hand on his leg and smiled at him, I knew he'd not even be leaving for the night. He shifted his legs. She bit her lip. He put his hand on her shoulder and leaned into her. She leaned back.

"Too many distraction?" she said.

He laughed and kept going.

She artfully slipped free from under him and moved toward her quarters. When she reached them, she turned and faced him.

"Too many bad influence?"

"Well, I have never been a church-going man, ma'am."

It's him! I wanted to yell. *The cheater! The whole reason I'm here!* But I held my tongue. Maybe it was some filial loyalty to Lex. Maybe it was that sweet two percent.

She disappeared through the doorway. Lex paused, turned to me, winked from across the room, then disappeared after her and pulled the door shut.

I stayed where I was for a long time, or maybe it was a short time; I couldn't tell and it didn't matter anyway. When the noises started behind Ah Toy's door, I rose and exited the house, desperate to gain the fresh air and leave Lex behind me. It seemed as though the Garden, I surmised with equal parts relief and disgust, would live to see another night.

ARREST OF A ROBBER! EXECUTION ON THE PLAZA!

by James King of William

Daily Alta California

Jul. 1, 1851

Last evening about nine o'clock, a man called John Jenkins came down to the boat station with a bag containing some heavy article, which he loaded in a boat and rowed off. A few moments afterward a gentleman who keeps a shipping office upon Long Wharf came along and stated that his office had just been robbed of his small iron safe. Suspicion immediately fell upon the man with the bag, and some of the boatmen jumped into their boats and started in pursuit of the fellow. After a sharp race they succeeded in capturing him and upon getting him on shore gave him a pretty severe drubbing and walked him off to the Station House.

Soon after the arrest of the person above-mentioned, he was taken possession of by the committee of citizens, and by them was tried in their headquarters. About 12 o'clock it was reported that he had been convicted, and sentenced to be executed upon the Plaza.

At about 2 o'clock the prisoner was brought out pinioned, and accompanied by a strong guard, was conducted to the Plaza. There was much excitement on the Plaza, and a great deal of noise, and a rope was woven through a block attached to a beam upon the end of the old Adobe building. The rope was placed about his neck by a dozen willing hands, and he was immediately run up, struggling furiously. His death occurred speedily. As we close this article the corpse of the doomed man is swinging in the night air, surrounded by a guard of the committee of citizens.

A spirit is aroused which will not be suffered to slumber until the city is purged from one end to the other. The orderly, quiet and honest citizen has nothing to fear, but for all others a reign of terror has commenced. On the whole we feel constrained to acknowledge that the ends justified the means.

July 1, 1851
San Francisco
Bright and sunny, followed by fog and wind.

Tonight, Lex was in high form, topping even himself. He put on a performance for the ages, a *tour-de-force*, one that would win him awards were he acting it out intentionally. But I knew he wasn't. Not this time.

It all happened in the span of an hour. That was it, only an hour in which so many events occurred that it sucked the vitality out of my body, until my ultimate state at the end of it all was a mere pile of bones with nothing left to animate them.

The evening and night proceeded routinely by Garden standards, though there was no denying that the vigilante business that occurred last night was suppressing the turnout. The judges, aldermen, and the law enforcers, as well as most of the well-known merchants, stayed away. These days it's not politically expedient to be sighted in a brothel. Of course, that hasn't deterred the determined in the town—the miners, the newly-arrived, essentially all those who don't have reputations large enough to deflate.

In the latter half of the night, Lex reeled through the door.

Oh no, I groaned. *What fresh drama will he inflict upon us now?*

Then my stomach sank further. Lex wore a sloppy grin and reeked of alcohol, and my mind raced with all the ways the night could go sideways. I ran up to him and attempted to push him back through the doorway. "Get out of here! You can't be here in your state."

"I'm in a state all right. The great state of Californiatucky!" Lex exploded with laughter and draped a heavy, swaying arm over me.

Ah Toy came into the room with a coquettish smile that turned to bemusement the moment she realized her paramour was stumblingly swizzled. Yet rather than call the Celestial over to heave him out the door, she cut across the room and, in a seasoned manner, lifted his arm off me and draped it over herself. "Well, hey there!" he bubbled at her as she led him to her quarters. Before they gained the hall, however, Lex's glassy eyes found me again and he stopped short. "Wait!" he blurted and struggled to right himself. "Everyone! Listen up!" Ah Toy deftly relieved him of the pistol resting in his holster without his noticing, and in that blink of an eye I had to wonder at what an experienced madam she was.

"Listen, listen, listen!" Lex exhorted those in the parlor. "I have an announcement!" The Celestial was immediately in the room, sensing trouble, his eyes darting from Lex to Ah Toy and back. His mistress shot him a look that told him to wait, a hesitation I reckoned owed to Lex's Committee status.

"Come, relax. You want the drink?" Ah Toy asked, gently pushing him toward the hall.

Lex swatted her away. "Everyone!" He hunted around and found me again. "There he is! It's his birthday today! His birthday!"

Everyone turned to me and I stood rooted to the spot. Heat prickled across my scalp.

"Don't ask me how I know, it's very secret," Lex winked sloppily at his audience. "Let's only say I know him from a previous light. I mean, life. A previous life!"

Ah Toy glanced at me. I uprooted myself and turned to leave the embarrassing scene.

"Cy! Cy! Don't go!" he called to me. "Don't worry, I won't tell 'em your true identity. It's your birthday!"

Mortified, I could only shake my head at him.

"I have a gift for you! No, two gifts!"

"Shut up, man, go sleep it off!" a voice called out in the parlor.

I groaned and winced all at once. "Who said that?!" Lex roared. "Who?" His head swiveled wildly around the room. *"Who?"* His arms twitched, itching to throw a good punch.

Ah Toy waved sharply to the Celestial, who jumped up, found the offender, and quickly led him out of the room while the man's angry complaints trailed after him.

"There," Ah Toy cooed to Lex, "find a place very comfortable."

"Two gifts for his birthday!" Lex said, undeterred. Ah Toy took an impatient breath. He shoved his hands into his pocket and roughly pulled out a crumpled bit of paper. "Here it is!" He unfurled it, tried to read it, then winced. He turned it the other way around, squinted at it, then gave up. "Oh well, it's a secret note anyway." He held it out to me. My eyes darted left and right; then I walked up to him to take it. The alcohol stench upon him was overpowering. He dangled the note around, playfully keeping me from it and prolonging the awkwardness, until Ah Toy snatched it out of his hand, handed it to me, and gave me a quick head jerk to tell me to leave. I was only too happy to, when Lex's slurred voice followed me yet again. "But there's more!"

By this time, a few people had left the room, but others were thoroughly enjoying the show. Lex's visage was beet red.

"As the older one," he rumbled, "it is my slalom duty—my slalom duty—my *solemn* duty—" He guffawed. "My slalom duty to give you this." He shoved his hands back in his pockets and pulled out a small bag of gold dust. "A man must grow up to be a man. It's your eighteenth birthday. Take this bag. Go on, take it! Take it." He shoved the bag in my hand. "And now give it to her." He pointed unsteadily to Ah Si, who up until this moment had been amusedly watching the spectacle.

"Me?" she cried.

"You heard me, baby doll. You take this man here and make a man of him. You," he looked around for me until he found me, even though I hadn't moved. "You have her for the night. Don't treat her too rough. No, treat her rough! Too rough! Do whatever! Break her heart, break her body! Live it up, birthday man, you're a kid now. A man now! Give her the goods!"

I flushed as the room became a furnace. Ah Si sidled up to me in a flirtatious way, smiling, the whole thing a game to her as the audience in the room whooped.

"Give it to her, birthday boy!"

"Like she deserves!"

"Show her that young energy!"

Ah Toy glared at me as if I'd orchestrated the whole thing, then pushed me into Ah Si, who grabbed my arm, flung it over her shoulder as though I were about to be conquered, and made a show of pulling me up the stairs to the hollers of those below. I could only stumble up the steps and, before we turned into the hallway, peeked over the banister. Ah Toy had already dragged Lex out of the parlor.

*   *   *

"You can't be serious," I said, sitting on Ah Si's bed.

Ah Si sat across from me. She took the bag of gold dust from me, opened it, inspected it, and placed it on her table. "He pay, you get."

"Give it to that drunk instead."

Ah Si scowled. "You know he?"

"Unfortunately."

"Very…" She mimicked a sloppy drunk.

I tried to laugh but I clammed up. What happened now? I was a stranger in this room, sitting. I was in her room every day performing the cleaning cycle between men, and now I was one of those men. What was I supposed to do?

"I should go," I said, standing up. "Keep the money."

Ah Si shrugged. A free night's wage was a free night's wage.

I made it to the door but stopped there. My hand rested on the knob, failing to summon the will to open it and draw me out of the room. *Maybe once. Just to know.* My ears burned as I stared down at my hand.

Ah Si gently lifted it off the knob. I hadn't even heard her cross the room. "Your *saang-yaht*. Day born," she said sympathetically. She'd dealt with plenty of shy guests and knew what tack to take. "Try!"

I let her lead me back to the bed. She lifted my chin and there we sat facing each other. Her painted eyes betrayed no disappointment at losing a night off; instead they stared straight into mine, in charge, yet still offering me the chance to play the lead. I returned the stare blankly.

"All the time work here, still do not know how?" she teased, but then smiled in understanding. She reached behind her and quickly unhooked the clasps of her dress, and the front of it fell away, revealing pale, small breasts. Despite working and living in the Garden, I was curious how little my mind registered nudity, it being around me every day. *Have I become immune to all shocking things?*

Now it felt that I saw Ah Si for the first time. This was what she did every night. I always cleaned up after her, always saw her in her rest and recovery mode. Now she and I were here, in the stage of her task I'd never seen. I was peeping into a scene forbidden to me, as if I was again seven years old with Lex and that girl groaning under his weight. I tried to swallow, but my throat had desiccated like one of the dunes in the western part of town. My arms hung uselessly at my side. My legs were rooted to the floor. What the boys at school wouldn't have done to find themselves in my position.

When Ah Si made an infinitesimal movement toward me, I flinched. She nodded to herself, then searched my face so deeply she could have been reading my very thoughts. She saw something there, for she re-clasped her dress and retook my hand, leading me to the head of the bed and rotating me so I was lying down. Then Ah Si reached over to the lamp and turned it low, so low I could make out only the outline of her body. She noiselessly unfastened my belt and tugged at my trousers until they rested at my knees. How expertly she'd done it.

I was petrified that this should be happening yet soothed as if entrusting myself to a friend. How she radiated such ease and safety amid such a profane act was wondrous, and despite my shivering I knew that this was something from which I shouldn't turn away. I didn't move, and that empowered her to continue.

I was surprised to find myself in an aroused state. Ah Si inched down the bed, moving her head to where my trousers had been. My nose was suddenly flooded with citrus as she brought her hand over and squeezed on me a few drops of juice. She watched my expression closely. Nothing stung, and when I didn't give any reaction, she said, "Very health!" and dried me with a towel. Then she pointed at my eyes and said, "Close."

I don't want to do it.

My breathing was short and frantic. She put her hand on my chest and gave a soft, soothing "Shhhhhhhhhh…"

But maybe it will help me forget about everything I've lost.

I closed my eyes.

"Think anyone."

I exhaled and immediately saw his face before me.

*   *   *

A faraway scream ripped through the house and shattered my blissful sleep. *"Aiya!"* Ah Si yelled next to me. She'd joined me at the pillow and was cleaning her fingernails. A glass shattered downstairs, followed by heavy footsteps and another wailing screech. *"Louh Ma!"* Ah Si said and ran out the door. Ah Loi's door opened, and feet pattered in the direction of the stairs.

"Hold him fast!" a male voice ordered, followed by muffled grunting and thumping. Bleary-eyed, I followed the curious patrons to the top of the stairs and peered over. There, trussed up like a hog, surrounded by the Celestial wielding his knife, a wild-eyed Ah Toy, and three other men, was Lex. A gag filled his mouth and his face was red.

"You." Ah Toy's calm voice sounded like yelling to me as she stood over Lex, and I winced. Her face had a large red welt across it. "I know you. No more fool me!"

I froze where I stood at the top of the stairs.

"You cheat. Two year ago. You pay brass." She bent down to his ear and yelled into it, "Thief! Liar! Then hit me?" She caught me staring down from above. "You?" she called up to me. "You know?"

Lex, on the ground and eyes bulging, tried to yell through the gag to me. Ah Toy kicked him hard in the groin and Lex convulsed, tears streaming out of his eyes as his muffled wail filled the room. Then Ah Toy turned and thundered up the stairs.

I turned away and retreated down the hallway to Ah Si's room. I closed the door, sat on the edge of the bed, and breathed deeply to still my pounding heart. The door slammed open and Ah Toy towered over me, seething. In flash her hand was at my throat.

"Your brother?" she growled in my face. Up close I saw swelling above her eyebrow and fresh, oozing red cuts.

Her hand choked me. I nodded through watering eyes.

"You plan? To *rob* me?" Her eyes were manic, dilated with rage. *"Again?"*

I tried to shake my head but her grasp was iron, and shimmery speckles materialized at the field of my vision. I started to lose sight of the room.

My hands came up to my neck and rested on hers, then slowly, finger by finger, unhooked her grip. She didn't resist even as her body trembled and her face contorted with fury. I moved her hand down to her side, coughing as the air rushed into my lungs and the room came back into focus. Neither of us moved, other than the heaving breath from each of us on that bed.

Through the door came the sounds of men stomping into the parlor and hauling Lex to his feet. Committee members, likely. How embarrassing for them; one of their own—the Brothel Inspector, no less—entangled in the Garden. Lex's gagged voice was a garbled mess as they led him out of the house. Ah Toy's stare never left my face.

I took a breath. "Yes, my brother," I said. My leg itched but I didn't move for fear of upsetting the balance we were in. "He's been back a few weeks now."

"My man not know him."

"He's grown a beard and mustache, and his face is darker now," I said. "You may not believe me, but I don't have a clue what he's doing. I truly don't. I thought, at first, he'd come to take me home. But each time he returned, it was more and more clear he didn't have anything planned."

"You lie. You do not tell me."

"I'd already paid his debt. I didn't want more trouble. He's crazy."

She was still for a moment, and maybe she understood. But then I opened my mouth one more time.

"But as much as I can't stand him," I said, breaking away to scratch my leg, "he's my only family. Do you know what I mean? He's the only family I have here, maybe the only I have left."

Ah Toy leaned away and a puzzling expression unfolded across her face, one I hadn't seen before. A mix of pride, pain, and stoicism, like an iron door slamming shut. I'd said something wrong. *What was it?* Lex? Family? She cleared her throat, and after a moment, she got up from the bed and moved to the door.

"Did he take anything?" I asked after her, but she was gone.

More voices filtered into the room from below, but I let them wash over me, distant and echoing. I got myself into Ah Si's bed and buried my head under the covers, wanting to feel contained and wrapped up, never to emerge into the light of day nor be sighted by the likes of humanity again.

Family. It had never been spoken aloud before in the Garden, not with any seriousness. What did it mean, and why was it elbowing me in a place like this? I closed my eyes and shoved my hands deep into the pockets of my trousers.

My fingers brushed a piece of paper. Numb and curious, I drew it out. It was the "secret note" Ah Toy had snatched away from Lex's teasing, stupid hands. I brought my hands out of the covers and unfolded it, and there on the wrinkled page was script that was unfamiliar to me. It read only three words.

"Await me soon."

July 4, 1851. Independence Day.
San Francisco
Cold and windy in the afternoon.

"The man is your brother, then?"

The crowd in Portsmouth Square raised a roar as a line of firefighters processed down Washington Street. Ah Toy's husband, the dapper Henry Conrad, was standing at my elbow, watching the Independence Day parade move its way through the German and British contingents. My mind elsewhere.

Await me soon.

Who? Lex? It wasn't his handwriting, and neither would he use words so fancy as "await." Nothing about my brother betrayed sophistication.

A small band of Welshmen shuffled by to mild cheers.

"Strange, and rather unfortunate for you, that the men who subdued him called in the Committee. The Committee does not wish to invite charges of hypocrisy by harboring a ruffian. If she could have, Ah Toy would have dispensed her own brand of justice." He cocked his head at me. "Like she did to you."

Firecrackers exploded somewhere to the left of us. The crowd near us jumped and then laughed.

The Vigilance Committee had locked up Lex at their headquarters. Now we were both wasting away—him in a cell for assault, me in a brothel wondering where my morals lie, with my two percent and a mysterious note.

Whom am I "awaiting?" Who cares enough about me to send for me?

For a second my heart leaped. *Could it even be possible? From that far away? But how would he know where I live? I haven't communicated with him since I left.* I shook my head. *No. Don't let it in. That hope will kill me.*

"Have you attempted to secure an audience?"

I snapped my head to Henry Conrad. "What?"

"Your brother."

My brother. *What could I say to him?*

We were quiet for some time, watching the parade marchers. The Chinese contingent passed, to a noticeably less robust response from the crowd. "Do you see that?" Henry Conrad said with a sigh. "The era of good feelings toward the Chinese is waning. It was only a matter of time."

For a while we stood in silence while they filed by, their baggy cotton trousers swishing silently and their braided plaits swinging to and fro. Henry Conrad pulled out his pocket watch and motioned that it was time for us to return to the Garden. We pushed through the throng of people to retreat from the parade. Committee members were everywhere, on the lookout for nefarious deeds, their self-made badges glinting in the sun. More firecrackers popped at the east end of the Square, and a member hurried off to investigate.

We walked up Clay Street and turned left on Pike, and were nearly at the Garden when Henry Conrad asked, "Did you notice anything else about the Chinese in the parade?"

I searched my mind yet couldn't come up with anything definite. They'd marched in parades for as long as I've been here.

How soon is "soon"?

"Someone who used to be very important in Little China—a 'respectable citizen'—now appears to have been pushed aside. He was missing from the procession." He smiled and walked through the door.

July 5, 1851
San Francisco
Similar to yesterday.

Surprisingly, despite copping a mouse from the shenanigans earlier in the week, Ah Toy was in a fine mood today. She didn't acknowledge it nor speak of the incident, which led to speculation among the girls about the reason. Over midday dinner, while the madam was presiding over the accounting in her quarters, they ventured their guesses. Ah Loi thought it was because of the bump in business from the Independence Day festivities. Given the anxiety surrounding the Vigilance Committee, last night had been strangely busier than normal. Ah Si theorized that she'd spent a splendorous night with Henry Conrad. Li Fen surmised that it was Lex's incarceration by the Committee that had buoyed her spirits. The tall girl, as always, said nothing and looked only at her food.

I stood to leave the table, but the girls turned to me and asked, "What you think?"

I didn't wish to be drawn into the conversation. I sighed and said, "It's obvious, isn't it? Norman Ah-Sing wasn't marching in the parade yesterday."

The girls looked at each other for a quiet second, then burst out laughing simultaneously as if on cue. Ah Toy swished into the dining room. The girls went quiet like a flock of swallows espying a cat. "Why laugh?" she asked. Before any of them attempted an answer, she pointed at me. "You sit. We talk."

I sat.

"You all go. Go wash. Now!"

The girls rose from the table. Ah Si winked at me as she

departed.

When it was just her and me, Ah Toy, with her almost-perfectly-concealed bruise, drilled her unblinking eyes into me. I knew what this would be about before she even opened her mouth. I'd ruined something, blurted out one too many sentences. However awfully in the past she'd treated me, however warped her understanding of relationships were, I was about to pay for it. She opened her mouth and spoke.

"The trial tomorrow."

I furrowed my eyebrows.

"He your brother, but think smart. They ask many question. You take care yourself. Your own good. What else to do? Two year you work his debt. He need work here, not you." Her eyes glanced down at my "prisoner" tattoo.

I tried to comprehend what she was telling me. "I should testify for him so he's released? Then you have the chance to catch him yourself?"

"*Aiya,* you say what?" She scowled as if she'd just bitten into a rotten vegetable.

"You have your own justice."

"You right, but also fool. Think! Hold the Committee man? Bad look!"

"Then what should I do?"

"The thing best for you. Think for yourself. Not him, not me, you only. The only way. What *I* get from him? He very broke, only know how to drink. Tomorrow they ask you; you decide." When I didn't answer, she pressed on. "Your future. Think! What you want? Stay? Leave? What come after? What help you? The drunk who beat a woman?"

"I can leave now, skip the trial. Just take off and get out of here."

"Not help him, not help you. Who know what the Committee do? Chase you like the Hound? Also know what you lose when leave." She held up two fingers.

I stared through the wall, my mind jumping left and right. She didn't mention the word *family*. Was it still part of her equation?

"Look," she said, spreading her arms wide. "I have very much.

I choose good thing for me. My husband die, I should go home. But the Chinese widow not make her own life. So I stay. In China you see my auntie. Say I stay in Gam Saan, betray family. But I choose for me. You now choose for you."

Her words rolled over me like fog, and I couldn't organize them. "What do *you* want me to do?" I asked.

"No matter. I both way lose and gain. You stay, I lose two percent but you help with the business. You leave, I gain two percent but lose you."

"Can't I leave but keep my two percent?"

She just chuffed and waved me off.

Do I really want to keep my share? My wallet was fat from the Garden. In fact, I could leave now on the next steamer and make it home with a respectable amount still to my name, enough to live on while I looked for employment.

The door opened a crack and the tall girl peered in, saw we were still talking, cast her eyes down and withdrew, closing the door without a sound. *But there's the cost*, I thought. *The human cost of it all.* Ah Toy didn't see it that way, but I did.

"Last thing," she said, "the lesson I never forget: Cut all thing too heavy for you."

I thought for a long time, bouncing in my thoughts between everything holding significance to nothing mattering at all. She was giving me permission to act for myself. The irony almost stung. What I wouldn't have given to have this choice two years ago.

"What if we made it three percent?" I asked.

She rose from her seat. "Think very fast," she said, and left.

*　　　*　　　*

Later in the evening, much later, something startled me awake. I swayed groggily and it came again, a tapping at my window. The room was dark and the house was quiet, the exception being only a couple of soft voices upstairs. I shook my head to clear the fog. It had to be just before dawn, that ethereal, small window of time in a brothel when a house has bedded down before light creeps over the horizon. I must have been asleep for only an hour or two.

The tapping came again, and I turned to a silhouette in the window, the creepy sort of image that reminded me of that headless horseman in "The Legend of Sleepy Hollow." In my drowsy state, I reached over to the window and carefully pushed it open.

"Lex?" I whispered.

"Hush, boy," a harsh whisper came back. "Quick now, climb out of this window and let us get started. The sun rises in an hour."

It wasn't Lex's whisper. "Who are you?" I asked.

"Don't say my name out loud. You received the note?"

I slipped on my coat, my trousers, and my boots, and climbed gingerly out the window into the rear yard of the Garden. Two hands roughly pulled me out and stood me upon my feet. Standing there in all black, barely visible, was the newspaper reporter, James King of William.

"Hurry now," he murmured. "Where is this Queen's Room?"

My stomach jolted but I refused to move. *How did he know?* "Queen's Room?" I asked in my best casual whisper.

James King of William sighed like a man resigned. "Son, let's not play games here. I know you've worked for that Chinawoman going on two years now, so you're invested. You're in it. You're either a dedicated employee or you're financially tangled with her. Maybe both. I respect that. I'm a businessman myself—I appreciate a good deal and hard work, and I don't fault you for doing the same."

He took a breath and plowed forward. "But how you do it matters. Lord knows there's nothing wrong with earning a buck, but Lord also knows the right way to do it. And your way," he lowered his voice, "is abhorrent."

"What way is that?" I asked. "A boardinghouse?" Pricked though my conscience has lately been, I wouldn't let some nosy outsider have the honor of deflating it.

"It's no more a boardinghouse than a nunnery is. Let's call it what it is—a pleasure plantation with slaves' quarters."

Someone whooped distantly in the Square.

"I don't think I can help you. I'm sorry."

He grabbed my arm. "I know you were in China with the madam."

"We were getting supplies." I wrenched my arm free.

"Is that what you call little slave girls?"

"Give her," the old woman had ordered.

"It's not like that," I answered. "She treats them well. They have a room, a roof, meals, and employment. She pays them."

"You wrenched them from their families."

"Their families sold them."

"Did they have a choice?"

"They would have starved."

He studied me long and hard. "I see. You've bought into it."

"Bought into what?"

He shook his head. "I'm only surprised you haven't started throwing scripture at me yet, like those yokels south of Mason-Dixon."

"This is nothing like that."

"No? They like where they are, do they? They're here of their own free will, are they? They tell you that?"

"If it's such a big problem, why so many harlot houses? They operate in plain daylight, don't they?"

"Indeed they do. Your sacks of gold dust making their way into certain hands wouldn't have anything to do with that, would they?"

I didn't answer.

"It's all rotten, up and down, to the core. But not when I'm through with it. I'll find the Queen's Room soon enough, with or without your help, and when I do, the public backlash to such an immoral business will be swift and thorough. I just have to expose it and let the Vigilance Committee do its work."

"The Committee isn't as pure as you might think."

"Nothing is. But it's better than any crooked officials your mistress has on her payroll."

I was silent. My mind raced but couldn't land on anything.

He took a step toward me. "Help me out. I'll have that Queen's Room exposed within the week, and I'm drawing a line straight to this place," he gestured at the Garden. "If you help me out, I'll get my story sooner, and I'll give you a week's worth of wages when this place inevitably folds. Might be enough to get you back home to New York."

My head jolted up. "My brother tell you that?"

"I'm a good journalist." He folded his arms across his chest.

"Then you'd know I already have enough to get home."

"Do you, now? Then 'financial entanglement' it is. In that case, I'll ensure you have enough to reestablish your life back home. More importantly, I'll keep your name out of the paper. *Most* importantly, you'll sleep at night with a clear conscience. Make yourself good with God, or whatever it is you believe."

The street was dark, save for a pinpoint of light in the eastern sky behind us. The persistent wind had died down to a breeze, which had shifted direction, bringing with it the stench of the garbage castings and sewage collecting at the bay's edge. My mind wandered to the trial only a few short hours away. And my summons to testify at it.

Lord, what am I to do? Lex, my useless brother, sitting in a cell in the Vigilance Committee headquarters. A surge of vengeance filled my guts and limbs. *I should hammer that nail in his coffin. "Yes, he cheated!"* I will say to the Committee. *"He drank! He battered! He lied! He abandoned! He wanted more, always more, damn the family, damn the consequences, damn it all. Do what you have to do. Banish him, set him in a skiff and push him away from shore, push him through the Golden Gate, through the shark-infested Farallones, and push him far, far beyond. To China, let the Taipings have him!"*

"Will you kill him?" Leland asks. *"Will you hang him from the Old Adobe House? Certainly a man can better atone for his roguish behaviors standing on his own two feet than he can dangling from a beam? Certainly he can better pay back those he has harmed? How can he feel remorse with an unbeating heart?"*

The open air of the night carried in the rot of refuse from the bay.

James King of William leaned forward. "Well?"

I forget why Leland and I were in the privy. We were primary school age, spending the day in play and mischief. The privy was off limits to any purpose than the one intended, which is likely why it attracted us; Mother and Father would not think to look in there, and I was always trying to hide away from them. I'm sure they didn't mind me being out of their sight.

We were doing things only children do: holding our noses, flicking pebbles into the hole, awarding points for those that went in without hitting the rim. It was foolish, from an older person's perspective, that we should have been in there when a similarly sized hole gaped in the street outside, yet there we were. I was in the midst of taking careful aim when I was shoved forward and my forehead rapped upon the seat. My ears exploded with shrill ringing, the first time I'd ever experienced such a thing. I pressed my fists to my head to quell the awful noise and lay on my side to stop the ground from tipping.

Leland was pushed next and landed on top of me. The door slammed shut, followed by footsteps striding, accompanied by Lex's evil snickers. Only when the ringing in my ears subsided somewhat did the privy's stink overwhelm me.

We were entombed there for hours. I vacillated between yelling, pounding upon the door, and, after my initial hesitation of doing so in front of Leland, crying. Leland, however, sat still, so still and serene, saying nothing but soft words to soothe my frayed nerves. At one point, in a fit of angry tears, I growled that I would do anything to kill Lex. Leland put a hand on shoulder—or maybe it was already there—and exhorted me to not mind my tormentor. "He's your brother," he said, as if that were enough. "He's your family. Don't mind him."

LYNCH LAW IN SAN FRANCISCO
by James King of William
Daily Alta California
Jul. 6, 1851

The time has arrived when the people feel compelled, for the safety of their lives and the protection of their property, to take the law into their own hands and mete out a terrible punishment to the guilty. Extraordinary circumstances justify extraordinary measures, and the administration of severe punishment.

In conclusion, we indulge in the hope, and with some degree of confidence, that the dark days are over, that crime which has stalked in our midst unchecked and unpunished for so long is in a fair way to be speedily extirpated, and that our city shall not be regarded in the future as a resort for villains of the blackest character.

July 6, 1851
San Francisco
Cool morning and evening, warm midday.

The Vigilance Committee headquarters was crammed with people desperate for any sort of depraved entertainment, and those people spilled into the street. I don't know how many of them knew or cared about my brother, yet that was no barrier to witnessing the event. A show is a show, and the price was right. The Committee prosecuting one of its own! Who could resist?

I was shown into the headquarters, a Committee person pushing aside the hungry audience so I could shove my way in. "Witnesses for the defendant stand here. Witnesses against stand there," another Committee person shouted above the scrum. I positioned myself somewhere in the middle.

Mr. Payran, my old schoolteacher, was seated at the front of the room at a table raised as if upon a stage. He had papers resting in front of him, though he gazed calmly upon the jostling crowd before him. He was taking in the moment, a man without a care in the world, looking as though he'd rather be in no other place than this. It was the same aura he projected at school back home when he'd take the switch into his hand and was about to commence justice upon the body of some prepubescent deviant.

A loud jeering and laughter erupted in the back of the room. A Committee member escorted Lex into the main room, past James King of William standing near the doorway with pen and paper ready. Some in the audience slapped at Lex as he shuffled by, bound by rope with Committee members surrounding him. The escorts kept straight faces in an attempt to add gravity and legitimacy to the proceeding. This was grand theater, and they were a part of it. They settled Lex at the front, to Mr. Payran's right, close to one of the holding cells, just in case he became unruly and the situation necessitated his being shoved into it. For the time being he was put on display in front of the assembly.

Once the catcalls subsided somewhat, an even louder roar arose to my right. The Red Sea parted and Ah Toy entered, dressed in her finest gown, her nose held high. Her hips swayed in a calculating way that sent the men to howling, as in her dancing days of old, yet the expression on her face was a sea on a windless day. She glided to a spot near me, and behind her, following with a chair, came the Celestial. He placed it down and Ah Toy sat, seemingly oblivious to the hooting animals surrounding her, then adjusted her sleeves, her arms, her wrists, her bangles, and folded her hands in her lap, eyes forward as if she were only mildly interested in what was about to happen.

Mr. Payran stiffened in his chair. He had to be miffed that the brothel madam was commanding the room, and so, without letting the moment linger, he announced, "The case involving Mr. Alexis Kirkpatrick is now in session!"

A man stood and in a ringing voice pronounced, "Mr. Alexis Kirkpatrick, a citizen of the state of New York, is hereby accused of assault and battery upon the body of Ms. Ah Toy, manager of the boardinghouse on Pike Street; of disturbing the peace; of parading about in a drunken state; and of thus violating the sacred social contract between the people, the town of San Francisco, and of God Himself by shattering the expectation of public security, peace, and the freedom to exist in the town."

Lex wilted.

Mr. Payran, eyes glittering, stated, "We will now hear witnesses against the defendant, commencing with the victim." A rousing, sarcastic cheer exploded in the room as she stood, yet a wave of Mr. Payran's hand commanded silence, and Ah Toy, taking her time and several breaths, began.

In a powerful, Chinese-accented voice, she described it all: how she'd met Lex a few weeks previously; how he'd introduced himself as a member of the Vigilance Committee (the "most glorious Vigilance Committee" she called it); how he'd arrived drunk and made a scene in front of her scandalized clients; how he'd followed her into her quarters; how he'd advanced upon her; how she'd pleaded for him to stop and cried for the Celestial to come to her aid; how Lex had struck her with several blows to her face and torso; how the Celestial and some of the more chivalrous clients had finally subdued him.

Much of what she testified was exaggerated for an added degree of effect, and the crowd moved emotionally with her. Where at the start she was a shiny object, a plaything at which to gawk and to mock, by the time she concluded the audience was ready to wrap its collective arms around her as one would a younger sister desperate for protection. The sentiment against Lex coalesced into the beginnings of rage, and the following testifiers, none of whom were present at the Garden that night—for that would have been too risky to admit—only added to the pile of charges lying at Lex's feet. By the time Lex's accusers were finished with their statements, the crowd was dangerously close to grabbing Lex and the executioner's rope and doing the deed itself.

"Gentlemen!" A stern voice cut through the din, and it was not Mr. Payran but Selim Woodworth, the merchant from the Long Wharf, who stood at the dais. "We are a town and a committee of laws! We must hear from Mr. Kirkpatrick's defenders!"

The room exploded into boos, and I deflated. How formal, how ordered the Atchoung trial was, and now, how distant. I saw no chance that Lex would get a fair trial from this hearing. Couldn't anyone see it? It was as if the children had chased the parents away and were trying their best to play house. But the consequences were real.

Woodworth frowned and waited until the protests dissolved and relative quiet returned.

"We will now hear from the Defense," Mr. Payran commanded.

Heads swiveled, trying in vain to locate who in his misguided mind would dare thwart the will of the people. I resolved to speak second, or maybe third, after I'd gathered my legs and my resolve, though perhaps there'd be such an outpouring of support for Lex that mine would not be needed. To none of my surprise, and very much to my dismay, no one made the smallest move to step forward. The crowd murmured.

"Will no one defend this man?" asked Selim Woodworth.

Someone shoved me, and I tumbled forward into the front of the room and into everyone's attention. I glanced behind me and saw that it had been Ah Toy; she waved me to the front and flashed an encouraging look. I faced the front again, and with every eye in the place boring into me, I attempted to swallow. My throat caught. Heat and spiders crawled over my scalp. Mr. Payran, Selim Woodworth, and the rest of the panel rose miles into the air, casting down harsh, disbelieving stares. And then, with the circumstances at their most dire, my mouth creaked open and my voice tumbled out. It rang in my ears, taking on a life of its own. Even worse, the room had quieted, leaving only my words to bounce around the walls, again and again, making circles around the room, so that each listener heard it four or five times and had ample time and opportunity to judge it the most offensive, unreasonable, and blasphemous voice ever spoken.

"I am Cyrus Kirkpatrick. Lex is my brother."

No one answered.

"I...have..." I cleared my throat and took three long, deep breaths. I took control of my body and started again.

"I have long hated him, for many reasons. Growing up in New York, he tortured me. He hid my clothing and shoes, forced me to complete his chores, beat me whenever he saw fit, and swiped my food at mealtimes. He relentlessly bullied me about my best friend. He was merciless, throwing things at us, knocking us down, rubbing our faces in the dirt, voicing aloud my most humiliating secrets. He claimed that my friend and I..." I took a shaky breath, "...that we were in love with each other and threatened to spread that rumor if we didn't do his chores for him. He once shoved us into a latrine and locked us in there for hours. I took to staying away from home as often as I could. And when my friend was *not* around, Lex ignored me. I hated that the most, the ignoring. He mimicked our parents, who saw me as nothing more than an extra mouth to feed. He gave me no guidance, no love, and no support."

I stared at my feet. I couldn't look Lex in the face.

"He's matured since, yet even now I'm only an impediment to him. Upon arriving in California, he abandoned me though I was barely sixteen and inexperienced in the world. When he returned from gold country two years later, he used me for access to a brothel. He said he'd take me home to New York, yet there he is, stuck in a cell, and here I am, speaking his failures.

"He drinks all the time. He pursues women. I'm fairly sure he gambled away our wealth. And now he assaults those who refuse to give him what he wants. He's a rascal, and I'm ashamed that I share his family name."

I swiveled my head around the room to the hundreds of pairs of eyes staring back at me with confusion. *Is this a defense?* I found Lex, his eyes wide and full of despair, like those of a cornered animal. He mouthed something but I looked away.

I waited. And waited. And waited. The crowd shifted its feet, and the moment still hung there, and the awkwardness grew until the room could no longer contain it. It leaked out through the windows and out through the doors, misting like a fog over the late arrivals in the street. Inside, Mr. Payran's facial muscles gave an initial quiver and his lips parted ever so slightly. His chest expanded, but just before it all came together at the peak, my voice issued forth again.

"He's made mistakes and grave errors." The room exhaled but still stood on edge. "But he's my brother. He's my only family now. We are here clinging to each other in a land foreign to us. All of us have come from somewhere else. All of us are trying to better our lives. And all of us here have screwed up. Me included. Members of this Committee too. And my brother. But you've singled out only *one* man to pay for it?

"Is he remorseful for his actions? Ask him; he's sitting right there. Who will ask if he'd choose a different path if he could?"

I finished speaking and the room remained silent. Men ogled me. Were they ashamed? Contemptuous? Did they hear anything I'd said?

I sighed. *Has it all been for nothing?*

A soft murmuring rose behind me, followed by a shift in the crowd. Then a voice pierced through the thick quiet and broke it into halves.

"Do not listen to this boy! Do not listen, for he, too, is a criminal of the worst kind!"

The audience turned to find the voice. Selim Woodworth, at the front of the room, groaned. "Mr. Ah-Sing, we don't wish to hear another of your false accusations—"

"Do not believe him! Do not listen to him! He is leading you astray!"

There he was, dressed in a baggy cotton suit with a top hat crowning his head.

"No, Mr. Ah-Sing, you do not have the floor—"

"The boy is a murderer!" he spat. "A murderer! He and his brother both, and I can prove it!"

July 6, 1851, continued.

The crowd murmured in excitement; it was only too delicious! What a bargain performance they'd happened upon, such dramatic twists and turns!

Selim Woodworth looked pinched. "No, Mr. Ah-Sing, we have heard quite enough. This hearing will not be interrupted."

"Murderer?" The word was muttered, echoed, and shared like a dirty secret around the room. Like a wave it made its way to the back, to the door and out, and soon it was on the lips of those outside straining to get in.

"Let us hear it!" demanded an anonymous voice.

"Out with it!" cried another.

"Speak, Celestial!" added a third, and a cascade of calls began, overwhelming Selim Woodworth's protests. Woodworth shouted for order, and in the confusion Norman Ah-Sing moved to the front of the room and waited for quiet. Ah Toy's man stood, but she shook her head. He melted back into the crowd. The room slowly hushed. I stood frozen to the spot. The entire moment felt otherworldly, as though my soul had fled and left only my body standing there to bear witness.

"It is true!" Norman Ah-Sing began. "Two years ago, almost to the day, on the horrible occasion so many of us remember so well, when the criminal element of our beloved town, those called the Hounds, raided the peaceful Chileno neighborhood and terrorized the population there, causing horror, injury, and yes!" He spun to glare at me, and all the eyes followed as he paused for good measure. "Even death."

I listened in a panic. *What is happening?* It was going too fast, as if the events before me weren't real but rather played out on a theater stage, and I in the audience.

"Mr. Ah-Sing, enough of this!" Selim Woodworth bellowed.

"You have worn out your welcome here!"

"Let him speak!" the crowd shouted him down. "Let the Celestial speak!"

"I was not part of that mob!" I protested, but Norman Ah-Sing drowned me out.

"Yes, murder! Friends, I was there that fateful night when the mob ascended the hill and set upon the poor Chilenos. Frightened for my life, I hastened down the side streets and was compelled to duck behind a tent. Inside I heard a row and the sounds of a terrific fight. Wishing to avoid being drawn in, I made to flee, yet as I was passing across the entrance there was a flash and the report of a revolver. Startled, I turned and saw this man"—he pointed at Lex—"and this boy"—he spun and pointed at me —"with a slumped man between them, blood spilling onto the ground. Never have I been witness to such an action, and never more frightened of my life have I been than at that very moment!"

It happened for me all over again. The Hound had beaten Lex to a pulp and was about to set upon me. The revolver in my hand had inexplicably fired, though my fingers had made nary a twitch, and he'd fallen. It had been so long ago. A Celestial had materialized at the door and told us to get away.

"That…" I said, trying to gain a hold on my thoughts, "…that was self-defense. The man came at me with a club!"

"Self-defense? You had a gun!"

"Everyone here has a gun!"

"It was drawn, seeking a victim!"

"It was a riot, of course I had it ready!"

"You killed a man, which you have just admitted to!" Norman Ah-Sing roared. "The Hounds were after Chilenos that night. You are not a Chileno; what had you to defend yourself against?"

The Hound had called me something. Just before he charged. What was it? "'Filthy Chileno-lover.' He called me that and then attacked. My brother was grievously beaten."

Norman Ah-Sing turned to the audience, which was eating it up. "Even so, friends, even so, let us suppose for a moment that this scalawag is speaking truly. Explain, then, another event this most recent April, a horrendous occasion that I would not otherwise make public because of its unspeakable nature, yet I must do so now to reveal to you the danger of this boy."

"Is this even a *trial?*" I asked.

"Mr. Ah-Sing!" Selim Woodworth yelled.

"What did he do?" someone yelled back.

"Tell us what he did!"

"Speak! Speak!"

"I didn't do anything! I came here to testify for my brother, and some old man is allowed to interrupt—" A Vigilance Committee hand clapped over my mouth, and the crowd cheered. I shook my head to free it but the man clamped harder and restrained me. My muffled curses died in my cheeks.

Norman Ah-Sing waited for the attention to return, for the calls to multiply, then spoke up. "It was...It was..." His voice cracked.

No. He couldn't say it. *Don't say it.* But of course he would, because he knew. James King of William knew, which meant Norman Ah-Sing knew.

The crowd leaned forward, ignoring my stifled screams. He was really putting on a performance, and there was nothing I could do but watch as his mouth opened, his next words spilling into the air, never to be mopped up again.

"Stealing and enslaving little girls."

I thrashed and moaned but the arms held me tight and a slap stung my face. "Did he say 'little girls'?" someone near me asked. Even the Committee members were at a loss, unbalanced by the weight of Norman Ah-Sing's charge.

Selim Woodworth was the first to recover. "This is an outrageous accusation, Mr. Ah-Sing. This time you have really gone too far."

"Little girls?" someone repeated.

"Enslaving?"

The room shrank and pressed in upon me, squeezing the air from my lungs. The air itself was sticky and hot and stifling. A horse whinnied outside.

I looked to where James King of William had been standing, but he wasn't there. He and Norman Ah-Sing were acquaintances, and the reporter must have leaked it to him. But that didn't make sense. He'd wanted to make a splash in the paper; he wouldn't have leaked a scoop like this. No, of course the well-connected Norman Ah-Sing already knew about the Queen's Room. He was the Mayor of Little China, diminished though he was, and he'd have heard about Ah Toy's delivery that day, the money paid, and the scrawny *gwai-lo* who refused to help a clinging, desperate girl.

"Yes," Norman Ah-Sing said, looking straight at me, "little girls. He and the brothel madam Ah Toy traveled to China to smuggle little girls, stole them from their crying parents. Transported them in inhumane conditions, some to be sold off to the highest bidder right here in San Francisco. And some," he narrowed his eyes, "no older than ten, to be grotesquely defiled in the brothels."

The room turned into indignation, into the emotion itself, as if a swarm of bees had blown in off the bay and eclipsed all other thoughts and feelings. The furious buzzing enveloped me, pushed toward me, raged at and suffocated me. Norman Ah-Sing was close to extracting his vengeance.

Off to the side, I noticed Ah Toy standing stock still and making no sound. She hadn't made a peep this whole time, not since her earlier testimony. *Why isn't she defending herself? Defending me?* I grabbed wildly at the first idea that flitted into my brain. I gave a sudden lurch that shook my mouth free. "Ask her!" The hands clamped on me again, pulling me roughly back. I knew my boss, the businesswoman, would outsmart her rival, just like she had every other time he came calling to the Garden. She'd give him the dressing-down he needed, in front of all these people.

Everyone turned to her.

"Miss Ah Toy, you do *not* need to answer these accusations. That's not the purpose of this trial."

"Stuff it, Woodworth!" a voice hollered.

"Speak! Answer the question!" another added.

Ah Toy gave me a long, steady stare that was hard to read. The hush remained over the crowd.

"She will only deny it. Ask the girls!" Norman Ah-Sing protested, but he, finally, was shouted down.

Ah Toy brought her head up high and stared defiantly at the

Committee members seated at the dais.

"All true," she said.

The crowd devolved into shocked chatter. Mr. Payran pounded on the table for silence.

"Miss Ah Toy—" Selim Woodworth started.

"All true." Ah Toy was fiercely still and composed. She spoke quietly, but her words rang clearly. "Girl come from China, from poor family. I buy them, take here for work."

What is she doing?

"What are you saying?" asked Selim Woodworth.

"Girl in China starve. Parent think I work for the God man. They sell to me to take to the mission, but I bring here. To work, and sell."

"Like slaves!" Norman Ah-Sing shouted excitedly. "You buy and sell them like chattel! You hear that?" he appealed to the Committee members. "She's admitted to it!"

Selim Woodworth waved him off and kept his gaze on Ah Toy. My stomach churned with acid. *Is she trying to lead the accusation away from me? Is she doing some sneaky end-around on Norman Ah-Sing?* My brain was mush.

"Are you the sole owner?" Mr. Payran spoke. An amused, shrewd look played on his face. "Of the boardinghouse, are you the sole owner? Do you make all the business decisions?"

"Not only owner, but I make all the decision."

"Who else owns the house?"

"My husband."

"What is his name?"

"Henry."

"Henry…?"

"Conrad."

"Henry Conrad." Mr. Payran pointed at a Committee member seated at the end of the table. "The clerk will record this name into the record. Let us locate him and follow up."

I couldn't believe the proceeding had taken this wild turn, yet when I glanced at Ah Toy she was as calm as ever, in complete control while the chaotic energy whirled around her. She *had* to be scheming something.

Mr. Payran pointed at me. "And this boy. He works for you, does he not?"

This boy. I'd been his student, for God's sake.

"Yes."

Mr. Payran talked over the buzzing. "Is he involved on the ownership level at all?"

Selim Woodworth spoke up. "Stephen, the trial is for assault —" but Mr. Payran held up a silencing hand.

"Does he own any portion of the business?"

"Little bit part."

Selim Woodworth threw up his hands.

"Does he participate in the buying and selling of children?"

Is there any way I can fight off these men? Any way I can wrench myself free?

"*That* man," she pointed at Norman Ah-Sing, "he in the Queen's Room. He know how to buy the girl. Buy for the other men. There all the time. Ask him."

"What? A lie!" Norman Ah-Sing yelled. The audience once again burst into scandalized gasps. Norman Ah-Sing's panicked eyes darted around the room while part of the crowd moved in to surround the old man.

Mr. Payran grinned as he silenced the room after a prolonged effort. "Well done, ma'am. Yet you are still in a risky predicament. It is no secret that information spreads like fire through the underworld, of which you are a part. In fact, this Committee ought to shut you and your little den of iniquity down, finish the work so inadequately begun by our disgraced former member here." He cocked his head toward Lex. "So think hard. Is this boy involved in the buying and selling of child slaves?"

Ah Toy paused. I closed my eyes and said a prayer, for the first time in years.

"Well?"

Too many holding me down. Is the entire town here? How have they all fit into this room?

Ah Toy looked at me. Her eyelid gave the briefest flutter before her expression returned to iron.

July 7, 1851
San Francisco
Hard to tell the weather from a cell.

"Hey Cy, how are you over there?"

Lex, for once in his life, had attempted to do the right thing. While a hundred hands came down upon me, he jumped up and confessed to all of it—the killing of the Hound, the beating of Ah Toy, even the buying of the Chinese girls. Yet as usual with Lex, it wasn't enough. The focus was on me; he was forgotten and drowned out by a hundred voices shouting a hundred commands, yet they all added up to one thing: I was thrown into a cell at the opposite end of the headquarters from him, and the Committee posted a member around the clock to watch us. But not before I'd connected my fist to someone's head.

"Take care you don't do something more stupid, Child Slaver," the Committee guard said, rubbing his temple. "You're marching to the gallows as it is."

"Then what's it matter?" I sneered at him through the bars.

"Not one bit, lad!" a voice echoed from down the room. It wasn't the guard or Lex. I couldn't see the fellow, though the gravelly timbre was clear. "We're in Purgatory, aren't we? A waypoint! This is only a break on the way to the noose. So rest up! They've already decided our fate."

"Don't discourage him!" Lex called from the other end of the headquarters.

The person spat. "He should be discouraged, shouldn't he? What hope does he have? Or any of us?"

"I'm not giving up," I said.

"Ha! You should!"

"I won't. I've been unfairly damned!"

The gravelly voice exploded in laughter that echoed off the walls and made me wince. "Such big talk! You want to talk fairness, boy? Fairness? Take me and Mac here. We got wrapped up on the wrong side of fairness. We ain't no angels, and maybe we plucked a goody here and there, but nothing to deserve the V.C.'s attention. But a weasel squealed on us to save his own hide, and here we are. Trial was a joke. Now we're on the last stop before the end."

"I don't know who you are, but I'm not joining any dead men." I hoped to God they weren't Hounds, not after I'd pulled a trigger on one.

"Whittaker. Mac here don't talk much anymore, and who can blame him?" He coughed and spat. "Anyway, you already had your trial. Saw the whole thing. What a crowd! Stealing children brings out the sickos, don't it?"

"I was betrayed!" I protested. "I followed her orders and she turned on me. *She* should be in here, not me."

"'Turned on'! You, Mac, and me, boy! All of us in here! Though maybe not your brother there; he did himself wrong, didn't need no help."

"Get off it, Whit, you backbiting scrub," said Lex.

"Boy," Whittaker continued, "you're in here means you hit the end of the line. You did it or someone framed you, ain't no difference. We're all dead men sitting in here, ain't we? Right, Mac? Right? Hey Mac, if you know you're a dead man, don't say nothing."

There was no reply. Whittaker's laugh split the silence.

"Screw you, Whit," said Lex.

"Yeah, ol' Mac knows."

I eyed the guard, who'd taken a seat and kicked his feet up on the table. He didn't see a need to stoop to the level of prisoner talk, and instead took to cleaning his fingernails with a knife. "Excuse me!" I called to him. "Excuse me! I need to see Selim Woodworth, please."

The guard ignored me. Whittaker chuckled.

"Sir, I must see Selim Woodworth!" I tried again. "It's

important and urgent!"

"My, important *and* urgent!" Whittaker said. "I don't know, boss, sounds like you better listen to the boy, don't it?"

I ignored him. "Please, sir. How about Sheriff Jack Hays? He knows me. I must share some information with him. May I please see him?"

"Boy, the sheriff has no say in here. These boys are the law now," Whittaker answered.

The guard may as well have been struck deaf, for he continued leisurely picking at his nails.

"Hey!" Lex yelled. "My brother is talking to you!"

"Yeah he is!" Whittaker joined in. "Listen to the boy, won't you?"

The guard put his hat over his face and reclined.

Whittaker guffawed. "There you go. Justice!"

I looked around me and spotted several pebbles on the floor of my cell. I picked one up and tossed it through the bars toward the guard. It hit the ground in front of him and clattered sideways. I picked up another and attempted again, this time hitting the side of the table.

"Boy, don't go doing that unless you want a wallopin'," Whittaker warned.

I snatched up a third and flung it; this time it bounced off the man's hat. From somewhere to my left Whittaker muttered something. The guard stirred, calmly took his hat off his face, picked up a rifle, stood up, and sauntered toward my cell.

"Here we go," Whittaker mumbled.

As the guard drew closer, I said, "Excuse me, sir, I must see Selim Woodworth. It's vital information regarding a brothel." Ah Toy was about to be done if I had anything to say about it. She may have taken Norman Ah-Sing down, but she wouldn't take down me. I had too much information on her and I wanted to use it all.

The guard drew up to the bars and stopped, resting the butt end of his rifle on his shoulder.

"Shut up now, boy," Whittaker said.

"You see," I continued, "Mr. Woodworth will want to know

what I know. Or the reporter, James King of William."

"That so?" the guard asked.

"Cy, shut it!" Lex hollered.

"It is. I know he's on a crusade against girl slavery, and I happen to know—"

My ribs split open with a crack of exploding pain as the guard slammed the rifle butt through the bars and into my side. I collapsed to the ground, gasping for air and choking on my own lungs. The world spun as the guard glared down at me. "Maybe you should listen to your fellows' advice, Child Slaver." He spat on me and walked away.

No more words came from Whittaker or Lex as I clawed some oxygen into my chest.

I didn't move for the rest of the evening. Instead I let the aching pain of my ribs, which *had* to be broken, stab me with every breath I took and rob me of any hope of sleep. The other inmates, one by one, began snoring, yet I stared at a single candle on the table, burning my eyes, even when the guards changed out and the new man let the light dim and nearly plunge the headquarters into complete darkness. But not complete enough. I held my hand out in front of me and could just make it out: the dim ink on my arm that condemned me and the rest of my short life.

*   *   *

I gasped myself awake, which turned out to be the most painful thing I'd experienced since I had a knife at my throat. The soreness in my ribs clutched at my body. My eyes watered as I grabbed my side and struggled to draw in air, and after a few shallow breaths, I rolled over and spotted something—a heel of bread and a tin of water. The pain drove away all thought of hunger and it was just as well, for the bread was like a brick: hard, dense, and would have doubled nicely as a deadly weapon.

I tossed it away, which tore a new twist of pain through my side, and I lay still. Any movement was torture, a knife in my side, and yet I had to get the new guard's attention. He was already walking away, his feeding chores complete, and so I did what I had to do. I screwed up my strength, took in as much air as my screaming bones would grant, and whispered, "Please, I must see Mr. Woodw—" but that was all I could muster before collapsing back onto the ground. The guard kept walking, lowered himself into his chair, raised his feet to the table, shut his eyes, and was soon heavily breathing.

He didn't doze for long before there came a loud rap at the door. The guard snorted as his head bounced up. Muttering curses to the dark, he shuffled to the door to admit a couple of silhouettes. In the dim light from the candle I could just make out their coats and the glint of a shining star upon their breasts, which could only mean the sheriff! They crossed the room, opened a cell to my left, and two men were led out of the headquarters. "Took you long enough, didn't it?" said one with the familiar, gravelly voice. Then, over his shoulder, he shouted, "Enjoy the waypoint, boys!"

"Where you taking them?" Lex called out.

The Committee guard banged his rifle against Lex's cell and growled, "Unless you write for the *Alta*, keep your nose out of it!"

"Sheriff Hays! John Hays!" I called out, my eyes watering from the pain. "It's me from the Garden!"

The guard turned to me. "You too! Quiet or you get it in the other rib!"

"Too late, friend," one of the men drawled. "Hays ain't sheriff no more."

Whittaker laughed like water over pebbles, and as he was forced out the door, he said, "Your justice is comin'!"

July 8, 1851
San Francisco
Hard to tell the weather from a cell.

A bread brick hit my face this morning. This must count as entertainment for those goons who keep watch over the two aberrant brothers.

Though my ribs were still painful, they'd settled into something of a dull ache, and though I winced through the entire ordeal, I managed to chip enough edible material off the block and swallow it. I was still ravenous, not having eaten for two days, but there'd be nothing more until dinner.

I checked under my shirt and found a massive black bruise on my left side. Each breath grated like a hot poker dragged across my ribs, so I lay on my other side to give my bones relief, which was scant. But at least my mind could wander to other things than my immediate health.

Like why, for instance, had Ah Toy done what she did. Why had she suddenly turned on me, just when I least expected it. *Because it was always going to be this way.* Lex's assault had nothing to do with it; he'd already been captured and neutralized. At the very least he'd be run out of town. No, I'd done something on my own. I'd betrayed her first. I'd claimed that Lex was my only family. What else could it have been? I'd done everything she'd ever asked, followed her across the world, propped up her flesh trade, buried my morals, yet those few words, *that* was the line I crossed. And she must have paid a fat sum to someone on the Committee to keep herself out of her own cell. There were too many gifts from Ah Toy to lock her up in here with me.

My head hurt, twisting around the ironies in our relationship, and I wanted to reach through my cell and throttle her. The nerve, the absolute *gall!* It was like snatching a puppy and beating it, then drowning it for not trusting you. How can a person be so delusional? I stared out the window in the direction of the Square, the glass reflecting my image back to me.

I sighed. *It doesn't matter, her motive. She got her final revenge on my family.*

My mind drifted to Leland. *What would he say to me now? Would he be shocked? Dismayed? Angry on my behalf, indignant at the injustice of it? Or...or would he shake his head resignedly, some unspoken prediction coming true in his head that I would inevitably end up here, that he'd known it all along, he'd seen it when we first met, in my eyes, limbs, maybe it was etched upon my forehead, or my actions betrayed red flags, signs that hinted at some rotten core that had always been there, that I was born with. Then why had he befriended me? Was I a project for him to improve upon, like some missionary tasked to save some backward native? Leland could never have chosen me for friendship. I'm so deficient in comparison that there had to be some other motive. It didn't otherwise add up. I'll never go home again, and perhaps that will ultimately be to his benefit.*

"*Cy!*" Lex shouted and I jumped out of my thoughts.

"Huh?"

"Are you alive? I've called you ten times!" Our voices echoed across the room.

"What is it?"

"How...how are you doing? How are your ribs? You really got plugged."

"Hurts."

Lex sighed. "Yeah. Don't do that again, all right? You have to stay alive."

"Really? For what?" I snorted. "So I can be hanged?"

"You can't make it out alive if you don't stay alive," Lex said. "So stop angering them. Just lay low."

"Lex, I *do* have information that would help both them and us. I just need to get Selim Woodworth in here to tell him."

"Find some other way then. Your way clearly doesn't work."

"What do you suggest? Hope he reads minds and waltzes in here? Tunnel into his store to have a chat? Start a fire?"

"That last one might do it."

"Got yourself a loco foco?"

Lex grunted.

I settled into a corner of my cell. "Yeah. The master of all talk and no follow-through."

There was no reply. Minutes ticked by and, assuming Lex had lost interest, or I'd insulted him into silence, I let my mind get back to wandering. *What will attract Selim Woodworth to the headquarters? He has to come by at some point, but I can't wait forever, or for days. Hours, even. What will get him here sooner?*

"You know, I get why you hate me like you do," Lex said.

"What are you talking about?"

"You don't take me seriously. You think I'm a nobody, that I'm a low-life who only chases girls and booze."

Aren't you? I thought.

"You don't respect me because I don't have education like you do."

You also take up oxygen.

"You think I just use up air and contribute nothing."

I said nothing.

"I know it. You don't give me the time of day. You barely speak to me. You want to be rid of me, free of your older brother."

I *have* wished it. But his words spoken aloud grated on my ears.

"Good news for you, you're about to get your wish."

"Stop talking that way. What are you doing?"

"It's the facts. What's there to deny?" He'd never spoken this way before. I suppose the hangman's noose has a way of loosening the tongue.

"Fine," I conceded, "you've made my life difficult. What do you want me to say?"

"Nothing. I already know how you feel. I only want to apologize before it all ends."

I rolled my eyes. "You're being rather dramatic."

"I have to. We've never really talked, and now I might not see your face again."

I squeezed my eyes tight until I saw stars. What was he doing? I was busy plotting ways to secure an audience with Selim Woodworth, and he'd rather wallow in his cell? What an atrocious way to spend his final hours. I'd rather skip to the hanging.

"Cy, do you hear me? We need to talk."

I groaned. "About what, Lex? What do you want me to say? That you bullied me? That you cheated and I had to pay it off? That you left me alone in a foreign town? That you promised to come get me but you showed up drunk and violent? Or do you want to talk about your loathsome character in general, how you never supported me as a brother should? Where should we start?"

Lex was quiet for a time, to the point where I thought I'd put him off and he'd lost his nerve. Yet just as I shifted on the ground again to get comfortable, he answered.

"I made you come to California."

I paused. "You did what?"

"I made you come here."

That hit me harder than the guard's rifle butt. My eyes darted around the cell, and I opened my mouth—

"Mother and Father were only going to send me. I convinced them to let me bring you with me to California instead."

My breathing quickened. My ears, my eyes, my head, and my entire body could not believe what was happening. The last two years flashed before me as my knees began to tremble. I'd had a knife in my eye. I'd been touched by filthy men. I'd seen girls sold for gold. I'd said goodbye to my best friend. I didn't know whether I should explode in anger or in tears, so I did both.

"What?" I sputtered, my face growing hot and my eyes welling up. *"What?"* For my brother's sake, it was good we were contained in separate cells, for had I had the access, I truly believe I'd have strangled him. "You're telling me…" My voice trembled, building slowly, as I stared through the bars confining me. "You made me come? *Here?* I could be home right now? I could be home *right now?* And you made me come…to this…to this…? You made me *come?"*

"I begged them. But it's not what you think."

"I'd be home right now!" My breathing was shallow and rapid.

"It's exactly what I think!"

Lex's voice was calm. "Cy. I know you think the worst of me. I know I took you from your friend. But you had to come."

My voice cracked. *"Why?"*

"Because..." he paused. "Because they were planning to send you to St. Patrick's."

I gulped at the air. "St. Patrick's? The orphanage?"

"No, the church. They were sending you to the church. To be a priest."

"What do you mean, to be a priest? Are you kidding me? That doesn't make any sense. Why would they do that?"

"Because of your friend."

"Leland? What about him?"

Lex sighed. "Cy. Mother and Father aren't good parents. They ruined us. Look at me, I'm a failure at life and I can't keep a job or a promise. Look at you. You were the good boy but you offended them. Nothing you did on purpose. The whole thing is a mess. It's no wonder we're sitting where we are."

Not a single thought could land. "What do you mean, I 'offended them'?"

"Your friend. And you. You spent all day together, never had any other friends. He's all you talked about. Mother and Father, their heads are all warped with religion. They got suspicious."

"Suspicious about *what?*"

I could hear Lex shifting in his cell. "The whole thing. They thought it was..."

"What?"

"You know."

"I don't."

"Um...different."

"Different how?" *Come on Lex, say it. SAY IT.*

"Different enough that it scared them, in all their old-fashioned thinking. They were going to pack you off to the church to become a priest. Father was already arranging it. Your life as you knew it would've been over."

I held my head in my hands while my rib cage screamed at me. The priesthood? Was I that disposable? "But I'd be in New York,"

I cried. "I could've seen my friends, I could have—"

"No, Cy," Lex said firmly. "It doesn't work that way. Once you're in, you're *in*."

"You don't know that!"

"We both know that. You would've been miserable. So I convinced Father to let me take you to California with me. I told him we'd earn twice the gold. I don't think he believed it, but it was his chance to get you out of New York. I had to get you out of there. I just..." He sighed. "I didn't know it would be like this for you out here. How could I know?"

Snot dripped out of my nose. "I could've seen my friends."

"Your *one* friend. And no, you couldn't have. Those tyrannical fathers at St. Patrick's wouldn't have let you out of their sight."

I pressed my fists to my throbbing temples.

"I'm sorry, Cy, for a lot of things. But not about that."

"Was, um..." My throat caught. "Did Leland know? About any of it?"

"I don't know."

For a long time I stared at the wall. Through the wall. It became shimmery and opalescent, and at any moment it would reveal to me what was on its other side. Some different life? Different people? Maybe a river. The Hudson River, and a bottle, and a raft. A button in my pocket.

"And now you got me in here."

"It wasn't supposed to happen like this."

"You showed up too drunk to stand, then you beat her up? My employer? Do you think *anything* through?"

"It was supposed to be for you. I got her in her room and I saw a bag of gold on her desk. It was just a quick swipe, to help you out on your way home. But I didn't expect—"

"—her to catch you?"

"I pushed her aside, and she fought back. I've never seen a woman fight back."

I shook my head to myself. "You're not the first man she's vanquished."

Lex gave a short chuckle, then was quiet for a long time. The excited voices of men yelled in the distance, but I paid them no mind. San Francisco is mired in noise.

Finally he spoke up. "What I wanted to say to you, before it's too late, is that I've made mistakes. I tried to toughen you up. I tried to keep you alive, like a brother should. But I failed. I've failed in so many ways, and here you are, with me, hopeless. I'm sorry for that."

"Screw you, Lex. I'm not hopeless. And just so you know, I didn't even need that money. I paid off your debt long ago. I stayed because she and I struck a deal, and I earned enough to take care of myself. I didn't need your help."

There was a long pause. Then he said, "Then why didn't you go home on your own?"

I said no more, and neither did he.

"One more thing," he said after a while.

"No, Lex. No more."

"One more. I was never Head Brothel Inspector. They'd never give that job to someone like me. I was just a foot soldier putting on a show, trying to get in to get you out."

As the sun rose into the midmorning sky, the door screamed open and a guard strode in. "Two more of you scum are dangling from the Ol' Adobe!" he announced. "If I were you, I'd get right with Jesus right quick!"

"Hey, jackass!" I yelled. "How about you shut up and get me Selim Woodworth!"

July 8 1851
San Francisco
Hard to tell the weather from a cell.

I awoke this morning naturally, with no stale projectile ricocheting off my head. It was a pleasant way to greet the day, with no bump upon my head nor rock-hard crust on which to chip a tooth, yet an inconvenience arose when my stomach began to growl and there was no rock-hard crust to satisfy it. Nor did a crust arrive in the evening, while Lex received both of his. The message from the Committee was clear.

Lex made pitiful noises from the other side of the room. "My stomach," he moaned. "Uuuugh. Why don't they open the windows, I'm sweating like a pig." I thought back to yesterday's conversation. I was here, in San Francisco, in a jail cell, my life ticking away with each minute, because of him. The thought of it cycled and recycled through my mind until it grew and expanded and filled all the corners of my head and limbs, before settling deep into my stomach like Edgar Allan Poe's "telltale heart" buried beneath the floorboards. At the core was Lex, my brother, who stole me out of New York. The priesthood? If it was true, that severed the scant remaining feelings I had for my parents. How desperate they were to be rid of me.

Yet there I would've been, in New York. No matter what Lex said, how difficult could it have been to slip out St. Patrick's back door and dissolve into the crowd?

I growled and hit my head with my fist. My brother intervened at the worst times. I had nothing to say to him, though even if I could've mustered a cohesive sentence, my strength was so diminished by lack of nourishment that anything I'd have

294

attempted would've been garbled by haze. Much better it was, then, to steady my spinning head by lying prone upon the ground. I dreamed of food and clear water.

* * *

"Lad?"

I cracked open an eye but saw only fuzzy outlines of the wall and the small window. The light had changed. Something made a rustling sound that could only have been Lex shuffling around, and as I no longer recognized him as someone deserving my time and thoughts, I allowed my eyelid to droop back down.

"Lad? Hello?"

I didn't know why Lex didn't answer, but I wanted nothing to do with it. I kept my eyes closed, dreaming of roasted beef and fried onions.

"You there! Wake up!"

I tried to roll over but my aching ribs protested, so I gave that up. Whoever was speaking persisted like an irritating fly. Why didn't Lex answer? My head tipped toward sleep.

"Rouse him, would you?" someone said, and then keys scraped and the door squealed open. A rifle butt jammed into my ribs and I jolted awake, filling the headquarters with my painful howling.

"That's fine, much obliged," the voice said, and the door shut with a metallic slam. There two figures stood, still out of focus, but this time due to the tears brimming in my eyes.

"Top of the morning!" said the same voice, and I became aware of the aroma of fresh-baked bread. My stomach made a growling plea for it. The man holding the prized morsel took a bite and came into focus.

"Mr. Woodworth," I mumbled.

"The same."

"You...um...I...you finally came." Hunger made me delirious.

"Indeed, and what an unfortunate reunion. Word has it you requested me, though your tactics in doing so raised a few eyebrows, including my own. Nonetheless, I was delayed due to other matters. There is no shortage of Committee business around the town, I'm afraid. You could say business is booming—why, only two days ago we put an end to two scoundrels who committed many of the atrocities here of late. Forgive my tardiness." He paused, then gestured for the guard to leave. Selim Woodworth turned back to me, and in a low voice, continued, "You must understand how distressed I am at your predicament. Norman Ah-Sing, it seems, has foiled me by using the Committee yet again to achieve his aims. But now he seems to have disappeared. Whether he's run off to the interior or back to China, only his China Boys know. And they're not telling me.

"As for your matter, most unfortunately, it is not one I can rectify on my own. This is a whole-Committee matter now, and as things stand, you are a convicted young man sentenced to hang. While I hold more sway than most other members, still I cannot overturn the wishes of the entire group. Neither was I able to successfully argue for a reduced sentence—exile from the town, for example. The town is thirsty for blood, and blood it shall have. This is no comfort to you, but can you blame it? Vagrants and delinquents have run roughshod over the good citizens for too long now. And it is not, after all, as though you have no blood on your hands."

He held up his hand as I started to open my mouth. "I did what I could to ameliorate your fate, to no avail, and so I am leaving you with my own token, this bread here to lessen your suffering. Peace between your soul and God must be your priority now, and so I leave you to that private task. I am sorry, lad, but you will not need to call for me again." He handed me the bread and rose.

My mind churned and bile coursed through my limbs. Selim Woodworth moved toward the door. My last hope for my life was walking toward the exit.

"Wait!" I called after him. "Wait!"

He paused.

"I have something more you can use. More information. Please, it will help your Committee."

He sighed and turned where he stood.

"It is true that I killed a man, but it was a Hound who was

attacking my brother and me."

"You have already claimed this in your defense."

"Yes. But afterward I was kidnapped, not by the Hounds, but by a Celestial employed by the brothel madam Ah Toy, who seized me at knifepoint and imprisoned me in her shanty. They marked me with this." I showed him my hand. "It means 'prisoner,' and they kept me for these past two years as a servant, forcing me to pay a debt that was never mine."

Selim Woodworth tilted his head. "This is a sad tale, and I offer my full apologies for your hardship."

"What I need is your assistance."

"I don't doubt it. However, as I mentioned, it is not my decision. You will have to convince the Committee that you deserve your freedom, and although your experience with the brothel madam is loathsome, there is nothing there that warrants your release. Your defense against the Hound is perhaps excusable, but what of your trading in children? Chinese children though they may be, this is nonetheless a free state. Even though I was sorry to have not convinced the Committee to go easier on you, I certainly cannot blame them for their refusal!"

"But I wasn't even the one on trial!" I closed my eyes and calmed my voice. "Mr. Woodworth. If you do nothing, if you stand by while I'm led to the gallows, there will be many more children doomed to the same fate."

He narrowed his eyes. "I am aware that the child trade is larger than you. It is a scourge to this country and humanity."

"I can offer you something to help stop it. Not in the whole country, but here in San Francisco. Information."

"What is it?" he asked.

"I can tell you the location of the Queen's Room."

His face flickered. "Truly? Where is it, then?"

"I'll tell you, but the Committee must cancel my sentence."

He studied me long and hard. Through clenched teeth he said, "I do not care to make bargains of this nature."

"This will further the work of the Committee, I promise you. Otherwise, while I hang from a beam, the trade of children will continue."

"You are not in the position to negotiate, lad. You have not even revealed the room's whereabouts."

"I'll tell you if the Committee helps me."

"You must reveal it first if you are to get the Committee's attention."

"With respect, I have it already."

His nostrils flared and he stuck his finger at me. "I am not your toy, and I will not be played with by a pup in a cage. Like it or not, your fate at this moment rests upon me. I highly recommend you choose your next words with care."

I raised my hands in a gesture of standing down. "I'm sorry. I'm hungry and distressed." I then breathed deeply and exhaled to slow the conversation. "I'll give you a taste of what I know. Then I must have your assurances about the Committee. If I'm released, I'll share the remainder of it."

"Full commutation is a prodigious ask. More likely it will be a reduced sentence. You might still be expelled from the town."

I'll take it, I thought, but said instead, "These are children's lives."

We stared at each other, neither of us moving forward nor backward. It was quiet at Lex's end of the room. Was he listening to every word?

Guilt then stabbed my gut; I hadn't made a bid for Lex's freedom. There he sat, alone in his cell, listening to my plea and my play for my life. He hadn't piped up once. *But I'm already asking for too much. How could I add Lex's plight to my own?* But I hadn't even tried.

"All right then, lad," Selim Woodworth said at last. "Tell me what you wish me to relay to the Committee. I will report it exactly as you say, and I guarantee the most prominent members, me included, will hear it and consider it. If this bit of information is helpful enough to warrant your release, you will then reveal the location of the Queen's Room and everything you know about it. Understand that your initial information must reveal enough that the Committee feels comfortable in granting clemency. Clemency for *murder* and *slave dealing*, mind you. Choose your words wisely."

I gulped silently, now feeling the life-or-death weight of how I'd put my next sentence. I realized that he'd turned the force of a heavy decision back upon me, and now I had to deliver. I took a deep breath and said, "The brothel madam, Ah Toy, has dealt in children before and will deal in them again if she goes unchecked."

"We suspected this, and she confirmed it at the trial. This is not new information."

"Do you know that she bribes people to turn a blind eye? Important people."

"I'm unsurprised," he replied. "There's a reason she's not in here with you."

"Some of those who've received her gifts also know about the Queen's Room. They make purchases there."

He blinked. This was new to him, and I imagined the gears turning in his head.

"Names?"

I shook my head. "That's for later."

"People in government?"

"Yes."

"The upper levels of government?"

I shrugged.

He pursed his lips and sucked in his cheeks. "The brothel madam testified against you. Is this retribution for that? Vengeance?"

"I'm trying to save my life. But I also want to sleep at night with a clear conscience."

"The gallows has a way bringing us around," he remarked with a smirk. He crossed his arms and held my gaze. I held his, too. This was not the time to back down. The seconds slowed into hours. My ribs throbbed. A cough issued from Lex's cell.

Without another word he turned and walked briskly out the door, at such a pace to prevent him from hearing any more.

When the headquarters door slammed shut and the guard took his usual place at the table, I tore a chunk of bread with my teeth and swallowed it whole, nearly choking on it as it made its way down.

*   *   *

[Author's Note: The following passage was written later that night, in an agitated state from what I can glean from my scribbled, sometimes illegible penmanship. —C.H.K.]

I've just aw— in a cold panic; s— is soaking through my shirt and stinging in my eyes. It's pitch black and I can't make out any sh— in front of me. Is the wall an inch from my nose or a mile? It presses upon me as though I'm being buried alive in a coffin or I —ht be floating in the vast darkness of the cosmos. I feel myself on the ground yet what —s that mean? Where is this ground? In New York? In the Garden? On the raft? I can't find a single point to orient myself to. The darkness is profound.

My mind w— not be still. It stirred me awake. No, it shoted me awake, —ing my head like a vise until my eyelids popped open and my eyeballs verged on dislodgement from their sockets. There was a shout in the dark, somewhere close by, I can swear it.

What have I done with my life? Have I b—n kind? Have I been selfless? Have I gi— joy? Have I improted anyone's mood by traveling through his orbit?

How do I answer these questions? Whom can I

ask now other than the one who brought me here, the one in the —me room as me, yet too far away to be reached? Were my parents' lives m— better by my presence? Decidedly not, yet what of Ah Toy? Did her life im— the day she captured me? Did she have —ces of war— and gladness when I was in her —nd? What of the girls? What of James King of William? What of Selim Woodworth, has his quality of life ticked upward? Or has everyone here been dragged down, depressed, res—ed by my anchor that causes them to stoop and bend under my weight? Lex, as you languish in a —ll, was I w— the trouble to save? Leland, has the dr— of your life been realized or has my time here in S. F. freed you of s—w and negativity? Has the c— around your neck —en broken, and do you feel liberated?

I sh— have —ed in that river. L— should have been elsewhere, too far to assist, too engrossed in another's attention to notice I should have s—d beneath the surface and s—d there, and the only mention of my ab— should have been one of the other boys from school, looking around in a mildly cu—s manner, asking the ne—st one to him, "Wasn't there someone else with us? I count only five." It w— have been my greatest cont— to the world.

July 16, 1851
On board the Pacific
Warm and breezy.

[Author's Note: For 77 long years, until the mysterious package arrived, the following was the only entry in my possession. I had believed that everything preceding this date chronicling my time in S. Francisco had been lost to me forever in the events of July 10th. —C.H.K.]

My ears are ringing and it's all I can do to keep from pressing my fists into my head. My five deep breaths were useless. I'm *dismayed*, for so many reasons, more than I care to spell out, not least of which is the loss of my dearest possession on July 10th— the journal in which I recorded all my thoughts and happenings over the previous two years. Part of my soul is lost with it, and most of the days since have been spent lamenting it. Nothing counts now. My time in San Francisco was an illusion, or a dream, or a shadow. I can't pick out what was real and what were figments in my mind.

It took me six days after that fateful day and generosity from sympathetic souls around me to locate a bit of parchment, a pen, a bottle of ink, and the spirit to put words on blank paper yet again. And so, here, I've attempted to recall the events of July 10th in all their detail. I don't know why I do this, because really, what use is a travel journal with only one entry? But here I am, my head aching, my hand itching to record, before I lose it, while I have all the time in the world to do it. At least part of my time in S.F. must be recorded as real, and the most dramatic day may as well be the one I capture.

If nothing else, I've got to break the tedium of the constant rocking of this blasted steamer.

* * *

July 10, 1851
Recorded in retrospect.

Today was the most bittersweet day.

I wasn't given any bread this morning, maybe because I'd had Selim Woodworth's loaf last night and *that*—per the power-hungry vigilante guards—was more than enough for the likes of me.

Lex though, from the moment he woke up, was agitated. "Something's off. Something's off," he muttered in his cell. I didn't reply. I was slated to die, and I didn't wish for the remaining words in my life to be wasted on him. I ignored him and instead reviewed my conversation with Selim Woodworth. Surely he must have relayed my request to the Committee by now. Maybe even now they were meeting to consider it. Maybe they'd even decided! I stared at the headquarters door, praying he'd burst through it, waving some piece of parchment in his hand, crying, "I've got it! I've got it! You are to be released!"

The door remained fastened shut.

The morning unfolded slowly. Lex attempted to get my attention, and I denied him the satisfaction of a response. By and by, however, his disposition increasingly mirrored my own.

"Today's the day, I know it," he fretted. "Something's different."

I didn't respond.

"Something's in the works, I feel it. Everyone's acting queer. Are they tying the noose? I'm a goner, I know I'm a goner."

A minute went by.

"Oh, I just know it. Today is hanging day. They must have gathered everyone at the Square. On the Plaza, saving spaces, staking their good seats. This is my last morning, it has to be."

I put my hands over my ears.

"It's today, no doubt about it. Cy, listen. I told you I'm sorry. You have to know that before they take me. Do you hear me? I'm *sorry!* I did what I thought a brother should, but I've lost you anyway." His breathing was labored. "Why won't you talk?"

I couldn't bear it any longer. "Shut it, Lex."

"Cy, you have to believe me. I'm sorry. I didn't know. I thought I was rescuing you from misery but I've only led you straight to it. I swear, it was only my best inten—"

A humongous explosion from nearby concussed through the cell and rattled the windows and the doors on their hinges. Something metallic creaked, the wooden walls crackled, and dust floated down from the veiling.

I froze. The Committee guard jumped up, grabbed his revolver, and ran out the door. Lex wailed in consternation, "What is it? Are they shooting? Who? Are they breaking us out? Are they killing us? Is it the Hounds? Cy!"

I crept up to the window and peered out. Only a small cloud of dust drifted up from the west side of the Square. Otherwise everything seemed the same. Peaceful, even. Had it even happened?

"Do you see anything, Cy? What's happening? What's going on?"

I came away from the window and sat, wondering. *What does it mean? Is someone firing upon the town? Is it an earthquake? Maybe a steamer exploded? No, the dust is to the west, not over the water. Does it have anything to do with Selim Woodworth and the vigilantes? What can it possibly be?*

Then the screaming started.

I jumped back up and raced to the window. "Oh God, oh God, what is it?" Lex cried. The small cloud of dust had turned into a tailing wisp of black smoke. I eyed it with suspicion as the screams came muffled through the window glass. *Another fire,* I thought, and on cue the bells in the town began to clang.

"No, no, no, those are for us. Those are meant for us! Cy!"

I glued my eyes to the window and watched a man run by toward the smoke, which was already billowing into a fat column. *How had it grown so quickly?* I stared at it, and right before me the column widened and undulated, and beneath it, just visible now, were the first flecks of orange. Then a realization slugged me in the stomach.

The Queen's Room. I stared so hard through the window my eyes watered. I was almost sure of it. *The fire was in the direction of the Queen's Room.* What could that mean? Did the Committee do it? Did they take my breadcrumbs and sleuth it out? *Maybe they paid Ah Toy a visit,* I thought, torn between savage joy and lingering regret. *Maybe they drew it out of her and they blew it up. She could have traded the location of that awful room for immunity. She doesn't need some gloomy, secret room to ply her trade.*

I felt a stab in my gut and I almost doubled over. *The girls! Oh no, the girls.* Were any still in there? Did any get caught in the blast? *Oh God.* I thought I'd be sick.

"Cy! Flames! They're coming this way!"

I looked back through the window. They were shockingly and dismayingly larger and closer than only a minute before.

"Oh, I knew it, I knew it, I knew it," Lex babbled, "I'm to die today, either by noose or by flame, today's the day, I'm done for…"

I could only watch, mesmerized, as the flames marched and leaped, building to building, like frogs after flies, while men flailed buckets of water at them or fled from their warpath. The fire begat more fire, and it was soon a wall, unchecked and rampaging through the town at its demonic will.

"Not this way, no, not this way. It's today, it's all over, everything is all over—"

The metallic screeching of door hinges cut Lex off, and he groaned in agony. I instinctively shrank to the rear of the cell as the door opened and a man appeared in silhouette against the light. The door closed, and my unadjusted eyes lost the man in the darkness of the headquarters. Footsteps came toward me. My breath caught, and it sounded as if Lex's had too; perhaps if we were silent enough it would delay our fate. The footsteps, although quiet, still headed for me, and before I knew it, a face showed between the metal bars. I held still, hoping to not be spotted. Then I stared, not believing my senses, for it was no Committee member who gazed back at me. It was the Celestial.

There he stood, the stocky, braided, glowering man who had captured me time and time again. And here he stood again, tormenting me as one of the last faces I'd see in my life. I was doomed to be followed by him until the end.

"Who is it?" Lex whispered. "Cy, your time is up! Forgive me, *please!* I couldn't have known my actions would lead to this! Cy, look at me!"

"Hush, Lex!" I barked, then turned back to the Celestial and growled at him, "Why are *you* here?"

The Celestial, true to form, said nothing. Instead, he fished something out of the folds of his jacket and stuck it in the lock. It scraped and clicked and clacked, and suddenly the door swung open with a squeal. I stayed put but my eyes darted left and right.

"What is this?" I said warily.

Calmly but swiftly he pulled out something else and handed it to me. It was a burlap sack that weighed heavily in my hand, the coins inside clinking and the dust crunching. What was this? The money Ah Toy owed for my work? My two percent share of the Garden? "Is this...?" I started, but then he did something that *really* surprised me and struck me dumb. It was only one word, but he spoke.

"Wharf."

I stared at him. My mind didn't grasp his words. "You speak English?"

"Wharf," he said again.

"Cy?" Lex called, "What's going on? They can't take you! It was me, I confessed to all of it!"

"I don't understand," I said to the Celestial.

"Wharf."

"Long Wharf? How...? Where are the guards?"

The Celestial pointed through the window at the advancing flames. *"Wharf!"*

"Hang *me!*" Lex yelled. "He didn't do anything!"

I stumbled out of the cell. As I got to the middle of the headquarters, my eyes fell upon my brother. He was squatting in his cell, shaking, sweating, and scratching his arms obsessively. The Celestial noticed my gaze and shook his head. I glanced again at the fire through the window, then ran out the door.

"Cy? What—?" Lex shouted behind me as the closing of the

door cut off his question. The brightness of the outdoors, where I hadn't set foot in days, dazzled me for a moment, and right then someone knocked into me hard.

"For God's sake, man, move!" a man yelled. The noise of the fire rushed into my ears—the deep roar, the crackling, the cacophony of shrieks, screams, horses' whinnies, birds' screeching, clanging church bells, all of it exploded in my head. The air was charred with smoke that assaulted my nose and lungs. Wiping my watering eyes, I scoured the ground and came across a rock the size of my hand. I picked it up and ran back inside the headquarters.

"Cy!" Lex yelled, wide-eyed. "What's happening? I thought you left me!"

"Stand back," I said and slammed the rock into the lock of Lex's cell.

"What are you doing?" he asked yet I answered only by raining more blows upon the lock to bust it open. The lock, however, was too strong and my arm shook from the vibrations of mineral striking metal. I shuddered to think what my fate would be if a Committee member walked in at that moment, but then I remembered I was doomed anyway, so I doubled my efforts and crashed the rock down on the iron again and again.

Both lock and rock, however, were as stubbornly intact as before. The shouting outside intensified, and I wasn't doing any damage. I groaned and said, "I'll find something bigger."

Lex wailed, "Cy! Don't lea—" but I was already again outside. The smoke and the flames were closer. The Celestial was gone, having done his duty and delivered his message. I looked around frantically, then glimpsed something long—a shovel leaning against a building. It was better than nothing. I retrieved it and returned to Lex's cell.

"Cy, help me!" he cried.

I slid the shovel through the bars to him, then grabbed his quaking hands. I couldn't look him in the eye, but I gave him a squeeze and said in a shaking voice, "You did what you could. That's all you ever did. Good luck, brother." Then I turned and fled.

Outside the headquarters, I paused to wipe my eyes and reset myself. The conflagration was to my right, now only a few streets away and churning toward me. To my left was Long Wharf. I hoisted the bag of gold under my arm and ran toward the Wharf and the steamer docked there.

The Wharf was filled with panicked people when I reached it, breathless. What few women there were in the town all seemed to be here, some crying, some stone-faced, all dragging whatever precious possessions they had thrown into their trunks to the last bastion of safety before the water. The captain of the steamship stood on the gangway, fingers rapidly tapping, eyes wide as he stared at the fire.

The good citizens of San Francisco ran hither and thither, some with a calm that demonstrated their seasoned experience with such disasters, and others—the newcomers—bucking about in terror. Merchants stood framed in their store entrances, one eye on the advancing flames, offering passersby twenty, thirty, fifty dollars a load to transport their valued stock to safety. The able-bodied were either too distressed to take them up on the offer or negotiated for fees still higher. Only the Chinese dock girls were unperturbed, staring idly at their nails and sitting quietly.

I didn't see Ah Toy, and I wondered briefly if the whole thing was some strange setup, or perhaps she'd been delayed by the Vigilance Committee—arrested, detained, passing small gifts over...but then I turned and there she was, standing calmly, appearing out of nowhere as she always did. She was beautiful, as always, in her madam's robe, and serene. Nothing wrinkled nor out of its place, everything smooth, contained, and unflappable, as if the chaos swirled above and around her but could never pierce that space she resided in, that which buttressed her strength yet kept the world at arm's length. I flushed with anger when I saw her and then was just as quickly doused with relief, then settled on resigned confusion. I rubbed my tattooed hand.

"You have gold," she said, eyeing the sack in my arm. "Good. All you earn."

The noise around us pounded my ears, but her soft voice still carried so much power I could hear it like a bell. Yet while I admired the presence she commanded, a burning question scorched my mouth, and I had to spit it out.

"Why did you do it?" I wasn't talking about the Celestial springing me from my cell, and she knew it. She paused while a man howled nearby.

Then she answered, "You."

"What do you mean, me?"

"You. At the trial, you are in trouble. After old dog talk, all *gwai-lo* say you are guilty. They ask me, 'He do this? He sell the girl?' but what I say, no matter for you. Only me. Say yes, you go to the jail. Say no, we *both* go to the jail."

"It would have been you in there, not me."

"You go to the jail. All say you are guilty, no matter how I say. You go."

"So you gave me to them and saved yourself."

She nodded.

My nostrils flared and I spat to the side. "Well, thank you for that explanation. I suppose you now want me to thank you for springing me out."

"Yes."

I shook my head in disgust. I looked over her at the blaze pushing steadily toward the Wharf.

"All steamship passengers aboard!" the captain announced. "We must depart early to avoid the flames!"

"I save *me* to save *you*," she said, poking my chest hard and refusing to follow my gaze over her shoulder. "Who will save? No one. I do not go to the jail, then I can save. You see?"

Was she telling the truth? Was it a bigger plan she'd concocted? I didn't answer her. I didn't want to give her the satisfaction that I owed her anything.

"No need to thank now. Someday."

Still burning, I said, "Then what are we doing here? Why are we standing on this dock having a chat while the town burns?"

"You choose."

"Choose? Choose what? What's there to choose?"

"You listen," she said in her soft, commanding way. "This town—too many trouble. Too many fire. Too many *gwai-lo* with bad idea, do not like Chinese. Soon not safe. I go to San Jose, bring the man and all the girl." She dug her hand into her robe and pulled out a sheet of paper. "This the deed to land at San Jose. You come with me, help build the new house. I double the percent."

She handed me the paper, and I glanced at it without really focusing. "You want me to go to San Jose with you and set up another brothel?"

She nodded. "Later this town more safe, maybe I come back. Maybe you stay at San Jose, in charge the house, make more money, become very rich!"

I flipped the paper over, then back again. *So simple everything is, written on paper. But so complicated what it stands for.* I felt the weight of the sack of gold and said, "I already have money. I don't need any more."

Ah Toy smiled. "'People who know they have enough, always happy.' Very smart. But you have *everything?* Friend who like you? Family who love you? All at San Jose. Come with us."

I met her eyes but couldn't get my thoughts straight. There was too much noise, too much flickering light, too many bees buzzing in my head. San Jose? The fire bore down on us all the more.

"Would we buy more girls from China?"

"You know already."

I took a deep breath of burnt air and let it out. I tasted the ash. "You said I have a choice. What's the other option?"

With her other hand, Ah Toy pulled a smaller piece of paper out of her robe. "Ticket to your home," she said simply, gesturing toward the docked steamer, and waited.

"All steamboat passengers, aboard now!" the captain yelled. The crowd surged forward and had to be blocked. "Only those with tickets!"

The number of times I've come to this very Wharf, praying that one day I'd be able to do this very thing, to step aboard and convey myself home, and the number of days, weeks, and months I've had to think and dream of it until it turned to years, only now to have the actual possibility of it compress back down to minutes, and now seconds. I know I can't stay in this town another moment if I wish to—quite literally—save my neck. But which way to turn?

The steamer gave an earsplitting blast from its pipes. *"All passengers, please hurry! Only ticketed passengers! We push back in one minute!"* The fire was nearly upon us. Yellow, orange, and red swayed, undulated, swallowing buildings and people in its path, vomiting black smoke, resembling nothing less than the yawning mouth of Hell.

Ah Toy stood there patiently, immune to the chaos, watching her big question torture me.

I pushed her out of my head. I pushed Lex and my parents out of my head. I pushed Leland out of my head. What was left was me. What did I want, and what would I do to get it? No, that was the old question. What *wouldn't* I do to get it?

Three quick blasts of dynamite at the foot of the Wharf shook me and brought me 'round to the present. The crowd screamed, and a two-story dried goods building collapsed upon itself, coughing up a billowing cloud of dust.

"Departing now!" the captain bellowed. The steamer's whistle blared a second time.

I stepped up to Ah Toy and looked into her face for a long moment. I reached out and took the smaller piece of paper, then said, *"Li-douh m-joi hai ngoh uk-kei*. This is no longer my home."

A subtle smile curled the corners of her mouth on her smooth face and she nodded ever so slightly as if, in that moment, some long-held hypothesis had at last been confirmed. It all added up to an undeniable message, one spoken without words, and one I would never forget.

You are cutting the dead weight. You have finally learned.

*   *   *

Amidst the panic the steamer was already beginning to move, and seeing the dock lines undone and the gangway stowed, I shoved my way through the crowd to where the ship had just been docked. The gap between it and the Wharf was close to five feet but growing quickly, and in that handful of seconds I hesitated, it became seven, ten, twelve feet. I looked over my shoulder but could no longer see Ah Toy, and when I turned back the gap was at fifteen feet. I looked down to the water and my stomach clenched. The gap was now twenty feet. I took three deep breaths. Twenty-five feet. I closed my eyes, coiled my legs, and paused. Then something pushed me from behind and I was falling, suspended in the space between the Wharf and the water, and the awful, insane thought seized me and squeezed me in an iron grip. I was back there, back in the river, the raft drifting slowly yet resolutely away, my sodden clothes restraining me, entrapping me, like weights tied to my arms and legs, pulling my neck, my chin, my cheeks, my nose, my eyes, my forehead underwater. And then he was there, pulling me limb by limb out of my clothing until only my undergarments remained and the freedom of movement came like a bird first learning to fly.

This time, however, it was just me. Automatically my legs kicked and my arms hugged the water in front of me over and over. But rather than rise, the water level settled around my neck. I barked a short, hysterical laugh. *I'm not sinking! I'm floating!*

It was then that my heart plunged through my stomach. The sack of gold.

No no no no no no...

I searched about like a madman, looking to my left and right. Nothing. *Where is it?! Where did it fall in?* I spun myself around and then spotted it through the water, shrinking and shrinking as it sank to the sandy floor and settled there. I looked back at the steamer, which pushed onward, unconcerned with this horrible development. There was no time to dive for the sack. All those bits of gold I'd earned over the months and years. What would I use to reset myself in New York? How would I live? What about food? Drink? Clothing? Bill collectors?

Groaning in exasperation, I scanned the Wharf. Many in the crowd peered over the edge at me, their faces still shocked from my fall. I heard shouts of "Someone save him!" and "Throw him a line!" but I ignored all that. I didn't know what I searched for until my eyes found her. In the midst of the throng, her face stood out, young but jaded, that of one of the Chinese dock girls.

My brain spun. *How do I tell her?* I ran through the Chinese words I'd heard at the Garden. So many I didn't know and didn't think to ask their meanings. *Why hadn't I paid more attention?* But three came to me.

"Heya! *Siu-je!*" I yelled up at her as loud as I could muster. "Heya! *Siu-je! Siu-je!*"

I saw her brows furrow and she pointed to herself with a questioning face.

I nodded with exaggeration. *"Gam! Gam!"* I dared not yell out in English.

Her puzzled expression didn't change. I took my arm, lifted it out of the water, and pointed toward the water in big motions. *"Hai-douh! Gam hai-douh! Gam hai-douh!"*

Her face melted into understanding. She made a fist with her left, covered it with the palm of her right, and bowed slightly toward me. "Thank…you!" she mouthed.

The steamer gave another blast of its whistle, and my arms and legs started churning forward. The waves were choppier than normal on account of the summer wind and the vessel's wake, but I settled into rhythm and pushed through them. The manual labor at the Garden paid its dividends. The steamer was moving slowly but picking up speed, and soon it was all I could do to keep pace with it. I had to reach it. I *had* to. If I stopped swimming, I'd miss my chance to go home. I could go back to Ah Toy, but that would mean going backward. That was behind me. My life was mine to save. I checked my progress again, then doubled my efforts, my arms pumping harder than ever. I ignored my rib twinging under the strain. The fishy aroma of the water didn't bother me. My lungs pulled salty air in and pushed hot air out at a torrid pace. But another few seconds later, the ship began to pull away. Panic sprouted in my belly and I remembered to breathe deeply to keep myself under control, but it was slipping from my grasp.

The steamer was shrinking and I lunged with the last bit of strength I had. Winded, my limbs were turning into anchors and my ribs were about to split open right there on the water. On top of it all, the waves pushed me ceaselessly back toward San Francisco. *After all this, is this the wicked fate I've been assigned?* I growled in frustration. The steamer stayed on course.

At that moment, something caught my eye and I looked upward. A flock of pelicans, brown, long-billed, and graceful, soared above me on the wind. Their progress was effortless and beautiful, exquisite and natural, and although I expected to resent them for it, I could only smile as tears ran down my cheeks. Their outstretched wings and their coordinated formation created their own glorious freedom, and it was heavenly. God did not disappoint. If it were the last image of my life to behold, so be it.

I nearly dropped my eyelids in exhaustion when a figure on the retreating vessel caught my attention. It was waving both its arms and pointing in an exaggerated manner into the water. It might have been yelling something, but I could focus only on the wild gestures. I regarded him with only a calm puzzlement, which struck me as a ludicrous juxtaposition—he, safe on a ship yet gesticulating in a panic, and me, any number of moments from an oceanic demise, bobbing in the water with an air of serenity. Having only the energy to smile, I tipped my head back to feel the warmth of the sun upon my face. *There can be worse ways to die. Better to go out giving one's all in the midst of God's green earth than to waste away, alone, imprisoned, in the dark, or dangling, swinging slightly, to the roar of a bloodthirsty crowd.* At least I had escaped a dull demise. Mine would be adventurous, memorable.

Something brushed my head as it dipped into the water. *Sharks, perhaps.* The bay's waters were filled with them. *That must be what that figure on the ship was pointing at. Well, let them come.* The waters around me churned. I inhaled, waiting for the first strike of sharp, serrated teeth to cut into my flesh, to be dragged underwater and feasted upon. My only hope was to die quickly, before my body was mangled and transformed to chum. *Let them return my body to the earth. I would rather* this *be my bloodthirsty crowd than the one gathered in Portsmouth Square.* I closed my eyes and prayed that it would be quick.

I waited, and waited, and waited. I exhaled, ready for the end, with no panic and no apprehension. I thought of Ah Toy, packing for San Jose. I thought of New York. *Well, Leland, I regret to inform you that I won't be making it back. Your friendship has meant the world to me. As consolation, though I be thousands of miles away, please know that thinking of you was my feeble mind's final act.*

When the attack came, it came not as jagged ripping or feral tearing, but a coarse burning. Absentmindedly I moved my hand toward my attacker, wondering what a shark truly felt like, when the most curious sensation met my hand instead. It was rough, and ribbed, and moving at a great speed, not toward me yet past me. I clenched my hand around it and was pulled forward, so I brought my other hand up to clench it as well, and with the stronger grip I began to move, dragged along with whatever was in my hand. When I looked down through the rushing water and adjusted my eyes, I saw it was no shark, nor any animal at all. Rather it was a rope, thin and taut.

Keeping my grip, I followed the length of it with my eyes and realized it led to the steamer, the steamer which had, remarkably, ceased gaining distance on me. Its sidewheels still churned and its smokestacks still billowed, yet it held still at a steady length. The frantic figure on the deck no longer danced about and instead heaved on something. Another figure joined him, and another, and another, until half a dozen or so of them were pulling, pulling, pulling, and before my waterlogged brain could make sense of it, the ship's size doubled and the length between it and me halved. This was a welcome turn of events, though I couldn't spare it any energy nor thought save for gripping the rope with my life. The length halved again, then again, and another jerky heave, and a heave, and a heave, and I was lying on my side on a smooth, warm surface, trembling violently while dark shadows closed in on all sides.

*   *   *

The ship turned left to follow the coastline, and as it did so, Long Wharf and that side of the town became blocked by Telegraph Hill and the hilly terrain of the peninsula. The golden glow silhouetted the ridges and the black smoke swelled above them. The passengers watched, grim-faced, as the town receded into the distance. Wrapped in a blanket and shivering violently, my gaze traveled over the water to the town I'd just escaped. The fire had reached the water's edge. A knife stabbed my heart as I realized that the Vigilance Committee's headquarters must have already been consumed. I turned away and wiped the tears streaming down my face.

The Golden Gate, buffeted on both sides by rocky slope, loomed in front of us and expanded as we neared. In front of us a steamer churned in the opposite direction. It started as a speck upon the water and grew until it became a full-sized vessel with a sidewheel and smokestack like our own. It passed on our port side, between us and the old Presidio, and as is customary, the passengers on our ship flocked to that side of the deck to wave their greetings. Through my watery eyes I watched the interaction play out. It was an international collision of cultures, for face after face on the passing steamer was Chinese, each one with a golden-brown complexion and a braided, ebony queue gracing his neck and back. Each one, I imagined, contained a sparkle of hope in his eyes and longed for the good fortune he'd given up everything in his previous life to find. What a day for them to arrive. At the stern of the ship sat a crate—bulky, sturdy, and clearly marked "Fine China."

The steamer passed us and we were on our own. In another few minutes we were through the Golden Gate and steaming into the open ocean, toward the Farallones, Panama City, and beyond.

Afterword

I closed the last of my San Francisco journals. In the seventy-seven long, intervening years between that time and the delivery of these lost volumes, I'd countlessly wondered as to the fates of those I knew at that time—Ah Toy, Ah Si, Ah Loi, Li Fen, the Celestial, Henry Conrad, even the tall girl. Primarily, did they escape the fire? And supposing that, did they continue on to fortune and happiness? Many was the day I scoured the newspaper for those names, surprised at myself for contemplating so often that town, and those in whose orbits I spent a mere two years of my life.

The *Oakland Tribune* obituary was my only window into any of their lives, and that only of Ah Toy, who'd apparently gone by "China Mary" later in her life, moved to Alviso, kept a house for her brother-in-law—she had relatives?—sold clams to tourists, had a number of children in China—children too?—and lived to be ninety-nine years old. It's unfathomable that she was only in her early twenties at the time I knew her; she lived an entire lifetime after I left. She's buried in San Jose at Oak Hill Cemetery, and I've wondered how it would be to travel to her grave and hold vigil for her. But I'm an ancient man now, hard of hearing, hard of sight, and hard of locomotion, my stiff, brittle bones protesting every movement. My place, as it's always been, is here, with my memories, for the minuscule amount of time I have left.

Though I'm an East Coaster through and through, there's something that still bubbles in me whenever the City by the Bay materializes in the news. And in the news is where it frequently resides, through earthquakes, political scandals, entertainment, crime, race riots, the law that bans Chinese laborers, all the headlines that are the hallmark of an established city. What's caught my attention most, however, is when those stories mention

Donaldina Cameron, that magnificent matron of the Mission Home who rescues Chinese sex slaves and cares for them in her Presbyterian mission. She's done what I could not and cannot, which is to wrangle her fiery passion and burn brightly as a beacon for the broken. I send her money every year. There is some weight that can't be cut.

Then there is Lex. All these years later, there's no word of him. I've received no letters or other sign to prove he's alive. Yet neither is there any evidence he's not. I've not received any of his possessions nor notification of his demise, nor do I glimpse his full, Christian name in the obituaries, though my heart always misfires when I catch an "Alex" or "Alexi." He could be anywhere, or nowhere. Regardless, I hope he's had a peaceful life. I may not be here without him. He's shaped my life in more ways than I can count, and in many more ways I don't fully understand.

One story remains. On the day I received the package at the door, I spent the rest of the evening and deep into the night reading the journal entries of my sixteen-year-old self. I was an emotional tornado as I came face-to-face with memories that had laid dormant for decades. When I at last reached the end, I retreated into my study, dug into my files I'd archived long ago, and located the entries I'd written on board the Pacific, those accounting my watery escape. Taking great care, I took a bit of book-binding glue and adhered the final entries to the end of my last journal. After seventy-seven years, the journals, like Odysseus returning home, were complete. I was bleary-eyed from lack of sleep, and though I cringed at so many of the actions and thoughts of the adolescent memorialized within, I experienced a calming sense of closure. Just as I was about to place them on my shelf, however, my eye caught something on the inside cover. I examined it closer and discovered two things.

The first was a button, small and gray, adhered into place. I was flummoxed, for I owned no garment to match it. I stared at it for a long while, turning it this way and that, until my mind jogged back to the beginning of the first journal. Then I had it. This was Leland's button I'd picked up from the ground at the front of his house! My cheeks flushed at the thought of my boyhood obsession. But where had it been, how had it been retrieved, and by whom? Who was this anonymous benefactor who sent the journals and this button that embodied my youthful yearnings? I rubbed the button and marveled at how simple my mind was then.

The second was a small Chinese character, hand-drawn in decent calligraphic script. I recognized immediately the character for "prisoner," identical to the faded symbol tattooed upon my arm. I hadn't drawn this, though with so many years passing I couldn't be sure; but then I noticed something else. On the left side of the character there were three additional marks, marks I hadn't seen before and were not mirrored on my hand. Two angled up to the left and the third angled to the left and down. The additions were clearly someone else's doing.

Perplexed, I rooted around my study until I found my copy of *Morrison's Chinese Dictionary.* I blew the dust off the cover and opened it, and, using my limited knowledge of Chinese roots and radicals, I scoured the book for the word. About an hour later, I saw it. When I read its definition, I had to put the book down. My hands were trembling.

The root word, the character in the middle, is "person." When the box is drawn around him, he becomes a "prisoner." Add the three additional strokes, and the word is transformed into "swim."

I dedicate these journals to my brother Lex, to all my family from the Garden of Fragrant Flowers, and to Lee, the love of my life.

C. H. Kirkpatrick

1928

Historical Note

On January 24, 1848, James Marshall found a nugget of gold in the American River near Sutter's Mill in Coloma, California. Gold had been discovered in California before, mostly by Mexicans and Native Americans, but it was Marshall's discovery that caught the world's attention. Two months later and one hundred and nine miles away, businessman Sam Brannan paraded through the dirt streets of San Francisco, waving a bottle of gold dust and yelling, "Gold! Gold! Gold in the American River!" The town emptied and headed for the hills.

Eleven months later and 2,400 miles away, President James K. Polk gave his annual State of the Union Address, confirming that "the accounts of the abundance of gold in that territory are of such an extraordinary character as would scarcely command belief." The rest of the country, and soon the world, rushed in.

San Francisco, a sleepy hamlet of roughly 400 residents just before Marshall's discovery, suddenly became a funnel to a massive migration. By 1852, the town burst with 36,000 people, mostly men, who came to live, work, mine for gold, sell supplies at inflated prices, drink, gamble, and better their circumstances in whatever ways they could. "It is an odd place," pioneer J.K. Osgood wrote, "unlike any other place in creation, and so it should be; for it is not created in the ordinary way, but hatched like chickens by artificial heat."

Into this chaotic environment, enter Cyrus and Lex Kirkpatrick. Fictional characters though they may be, I modeled them on the thousands of hopeful adventurers who wagon-trained across the continent or sailed from the Atlantic to the Pacific, leaving families, friends, jobs, and homes behind to make their fortune. Once in California, Lex takes the typical miner's route by joining a gold company—a group of people who banded together to share in the costs and the profits of mining—traveling to the gold diggings in the foothills. Lex comes back empty-handed, which happened far more often than not. Cyrus stays in San Francisco to make his living there, a path no less common.

Ah Toy was a historical figure, and her journey to San Francisco was easier transportation-wise, but no less mentally taxing. Boarding the ship in 1849 was already a small victory for the twenty-year-old. China's Qing rulers forbade women from leaving the country, so bribes had to change hands for officials to look the other way. With her husband, Ah Toy sailed into the Pacific with other Chinese prospectors in what would have been a sixty-day journey. However, along the way, her husband, whose name we don't know, became sick and eventually died.

Rather than return home, Ah Toy decided to stay in California, opening a peep show on Clay Street in San Francisco's Portsmouth Square. The attraction became so popular, according to Curt Gentry in his *The Madams of San Francisco,* that "whenever a boat from Sacramento docked, the miners would break into a run for Ah Toy's." But when her accusation against various miners for cheating her with brass went nowhere, she pivoted and opened a brothel in an alley on Pike Street (now Waverly Place). This caught the attention of neighborhood boss Norman Ah-Sing—a historical figure himself—who attempted to extort her and her successful business. Much to his irritation and wounded pride, she rebuffed him.

As for her appearance, we don't know what Ah Toy looked like. There are no photographs of her, nor are there paintings, drawings, or sketches. This is too bad, because accounts at the time have it that she was a real beauty. Elisha Crosby wrote, "The first Chinese courtesan who came to San Francisco was Ah Toy. She arrived I think in 1850 and was a very handsome Chinese girl. She was quite select in her associates, was liberally patronized by the white men and made a great amount of money."

Albert Benard de Russailh agreed, writing, "There are a few girls who are attractive if not actually pretty, for example, the strangely alluring Achoy, with her slender body and laughing eyes."

Charles Duane remembered her as a "tall, well-built woman. In fact, she was the finest-looking woman I have ever seen."

And, reporting on one of her many court appearances, the *Alta California* described her as "blooming with youth, beauty, and rouge," adding, "It would be well for the female dress reformers in the Atlantic States to send out here for a Chinese woman as a specimen."

There are conflicting reports about whether or not she had bound feet. Foot binding, the bygone Chinese practice dating back to the 11th century, was still *en vogue* for middle- and upper-class women in the 1800s. For Ah Toy, however, signs point to normal feet. She was likely a peasant in China, and likely part of an ethnic group of people called Hakka, who did not bind their women's feet. But the biggest hint that she didn't have bound feet comes from this newspaper story in 1851:

Last evening, about eight o'clock, that portion of the city in the vicinity of the Plaza was aroused by a certain nondescript noise…. When we arrived near the spot whence the outcry was proceeding, we found her in full chase after a suspicious looking individual, who had the appearance of being a volunteer to the Indian War. The thief kept ahead for a time, but Atoy was too swift for him, seized him by the collar very much in the style of a police officer, and demanded a diamond pin which he and his party had taken away from her.

Could a foot-bound woman have moved like that? Possibly, but I'm skeptical.

Not surprisingly for a woman in her business, Ah Toy continually pushed up against the law. In 1851, two years after her failed brass filings court appearance, she showed up in court again. This time it was to denounce the letter from her supposed Hong Kong husband "Atchoung" and to defend herself against efforts to deport her to China. This time she won, when one witness claimed that three men, including Norman Ah-Sing, "conspired together to abduct the above named Atoy, against her will, out of this country, and carry her forcibly to China." Norman Ah-Sing would try again to rid himself of the madam, using the Committee of Vigilance in an attempt to deport her, but Selim Woodworth, a member of the Committee, saw through his efforts and quashed them.

Other events in Ah Toy's life that are depicted here are true. She did make at least one trip back to China to acquire more girls for her brothel, and the deadly Taiping Rebellion did start its destructive path through the country at that time, though I fabricated the details of her return there. The same is true for her love affair in San Francisco. Yes, she dallied with the Vigilance Committee Head Brothel Inspector, and yes, he did beat her, but for the sake of this story, that man, John Clarke, became Lex Kirkpatrick.

One aspect of her life that I hope shines through is her absolute refusal to suffer fools. Ah Toy was forever shoving uphill against forces attempting to push her down, and she refused to follow the mid-1800s norms and expectations of a female immigrant. If a white man cheated her, she took him to court. When she was laughed out of court, she established a brothel in response, making even more money. If a neighborhood boss attempted to extort her, she refused him straight to his face. If that same man tried to have her deported, she went to court again to defend herself. If someone stole from her, she may not have kidnapped him to repay a debt, as she does in the novel, but she *did* chase him down and press charges. If a lover beat her viciously, there she was, back in court and on the record. She won some and lost some, but she never gave in to the pressure to soften her stances or leave the country.

Ah Toy's time in the prostitution business ended in the late 1850s due to increased competition from the Chinese tongs, who imported their own girls; but she continued to call the Bay Area her home. She eventually moved to San Jose and, according to her obituary, made a living "selling clams to tourists and yachting parties" until the impressive age of ninety-nine. She is buried at Oak Hill Cemetery in San Jose.

Other events and people that are true, if slightly embellished for the story: the Hounds' riot in Little Chile; street preacher Reverend William Taylor; the Garrett House; the Christmas Eve fire in 1849; California statehood in 1850; the statehood and Independence Day parades; Selim Woodworth and Stephen Payran; and the Vigilance Committee hangings of McKenzie and Whittaker.

Aspects of the story that are more flexible (and in some cases completely fabricated) include: James King of William, who was in California but didn't become a reporter until later; Ah Toy's traumatic reunion with her mother in China; Lex's Vigilance Committee trial (the Committee did hold sham trials, but not this one in particular); and the fire at the end of the book. However, that fire that sent Cyrus chasing after the steamer is based on accounts of the countless conflagrations that beset San Francisco in the 1850s. Those fires are the reason a phoenix graces the city's flag today.

Lastly, and probably most importantly, human trafficking was a very real phenomenon in Gold Rush San Francisco. Ah Toy did import young girls, and unscrupulous businessmen and gangsters did the same. Some of the Chinese girls became house servants and some became prostitutes. Many of them were sold like slaves and pressed into service with dubious contracts, and while the secret Queen's Room may not have existed so early, newspaper reports show that it did by 1873 and was subject to raids by the police.

The girls, wrote Charles Frederick Holder in *The North American Review* in 1897, were frequently tricked into believing that a husband awaited them in California:

> *The girl, who, perhaps, still expects to meet her promised husband, is taken to a boarding-house, provided with a rich wardrobe and rendered as attractive as possible. She is now...conducted to the 'Queen's Room,' which she is told belongs to her husband and where she is to receive his friends. The girl is now really on exhibition for sale, and is critically examined by high-binders, slave-dealers, speculators, brothel keepers, and others interested in the sale. Finally a price is*

agreed upon and she becomes the property of some man...

As admirable as Ah Toy's personality traits were, these business dealings complicate her legacy. Yes, China experienced famine and war, and yes, parents sold their daughters to survive and give their children a chance for survival. But that survival often meant a life of servitude—in many cases vile and invasive —and often an early death from overuse and disease, all of which Ah Toy and others exploited for profit. For more history about this topic in San Francisco, read about Donaldina Cameron and her Cameron House mission.

Human trafficking and all of its associated evils continue to this day. To report human trafficking in the United States, call the National Human Trafficking Hotline at 1-888-373-7888.

Here are some great sources for further reading about Ah Toy and San Francisco in the Gold Rush:

- *Men and Memories of San Francisco, in the "Spring of '50"* by Theodore Barry and Benjamin Patten (1873)
- *Bitter Strength* by Gunther Barth (1964)
- *A Year of Mud and Gold* by William Benemann (2003)
- "Free, Indentured, Enslaved: Chinese Prostitutes in Nineteenth-Century America" by Lucie Cheng Hirata in *Signs* (1979)
- *A History of the City of San Francisco* by John Hittell (1878)
- *From Canton to California* by Corinne Hoexter (1976)
- *San Francisco as it Is* by Kenneth Johnson (1964)
- *Becoming Chinese American* by Him Mark Lai (2004)
- *Mountains and Molehills* by Frank Marryat (1855)
- *Apron Full of Gold* by Mary Jane Megquier (1949)
- *Old San Francisco* by Doris Muscatine (1975)
- *Times Gone By* by Vicente Pérez Rosales (2003)
- *Last Adventure* by Albert Benard de Russailh (1931)
- *The Annals of San Francisco* by Frank Soulé, John Gihon, and Jim Nisbet (1855)

- *Eldorado* by Bayard Taylor (1870)
- *Unsubmissive Women* by Benson Tong (1994)
- *Unbound Feet* by Judy Yung (1995)
- California Digital Newspaper Collection for *Daily Alta California*

You can also read more about the rivalry between Ah Toy and Norman Ah-Sing:

- "A Little China Leader, a Brothel Owner, and Their Clashing American Dreams in Gold Rush San Francisco" by Noel C. Cilker in *Chinese America: History & Perspectives* (2018)

You will find a link to it and other historical musings on my website: **noelccilker.com**

Acknowledgments

This story took over twelve years to research and write, and was actually written twice: once as nonfiction and again as historical fiction, the version you now hold.

Plenty of people assisted, encouraged, and wondered out loud what was taking so long. These wonderful people are:

- Grace Choi for being the voice of Ah Toy in my head
- Shaochen Huang and Otto Yeung for translating Chinese words and sources
- Marcia Eymann for pushing me to think bolder about Ah Toy
- Dorothy Hearst and Pam Berkman for back pats and for talking me down from a few ledges
- Kurt Cyrus for helping me reimagine the story as historical fiction, and one of the many Cyruses who lent the narrator his name
- Nicole Giacinti, Megan Reif, Allen Choi, and Shining Hsu for beta and sensitivity reading
- Mario, my dear son, for trying his best to read the book but making it only a quarter of the way through
- Grace Ross and Michael Carr for making developmental edits on the various versions, and Carol Gaskin for copy editing the final version
- My friends and family, especially the Cilker clan, the Cyrus clan, and the Choi clan, for encouraging me to finish, even as they tired of asking me about it
- The folks who run and maintain the Bancroft Library, an excellent repository of western American history
- The folks at Google who made so many elusive historical

texts appear effortlessly on my computer screen
- Elaine Crane for telling me, "You want to write? So write!"
- And my mother and father for letting me do just that, write, and not pressuring me to do anything else

This book is dedicated to Allen, who sat me down one day in a coffee shop and told me what I needed to hear. I think he and Professor Crane were secretly working together.